Dedication

The book is dedicated to the short and passionate lives of Lois Elaine (Toni) Holstein and Shanon Lee Mason, *(two 'n's' not three)* who knew the love and pain of a being daughters of Lilith on earth.

First Montag Press E-Book and Paperback Original Edition October 2014

Copyright © 2014 by Bruce Lee Bond

As the writer and creator of this story, Bruce Lee Bond asserts the right to be identified as the author of this book.

Montag Press
ISBN: 978-1-940233-13-0
Cover art © 2014 Alison Hooper
Cover, layout, & e-book © 2014 Rick Febré
Author photo © 2014 Cheri Eplin

Montag Press Team:
Project Editor — Mara Hodges
Managing Director — Charlie Franco

A Montag Press Book
www.montagpress.com
Montag Press
1066 47th Ave. Unit #9
Oakland CA 94601 USA

Montag Press, the burning book with the hatchet cover, the skewed word mark and the portrayal of the long-suffering fireman mascot are trademarks of Montag Press.

Printed & Digitally Originated in the United States of America
10 9 8 7 6 5 4 3 2 1

~ A NOVEL ~

THE

BROKEN

COAST

BRUCE LEE BOND

MONTAG

Also by Author

Honor Thy Father, published by Sirens Call Publications in the Slaughterhouse, Vol. #2, Serial Killer Edition.

Girls' Day Out, published by Fox Spirit Books in the Girl at the End of the World Anthology in the United Kingdom and Commonwealth countries.

Midnight Lunch (a Lorelei story in modern Alaska) coming out in the Night to Dawn Anthology by Night to Dawn Magazine & Books LLC.

The Well of Souls, published in Bones, Vol. #2 by James Ward Kirk.

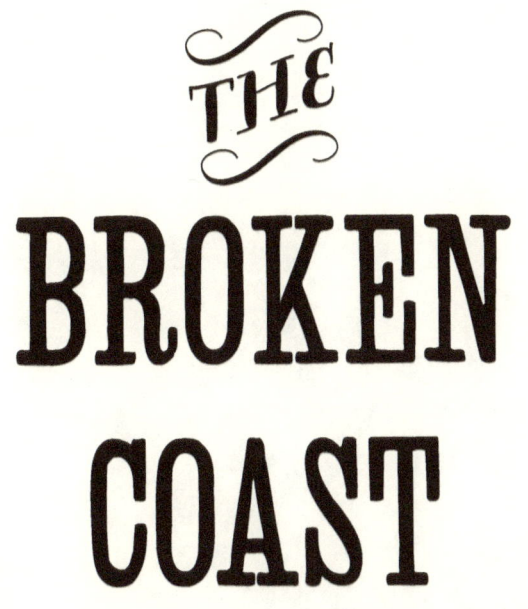

A NOVEL

THE
BROKEN
COAST

BRUCE LEE BOND

CONTENTS

CHAPTER 1.

The Slave, April 6, 1906 5:13 am

MAI LING COUGHED, AND THE tiny brass lamp flickered as she twisted on a straw mat watching ghosts dance across redwood timbers. From the floor above came the hollow sobbing of a girl, the shouts of a *boo how doy,* and the sound of a slap. Cruel laughter echoed off the walls, followed by the grunts of a man and a low moaning from the throat of a girl.

She rolled on her side and reached for the cup of water. They had given her that when they had left her on the shelf, along with a small bowl of boiled rice. They would return in the morning, or whatever time they had chosen. By then she must be dead.

She sat up in the windowless room with limbs like lead and head thick with opium. She wheezed, as her lungs strained to breathe against pneumonia locking them like a vise. She shivered, naked as she had spent the last eight years waiting for any and all customers within a tiny pen in a dark brick building at the end of Butcher Alley.

Mai Ling would remember forever the journey to Canton, and the shove her mother had given her toward the man who had taken her to the boat. Her mother's face had been blank as a wooden mask as her daughter's small hand was crushed in the fingers of the leering stranger. He and his mates had been the first to ravish her.

The crewmen had threatened her with horrible death should she tell the agent of her buyers in San Francisco of their deeds. She had not, hoping that it would bring some small measure of kindness from the slavers. She became numb and mute, stifled her cries of pain as she slept amongst other ravaged children in the bowels of the ship, and they hadn't beaten her.

Her hope had been that some good soul would buy her at auction in the Queen's Room, a basement of a building under Jackson Street where she and twenty others had been stripped and examined by a host of men. The old "doctor" who had certified her both healthy and a virgin to raise her value looked almost kind until he'd stuck his fingers up her with a leer. She could see his yellow teeth, and her nose twitched at the memory of his breath.

Mai Ling was given a sum of American money by a man who wore a black jacket, a silk shirt over a chainmail vest, and a black bowler hat, and told to immediately hand it to the captain of the vessel she'd come to California on. She did and was made to sign her name on a piece of paper, which due to an education imparted by her grandmother, she could also read:

> For the consideration of seven hundred fifty dollars paid into my hands this day, I, Mai Ling, promise to prostitute my body for the term of three years. If in that time I am sick one day, two weeks shall be added to my time. And, if more than one day, my term of indebtedness and use of my body shall continue an additional month.
>
> When my time is out, I shall be my own master, and no man may trouble me. But if I endeavor to escape I am to be held as a slave for life. If my Master, Mr. Sep Ye Hung, shall return to China, his partner, the honorable woman Dah Pa Tsin, shall retain my contract, and my obligation shall be fulfilled just as written here, with my continued labors for the term of my servitude.

> Signed, Mai Ling

She was clothed in a baggy cotton coat and trousers, and bundled into a wagon with two other girls for a ride through the streets of San Francisco. It was the last time she had worn real clothes but once in eight years.

Mai Ling discovered upon beginning her menses that those days were considered sickness, and for each day she bled, the weeks and months ahead were lengthened. She'd caught many an ailment from customers and spent days too ill to work also. It had become clear to her by the age of fourteen that the only escape from her contract was death.

She and Ah Tsin had become as one during their imprisonment. The two girls together were a popular diversion as they looked to be sisters and specialized in giving pleasure as a team, which afforded some protection for one another. Together they had plotted to escape to the near-mythical goldfields where some Chinese miners had managed to become rich before the *Fan Kwei,* the White Devils, could discover their claims and steal them by law or murder. They would find men who would take them as wives and return to China to live long lives in wealth and security, bearing many children who would honor their names. The dream kept hope alive as they yielded to the stinking bodies of strangers.

Each time she became pregnant, an old woman was called to induce an abortion with poisons forced up inside her with a rubber tube and poured down her throat. Mai Ling would lay on the bed and cry, imagining that day she and Ah Tsin would escape as the old woman barked at her and admonished her to remain still. The pain crawled from her womanhood and found a home in her heart.

When that day came, they were let out by a young man of the Hop Sing Tong for their weekly exercise in a courtyard where they were allowed to walk and do whatever they wished for a few hours clad in thin cotton gowns. Mai Ling and Ah Tsin had convinced him that they both would be his women, and their father would reward him handsomely when he arrived with them in Fairbanks in the distant mythical north.

On a signal from the girls that the yard was clear, he unbolted the iron door on the far side of the garden. The girls donned silk trousers and jackets, slipped their feet into sandals, and followed him to a wagon where they slid under a load of vegetables. Mai Ling burrowed into the bok choy, pressing her face against the side of the cart to peer through a crack in the boards.

They got as far as Portsmouth Square before the wagon was diverted into another alley across from the Hall of Justice by a gang of boo how doy. The girls listened to the protestations of the young man, then the croaking sounds of his fear as they were pulled from the cart. He fell to his knees and pled for his life before the four tong soldiers, who stood grim-faced with arms folded.

There was the noise of a melon splitting as a hatchet cut the middle of his forehead. As they bundled her and Ah Tsin away, Mai Ling glanced back at the pool of blood encircling the boy's head where he lay face down on the cobblestones. His long queue stretched across the stones like a butchered snake, having painted a red *S* upon them as he fell.

The torture went on for hours with hot irons across her back nine times and rapes beyond counting. One of the boo how doy almost slashed her face, but a boss man had shouted he would ruin the merchandise and then they could only kill her, losing many thousands of dollars that the Hatchet Son must repay himself. Still, she had come out of it with scars across her shoulders that lowered her asking price and lost much of her worth to the house.

Ah Tsin had taken her punishment until a very ugly man with the breath of a dog had forced himself into her anus while insulting her ancestors. She'd let out a scream as she twisted out from under him and tore bloody gashes down his face, trying to gouge out his eyes with her nails and fighting like a demon.

They carried Ah Tsin out of the room after the men had attacked her with blood pouring from her mouth and nose in a torrent. Mai Ling had never heard a word of her since and knew she was dead. Even her name was gone, passed from the world forever, and forbidden to be spoken. That was five years ago. Mai Ling hadn't tried to escape since.

The lamp flickered, and shadows danced across damp beams. Soon the oil would be gone, and she should be dead. She knew when they arrived and she was still breathing, that someone would be there to make sure she was ready for the ground or the sea no matter what. Then she would finally escape this place of slaves, to join the ancestors who even now must be watching her.

"Do you have any pity?" She hissed. Why then had they allowed her to come to *this?* Cracked lips spread in a sneer as she turned her head and tried to spit upon the floor. "To hell with you!" To hell with all the filthy men who had shown their yellow teeth and tossed their poison seed into every orifice of her body since she'd felt that shove of betrayal from her own mother's hand. To the deepest painful *hell* for her mother too!

She began to laugh, but her lungs locked up and air wouldn't come. She twisted on the frayed straw mat, gasping as she clawed at cold concrete. "Please!" she croaked to the spreading dark. The little light was sputtering out like her life as she fought to breathe. "Please!"

A radiant face appeared above her out of the stale air, glimmering like it had taken the sputtering light of the lamp and rekindled it within its pale flesh.

Mai Ling jerked upright from the soiled dampness as if lifted by a gentle hand. Air rushed into her lungs, resounding within her like a shout and filling her veins with light. She shuddered, raising trembling fingers to her face. "Ah!"

The woman held out a hand luminous and warm as the summer moon. "You suffer as my own, as my own flesh, Mai Ling, for surely all others have forsaken you."

Mai Ling's fingers entwined in those of the Goddess who had come to her deathbed, and all pain left her body. She stood upon the dirt floor of a miserable hole beneath Butcher Alley, stood on her own, proud of that which no crib or torture could take away. She was ten years old, running in the sun where mountains were green and full of birds and the sea sang in a secret cove for her. She was safe from the darkness, far from the little rooms where strangers laughed and used her as a dirty rag for their own pleasure. Mai Ling was going home.

"Show me how to get there!" Her voice broke, and hot tears streamed down sunken cheeks as the Goddess lifted her like a feather in her arms. Mai Ling saw that her eyes were many colors: like the sea and the sky, like leaves and the color of trees ... like the ochre earth of south China in her stolen childhood. *Oh* ... like the brightest, deepest red sunset!

She put her head against the high round breast of Guanyin, precious Goddess of Mercy, and was enfolded in her shining hair, a wondrous raiment that would keep her from the blades, from the cold and the sneering eyes of those who had passed her over like an insect upon the ground. She was taken across fragrant fields to a place where a river sparkled and flowed in a living rainbow. Mai Ling heard the singing of her ancestors who held no shame for her, those awaiting, those liberated and ancient ones whose only remaining burden was the love they held for her ... *to share*.

As the Goddess stepped into the water, she held Mai Ling up in glorious offering. The voices on the other side grew nearer, rising in peals of joy and laughter as they welcomed her, blessing her. Mai Ling was home at last.

Lorelei laid her down as close as she herself could come

to that other side. She brushed pale fingers across the stillness that had held Mai Ling, kissed her on the mouth, and stepped away from the light again to return to the world of the living.

II.

The Pilgrim

Audie slung his duffel bag on his shoulder, and stepped from the ferry's cabin to let the sea breeze purge the smoke of cigars from his blond hair and pea coat as he leaned on the gunwale watching the hills of San Francisco appear like ghosts out of breaking fog. A shaft of sun caught the tower of the Ferry Building at the foot of Market Street over a forest of masts. The golden hands of the tower's clock were on twelve, and a half-dozen ferries jostled for moorage at the crowded wharves. The boat tied off, and the rattle of the gangway echoed off the wall of a warehouse filling the Washington Pier proclaiming **NORTH STAR STEAM LINE** in brilliant gold letters.

A wizened Chinese man stood where the dock met the street before a red-lacquered wagon that had carcasses of small smoked pigs and fowl dangling from twine below chicken-scratch writing. The man's head bobbed as he removed a long ceramic pipe from his mouth to let loose a stream of pidgin English or flowing Cantonese at his customers. Chinese were as common as dragons in Audie's hills of West Virginia. He inhaled the air of the vast Pacific flowing over the peninsula before him, resolving to see the Far East as part of his gentleman's education. But first he had to spend a few days exploring the fabled San Francisco and write his great novel of the North this summer in the far Klondike. He'd devoured everything Jack London and other adventures in the gold rush could put out, and rather than wait for more, intended to see it himself. His study of classical literature at Marshall University in West Virginia had begun to bore him, and Audie had accumulated enough to make it to Dawson City now that the railroad was running to White Horse from the port of Skagway. He checked his wallet and money belt, shouldered his duffel, and struck out into the beckoning city.

There were small hotels aplenty in the area along East Street with saloons on every block. Audie stretched his legs and scanned the signs. A pretty red-haired girl spotted him as he stood waiting for a hole in the procession of horses, wagons and motorcars on the cobbled street, and was at his side in a ruffle of green skirts. Her freckled breasts seemed to burst out of the low-cut bodice of the dress and whalebone corset she wore holding her slim waist in its grip. Audie gazed into the cleavage, he being six-feet three inches tall and the girl but a slip of a thing. He swallowed as soft fingers slipped through his own, and his fair complexion waxed red.

"Just off the boat, fellow?"

"Yes ma'am, the name's Audie Mitchell Bond. I'm headed to the Klondike."

"Wonderful, and I am Leah … Hayman. Where are you from?"

"Charleston, Charleston West Virginia. My family's been there for generations. Bound for Dawson City to write a—"

Her hand stroked his back, and a thrill ran up his spine, for at the age of twenty-two Audie had never been familiar with a woman in such a way. Audie's father was a Methodist minister, and marriage wasn't in his plans yet. His brother had waited until he was well-placed in business and married a perfectly acceptable young woman at the age of thirty. His parents expected Audie to do the same. He stumbled, and excused himself to musical laughter.

"Audie you're a charming fellow. Would you like to spend some time with me while you're here? I should be delighted to show you the town."

"Urn, I need to find a boardinghouse where I can put up. I'm to book passage on—"

"I'll show you a place to hang your hat, Mister." She gave him a coquettish wink."Just don't expect to get a lot of sleep." Leah again took his hand, and he began to pull away, but surrendered as she blinked large blue eyes with mahogany lashes and led him up the cobbled street.

As they passed a saloon, a man leaned out."Don't waste time on her! The women in here are on the house, sailor!"

She yanked him forward, and he staggered under the weight of his duffel bag."Shanghai joint!" she hissed."If you want to keep your freedom and your purse, keep moving!"

Audie stared at his hand in her small one, marveling at the unseen force that gave it such power.

"Bet you've got a big one there. I can tell from the hands."

"What?"

Leah winked again as she steered him to a stairway barred with an iron gate. She produced a key from between lovely breasts, opened the lock, swung back the gate, and led him in.

He followed with his bag on his shoulder and his heart in his throat. The idea of losing his virginity was a thrilling possibility coupled with fear. All his fantasies of women hadn't prepared him for this. Leah wasn't a girl on a French postcard. She was here in the flesh, and her hand in his made his palm sweat to an astounding degree.

There was a heavy footfall above, and his hand went to his grandfather's cap and ball .44 under the navy pea coat.

She gave him a quick laugh."Don't be nervous. Here we are."

The room had a wainscoting of dark redwood with walls papered in red velvet rising to a high polished tongue-and-groove ceiling from which hung a bronze chandelier. In the middle was a huge bed with a brocade of green Chinese silk that had thick square posts carved into lions' feet. On one side was a dark dresser with a mirror, and on the other a high credenza with a drawer open to women's under things. Beside the bed was a table with a green travertine top, a pitcher of water in a chipped enamel bowel, two washcloths and two towels. The sound of a man gasping came from beyond the wall, followed by a woman's laughter.

She untied the back of her corset. "Ready to spend a bit of the cash tucked in that money belt around your middle, Audie?"

"Miss, I—"

"Here." Auburn hair fell to her waist over fair freckled shoulders as the bodice came off, revealing a silk undergarment her breasts bobbed in deliciously as she opened the mirrored top of the credenza. She took out a crystal decanter filled with dark golden liquor and poured it in two fat glasses. "This is real Irish whiskey, not that shit they sell in saloons. Just like Mrs. Mark Hopkins serves at her place. In fact, this *is* what she serves. Got it from a rich fellow who thinks I look like some princess in England ... or at least he says so."

She began to unbutton his pants, and he grabbed her hand. Leah stroked his fingers and smiled. "It's quite all right, sir."

Audie shivered as her hand slipped beneath his belt and squeezed. He dug teeth in his lip and tried to say something, but the knot in his throat stopped him. He swallowed hard.

Leah giggled as she held up her glass and pushed the other into his hand, clinking them so loudly that he thought they were going to break. "Go ahead Audie, it'll put lead in your pencil."

Audie rotated the glass in his hand as he gazed into wide blue eyes over lips that were incredibly inviting. His feet felt rooted to the floor. He let out his breath, and without protest, downed the glass.

Loud barking echoed in his skull. Audie squeezed a damp

clump of grass. He sat up, and a bolt of pain in the back of his head rewarded him for the effort. An ugly yellow mongrel bared its teeth six feet away, its silhouette square in the halo of a gas streetlight through the fog. The slope made Audie tilt. He put a hand out to steady himself, and it encountered something soft that oozed between his fingers. The dog snarled, and was gone. Audie tried to stand, but fell to his knees and slid on damp gravel. He put a hand to his face, dog shit smeared it, and vomit erupted from his mouth.

He found a fountain in a square where streets intersected at odd angles and old women spoke Italian, washed his face and hands, drank deeply, and pulled the pea coat around him. Audie leaned against the cold stones of the fountain staring at a near-full moon and wondering what had become of his plans. He'd had four hundred dollars and a ticket to Skagway in his purse and the money belt around his waist, both of which were gone along with his grandfather's gun. His journal of the trip across America he'd been engaged to publish was also—everything but his coat. A knot of rage twisted his gut like a knife, and he moaned. His skull was *splitting*.

Two men in dirty denim jackets appeared from an alley with the clubs in their hands reflecting the glow of gas streetlights. "There he is."

"Good size, ten big for that lug." There was a snort of laughter, followed by the slapping of wood across a horny palm.

Audie stared at their ugly faces for a moment and groaned. He tottered to his feet, and held his fists up before him.

The men seemed to shrink as they were yanked back into the alley, followed by the thud of bodies hitting brick walls and the clatter of wood. Audie blinked and glanced around. The street on both sides was empty, and disappeared in fog. He stared into the shadows, and collapsed with a sigh against the fountain with his hands to a throbbing head. A policeman must be some-where-someone in authority that could help him.

"Not really."

Audie gazed into a pale diamond of a face with eyes whose color he couldn't make out. From full lips, a beautiful voice had spoken. It was the face of an angel who seemed to wear a wonderfully good perfume that rose above the smell of restaurants and the gross smells of the street, filling him with the most pleasant sensations even now.

The woman chuckled. "All cops are corrupt on the Barbary Coast." She held out a long-fingered hand white as ivory.

He hesitated, remembering the soft and seemingly harmless hands of Leah. *Leah!* He was about to tell her he had no money or anything at all when her fingers closed around his own, and a rush ran through him.

"You are found, Audie. Fortunately, we have need of one another this evening."

Again he was being led by a woman through the city, this time by night and destitute. Drunken laughter, screams, shouts of anger and the report of guns all came to him from the streets, yet melded into a seamless fabric that had become music. All he could focus on was the wonderful rhythm of her breathing and the indescribable scent of her skin. It was all beyond strange, yet this time he wasn't afraid at all.

III.

The Guest

"You are my lamb." A tent of hair hung around him as he lost himself within her, thrusting farther than nature allows and never knowing the difference. "You are my virgin offering, and I am grateful."

Audie's eyes were closed to the room yet open on a realm where rivers ran to an endless sea. She took him to where lovely voices sang a song he had always known, but had somehow forgotten. Her laughter was full of love and caring, and he imagined some glorious saint come down from the windows of a cathedral. Somewhere else he struggled to make sense of it—to open his eyes on she who embraced him. He tried, but was stunned by the red light of a distant sun, and cried out to stars laughing with that angel's voice.

The scream of a girl struggling to breathe in darkness made him jerk awake as if an electric shock had run through him. Audie opened his eyes to the sound of hooves clopping on cobblestones, her marvelous scent all around him, and a horrible headache.

"Here." She held a tiny green bottle in her pale palm.

He blinked her into focus and sat up. Her gaze was a feather, stroking his body. He took the bottle and pulled the cork stopper, but it broke off in the neck. Audie tipped the half-plugged thing to his lips, and sucked at the thick elixir. "Damn," he wiped his mouth, "that's bitter!"

She offered him a steaming mug of coffee that he accepted with much more gusto. "Thank you." He glanced at tall windows covered by thick curtains. "Awful dark in here, isn't it?"

"You'll have to excuse me, but I have a problem with too much light. Breakfast is ready for you at the cafe downstairs, and I want you to eat well. You've had a rather draining experience since you arrived, Audie."

He stared at her lips as he searched for words of his own. "Nobody ever told me a woman could be like you." He stroked the fine-pored skin of her cheek in the dim light and almost forgot to breathe. Audie stood up, rubbed his eyes, and stepped to the windows to part the drapes.

The Bay shone green in morning sun, cradling the rocky shoulder of Alcatraz Island crowned in a nimbus of white and brown wings. Birds circled and roosted on its rocks and the army garrison on its crest as great brown pelicans scooped fish from the water. An old steamer moved down the middle channel into the Bay with her sails reefed on short masts, her twin stacks blowing dark smoke aft in the air of a clear spring day against the green mountains of Marin. Audie yanked open the casement and inhaled the sea breeze.

When he turned, she had a silken pillowcase over her face. Perfect breasts rose and fell in the morning light, and her long legs moved as the sun touched them, flashing on her ivory skin and painting the pure white of her flesh a glowing gold. Her voice came muffled from beneath the pillow. "Please, shut the drapes." There was a plaintive lilt in her tone, and a hint of pain.

Audie closed the curtains, and the room was dimmed. He sat on the bed and took her hand. Once more, that marvelous current flowed through him. She removed the pillow with a sigh, and her jet black hair fell to the carpet, a deep and shining black that seemed to pick up light from outside the dark room and reflect it like the wings of a raven in the sun. Her eyes were blue and green, and glittering with the strangest flecks of red. A shiver of glory shook him as a mixture of love, adoration and awe quaked his very bones that this was the woman who had plucked his innocence and begun his journey as a man.

"Don't wax too poetic. I haven't got you a new journal yet." A dimpled grin flitted across her face, and he bent to kiss her. Her breath was sweet as flowers. He ran his fingers down the silken skin of her stomach to be greeted by the hungry mouth of her body. She squeezed them in greeting. "Wait," She pushed him away with one hand easily as lifting a leaf from her breast. His pulse raced and his head began to hurt anew. "You very much need to eat first, Audie, and get some air. The sun will do you good."

"What about you … Lorelei?"

"I'll be fine. You're welcome to stay here, and money won't be a problem should you choose to. I want you to be around for a good long while. That is … if you'd like."

"No, I mean thank you. I don't know how this has come about, but of course I'll have to find work to earn my keep, and to book passage north as soon as possible. I may well do a bit of prospecting, and have solicited a publisher in New York to write a book about the Klondike like Mr. London. I don't want to live off a woman after all."

A peal of laughter rippled her white throat, and she put fingers to her lips. "Why not? I've been living on men for so long I could write you a version of history that would curl that lovely member there." She gave his cock a squeeze, and it leapt to attention. "Here, take some money and see the City. But remember Audie, tonight is yours and mine." From the nightstand, she produced a half-inch stack of bills. "Take the key to the door and don't get rolled by some thug. Watch out for the

shanghai bars along East Street and Pacific, and the one called
O'Toole's at the foot of Jackson with an anchor out front. I
don't want to have to pull you off some boat heading for Ma-
cao or fish you out of the Bay."

Audie flipped the bills across his thumb. He bit his lip,
shook his head, and began to hand them back."But ... why
would you give me this? Dear lady, you must be a very rich
woman indeed, but is it proper to—"

"Come love, let me show you the bath." Lorelei sprang up,
seized a red silk gown from the closet, took his hand, and led
him down a hall to a room with a huge tub upon green griffin's
claws of bronze. There was a commode with a tall brass pipe
leading to a polished oaken water box, a sink with hot and cold
water, and a brass shower head over the tub. She stepped away
from a shaft of sun falling from a skylight ten feet overhead
and pulled a silk cord hanging from the ceiling. A bell rang.

"You takey bath, Missie?" A voice echoed up the stairwell.

"Audie takes a bath, Wu." She kissed his cheek."Just we
two have this whole house. If you need anything, pull this or
the gold chain in the bedroom and Wu will be along shortly.
He's a dear." She gave him a dimpled smile and floated out of
the room.

Audie inhaled the last vestige of her scent, rubbed his
eyes, and tottered on his feet. He went to the toilet and began to urinate. A bright red stream of blood greeted him. The
muscles of his stomach tightened like a vise, as a hoarse croak
rattled his chest.

"It's all right." White hands were around his waist, with
their warmth entering him. She rocked him in her arms, and
pressed her breasts against his trembling back."Just piss. It'll
stop in a moment, I promise." Her breath caressed his cheek as
she kissed his ear.

He shivered and fought vertigo, wondering if he was going to faint there and then. Audie ground his teeth, closed his eyes, and emptied his bladder. After what seemed like forever, he forced them open. It was yellow, and his breath rattled out between his lips.

"You've just outperformed yourself. It happens."

"It ... *does?*" His mind raced, seeking some explanation to assuage a boiling panic.

She yawned, and her chin pressed his shoulder. "Things will become clear in time. You don't know what a help you've been. Everything will be fine, I assure you. Now, go and have a glorious day. I'll see you this evening, so just don't exhaust yourself my lovely man ... and eat!"

Audie got dressed, stumbled outside, paused to get his bearings, and looked around. He was famished. With a spinning head, he found the cafe next door, sat at a window, and watched a hawk-nosed man outside in a tattered coat with military epaulets and a hat like Napoleon's stopping people on the sidewalk who appeared to give him money.

Audie's head swam as his fingers wandered to his groin. There was no pain. He watched a prostitute accost a man on the street, and his jaw clenched at the thought of Leah. Somehow, he must regain his own money from two summers of haying, cutting wood and tending his uncle's orchards while studying nights for the university. He ran a finger through salt spilled on the checkered tablecloth, cracked his neck, and yawned. He actually felt quite good. He felt wonderful, except for being so hungry, yet a part of him hovered on the brink of abject terror and he didn't know why. It seemed wholly uncalled for emotion that called for critical thinking, but he'd deal with it after a meal.

A dark mustached man behind the counter motioned to a thin blond girl who hustled to bring a platter full of eggs, potatoes and ham. She poured steaming coffee into a chipped mug, placed fresh cream in a pitcher next to it, and returned with a basket of biscuits, butter and strawberry jam, then stood beside the table smiling as he attacked the food. "Lady upstairs said anything you need she's coverin' it. Want some fruit? We got oranges from Los Angeles just off the train. They're huge, and you can peel 'em with your fingers. They're real fresh and they smell so good."

Audie felt an answering thud in his groin. She was bright and fresh, lithe as a young deer, and he wanted to have sex with her. He put a hand over his mouth as the memory of Lorelei thrilled him to the point he couldn't chew. A shiver ran up his spine, and he straightened in the chair.

"Everything all right?"

He nodded as she leaned toward him, and her breasts spoke through the beige dress of a waitress. Her skin bled a perfume that he'd never noticed before, almost like Lorelei, but not as distinct.

"I'm Diana, like the virgin huntress in Greek mythology." She gave him a wink and went to the kitchen for the oranges. On her return, he asked about Leah. "Leah? Mister, every other hooker in town uses *that* name. She get you for your poke or somethin'?"

Warmth flooded his face. "She … picked my pocket when I got off the ferry. She's young, about this high, and she has red hair and a real … a real perky bosom."

Diana laughed, exposing crooked teeth in a pretty mouth. "Seen a couple girls look like that on Waverly Place over by Bela Cora's old mansion. They pay the Chink tongs for the territory, so you don't want to be hasslin' 'em. But there's a Navy ship in so she could be anywhere: Chinatown, the Coast, North Beach, the Tenderloin, anywhere on East Street or even on Market near the Ferry Building. I'd chock it up to experience if you got that lady next door takin' care of you. She's somethin', real class. Is she French? Tony thinks she's from one of those fancy places in New Orleans. That Leah's some jaybird with a bad bunch watching out for her if she's workin' down by the docks anyway, and if you're without any protection, you'll just end up at Land's End feedin' the sharks. I'd chalk it up to experience, buddy."

Audie ran a thumb under an orange peel, inhaling the fruit's scent. He shoveled eggs in his mouth as he digested her words.

"I'll get more ham." He nodded before she went on. "Besides, she probably spent it all at Dr. Shiftman's All-Night Drugstore. They sell ups and downs there allll night long." Diana said in a sing-song voice. "Those girls are all hopheads, so stay away buster. I don't know why Miss Lorelei is taking care of you, but I'd guess from lookin' at you what it is." Diana grinned in a way that made her look much older or made him feel much younger. The curve of her throat seemed to pulse in the morning light, and something in him took flight as she sashayed back to the kitchen.

When he finished, he left her a tip from Lorelei's money- a whole dollar as he had no change. He heard her gasp as he left the restaurant, and turned to watch her snatch up a day's wages and tuck it in her apron. Diana shot him a come-hither look that again made the blood rush to his groin as the door closed, then he was on the concrete sidewalk above the cobbled street.

He took a deep draught of the sea air and stretched. He felt great, as if the disaster of the previous night had reversed itself into a windfall beyond his ability to conceive, pushing from his mind the terrifying incident at the toilet and any idea that he was a kept man—as well as Lorelei's passing mention of a host of other men. How many men could she have had? She couldn't be much older than he, and was as fresh as any girl he could imagine. *Fresher.* What the hell, he had her now. Audie hardly wondered what he did have beyond the fact that Lorelei was astoundingly beautiful.

He found a stationer's, bought a pen and notebook, located a telegraph office by the docks, and wired his publisher in New York and his family in West Virginia that he had arrived safely in San Francisco and found decent accommodations. He caught a cable car and paid a nickel for a ride up Powell toward downtown. Somewhere, somehow, in this crowded metropolis he must find the whore Leah and regain his possessions. Then all would be right.

As they ascended a hill, he got a view of the Bay and the masts of sailing ships crowding the flanks of the peninsula. Coal smoke poured from the funnels of a hundred steamers. Telegraph Hill stood with the homes of Italian and Greek fishermen climbing its slopes with their tile roofs shining in the sun. Cables hummed under the street as the green-uniformed operator moved the levers to engage or brake the car.

They passed Sacramento Street, and he got a look at some of the mansions on the incredibly steep Nob Hill where pink, gray and whitewashed castles loomed with fine views of the City and Bay. A woman in a huge flowered hat was trying to arrange three boys on the red leather seats of a long black motorcar, who looked miserable in their tight-collared black suits as they rode to some uptown function. Audie got off at Market. He took in the tall twin hills at one end, and gazed down the canyon of buildings all the way to the Ferry Building's tower where he'd arrived a day before. He had to piss, and a knot appeared in his stomach.

Someone shouted, and he was nearly run down by a wagon that pulled onto the sidewalk to disgorge bundles of papers. He nimbly stepped out of the way, tipped his hat to the scowling driver, bought a copy of the *San Francisco Call* as a social gesture, and scanned the front page.

A drawing of Mount Vesuvius erupting behind a terrified mother hurrying her brood aboard a boat as flames rose from a generic Italian town greeted him. One of Mayor Schmitz's associates had been murdered at a 'renowned establishment' on Jackson Street while the mayor was receiving the Grand Duke of Russia. Two New York Opera companies were coming to town, and Clarence Darrow had won a big court case back East. A steamer had docked from France with several "actresses of repute." Muslim rebels had kidnapped three Illinois nuns in the Philippines and were threatening to behead them. Someone had robbed a stage along the Yuba River, and the story was accompanied by a paragraph on Black Bart's exploits decades earlier. A family of Pomo Indians had been shot by a rancher up by some place called Booneville who claimed they'd killed his stock. Several other killings and at least one duel over a "notorious woman" had occurred on the streets where he walked. There was an ad for guns at the Emporium on Market Street, and Audie decided to have a look.

IV.

Lucky Izzy

The Emporium was a block down Market across double trolley tracks and four lanes crowded with horses, carriages and motorcars. A display in its huge windows had dark woolen suits at one end, dresses and dry goods in the middle, and weapons at the other. Audie examined an elaborately inlaid sword cane before browsing the pistols, and entered through high arched doors wide enough to admit a train. A new automatic covered in bright chrome, a Colt .32 that held bullets in the grip, sat inside a glass case. It was flat and easy to carry, but he wasn't sure about something that complicated, it being full of springs and the like.

With some trepidation, he asked to use the water closet. He shut the door, stepped up to the ceramic urinal, closed his eyes, and opened them when he began to piss. Audie let out a long rattling sigh. Upon returning, he asked the clerk behind a counter to see one of the guns. The man placed a fancy wooden box lined with red velvet on the counter with a pistol, two extra magazines and a cleaning kit. Audie picked up the gun, and gingerly tugged at the slide.

A dark little man down the counter chuckled and held out a hand. "Here, let me show you pilgrim."

The clerk deferred to the man, who had large dark eyes, a dark beard, and a pronounced nose with gold-rimmed spectacles perched upon it. He wore a black bowler hat and a black coat over a silk vest with grey herringbone trousers. The little man took the gun from Audie's hand, pulled back the slide, and while holding it open pushed a lever on the side. He ejected the magazine and did something that released the slide from the gun, pulling it back, off, and catching a spring that popped out from around the barrel. He disconnected the barrel, and laid the gun's parts on a red cloth the clerk spread across the mahogany counter.

Audie shook his head as he tried to rebuild the gun in his mind. It would take some hands-on learning.

"Clever idea, but rather complicated," the man said to Audie's nodding agreement. "I'd get a short-barreled Smith and Wesson. Something double action with a top-break for quick reloading that shoots a bullet big enough to put a man down. Some of these lugs are all hopped up on stuff besides booze, and you've got to get their attention."

"I suppose you're right, sir."

"Oh, the name's Izzy Rothman." He held out his hand.

"Audie Bond. You know your guns, Mister Rothman, I—"

"Just Izzy, everybody calls me Izzy."

"*Lucky* Izzy." The clerk interjected.

"Thanks for the compliment, Frank, but that was all a long time ago."

"Yep, and you're still alive aren't you?" the clerk responded, holding up his hands in a gesture saying that alone was proof to his previous comment.

"People say I'm the luckiest guy in San Francisco just 'cause a couple a' lugs missed me in saloons." Izzy shrugged as if it were all a mystery to him.

"Hell, you took a forty-five Colt point blank in 'ninety-one. My uncle saw it with his own eyes."

"The drunk couldn't shoot, Frank. It went through my vest and hit the bar." Izzy turned to Audie. "Get one of these top-break forty-fives with a three-inch barrel. I've got one myself and I'll vouch for 'em."

"All right."

Audie left the Emporium in the company of Izzy with his new seven-dollar pistol in the holster Izzy recommended that hung from the shoulder below his left arm under his coat. Izzy took him to lunch at a place next to a huge melodeon, a show and dance hall called the Midway Plaisance that had posters for The Girl in Blue prominently displayed, billed as the *Terpsichorean Mistress of Hoochy-Kootchy, Unapproachable, and Beyond Competition.*

Izzy ordered porterhouse steaks, fried onions, and piles of crisp fried potatoes. The smell of cooking lit a fire in him, and when the meal arrived Audie began to wolf his food. He had to remind himself to eat as in polite society, though it was certainly lost on the crowd around him. As he ate in a cloud of cigar smoke staring out at Market Street, he thought he heard laughter and felt soft lips caressing the side of his face. His fingers went to his cheek.

Izzy pulled at his beard. "So, you think you're on your way to find your fortune this summer writing about the Klondike. Fairbanks is where the big strikes are these days. Dawson and Nome are claimed up or worked out, Audie," Izzy swallowed a forkful of meat, "and I suppose you're going to expand your education in our cosmopolitan Mecca of the West while in transit."

Audie rubbed his cheek. "Well, ah, yes, I suppose." He could smell her behind the odor of cigars, food and beer. Audie blinked, and concentrated on following Izzy's conversation.

"Son you're on a rite of passage, seen it a thousand times. People come here to do one thing, and then something else

reaches out and grabs 'em. I got here twenty years ago to invest
in a financial exchange and send away for some nice Jewish girl
from back East to marry. That was before people started calling me lucky. 'Course, if I hadn't succumbed to demon drink
and been in that saloon, I wouldn't have got the reputation in
the first place. Now, high rollers pay me to keep them company and watch their backs," he grinned,"and I do tend to win
at cards more than most." Izzy leaned back in his chair."I've
been in every bad and good joint worthy of its name, from
the Coast to the Uptown Tenderloin, from the old El Dorado
to Delmonico's. Rubbed shoulders with everyone from the hoi
polloi to the movers and shakers at the Pacific Union Club, the
Bohemian Club and the best parlor houses all the way back to
Belle Cora's—and Dolly Adam's place over on Ellis, may her
prematurely deceased soul rest in peace. Jessie Hayman has it
now, but Dolly's ghost watches the inventory and visitors you
can bet. And Maud Nelson's, Tesse Wall's, you name it. This
is an open town, son, comes from the spirit of the Forty-niners
and the Gold Rush. Hell, back East no Jew boy who wasn't filthy
rich would be allowed in places like those with the goyim." He
shrugged."You probably wouldn't be sitting here right now
yourself." Izzy's eyes twinkled behind his spectacles."Maybe
you've changed."

Audie saw his father's scowl when they'd passed Jews in
Charleston while riding to church, and swallowed. Izzy was right,
and the realization left Audie silent with embarrassment.

Izzy laughed, with a piece of meat wedged between
prominent front teeth."So, you got robbed by some little tart
right off the boat, and then ended up in the bed of some mysterious and beautiful woman, right?"

"That's ... substantially correct."

"Ha!" Izzy slapped his thigh."You're one of the lucky

ones. Don't you see? Don't you know what you are now, from one day's worth of trials and tribulations after a train ride across the country, and stepping off that boat?"

"What?"

"A gigolo, Audie, you're a gigolo!"

Something rose in his chest, and Audie sprang up as his chair bounced off the wall. He grabbed it, set it straight, and turned to Izzy. "I'm afraid you have mistaken my character. I cannot continue this conversation. Thank you for the lunch, sir. I'll be going now."

"Whoa, hold on!" Izzy's hand was on the sleeve of his coat, and Audie hesitated before tearing it away. "Don't get so het-up boy. You've just arrived, and I apologize," his eyes twinkled again, "especially after arming you properly."

Audie sat down feeling the senseless grin on a face still burning. Once again he felt light headed, and a laugh bubbled from his chest. "Damn, I suppose you're right."

Izzy guffawed across the table. Audie began to cough, and Izzy motioned to the waitress who brought a pitcher of dark steam beer from a bank of spigots at the back of the place. "Welcome to the next phase of your life, pilgrim." He lifted his mug in a toast.

"Thank you, I suppose."

"You should come here for breakfast. Best Virginia smoked ham in town. Praise the Lord that folks back East don't know my wicked lust for the lowly pig." Izzy said between draughts of beer. He wiped foam off his mustache, leaned over his plate and stroked his beard. "Tell me about your new woman. Sounds like a rich one who's come here from New York or New Orleans, or maybe even Paris, to set up a house."

"If she is she sure fooled me. She doesn't have an accent or anything. She just plucked me off the street after I was drugged and robbed by this little whore after getting off the ferry from Oakland, and there these were two thugs who—" Audie shook his head. "I don't know what happened to those fellows actually. Oddest thing. Anyway she cleaned me up, and … and then she gave me the greatest night of my life. Then she gave me a hundred dollars, told me to see the town, and to come back this evening."

Izzy whistled. "You must be some kind of cocksman, son."

Audie leaned back in his chair with a complexion waxing toward scarlet.

Izzy laughed. "Pilgrim, successful madams have picked up young fellows like you since the world began. And she sure must have loved *you* if she's throwing money around like that. You should be proud of yourself, son."

Audie toyed with his steak knife, twirling the point on the stoneware platter with his index finger on the handle while avoiding Izzy's eyes.

"What's the matter? You sure shouldn't be ashamed if you gave her that kind of a ride. Good God, you didn't expect a virgin, did you?"

"I-I'm not sure what I expected."

"Expected?" Izzy hooked thumbs in his belt below a grey silk vest with the golden fob of his pocket watch dangling. "Audie, you … " Izzy cleared his throat. His eyes grew serious, and his voice dropped to a whisper, "son … you were a virgin?"

"Yes, sir." Audie mumbled into his potatoes.

"Good *God* in the bosom of Abraham, Sarah and Hagar!" Izzy stood up across the table, reached over to grab either side of Audie's cheeks, and pinched them. Audie's eyes widened as Izzy kissed him on the forehead with a beard smelling of cigar smoke. "You were! You *were!*" He shouted as the entire restaurant turned to watch. "Mazel tov! This boy has become a man!" He proclaimed to the room full of strangers. He pulled Audie to his feet, tossed a bill on the table, and led him out of the restaurant by the arm waving his free hand expansively over the city like some patriarch of the ancients gazing across the fertile land of Goshen. "Come on Audie, let me show you our fine City of Sin!"

Izzy guided him across Market past the ornate marble facade of the Baldwin Hotel and up Ellis. "This is the Uptown, Tenderloin. Every great city has one, like a fat cut of meat along the spine of commerce where the more carnal of recreations reside." He pointed to a well-kept dark redwood Victorian where a beautifully dressed young blonde accompanied by a chauffeur in a charcoal grey uniform was ascending the travertine steps as they passed, having just disembarked from a Siemens limousine at the curb. The big car glistened like a black diamond with the red spokes of its wheels matching the red velvet cloth of its interior.

Audie watched the blue crinoline of the girl's dress shimmer across her slim body as she sprang up the steps an unladylike two at a time, to arrive at a polished oak double door set with stained glass that was immediately opened by a Negro maid in a gold uniform and white apron.

"Two twenty-five Ellis Audie, Diamond Jessie Hayman's Parlor House and Resort. It's home away from home for some of the wealthiest gentlemen on *any* coast."

"That's ... a whore?"

"Shhhh!" Izzy put a tobacco-stained hand to Audie's mouth. "She's one of the *demimonde*— a cultured pearl that may be handled for a substantial fee, but not without very specific rules as to one's behavior. If Jessie heard you, she'd probably have the coppers tossing you off this block entirely."

"Sorry. Where are we going anyway?" Audie glanced back at

the dark three-story building with gilded columns around bay windows that were set with stained glass flowers. A red silk curtain glowed from the top one.

"To a tailor's to get you properly attired for the better company in which you are to run, and of course for your fascinating lady when you return to her attentions this night."

"Oh."

They passed a five-story pale green Victorian at the corner of Mason where a well-dressed man with another beautiful young woman on his arm was alighting from a Hansom pulled by a bay Clydesdale. A gilded sign over the door at the top of the marble stairs proclaimed **Poulet d'Or.**

"People call it the Poodle Dog." Izzy said, tipping his hat to the couple. "She's another of the demimonde and he's one of the mayor's pals, probably here to have a confab. Hear a partner was killed at the Municipal Crib last night on Jackson. Usually it's just one of the girls. That's the cowyard the Mayor's got a stake in. They have ninety girls working their tails off for him and his buddies, although she's definitely not one of them-too high class. Abe Ruef is the guy behind the throne and his boys call this place headquarters. The cost of their nightly refreshments could keep a working family in the chips for a year." Izzy swept a hand across the building. "This is where the real business of town is conducted. They run everything: who gets the contracts, permits, stuff from the railroads and docks, which of these restaurants gets the best champagne and caviar off boats, and who gets the leavings. They got their hands on a half-dozen boatloads of stuff headed for Panama where they're building that canal and resold it in Oakland. Hell, they own locomotives, ships, you name it. Hear they even fixed a fight at the Mechanic's Pavilion Wyatt Earp and Lucky Baldwin put on. Earp's got a rep as a straight shooter, but he knows which side his bread's buttered on. Mayor Schmitz is Abe Ruef's man and he takes care of the public side. They run the Union Labor Party that the lumpenproletariat call the Workingman's." Izzy slapped a wool-covered thigh."Ha!"

"What's the lumpenproletariat?"

"Most folks Audie, that's from Marx." Izzy turned up Taylor Street past a theater from which music issued. A boy in a sailor suit waived them in, shouting in a hoarse voice that the one and only Little Egypt had just arrived. Izzy stopped two doors down in front of a narrow shop whose windows were filled with suits, vests, top hats, bowler hats and canes."Right here, pilgrim." He ran his right hand over an ancient bronze mezuzah in the doorway and motioned Audie in.

An old man sat at the far end past a plethora of hanging garments that made the place look like a cave. He had a full grey beard, a blue yarmulke decorated with gold thread upon his head and wire-frame glasses not unlike those Izzy wore. When he saw them, he cleared his throat with a low rumble, and put down the garment he was working on."Israel, you apostate sonofabitch, vat are you doing?"

"Moshe, I love you too. This is my friend Audie Bond. He has just arrived from the East, and already is the kept man of a lady of means. He needs new clothes to go with his new station, and I couldn't think of a better soul than yourself to help him in his time of need."

"Liar. You vant that favor I owe you, and if you run over the bill you know I'll trust you, you sonofabitch."

Audie glanced from one to the other, then to the door.

"And you know my word is like gold, Moshe."

"It had better be. Your father gave you a name that speaks for us all, bless his soul."

"Next year in Jerusalem, cousin."

The old man squinted in Audie's direction. "Well, come here boy." Moshe stood and reached out with a measuring tape to Audie's shoulder. "You're a big one. Lucky for you I have one I can alter that a fellow ordered and never came back for. He got shot over on O'Farrell in front of Delmonico's three days ago over a worthless woman, and they buried him in a suit I sold his father for the occasion. This one is taupe herringbone with a nice hat to match. I can do it for … " He mumbled under his breath in Yiddish as he measured Audie's leg.

"I'll give you twenty dollars, you old bandit. I know he paid for the suit ahead of time. They always do. All you have to do is the alteration."

"Israel I'm wounded. In actual fact, I was forced to give them a much more expensive suit for the aforementioned payment, leaving this one made but not paid for. But because you are destined to return to the fold and give up your life of sin eventually, and this is your new friend who certainly doesn't want to listen to your miserable haggling, I will give it to you for thirty-five."

"Thirty-five! Oy! Twenty-five and not a dollar more! A man can rent a house for a month south of the Slot for less than that!"

"Yes, and be set upon by Irish wags or rolled by greaser whores before he gets back to Market my foolish cousin. If you are polite, I will make it thirty."

"Gangster!" Izzy huffed. He reached into his coat and produced a wad of bills as Audie stood speechless.

"I'll have this done in an hour, you being my favorite cousin, Israel."

"Only in the most extreme sense, Moshe Ben Hillel."

"That is overly generous, Izzy. Why are you purchasing a suit for me?"

"Because of someone did the same for me once upon a time

amongst the travails of the Coast, pilgrim. He was a righteous gentile who rescued me from a certain den of iniquity, and I swore that day to do the same should the opportunity arise. Consider it the superstition of a gambler, of one who has witnessed fate take furious and random turns, perhaps." Teeth flashed in his beard. "I suppose a couple of arrant bullets made me somewhat of a believer also."

Moshe produced a bottle of Chilean brandy from under the counter and poured the liquor into three remarkably clean glasses that appeared from the same place. "Now, a toast to your young friend Audie, who is the kept man of one of the demimonde I take it."

"Not only that, but one whose innocence was taken but last night by this mysterious woman, who certainly sounds like someone come to establish herself amongst the preeminent of the profession right here in our City."

"Indeed?" Moshe's thick eyebrows waggled. "You were but an innocent abroad far from home, but an innocent no longer. Tell me about this woman."

Audie fooled with his glass as he watched Moshe deftly cut out a seam and move the pants to the sewing machine, working the treadle with his feet. "I don't know if that's her-her profession or not. She's a rich woman indeed, but there was no mention of such a pastime. All I know is her kindness, and her beauty, and her first name only."

"Which is?" Moshe asked without looking up.

"Lorelei, her name is Lorelei. And she is very fair-skinned and black-haired, with blue-green eyes ablaze with the most beautiful fiery flecks of red, and a fine figure ... rather tall too."

Izzy laughed. "What type of woman would pick you up off the street where you lay robbed by a common whore, bathe you, put you in her bed, ravish your innocence, and afterward give you a hundred dollars but one who has known such misfortunes?

One whose heart is not hardened, and whose sense of kindness is indulged by such acts of spontaneous charity? Sounds like one of the best, to be honest, the kind this city is duly famous for. Perhaps she will become one of our renowned madams if that is her object. I'd definitely like to meet her."

"I'm certain she wouldn't mind."

Izzy held up a finger. "Lorelei is the name of a siren in Germanic mythology, a beautiful creature whose very voice lured unwitting mariners onto the shoals of the precipice upon which she dwelt to die in the waves. I would think that a lovely and fitting name for a woman in the unmentionable profession. Wouldn't you Audie?"

"It's a lovely name notwithstanding."

Moshe nodded over his work. "That it is youngster. That it most certainly is."

V.

The Second Night

Shadows of evening spread across the Bay from the east and joined with coal smoke from powerhouses and furnaces to shroud the City. Gaslights and electric lamps came alight. Doors of homes locked, and deadbolts were thrown as footpads and whores moved onto the streets of San Francisco.

Lorelei stretched in the tub, luxuriating in the strength flowing through her from feeding the night before. The reflection of Audie danced softly within her, churning in her soul. She yawned and closed her eyes, relishing his youth and innocence. A chuckle rippled off the high glass skylight like a string of tinkling bells. Thankfully, no man could hear it but Wu who thought her a demon, for if one chanced to catch the sound it would draw him like a moth to a flame.

Her brief exposure to sunlight when Audie had opened the window had reddened her skin, and she'd used the energy of his blood to heal as she slept the day. Her flesh was still tender to the touch of water, but she exulted in it. The too-raw feel of things was a reminder she was very much alive, carrying the lineage of one who had fought for millennia to bear her own child after the vengeful act of an upstart tribal god who'd sought to strike her barren. Alive beyond the multitudes who flickered like fireflies in her dreams living out their days around her, yet devoid of their one certain wealth.

For a moment, the loneliness of being the last of her kind abated as the tumult of souls throughout the city submerged in

the splashing of a tub. It was not that great familiar river full
of countless voices alive and dead, but only the sound of water.
She sank until her hair floated in a cloud around her, listening
to tiny bubbles breaking on the surface as she held her breath.
She went to the shower, stepped out, and patted her hair with a
towel before shaking it violently, flinging it about the room as
droplets covered the blue tile walls.

She would go out into the City and meet Audie, who, it
seemed, had met someone whose learning could be a bit of a
problem. Even one who fancied himself an apostate, being of
his particular people, might tend to bouts of fundamentalism
when confronted by the existence of such as she. Izzy's curiosity as a young man had led him to read many a tale of beings
like her, and to seek more from the lips of elders. Then again,
Jews had given up stoning women millennia ago, and hadn't
participated in that witch-burning thing in Europe at all. They
remembered her line at times, and had a word for her far more
appropriate than witch. Still, she should be careful around Izzy
Rothman. Jews had suffered almost as her own kind had and
had gained some measure of maturity from it, which in turn
could make one quite dangerous. She'd had Jewish lovers as
had all of her line, and some had the tendency to call her a
demon early in the relationship. But this was no rabbi, only
a player in the realm of the senses. Right now he was showing Audie the pleasures of fine drink while frequenting places
where all manner of other things were being ingested besides.
Hopefully he wouldn't get Audie too drunk or let him smoke
opium. It made the blood so muddled, and far worse, it made
the soul so clumsy and thick.

"Oh, well." She ought to get a cat. Find a promising kitten
and raise it with a few unique attributes. She was planning to stay
long enough to watch one grow as long as her new companion

proved useful. Audie was a clean canvas awaiting the colors of her pallet.

She donned her red silk robe and opened a window to gaze on the sails of fishing boats crowding the wharves. The air had the smell of the sea, and trembled with the voices of dolphins rising from the water as she focused on the Bay. The lights of a fishing boat caught her eye, and she felt the relief running through a young man gazing back from its deck at Russian Hill. He'd nearly drowned off the coast of Marin this day when his net had caught on a submerged mast in Drake's Bay, and his heart was fixed on the girl from Naples who awaited him. Lorelei felt a swelling in his chest for the unborn child turning in the girl's womb.

For an unguarded moment, she envied the girl with every fiber of her being, envied the brief flaring life of the girl's young flesh that was blessed with procreation, that state of grace that came as a package with aging and death. Such was not Lorelei's allotted place in the world, at least not yet. She moved away from the window, lest some passerby see the beautiful woman in a red robe and assume she was a common woman of the night. She had her consort for the months ahead.

Izzy was showing Audie what his moniker meant at Daroux's Resort above the Orpheum Theater on O'Farrell. The dice seemed blessed in the fingers of the little Jew; the other players treated Izzy with an ample amount of respect and Audie was included being his companion, which was good as Audie was rather drunk.

Audie accepted another glass of champagne off a tray carried by a buxom waitress who received tips that disappeared within the folds of her skirts or between her breasts. A tall red-haired woman gave him an appraising look as he stood beside Izzy at the table.

"Eleven!" Half a dozen voices shouted, followed by a cackle from Izzy. The dice were returned to his hand by a thin white-shirted man with sleeves held up by red arm garters, who chewed his mustache at one end as Izzy continued to win.

A stouter fellow in an expensive suit appeared out of the crowd, put his hand on the thin man's shoulder, and whispered in his ear. The man nodded, and left the table to be replaced by another who could have been his twin.

"Time to fold, pilgrim." Izzy removed the butt of a dark robusto cigar chewed to a mangled stump from his mouth and swept his money from the table. The blank look from the man running the game was far more professional than the scowl of the heavyset one who now sat at a table with a bucket of champagne. He stared morosely at Izzy while attended by two provocatively dressed girls in their early teens, and was shadowed by a huge mulatto man with gigantic arms carrying two pistols.

"Mister Daroux isn't happy tonight," Izzy chuckled in his ear, "but there's still time for an excellent Chilean brandy before we shove off." He moved to the bar, where a young woman whose breasts were held up by something under the low-cut dress she wore immediately produced a crystal snifter glass and poured two fingers of brandy into it. "And one for my young friend, Jewel." Another libation was poured for Audie by the bartender, whose breasts were objects of fascination for his inebriated gaze. Izzy held up his glass. "To your continued enlightenment and success in San Francisco, Audie Mitchell Bond."

The brandy went down smoothly, warming Audie's stomach without burning his throat. It was something he could appreciate now that Lorelei had salvaged him from his previous misadventures with Leah and liquor. He smacked his lips and rotated the snifter in his hand. "Awful good."

"And there are others who would like to pour us a dram should we appear out of this cold night to grace their parlors."

"How do all these people make a living, anyway?"

"Off the labors of every miner from Sutter's Mill to the Comstock load. Off Bonanza Creek and Nome's gold. Off the silk trade without lifting a finger to go dicker with some Chinee fella across the ocean. Off the spices of the cannibal islands and the perfumes of Araby. Off the fertile valleys of California, and the vines those Guinea guys are planting. Off the redwood forests and the mills. Off the oyster beds across the Bay without ever having to cut their hands shucking the slimy goddamn things." Izzy made a face, and lowered his voice. "Personally, I always thought people who eat oysters used to pick their noses and eat their boogers when they were kids."

Audie burst into laughter, and the tall redhead stared at him from across the room. Izzy nudged him with his elbow and tipped his hat to her. She wore a smile on full red lips under a delicate nose between startling green eyes that were set off by the diamond and emerald choker she wore with a huge green stone hanging in the cleavage of her dress from a silver and diamond chain. "She likes your looks, pilgrim."

"Who is that?"

"Diamond Jessie Hayman. The girl who just poured your drink works for her. Mr. Daroux's paying for some extra help with the guests he's got from back East. Two senators around here somewhere," Izzy glanced about, "though I haven't seen either of 'em. They're probably keeping some of Jessie's girls busy. She keeps 'em working, to keep herself in those diamond dog collars."

"Hayman … that was the name Leah used. She's the one who owns that house?"

"A madam, and not any madam but *the* madam of San Francisco. Even bigger than Tessie Wall, although you can bet Tessie would have something to say about that. All these girls are hers."

"Why is she looking at me? I'm not a rich fellow or a customer."

"Well, you could be a rich guy, *and* a customer. You're dressed like a gentleman, you're obviously from an educated background, and you look damn good too. Or maybe it's just that other fabulous woman you've got on Russian Hill. Women seem to know when you're with one of the classy ones like they can read your mind."

"Really?"

"Sure. They leave something of them on you, something other women can smell almost even after you've bathed. I've had some good ones, and the women always know a goodly ways before men do. I think it's something we can't sense simply because we are men, something that goes way back to the pagan gods and the witches in the Bible."

"What witches?"

"Lots of it's in the Apocrypha that was taken out of the Bible. Great reading if you can find it. That's what's left of the really good stuff they took out."

"What?"

"Studied it, pilgrim. Of course it's just my opinion." Izzy took Audie's arm, with the glint in his eyes magnified by the thick lenses of his glasses. "Think I'll introduce you."

"Wait!"

Izzy pulled him halfway across the room, the other half being closed by Jessie who was approaching as if on a signal. "Kiss her hand when she holds it out."

She had a hand out as Izzy began an introduction, and Audie found himself holding the white eighteen-button evening glove in his own. He felt the warmth of her through the thin silk on his lips as they brushed the back of it, all the while hoping he didn't seem a total bumpkin in the process.

"Audie Mitchell Bond, what a lovely substantial name." Jessie's eyes seemed to measure him in ways they had no right to though he couldn't say how. Nonetheless, the flame-haired six-foot goddess before him had him instantly off balance. "And where are you from, Audie?"

"West-West Virginia … Ma-Madame."

She laughed, though he didn't know what he'd said that was funny. "You've been seen in the company of a very distinguished lady over by North Beach, one who must have reason to keep your company. Tell me, what is it?"

Izzy shot him a look.

"Miss Lorelei's business is her own, but I have the privilege of being her companion for the time being."

"How fortunate, but what are her intentions in San Francisco? Does she seek employment? Investors, perhaps?"

"As to that I don't think so ma'am. She appears independent in her finances as in everything else, but I'll mention your offer."

"Only a question, only a question. Do tell her I would like to make her acquaintance though." With that, Jessie nodded at one of the girls who floated up in a rustle of satin, and produced a card from between her breasts with a red embossed heart framed in gold upon it. It was warm from the cradle of her skin and smelled of perfume. Audie took it. His thumb rubbed the heart as Jessie continued. "I'd wager there's good reason she's keeping you. I'd like to find that out for myself perhaps, if the occasion ever arises."

He felt a lump in his throat, having never been politely propositioned by someone who appeared to be a lady though her actual profession was far from that. "Thank you, Miss … "

"Hayman, Jessie Hayman."

"Thank you, Miss Hayman."

Jessie removed her glove and held out a hand to shake his. She ran fingers through his palm, and a shiver ran up his arm. San Francisco was turning into a hell of a place to meet women. Might he ever meet any decent ones here, ones he could possibly mention to his family? Could he tell a decent one if he did meet her anyway?

She gazed at the far end of the room, and he relaxed. Audie noticed other people staring at the entrance and turned, expecting a senator or someone of that ilk to be commanding the crowd's attention.

Lorelei stood in a shimmering blue silk dress between the huge mulatto and the girl who had served Audie champagne. The big bouncer stood rooted to the floor, hands at his sides. Jessie's girl had a blank expression on her face that made her unblemished features seem as empty of character as un-kneaded dough beside the radiance of Lorelei. The silence in the room was broken only by the sounds of a vaudeville act in the theater below and the faint laughter of the crowd.

Audie blinked, and her image made a flash upon his retinas as if he had been staring at a bright light. He closed his eyes, and hers were upon him when they opened. A rush of sensation closed the space between them, a physical jolt that made his head swim.

She was saying something to someone as she approached, but he couldn't make out the words. The entire room seemed a tunnel with all others pasted to the walls like two-dimensional figures, mere paper cutouts rotating around her like clouds in the night. Then she was beside him, taking his hand. "Hello, love. Has Izzy been showing you a good time?"

He caught his breath. "The day has made me forget how beautiful you are."

"And the night awakens my hunger for your company dear Audie," came back in a voice like music. Her cheeks dimpled at their play of words. Her eyes shone. He again marveled how they were both blue and green, and shot with tiny flecks of vermillion as long dark lashes batted the air. Her lips were uncolored by anything but themselves, shell pink and moist. The aching need to kiss them was all there was in the universe.

She brushed his mouth with hers in the most sublime torture, her cheek but inches away. He fought to get his bearings, but her scent was a maelstrom in his senses. "Israel, I am Lorelei. I believe Audie's mentioned me."

She held a hand out to Izzy, who seemed like he was going to fall to his knees as he bowed to take it. His legs shook under his herringbone trousers.

"I am speechless, Madame, at your beauty." came from his mouth in a voice like wood splintering in a gale. Izzy cleared his throat and regained his composure. "Audie has spoken of you, but alas, he did not do you justice with words as I doubt anyone could."

She smiled. "Men can be so gallant. I see you've taken our young pilgrim under your wing, Israel Yacov Rothman, son of David, grandson of Ygail of the Pale of Kracow. Become my ally, and doors will open for you as you open doors for the one beside you. Only remember," she moved toward Izzy and gazed down on him. Audie could see he was in shock that Lorelei knew his name and family even as her presence made him tremble. "What is to be will occur with or without your aid. I honor friends, Israel, not enemies."

Izzy swallowed, inhaling the perfume of her skin far outmatching the expensive scents on others. He blinked behind his spectacles and tugged at his beard. He stepped back and cleared his throat. "Tell me, could you have passed through that door had there been a mezuzah upon it?"

She laughed. "Even if it held a Mishnah written in the blood of Adam himself."

Izzy's face blanched as he looked her up and down. "*Liliot!*"

Audie glanced from Izzy back to Lorelei's dimpled grin. "What's going on?"

"You are of her kind." Izzy rumbled. "She unmentioned who would not suffer the will of Adam, nor Adonai himself. Are ... you her daughter? How ... ?"

"How nice to have made your acquaintance." Lorelei's voice rose, and Izzy fell silent as if his jaw were clamped shut. "I'll leave you to puzzle whatever meaning you can find from your quaint tales of demons and succubae." She shrugged. "God knows there are enough of them to keep you busy for a few more millennia." White teeth flashed against her lower lip, and she shrugged. "I suppose we shall be seeing more of each other."

She took Audie's hand, and all the feelings evoked by Izzy's words melted as her presence flowed into him and the elation of her touch made them diminish beyond caring. Jessie Hayman stared hard as Lorelei led him from the gambling establishment, but Audie failed to notice.

VI.

The Pact

The neat facades of Victorian homes loomed out of fog through the Isinglass windows of the motorcar. The engine growled as the chauffeur geared down to ascend the steep grade, and the hard rubber wheels slipped before finding purchase on the cobbled street as the car topped the rise between two redwood mansions. They roared down the other side with compression slowing their descent accompanied by a loud string of pops from the exhaust.

Audie's stomach lurched, and his head spun. He closed his eyes and saw her next to him as if they were open, studied the curve of her face and the round rise of her breasts through a shimmering blue dress. He inhaled the indescribable scent of her, and his head swam as if he had smoked opium. *How did she pluck me out of where Izzy had taken me?* He rubbed his eyes. It was as if her heart were a compass, and he the lodestone. Lorelei had simply appeared unbidden at the club on O'Farrell.

His head was clearing from the drink, or perhaps the intoxication of her was simply stronger as if she could cut through the fog of alcohol like a light on wind-swept rocks, and find him anywhere in the real fog of this city.

How did you know Izzy's name?

"I know more than others about many things, Audie."

He stiffened.

"And I can find my lover anywhere, just as he cannot find

me without my wishing."

"Did-did I speak aloud?"

"You know you did not. Do you mind me knowing your thoughts? I hope not, Audie, for they have thoroughly pleased me."

Once again that icy serpent tickled his spine. He reached for the door handle as they stopped at the crest of a hill to let a wagon pass. He could step out and just walk away into the city around him, flee this woman who was more than any woman could be. Against his will he glanced at her, and those multicolored eyes held him tighter than bonds of steel. She smiled, and he let out his breath. He kissed her, and the car began rolling.

When they reached Chestnut Street on Russian Hill, the little cafe where he'd had breakfast sat closed. The red letters **RESTAURANT** across the window were the color of dark wine in the streetlights, or blood.

"It was arrogant of me to speak like that to Israel. I'm rather embarrassed at my own desire to impress him." She gave him that dimpled grin. Again it aroused an overwhelming need to kiss her as if a switch had been tripped inside him. "But I so loved the look on the little fellow's face. However, now he will be obsessed with the riddle of me. This very moment he's thinking about seeking out wise old men and ancient books, both of which exist in this city for someone of his intellect who spent a portion of his youth in a Yeshiva. His particular education can be a bit of a bother." She yawned. "I try not to fool with people's memories, but it's difficult." Lorelei glanced at children playing along the street and sighed. "Perhaps I'll make him very drunk to the point of blackout, and see how much he remembers in the morning."

Audie tore his eyes from her countenance and forced himself to stare at the wall as he tried to make sense of that. "Whatever are you talking about?"

Her eyes became a brilliant blue. "In time, love." She kissed his cheek and led him to the travertine steps of her building. "First you need more of me just as I of you. Understanding will follow eventually, I promise you."

She took him to her high room. He found himself trembling as she removed his clothes, and asked himself why as her fingers sent ripples of shock through his body. They knelt on the red satin sheets. Audie gazed into eyes now green as emeralds, and closed his own. She giggled as he mounted her. Their mouths met, and her breath filled him as he entered her with all his being.

The question of God was the last thing he wanted to dwell upon, but this night demanded it. The place where he had been was too real, too huge to not wonder upon the very nature of Deity as he lay trying to collect his thoughts and the person he had been. The utter force of that luminous river in which he'd feared drowning before her laughter had saved him, the sounds of voices beyond beautiful, all spoke of things he could not name without that most fundamental question arising in his heart; *Where is God?*

Audie watched shadows play, and heard a multitude of voices fading in and out of his attention knowing some of those voices were long dead. Brown-skinned children laughed on a beach as they skipped shells on the waves and played with horseshoe crabs in the sand. A white-sailed ship bobbed on a bay before green islands and wild shorelines swarming with birds.

Death stood over them. Audie could *see* it: a dark figure that kept shifting ... an abyss devouring the light eyes need for knowing. *Look,* her voice said, *those children died crying all the names they knew for God as they saw the end of their world, yet in this endless moment they play in the sand and the sea sings to them. They live within me, and I hold them close.* Her voice fell to a gentle whisper. *Of all born to woman, I remember.*

His heart answered in kind. *How do I know them?*

"This is my burden, love. How can I forget?" She lay like a pale flame in the night. His heart thundered against her flesh, bouncing the fine white skin of her arm as his fingers wound in her hair. "You have seen some small portion of who I am, for I relish the company of you and wish to share myself. It's not all that easy, such knowing, is it?"

He sat up, to be greeted by a jolt of pain in the back of his head. "Who are you?"

"Nothing, if not a woman." She rolled over and stared at the ceiling. "Izzy guessed in his way, so we'll have to speed things up a bit. It would have been my habit to not tell you until you'd come to it yourself. Most men must know me in ignorance for their own sake, though I adore only the bright ones. The rest are so boring. With the others I can get what I need to survive, but it's so damn lonely." She blew a strand of hair from her mouth. "Here I am taking you with me and you don't even know what I'm talking about, but you *saw.* I set you loose in time just a bit. Rather different from all you know, isn't it?"

"Like being a god," he furrowed his brow, "but a sorry one who knows too much pain. What is happening, that you can put such visions in me? And why don't I consider this madness? Those children … "

"Then consider yourself fortunate for a passing touch that does not bind. Though be warned; your hungry heart will ask for more, and as your body lusts for me so shall your soul. My soul lusts also, Audie. I am the prisoner of all souls I have touched, and shall never have peace until I reach the end of my own span and have borne my daughter to carry on my task. This is my inheritance. We all have our burdens."

He winced from the headache, and fell back on the sheets as a snarl spread his lips at his own weakness. "Is this madness? I feel like ... like I'm at the Oracle of Delphi, Lorelei, being riddled by some priestess. All I have studied of the ancients and theology are spinning in my head. Questions within questions, a head full of mysteries and no answers to what's happening ... and what of Christ?"

She brushed his forehead. "You're always free to ask him. I have myself at times, but I think you'll find him rather mum about this."

He stared. "Then am I bewitched? I attended Marshall University, I studied the Classics and letters. I learned to think critically. I'm an educated man. I know this simply can't be the sex of my parents, nor can it be what girls give in cribs and parlor houses for money. Certainly it can't be what people refer to when they make bawdy jokes either. Anyone who's been through this would be changed. *Utterly!* Even the greatest lovers have never mentioned such things in literature or song. This is all new to me, and you know that. Perhaps if I'd had more experience, I would have—"

Her laughter washed away his thoughts. "No woman can take you where I go, and no lover can love you as I do."

In every fiber of his being, he knew she was right. He glanced at her face, and with great effort, tore his eyes away. "Then ... exactly where are you taking me?"

"Places you've never been in this life, that's for sure. But you're right, I owe you an explanation." Her eyes were luminous in the dim room with tiny flashes of red lightning. Her hair glowed in the streetlight coming through the window, framing the pale diamond of her face in a soft halo. "I want to say this gently, love, but a portion of our connection is my need for blood."

"What blood?"

"Yours, Audie. Your present weakness is due to the loss of it. But you can keep strong. I'll show you how. I always stop before you're damaged. The Chinese here in town have herbs that help, and I've been giving you some." Her teeth were in her lip. "Please believe me, I don't intend to hurt you, but to cultivate you as a man."

Something rose in his chest, and his head filled with sparks. Audie fought for air, as the knowledge of what his mind had refused to know overwhelmed him. He felt a sickly rush as the pillow under him seemed to open up, and he dangled over an abyss.

Her hand was on his cheek. Lorelei held him like a leaf in her palm over a dark ocean. *"Do not fear, my love."* Her other voice echoed within him.

He was on both sides of a battle threatening to tear him asunder. Audie cried out all the names he knew for God as he shook with the awful revelation of Lorelei his lover. He glanced up.

She smiled shyly, and tossed hair from her eyes. "I am a hunter of men, born to wait centuries to learn my own fate. But while you are with me no one can harm you. Only give yourself up to me by your own free will. I stand before you, Audie, humbly begging for your company in this vast and lonely world." She was a blur of images and sensations. A succubus of Satan or an angel of God he could not tell, only that she was a being from another realm for certain.

"See me as you will. You sought learning, my virgin lover, adventure, inspiration, freedom from the bonds of your upbringing, a glorious justification of your time on earth. You don't have to go to the Klondike. I can give you more than you dreamed for knowledge. The wealth of lifetimes. I've lived them, and saved the good parts, and I long to share them with you," she grinned, "and I won't take your soul in payment seeing as you're so worried about that at the moment. I really haven't the slightest idea what I'd do with it, so it's yours to keep," she chuckled, "I promise."

Her words came when he had reached the point where it mattered most, like a soft pressure on the ground beneath his feet as he trod a path she knew well. Lorelei was leading him whither she would, across her own terrain.

He gave himself to her touch, and the peace and comfort was overwhelming. With a great effort of will, he pulled away, holding onto himself enough to strike a deal, as he now considered his very soul in the balance no matter what she said. "Tell me that you are not evil!"

Her cheeks bulged. "I'm not evil, but good and evil are the fabric of my life as for every one of us." She stared at the darkened windows. "That's not to say I haven't had a temper at times."

"Izzy called you a Liliot. What in God's name is that?"

"A daughter of Lilith, Audie, though to be more accurate a very great-granddaughter. I said his learning could be a bit of a problem. He was only partially right, and of course he was seeing me from a rather burdensome heritage with a very large litany of complaints about my kind."

"Lilith?"

"She was the first wife of Adam, my learned theology student."

"I never read that."

"Of course not, neither have you read the sacred books of three thousand years past, or your own Christian gospels before those Roman bishops decided to pick and choose what was allowed for the sake of a long-dead empire." She ground her teeth. "Would that they'd got rid of that damn fool John's Revelations and kept Mary of Magdala's story. We might have had a meeting of the minds long ago."

"Mary Magdalene?"

"There is a gospel of hers, also. Women have tried again and again to reach people such as your pasty-faced father who rapped your knuckles at the dinner table with a hickory rod when you reached for the cream." She bit her lip. "Excuse me; I'm using your memories a bit capriciously."

Audie opened his mouth, closed it, and rubbed his eyes. "I rather like the Book of Revelations."

"As have all who've sought justification for cruelty in the name of Christ." Her lips curled. "Izzy hates oysters. I hate John of Patmos. He had nothing to do with Christ and he makes me vomit."

"Has a lover ever turned on you? I mean, you're taking apart my religion and somehow I'm allowing it, but some—"

"There is no greater wound than to the heart. I can heal from things that would kill you, but to lose a great love to death is worse. And yes, a lover has turned on me. It was when your ancestors lived under England's crown. He took his King James rather seriously."

"Of what realm do you come?"

"Creation is as much a mystery to me as to you. My line goes back eons to a time of glorious sacrifice like a dream whose roots are within you. My years are longer than those of what you consider mortal beings, it's true, but I need their willing company to survive. To be alone is truly a doom for me, but I can't stand forcing men to give of themselves what I need for my own satisfaction. For my survival, yes, but I have come to loathe not having a lover who by his nature needs to know me." She shook her head. "In that I seem to be different from all those who came before me. Such is my gift, and my curse."

"How old are you?"

Her eyes were blue and bright as stars. "How old do I look?"

"Just right," he began. The absurdity made him grin in spite of the situation.

She grinned back. "I was conceived in Ireland in the fall of the year sixteen seventy-nine, and born in a log cabin west of the Massachusetts Colony the following midsummer's eve."

"Wha ... *really?*"

"My mother came as a rich noblewoman across the ocean, fleeing a death warrant put upon her for taking the life of the Lord who conceived me. Such is the way we are born, but you needn't worry about that and it's not something I need get into now. I spent my youth hiding amongst the Indians as the frontier was pushed west after my mother, my mother was hung as a witch, *twice,* Audie, and burned the second time that she not rise again." Lorelei's porcelain nostrils flared. "Let me be clear about that; I am in no way a witch as you conceive one, nor a monster, a demon, or an evil being. This is my true and natural form, as a young woman."

He took a breath as he fought falling into her eyes. "You're too beautiful for a witch."

Her laugh was a purling brook. "Thank you, although I could show you witches who would challenge that assertion handily. Neither am I cruel, though I have been sometimes given to anger as anyone born to woman. I know many languages and cultures, and the deepest thoughts of men, but only a select few I take for a companion." She put a palm to his cheek. "I can give you success and wealth, though I only tap the potential you already have and show you things you wouldn't have been able to guess except in your doddering old age when they would be of little use. It takes good material to begin with, and I see that in you Audie."

"Um, thank you."

The scent of flowers tickled his nose. "And the fact you were a virgin makes it rewarding for me, just as a man wishes for a virgin bride. You could say you're a clean slate for my brush, someone I can have a positive influence on so to speak." She smiled. "I hope I'm not going too fast, but I'd be truly honored if you decided to stay for a while." She mussed his hair. "We do fit quite nicely, don't you think?"

"You said your mother took the life of the man who fathered you."

"I was hoping we'd leave that for later. Yes I did, but it could be centuries before I produce an egg, and the man who gives himself to that task shall be wholly willing I assure you. It's the only way it happens, but I really wouldn't worry about that. I'll know when the time comes."

"Then ... I have a choice?"

"Of *course,*" she rose from the bed with a trill of laughter, "you can leave right now, although I'd recommend you eat first. You could most certainly have gotten out of the car when we stopped on the hill. In spite of what you felt, I wouldn't have held you. Your bonds were your own desire. And I'll give you money should you want it. You can leave for the Klondike today, Audie." She winked. "I thought I'd made it clear that only a willing lover shall grace my bed, oh proud young stallion of twenty-two years."

"It seems I have a wilderness before me to explore here, one rich with treasures I never imagined." He stroked her cheek. "You hinted at lives you've taken."

"Yes I did." Her eyes grew dark green. "I have killed, Audie, mostly for survival, occasionally when someone has refused to let go of their savagery, and sometimes to save an innocent life. Often much time has passed between such things. I wish I'd killed to save that girl you saw in your dream, but she never fought for herself and it left me powerless. And at other times I've killed when it is *ordained*, when in rare perfection a soul's sacrifice is more than willing, but that's really not killing as you think of it. Your own forefathers killed to have and hold the land where you were born, and sought to extinguish the memories and souls of those that were slain. What of those who prayed in the mountains of Appalachia for thousands of years? That to me is an abomination, although it is the way of men. I have seen family memories in you as I walked amongst your thoughts, but unlike that throne-polishing *God* of yours, I refuse to believe the sins of the fathers are branded upon the sons." She chuckled, "Lucky for you." Lorelei shrugged white shoulders, and he reached to stroke them. "At least I cherish the lives who are gone and do not seek to erase their souls from our own. We need keep them long after their physical forms have returned to the earth. What a wasteland the world would become if some men truly had their way." A flash of blood filled her eyes, and was gone. "You have no idea how much they've taken already."

"Am I amiss to say that my memories are private things?"

"No Audie, just blessedly ignorant. I am the only one on earth who shares so many lives, and yours is a beautiful repast. Better to be savored and tasted than wasting away on some table wholly unappreciated."

He glanced between his legs. "We're back to the subject of food."

She laughed. "Well yes, you are food if you insist my admitting again-living, breathing, wonderful *food*, Audie, but it's your heart and soul that nourish me. I'm not going to chew you up and spit you out, and I'm not going to kill you either. The pleasure you experience making love to me is greater than with any other woman on earth, and don't tell me you wouldn't do it now at the drop of a hat. It's my responsibility to keep you strong so you don't kill yourself in your enthusiasm. Men are so ready to do that. Besides, long after you have reached the end of your natural span, part of you will dwell within me … as I shall be in you to the last of your days and even after. That's already done, though you don't know it because this is new and you are young. But I promise that when your time comes in old age, and you *will* live to the end of your potential if you share yourself with me, but when your time finally comes, Audie, I will be there to take you to that other side. It's a promise I shall keep."

"What can you tell me of that other place?"

"You mean death. I can't go there myself. It always blinds me; it's so bright when I get close to it." She shook her head."People have their own ways of getting there, yet they deny that there are many ways of coming to death out of their own fears, even when they see others pass well." She gazed out the window."There was someone I helped the day you arrived, someone who touched your dreams," her white throat rippled, as she swallowed a lump in it,"and a part of me envies her even in her despair." She made an expression Audie couldn't read at all."All I can tell you is that at the end, there's nothing left but love."

"Then you actually have been in the presence of God?"

"Whomever or whatever. As I said, it's a mystery to me also. There's no describing it, so I can't tell you any more about it. Besides, it scares me."

"What does?"

"The totality. I know death in ways you can't conceive, and

parts of the dead that remain for the living after death as a gift or a curse. But there's a place where we cannot go while alive, any one of us. When it comes, most of it will be the same experience as everyone who has passed that way, although part of me shall dwell in my daughter to call upon in times of need of course."

"Then you shall die?"

"Of course, I'm not an immortal being. I just have a lot longer time to get things straight, thank God."

"Then ... you believe in God?"

She made an exasperated sigh. "Those words were habit Audie, *Wakan Tanka.*"

"What?"

Wakan Tanka, great mystery, the Lakota Indian name for God. I lived amongst them in the last century before the *Wasicun,* the Fat-Eaters as they call whites, made it over the Missouri in numbers." She chuckled. "Of course I'm the whitest of all, but when you're a sacred being it's rather different. They called me White Buffalo Calf Woman. It was a wonderful interlude, even if I felt the coming from the East with a surety that made my life seem like a passing play in the wilderness. I hid amongst them as I was not at all ready to go out into that world from which my mother had fled. I have the gifts of their seers in me and shall always carry a fondness for their sense of the Creator. *Mystery* suits God so nicely. There's nothing better. But enough of me, Audie, I've had to tell this story too many times and I'm boring myself. What about you?"

"Well." He gazed at the hollow at the base of her throat, watched blood pulse under skin like pale silk, and swallowed. "It's quite an offer. I suppose you're right that I won't get a better option at the drop of a hat, anyway, for the spring at least." He began to go on, but the words left him in the brilliance of her smile.

VII.

The Emperor

Audie awoke on his third day as Lorelei's lover while she slept through the sun's reign. He was careful to keep light from her high-ceilinged room once she explained how the sun was a bother to her white skin and singularly beautiful eyes. He accepted it along with everything else, solicitous of her well-being as any gentleman would be for a lady's welfare. The feelings were not in the least different. Of course, she was indeed unique amongst women. That just made it better.

He drank three bottles of the bitter elixirs she'd placed beside the bed for him, showered, grabbed his new journal, and made his way to the cafe where he hoped Diana would be working. A wry smile spread his lips as thoughts of ravishing the young blonde danced through his mind. Lorelei might have awakened such feelings, but surely they were his own. A flood of implications preoccupied him as he turned from the steps at the base of the stairway, and ran straight into the man with the odd military uniform he'd noticed standing on the sidewalk the day before. Audie and the man let out a gasp.

The man's curly brown beard quivered as Audie began to offer an apology. "Ooof, son, in a hurry to get somewhere?" He asked from under the shade of a tall military hat like an old admiral's topper or an upright clamshell. The gold tassels on it were frayed, and one of the epaulets on the shoulder of his blue coat had been sewn back on.

"Actually sir, only breakfast."

"Ah, a late riser. You seem rather fresh-faced for one of the local night life, but there are always new recruits I suppose. Nonetheless I wish you a pleasant repast. My name is the Excellent Joshua A. Norton, Emperor of the United States and Protector of Mexico, of late ensconced in this golden City which has deigned to be my capital. May I join you?"

Audie found himself without an answer as he tried to make sense of what the man was saying. Obviously the man was completely insane.

"And let the meal be upon my treasury," the Emperor offered before Audie opened his mouth, "provided by donations from this glorious metropolis of boundless opportunity and sin."

"Well, all right I suppose. My name's Audie Bond." Audie offered his hand, which was promptly seized with a force that almost pulled him off his feet.

"Excellent. This cafe just to my rear is a wonderful establishment."

"I was going there myself."

They sat at the same table he'd occupied the day before. The place was filling for lunch and the smells of fish frying, cabbage boiling and cigars provided a heavy olfactory background to the rough and varied crowd. Two girls looking the worse for wear were eating steak and eggs at the table next to them. The thin brunette caught Audie's glance, and gave him back a tired smile out of habit as if she were standing on the street outside, before turning back to her companion and cutting herself another bite. He supposed if he approached her with money, she might get up from the meal and follow him to some room as easily as stirring cream in her coffee. Audie imagined her returning to her food after the quick and uncaring sex to which she was used, scowling at a cup grown cold. He turned to Emperor Norton.

"I recommend the cioppino," the man was saying, "an excellent fish stew which does justice to the ethnic origins of the proprietor. It provides all the essentials of survival for a body when accompanied by a generous helping of our local sourdough bread whose recipes are handed down from the original Forty-niners, along with butter and a simple Chianti wine. Please, allow me to order for both of us."

"Sure ... I, what do you *do,* Mr. Norton?"

"What?" The man smoothed his ragged blue coat before answering. "I administer and protect the good citizens of the North American continent, Canada being a protectorate of my realm, as of course is Mexico. This City recognizes my reign, and thusly I have graced it with my continued presence."

"That's wonderful, but how do you, ah ... make a living?"

"The Imperial mint prints all the money I need, young Audie. Observe," The Emperor pulled several hand-drawn sheets of paper from his breast pocket, each a bill for fifty cents with a toga-clad picture of himself surrounded by olive branches and his right hand grasping a bundle of sticks with an ax head protruding from it.

"What's that?" Audie pointed to the ax thing.

"A caduceus, the Roman symbol for the power of many standing together as one. It says that one stick may be broken easily, but many together are stronger. It is both a weapon and a badge of office in the hands of the wise ruler."

"Oh, I thought a caduceus was two snakes, with—"

"Royal tender is accepted in many fine establishments in this town. This, my friend, is one of them."

Diana appeared with her hands red and cracked from cleaning the kitchen. Fine lines were around her wide blue eyes from not enough sleep, but she seemed enormously more attractive than the two whores at the table. She was young and real, and full of life. Audie wondered if that was how he looked to Lorelei: young and fresh, and full of what she needed simply to stay alive.

"Hi Audie, good to see ya."

"You too, Diana."

"That rich lady treatin' you right? You look kinda tired today."

Audie's grin grew wider."I had a somewhat taxing night. I guess the gentleman here is ordering for me."

"Correct. Young lady, I'll have my regular repast for myself and for this young man who is my guest."

Diana put hands on her hips and cocked her head."Emp, you tryin' to pass that goddamn scrip again?"

Audie imagined the blond bush beneath her hard belly, and his lust rose up in a fire ready to explode like some goat-thing on midsummer night's eve. He was a satyr of pure desire, ready to spread his seed and secure in the love of a Goddess. Did Lorelei know his thoughts, even in her sleep? *Is she really that old? Where does she go as she lies sleeping?*

"Tony is quite sanguine about royal tender, young lady."

"It's crap. And it ain't no goddamn tip, buddy."

"That's all right Diana. I'll get this."

She glanced at Audie and shook her head."Okay, if you're payin'. One royal repast comin' up or somethin'. Lucky you got him this time Emp." She tossed a lock of hair from her eyes and returned to the kitchen.

"You seem like one of those who finds himself in a great state of transition, Audie," the Emperor went on as if having never been interrupted by a mere wench of a waitress.

Audie blinked, pulling himself away from a vision of Lorelei asleep in the dark with the air circling her body like a host of angels. *What is she? Am I damaged? Cursed? Is she really what she claims? What's a Liliot?* He ran a hand across his face and tried to regain the thread of Emperor Norton's conversation.

"No? You look like someone who might be headed for the goldfields of Fairbanks, or the treasure beaches of Nome."

"What? I'm sorry sir. I lost the conversation for a moment. I was thinking about someone."

"Ah-ha. The rich lady aforementioned by yon serving girl?"

"Yes, sir. I suppose you could say I am presently living in sin."

"A sojourn as a gigolo so to speak?"

Audie chuckled. "I should hate to describe it as that."

"Of course, of course. The better madams of this great city are prone to lavish their favors on a select few young men. You lucky devils are evening the score I suppose. I could think of worse ways to pass the time myself. I would admonish you to watch your back, though. Many a young plaything of the demimonde has ended up in the Bay at the hands of the next paramour after falling out of favor. The ways of a woman are most fickle, I assure you."

"I shall take that advice to heart, sir."

"Good. You are a promising young chap. Now, didn't you say you were headed for the Klondike?"

Audie blinked. He was sure he hadn't mentioned it. "I-did I? I was planning to go straight up there to write a book, but I lost my kit upon arriving to a … a scoundrel. Then I was going to work here and book passage on a steamer or salmon packet come May. I hear there is still gold aplenty in the Fortymile country. Enough to fill a mule train with a summer's labor. Things have changed remarkably for me in the last couple of days though."

"It does seem you are well provided for this very moment. I have seen the woman you are presently residing with, though only at night. Quite remarkable I must say. Where is she at this moment?"

"She's-she's resting."

"Ah," bushy eyebrows rose under the dorsal fin of a hat, "she sleeps the day, I take it."

"Yes, she does most of the time."

"Strange, but her beauty evokes a sensation in me I cannot describe, as if she were truly of another time and place almost. I've seen her comings and goings by night. I see all that happens in this town eventually and am privy to many secrets that the common passerby would not know, being considered mere local color and a total fool by some."

Audie blinked. The self-knowledge of the man across from him seemed out of character in a way. What kind of life did this man lead on the street? Where did he sleep? "How did you end up here?"

"Being from a family of good standing in the East, I was an investor. Trusting the wrong people, I lost it all, and one day was left standing at the foot of Commercial Street shouting at the uncaring waters of the Bay while debating with myself the prospect of taking my pistol and ending it all. It was then I became aware of someone who was quite distraught at my condition, a well-dressed lady of the demimonde. She took pity upon me, and gave me five dollars in gold even as the 'better citizens' scowled as if I had fallen from the moon like a piece of green cheese.

"I stood there ready to throw the filthy lucre into the sea, when I realized that I did not have to play the wretched game of dishonesty that is business and finance in this world of greed, lust and avarice. Thusly I held my hands out over this great amoral City before me and proclaimed myself ruler of all this domain to the applause of several miners who had just arrived off a steamer from the treasure sands of Nome. They showered me with gold and good wishes as they being just back from the hardscrabble world of the north recognized my baptism in sin you see, the epiphany of my bankruptcy in the world of Mammon so to speak." The Emperor scratched his beard and gazed into the street. "Every city needs one fool to know itself as a community. Verily it is part of the ancient harmony of the spheres that keeps a society together, and so I have assumed that mantle in this town: King of the Fools. Though I own nothing, I go wherever I please. I am welcomed by some of the rich and notable in the mansions of Nob Hill, in the honky-tonks of the Barbary Coast, and even the occasional Parlor House." The Emperor winked. "Things could be worse."

Diana reappeared with warm sourdough bread and placed it down with a cube of butter in a cracked dish. Emperor Norton tore loose a slice, and spread butter across it as she put two glasses on the table and poured red wine into them from a green bottle in a frayed straw basket.

The Emperor nodded his approval and held his glass up in a toast. "To a long life Audie, and the answers to your own singular dreams."

Audie held his glass of blood-red wine from the hills of Napa and gazed at its rippling surface. He cupped it like a chalice, and put it to his lips while watching the pout of Diana's mouth.

VIII.
The Boss

The hiss of a Stanley's boiler alerted Sergeant McCauley to rise from the pillow between him and the damp stoop. A long black motorcar was crossing Dupont, climbing the hill from the direction of Portsmouth Square in the fog, and the overflow from its engine left a steaming stream like a great overheated horse pissing on the cobblestone street as it rolled to a stop. A gray- uniformed man got out and opened the door at the curb.

McCauley motioned to Patrolman Grady to return a flask to his pocket and fumbled with the buttons of his coat as he tried to hide his un-tucked shirt. He hadn't recognized the car, having expected the Rolls Phaeton. He straightened his waxed mustache, and saluted as a passenger in a gray overcoat and bowler hat emerged with a large leather valise in hand.

"You won't be long?" came a female voice from the big black car.

"Not at all, Violet. You're welcome to come in."

"Don't even joke Abraham! I wouldn't be seen *dead* on those goddamn steps!"

"My apologies." Abe smiled, and leaned in for a kiss.

The two cops blinked as the flash of diamonds from a jeweled dog collar necklace adorning the throat of the very young and beautiful woman within caught their eyes. She huffed."I can't believe you'd have the gall to bring me here!"

"Violet my dear, I beg your pardon, but time is of the—"

The door slammed cutting him off, and the car sat hissing

steam on its tall tires.

"Evenin', Mr. Ruef." Sergeant McCauley said.

"Good evening Robert."

"You'll be needin' an escort?"

Abe Ruef nodded, ran a hand over his balding forehead, and straightened his hat. Since Jones had been killed here, he wasn't taking any chances. The occasional dead girl was one thing being a normal part of business, but Jones' murder had put everyone on edge. McCauley motioned to the younger cop who reached for the valise, but Abe pulled away and shook his head. Patrolman Grady shrugged, walked up the travertine steps, and opened the door for the Boss of San Francisco. He followed Abe into the building and stood by the door at parade rest.

The huge seaman doing duty at the door picked up a black truncheon with a smoldering cigar still held between the fingers of one big hand, snatched up a newspaper-wrapped bundle of fish and chips with the other, and stepped out of the way. A haggard blond woman holding a ledger sat on the hardwood bench. She grinned, exposing an incisor tooth inlaid with turquoise.

He nodded, avoiding her eyes. At the far end of the foyer was a door leading to a long hall opening on three dozen more doors from which the sounds of women moaning, men grunting, loud expletives and the wet slapping of flesh sporadically issued.

Abe unlocked the stout door to the left of the foyer with a large brass key, and stepped into a room holding three desks and two green-visored clerks who stood immediately. "Sit down. Where's Jules?"

"Downstairs, Mr. Ruef."

Abe nodded and stroked his drooping mustache. He crossed the office and climbed four steps into a narrow hall dimly lit by yellow bulbs every twenty feet. On his right were small peepholes allowing someone in the passage to look into each room where girls entertained customers. He snorted, put a handkerchief to his face, and hurried toward the stairwell at the other end of the building.

As a young man, Abraham Ruef had been a brilliant student and would-be reformer. He'd graduated from the University of California at Berkeley at eighteen and the law school at twenty-one. He spoke and read eight languages. He'd memorized more great speeches, court rulings, musings on democracy, the human condition, and dignity in the entire Western World than any damn one of those nabob neighbors of his on Nob Hill made rich by the Comstock Lode, the redwoods or the railroads. One day, there had come a time when the cynicism that had once insulated him from their doings had found a home in his heart and had settled with a vengeance. Now he was getting his.

Abe sighed. Perhaps it had been there all along and had only emerged with that epiphany, that *moment* when he realized no one, not *anyone*, was worthy of their own pretensions. Every rich sono-fabitch in California had skeletons in the closet and mistresses in the bed, perhaps even boys, and every business needed greasing from the lubricant of graft whether or not anyone cared. They usually did anyway only in regard to getting a piece for themselves.

He rubbed his nose. The world would grind to a halt without it. He'd seen far too much wealth going to men with not a fraction of his intellect to be squandered on idiot baubles and tawdry delights. The "People" were apathetic louts, more concerned with self-gratification than some rhetorical chimera of brotherhood spouted by their self-proclaimed leaders who were usually no more than carnival barkers anyway. Abe knew the Law, and he knew History, and was sure from the time of bread and circuses that the masses had been the same. Women were heartless in the end and cruel about a man's lot when it came to the endowments he might have been born with, most especially such a magnificent specimen as Violet. Only great wealth could buy a man such company … along with the concurrent pleasure of having her do his most carnal bidding.

He held the handkerchief to his face, blinking at the smell of used women and the pine tar cleaner used to scrub down the wretched facility the hoi polloi referred to as the Municipal Crib. Let his mayoral stooge wear that moniker along with the job Abe had planted him in like a palm tree at the Palace Hotel. And now he and Gene Schmitz, his handsome, dapper, orchestra-conducting cipher of a mayor were court-ordered to a hearing on the 18th by the damnable triumvirate of ex-mayor Phelan, Fremont Older of the Bulletin and the money and prestige of Rudolph Spreckels backed by the very considerable sugar fortune of his father Claus. Abe had received the subpoena from their hand-picked prosecutor this morning.

A shriek came from one of the rooms as he passed. "Ow! Ya pig! Not *there!*"

Abe swallowed. To imagine Violet working on the other side of that wall, being of the same ilk soured his stomach. He'd leased her from Jessie Hayman complete with a rather excellent pedigree that included time in a Catholic girls' institution, and had become quite habituated to her company. They'd had a wonderful dinner this evening while conversing in French, Spanish, and German over a bottle of Mumms at the Poodle Dog as every other man eyed her perfect skin, sparkling eyes and youth. He could take her anywhere, as long as word didn't get back to his wife. Violet was a glittering trophy who could hold her own in any social repartee as well as sex. Her manners were impeccable, and her price showed it. And he could make up for it all by making the girl do things no wife would suffer, that no well-heeled husband would dare even *ask*. He sighed. Where did Jesse *find* these girls?

"Ouch, sonofabitch! You're gonna pay another goddamn dollar or get the hell out!"

There was a loud slap. "Shadup!"

"Goddamn ya ta hell! I'm callin' the fuckin' bouncer!"

As a bell rang from the crib for an enforcer, Abe got to the end of the hall, unlocked the door, shut it on the wretched cacophony of the Municipal Crib, and descended an iron spiral stairway to the basement. He reached the door at its base, used two keys to release the deadbolts, and shoved the iron-sheathed portal open on a darkened office. "Jules!"

Abe cursed, fumbling for the light and cradling the pistol in his overcoat pocket with his other hand. There was a meow, and the big notch-eared tomcat Jules kept at work brushed Abe's leg. He bent to stroke it, and a purr as loud as a Southern Pacific engine erupted under his hand. Abe began to relax. He should take it easy, but he hated coming here. Someone from the upper classes who wasn't a customer seeing him step out of or into a car in front of the Municipal Crib was a reoccurring nightmare, and Violet's anger only served to reinforce it. He flipped the light switch.

The room was illuminated from the six lamps he'd installed so as to leave not a shadow while counting money, and he brought a hand to his face as his eyes closed against the glare. Abe opened them, gasped, and grabbed for his .45. It caught in his coat, and the pocket split.

Jules was draped naked on his desk at the far end of the room, and bills of all denominations, silver and gold coins, bonds and stock certificates were piled like garnishment at a ghoul's banquet around him. He looked like the roast pig at the Crocker's Christmas party with an apple in its mouth, but this apple was his penis and testicles red with blood. Milky blue eyes stared blindly over bulging cheeks at Abe's trembling pistol.

"Meow?"

Abe jumped as the cat glided across his pants leg, and he felt a dampness there.

IX.

The Wisdom of the Jew

Audie finished the excellent cioppino and was about to ask for more when he spotted someone on the other side of the smudged window. Izzy lifted a hand to the brim of his bowler hat. His eyes had a look of worry that was magnified by his thick glasses as he absently pulled at his beard.

"Excuse me." Audie pushed away from the table.

The Emperor made an expansive gesture. "Your worthy company has been appreciated young man. Remember: watch your backside as you become familiar with the peculiar qualities of our town. Scoundrels and sneak-thieves perambulate the streets at nightfall, and I have seen many a young sojourner such as yourself come to tribulations that I would wish upon nary a soul. Do not stray into Chinatown after losing your wits to drink, and down along Pacific they—"

"I surely shall, sir."

"Good. I hope to see you again, and listen to further tales of your progress."

"You too sir." Audie saluted and slipped Diana a dollar as he brushed by. Her hand squeezed the left cheek of his buttocks, and he turned in time to see a grin on her face as she disappeared into the kitchen. Then he was out on the street.

"Pilgrim," Izzy seized both of Audie's biceps in his hands, and the gun under Audie's arm dug into his flesh, "I tried to call you, but some Chink said you couldn't be disturbed."

"Call me?"

"The telephone at your place. That woman Lorelei gave the number to Jessie, so I—"

"She did?"

"Yep. Plenty is moving in the world to which you aren't privy pilgrim."

Audie grinned as what he'd been through in the last two nights burned in him like a flame. How could he even hint at it? How could he ever write about it?"It sounds as if you still consider my paramour some accursed denizen of the night, Izzy."

"More than you know." Izzy stroked his mustache and gave Audie a measuring stare. He took a deep breath."Did you know that she was here in fifty?" He gave him a look of importance that faded as he waited for a response."*Eighteen-fifty* Audie, that's *fifty-six years ago!*"

"What do you mean?"

"I mean she appeared over a half century ago, right here." Izzy reached into his coat and produced an ancient yellowed page of the *Alta California,* dated June 7, 1850."The Gold Rush is quite a tradition here. I got this from the private library of a friend of mine who has a theater on Pacific." He unfolded it and motioned Audie out of the breeze into a doorway."Look, look at this." He held the page out.

NOTORIOUS SYDNEY DUCK DISAPPEARS WITH DEMIMONDE

The Sydney Ducks have been cackling in the pond since one of their leaders,

Bobby Giles, lately of the penal institutions of the Far Pacific and Australia, was said to have absconded from the City in possession of some three hundred pounds of gold dust, nuggets, and coin stolen from the guarded offices of Alcade

*John W. Geary after Giles escaped from the prison brig Eu-
phemia anchored in the Bay. Rumor has it that the hoard was
to be divided between Giles and Several associates from the
sinks of sin and bawdy carousal known as Sydney Town, located along Sydney Cove.*

*After stealing the hoard, which surely took several ac-
complices, Giles was seen in Portsmouth Square in the company of a tall and striking woman, a recent arrival rumored
to be from the vicinity of New Orleans, France, or Ireland,
and known as Mademoiselle Lorelei.*

*Mlle. Lorelei is said to be above average height, have
long black hair, and skin as white as the finest Lady of Station, but her most identifying characteristic is said to be her
eyes, which are of several colours, being blue, green, and sparkling with flecks of red or vermillion.*

*Nine armed men under the aegis of the Alcade searched
the premises of the Fierce Grizzly Saloon for the bandits, and
were soon involved in a gun-fight that left two desperados
dead and several citizens wounded. The grizzly she-bear kept
chained at the door of the disreputable establishment was
said to have been put into paroxysms of rage by the alterca-
tion, and to have fed upon one of the dead until the man was
removed by his associates. A reward of five hundred dollars in
gold is offered by the office of the Alcade to anyone who has
knowledge of the thieves' whereabouts, payable upon appre-
hension of the pair Bobby Giles and Mlle. Lorelei.*

*Outgoing ships are being thoroughly checked in the Bay, as
well as all transport to the Goldfields and to the South. The rarity
of a comely White woman in these parts is sure to bring swift
capture of the two according to the general opinion of the Citizens of the City.*

There was more, but Izzy folded his arms and fixed his

gaze upon Audie."So, what do you think of that?"

"What am I supposed to," a vision of Lorelei walking this very street before he'd been born flitted by as it were this moment,"and what's a Sydney Duck?"

Izzy blew through his whiskers and fumbled in his pocket for a cigar."Some Aussie lugs that burned the town down a couple of times in the fifties and ran roughshod over folks. They're why we had the Committee of Vigilance—the *Vigilantes*. They hung a few in Portsmouth Square from lampposts to settle things down. But you're not surprised. That in itself tells me more than any reaction you could give me, Audie." Izzy lit the cigar, puffed it to a burn, and waved the thick maduro at the gray redwood façade of the house where Lorelei slept the day."That place was called the House of Blazes thirty years ago by the way. Hell of a bagnio and now she's in it." Izzy shook his head."She's got you good son. We should have a talk." He waved toward the docks and motioned for Audie to follow him.

Audie stood his ground."About what?"

"About that *Liliot* you're sleeping with! She's been around for a very long time and by many names. I truly think you could use some of what I've learned studying the ancients and their own peculiar experiences with her. I'd hate to see you a servant of Hell, Audie."

"She's not from Hell, Izzy, I can assure you." Audie hadn't budged from his spot on the sidewalk.

Izzy sighed, and pinched his nose."Then … where the hell *is* she from, pilgrim?"

"I can only speculate. Perhaps my capacity to conceive is limited by my education rather than aided by it, or perhaps my education is simply too limited in itself. She's very different from other women it's true, but she's not from Hell, Izzy, not by a long shot. But tell me what you think."

"Let's find a good place for a confabulation."

Izzy led him down to the wharves where fishing boats
with red sails clustered below drying nets and wire traps used to
catch shrimp and crab from the fecund waters of the Bay. Voices
shouted out in Italian, Greek and Portuguese above the smell of
steaming shellfish in great pots over earthen stoves built upon
the ground where men and women in stained canvas aprons were
selling it. Women in calico dresses, men in dirty overalls and
Chinese house servants filled the quay shopping.

Audie leaned on the gray redwood railing built above
a steep plank-way leading down to the wharves. The ramp had
small slats nailed crossways to prevent people from slipping as
they ascended it with their burdens or went to the boats below.
On the docks a bald eagle screeched, landed with a thump of wings
in a crowd of seagulls fighting over fish scraps, and the gulls flew off
crying in every direction.

Izzy chewed his cigar and studied the boats for a while,
leaning over the water lapping at ancient redwood logs driven
into silt twenty feet below. He puffed clouds of smoke as gulls
wheeled and cried and the fog burned off, and absently flicked a
wad of ash at the water. One of the gulls who'd lost a meal to the
eagle dove at the falling ash and a cloud exploded from its beak.
Both men laughed. "Ever heard of Lilith, Audie?"

Audie let out his breath. "Not until last night."

"She was the one Adonai, *God,* whose true name I should be
struck down for uttering," Izzy blinked at the sky, "Yahweh,"
he muttered, "chose for the Mother of Mankind, to be the wife
of Adam, the Father of Man."

"That was Eve, Izzy."

"Nope, Audie, it was *Lilith.* In those days, our Lord was a
tribal god you've got to understand. This was long before he was

this great omnipotent deity we think of as God today. He had his chosen people, but that was about it."

Audie rubbed his neck. "God has always been God, Izzy." He slapped the railing. "Last night, she's cursing John the Divine and today you're attacking Eve! I can't believe that I'm even *having* this conversation!"

Izzy stroked his beard. "Nor I, pilgrim. Here I'm falling back into things I grew up thinking were *maaseh,* what you'd call old wives' tales, but they're the only things that explain it. I never really thought a Liliot actually existed." He shook his head. "I think our concept and sense of God evolves as men do, but that woman certainly doesn't fit my conceptions either. Have you read Mr. Darwin's work?"

"The Origin of Species? Yes, and I find it utterly fascinating. In fact I believe it only serves to prove the infinite mind of God as I alluded to before. Creative to no end, and infinite to the furthest reaches of the—"

"Once my people were a wandering tribe, still are in a way, and we needed a strong and vengeful Lord to protect us. Lots of murder and mayhem in those days, let me tell you. Our God has evolved as people have and with a little help from that Nazarene the world embraces some version of him, but his roots are more humble I assure you."

"Yes, and what about Jesus?"

"He's not to my present point. I've got my own take on Mary Magdalene by the way that you might see a lot of sense in now, but let's return to Genesis. In the original version, God created Adam as first man and chose a goddess named Lilith as first woman. They found tablets in Mesopotamia a few years ago with one of the stories, in Ur, Audie, where Abraham came from. I can show you the research. Anyway she'd been around pretty much forever and was deeply ... *invested* in human events guess you'd say. God gave them the same instructions he gave them in the Bible we know today. You know; all things of the earth were there for Adam, every animal to tame or use for meat, every green herb for food, or medicine or clothing. But when he turned to Lilith and told her she was a vessel for Adam's children, and to follow him dutifully anywhere, she up and refused."

"Refused?"

"I think she told him she'd been around just as long as he had ... maybe longer." Izzy took the cigar from his mouth."-May the Lord forgive me for that sinful if well-founded speculation. Anyway, she wouldn't surrender her territory without a tussle. Well, that posed a problem for God you can imagine, what with her refusing to do the job for him and to bear Adam's children like that."

"The idea her kind came before the Lord on High never occurred to me." Audie gazed at an eagle soaring overhead."She sounds like a handful ... and of course she must have been beautiful to boot."

Izzy nodded."There are many stories of her, thousands, Audie. I grew up listening to them from the Old Country. One says she simply wanted to have sex from the top position."

Audie chuckled."Lorelei's a lot like her."

"This was a real quandary in those days and no joke by far. The Lord even killed a guy for spilling his seed upon the ground, and as far as Lilith went, he had to get rid of her."

"Why couldn't he simply ... destroy her, and start over?"

"Like to think he did, eh, pilgrim?" Izzy puffed on his cigar, rolled a mouthful of smoke, and blew it toward a ragged steamer at the docks with bandana-wearing men painting the funnels red while singing in Italian."But he wasn't the all-powerful *God* you're thinking of. He couldn't totally overcome her, but he could imprison her. His power was waxing in the world, and hers, of the days of pagan goddesses and such was waning, so he did. One version says he bound her at the bottom of the ocean with everlasting chains. That's what Mr. Jung calls the 'collective unconscious' nowadays. He's a fellow over in Europe like Mr. Freud who studies such things. Read him in the original German. 'Course Lilith didn't like that, and the girl had a famous temper. After that, some say God struck her barren, that she would never give birth to an alternate line to challenge his creation. But in spite of everything she retained terrible powers, to give birth to demons, to steal little children and devour their souls, and to take the firstborn son of each generation of Adam and Eve, whom God made from a rib of Adam to make sure *she* was of the same stuff and compliant to his bidding, and *curse* that man." Izzy tapped his cigar on the railing and glanced at Audie. "You didn't see her around any babies, by the way?"

Audie shook his head. "No, and she loves children. So … does that mean that I carry the mark of Cain?"

Izzy shrugged. "I never considered that. It's an interesting supposition. You're following this well, by the way. I don't see anything on your forehead, but I suppose it's symbolic anyway. Oh, well. 'Course Cain was the firstborn of Adam and Eve and he went and killed Abel. It was Lilith's curse did it, and none other, *Lilith,* whose name was struck from the Bible except as an accursed witch and succubus, who is said to be married to Asmodeus, the King of Demons, whose daughters make whores of women and destroy the souls of godly men to turn them away from their wives and children. Her story's in pieces, but I know a goodly part of it." Izzy shrugged. "My aunt used to tell my lovely cousin Tovah that if she stared in the mirror too long, she'd open Lilith's cave."

"Sounds like she's got quite a history," Audie rocked on

the balls of his feet, "I want to know it."

"She's got you good, pilgrim. Ever heard of the Kabbalah?"

"What does all this have to—"

Izzy snorted. "You know in your heart, you *must*. That woman is Lilith's spawn, a *Liliot* Audie, and one of her servants on Earth. Look: I am considered a heretic and apostate by the Orthodox of my faith, unworthy even of my clothes, and nothing but a damn lucky little Jew sonofabitch by most of the Goyim, but I *studied* it. It was just folk tales on the side while I was immersed in the Torah and Talmud and all but it was fun, and I delved into it. I ate it up. Hell, my grandfather wouldn't leave uncovered water out on the spring equinox for fear the menstrual blood of Lilith would fall into it from the sky, and he was an educated Rabbi. He wrote sixteen books in two languages. And Rabbi Judah Lowe was said to have rescued young men from just such a Lil—" Izzy puffed on his cigar, and tugged his beard. "I've felt her power. I'm surprised she hasn't come for me, if I'm an impediment to her plans. Hell, I can feel it surrounding you this very minute." He shook his head. "Son, I'm telling you from the bottom of my heart, that she is *it*."

"If you'd got to me yesterday with all this, I most likely would never have gone back to her, but it's all changed now. She's wholly honest. She's shown me many things that you're simply confirming from a perspective that appears quite limited from my new one. We … we have an understanding, Izzy."

"That quick," Izzy sighed. "Listen, you've got to understand her power, her ways. A Liliot—"

The memory of sharing blood made Audie shiver, but was obliterated by the memory of her skin and the sound of her voice. He straightened, and cleared his throat. "And if she is? What? Do you want me to help you hurt her? I shan't, Izzy. She is the wisest woman in creation as well as the most beautiful and has shown me things you cannot conceive. Just as she knew your lineage, she certainly knows your schemes, and shall be untouched by them," he stared at the long black slash of a clipper ship gliding under steam with her sails furled, "and she is not a demon! It's true that our minds and hearts are like an open book to her, but she's trying to be responsible with them. Her character is sterling, I must tell you, and I won't let you harm her. I doubt you could even if you tried."

Izzy waved his cigar at Russian Hill. "Didn't say I'm fixin' to kill her. I'm not a *Besht*, brother, far from it."

"What's that?"

"A *Baal Shem*, Audie. That's a guy who's righteous in the ways of the Torah and has spent his days in study, like a great rabbi who can call out demons from their disguises and banish them from doing mischief." He chuckled. "That's not me. You're looking at some pretty damaged goods before the throne of the Lord." He glanced over his shoulder, and fingered the gun under his arm. "But you're young, and not sophisticated as to the ways of our town. Look how that bum emperor hit you up for lunch. He's not even the original Emperor Norton. That fellow was one of the original Vigilantes who lost his mind decades ago and has been dead for twenty years. I'll show you his statue. There's been a half- dozen of those guys since. But then, you don't deny what I'm saying?"

"I see some truth in it, although there's no picture of her on that old newsprint."

Suddenly Audie saw himself bathed in blinding light before the throne of God, attempting to defend the very one God had judged eons ago and waged war on since. He heard his father's voice from the pulpit, admonishing young women to hold close the power within them lest it sunder a man's soul and ruin the path of righteousness. His Klondike quest had been intended to take him as far away from that as he could get in a way and now he was, but he couldn't see himself as a supernatural version of Daniel Webster or Clarence Darrow in the court of the Deity winning his case.

Is she actually the female incarnation of Satan? What about my blood? She's taken my blood!

An icy wave roiled his flesh. Was he speaking to a messenger of God? This brilliant little Jew who had appeared in the Emporium on Market Street? Was Izzy a guide sent by God to lead him from the seduction of Lorelei? Audie's hands closed around the railing and squeezed until splinters pierced his flesh. He made a noise like a branch torn from a tree in his throat, and squeezed harder. "Her heart is too full of love to be evil! She is so full of love for those she has known, I can't begin to tell you. She has shown me little children, Izzy, children who died centuries ago, and I could feel the compassion living within her today, her caring. It was … it was *Christ-like*. Could Satan hide evil in the cloak of love so perfectly? Could love be so wrong in its fullness?"

"We're both children in that respect. I truly do not know, Audie."

"Milton writes that Lucifer created his Hell out of misdirected love, doesn't he?"

"I'm familiar with the sacred, the secular, and have read Dante, Milton, and about everybody else who's speculated on Hell in the last two thousand years. That's an insightful question, and I'd have to say yes." Izzy relit his cigar and leaned on the railing. He gazed at the flag flying over the little garrison on Alcatraz, and stroked his beard. "You'd better get those splinters out of your hands, by the way. Redwood splinters infect no matter how old they are."

"Oh, thank you."

Izzy blew smoke. "Did you ask her?"

Audie clasped his hands in front of him and leaned on the

railing. "Yes."

"What did she say?"

"She doesn't deny it, but she's more of a great-great grand-daughter of Lilith. She told me some of her history, and it's utterly remarkable I assure you. I—I feel as if I'm the luckiest man on Earth at this moment, that she's given me the opportunity to know her. As I told you, I'm going to learn more."

"Damn."

"I must ask her if she really helped a scoundrel like Bobby Giles. It doesn't seem like her at all, somehow."

"What kind of men does she like?"

Audie exhaled in the damp wind. "Virgins, preferably."

X.

A Successful Quest

He very much wanted to find Leah, driven to confront her from the perspective of his new position with Lorelei both out of principle and a wholly un-Christian desire for revenge. A vision of Leah's blue eyes and the sound of her laugh plagued him, though he otherwise felt quite content in spite of Izzy's warnings. An entire world he never knew existed was there for his exploration, awash in pleasure beyond measure, and he trusted her. Audie grinned at the clear spring sky. He should retrieve what he could from Leah. Perhaps even his journal. He excused himself to Izzy's protestations, and promised to meet him at the gambling establishment of Mr. Daroux.

"Watch your backside and keep your pistol ready pilgrim!" Izzy called as Audie walked down Columbus toward Chinatown and the Barbary Coast.

Audie wasn't sure what he'd do when he found her, but he had to. He seemed to sense the thoughts of the women he passed: from the old crone under a purple scarf selling dried tomatoes, anchovies, and artichokes who admired his youth, to the mulatto whore a good inch taller than himself in a bay window above the street watching from between red lace curtains. He could feel the power of Lorelei in his veins, as if she had endowed him with some miraculous ability to move in the world with a piece of her own unique and imperishable nature. Perhaps it was his imagination, but it was something to contemplate. He simply felt incredibly *good.*

Music spilled into the street from saloons and melodeons, most too small for a dance floor that still packed a band onto a stage. As he headed southeast on Columbus, the delectable smells of Italian restaurants gave way to the coarser smells of cheap liquor and the stench of urine in alleyways. He passed penny arcades and nickelodeons, and a bawdy theater with a huge red sign shouting **Naked Cannibal Women of Borneo.** The rowdy saloons became more frequent, and the number of sailors, whores and assorted shady-looking types thickened as he neared Washington Square. By the time he made it to where Columbus, Dupont, and Broadway met, he knew he was entering the 'Gut of Depravity', as a wild-eyed street preacher was announcing just that from atop a packing crate leaning against one of the gas lamps lining the length of Broadway as it descended to the Bay.

Shouts came from a dilapidated building followed by the report of a pistol, then silence. He had a vision of the denizens looting the corpse of some unfortunate before throwing it like garbage into the alley, and Audie stroked the butt of the Smith and Wesson under his coat.

There was a cluster of whores on the corner of an alley connecting Dupont with Columbus where it made a diagonal through the grid of north-south streets. One was a slight red-haired girl in a green satin dress, wearing a low-cut bodice that made her breasts seem ready to spring out of her clothes. The girl glanced over her shoulder, and disappeared behind a phalanx of six Chinese coming down the alley in black padded coat-shirts buttoned to their necks wearing wide-brimmed fedoras. Their hair hung in thin dark queues that swayed as they walked in unison like a military formation, and they scowled fiercely as Audie sought to see around them. A heavy door slammed after someone darted through it.

He crossed the alley after they had passed, but the red hair and green dress disappeared into another doorway. He skirted a horse and wagon loaded with produce. The heel of his boot slid on the cobblestones, and two Chinese boys in the back of the wagon laughed. They shouted in Cantonese at him as he stepped around another pile of horse droppings and onto the opposite curb.

Sounds of a piano and fiddle came from the door into which the girl had gone. He tried the handle, stepped inside, and found himself on a narrow stairway descending into the bowels of the earth. The stench of cigars, sweat, liquor, and filth mixed in his nostrils, along with a sweetish aroma he suspected was opium.

Audie paused to get his bearings in the dimness, and was nearly knocked sprawling into the room below by two sailors stumbling down the stairs behind him. He caught himself, palms to the wall, and let them pass as his eyes adjusted.

There was one large room with a bar against the back. The center was filled with rough tables and benches occupied by a collection of motley types in various stages of drinking from carousal to unconsciousness. Girls were sitting both beside and in the laps of customers. One had her skirts up and her legs around a man, bouncing with blotched arms wrapped around his neck as she shrieked in feigned passion. The loud grunts of the man were accompanied by the awful music being played by a haggard blond woman with a battered fiddle. A rail-thin black man in a pinstriped shirt wearing a black derby sat at the piano, doing his best to keep a ragtime tune as the fiddle yowled.

When her customer was finished, the girl leapt off his lap. The man fumbled with his pants as she disappeared in a doorway that was guarded by a huge Irishman in a derby hat bedecked with a paper clover who was wearing two pistols in his belt.

Audie approached the bar, careful to keep his back to the

wall at the near end of the room. He motioned to the woman
behind it, who responded with a look he couldn't read. Whatever perceptions had been stimulated by Lorelei seemed to have
worn thin in this particular environment.

"Whiskey?" came in a clipped snarl.

He gazed at freckled breasts in the garish red dress before
raising his eyes to hers, and nodded. "Not poison please."

She grinned, exposing a crooked incisor tooth inlaid with
turquoise. "Sure sugar, only the good stuff." She grabbed a bottle from under the bar.

He scanned the room. There wasn't much he could do in a
place like this, and would have to deal with that fierce-looking
Irishman if it became a ruckus. "Did you see the little redhead
who came in a moment ago?"

She held onto the whiskey and demanded a dime for the
drink.

Audie slid a dollar across the bar. "Keep it."

She scooped up the silver coin. "Who?"

"In a green satin dress, about this tall, perhaps a little taller. I
think she goes by Leah."

"Leah? Might as well be a Chink bitch named Au Toy."

"Say what?"

"Leah's the name half the girls in town use, like Au Toy
if they're Chink trade. Leah in this town means *whore,* sugar."

"Oh, I guess someone told me that already."

"They're fuckin' right. But if you're lookin' for a good time,
there's plenty more where that came from. I know where a hundred girls are who're just waitin' to make your acquaintance on
Jackson Street. The coppers even guard the door so there ain't
no problems. Want a redhead?"

"I want to find that one."

"Well ... maybe I'll let her know you're here then." She motioned to a man leaning against the wall behind the bar, who promptly disappeared into the door the girl had gone in.

Audie lifted the whiskey to his lips, swallowed, and gasped. It had a foul taste, and could be drugged indeed. He looked around the room for the man or for Leah, saw neither, and decided to leave while he had his senses. He put down the whiskey and headed for the stairs.

"Hey fella, don't cha want Leah?" The bartender's shout was followed by loud laughter from the dank room.

Audie bounded up the stairs and burst into the alley, stumbled into a passerby, and went down on the cobblestones in a tangle of scented skirts accompanied by a girl's shriek. He pulled the girl to her feet, and began his apologies.

His voice stuck in his throat as he stared into the startled blue eyes of Leah. She had a look of amazement bordering on terror. She glanced up and down the street, whether for help or in fear he had accomplices in finding her he couldn't tell. She tried to pull out of his grasp, but he held her wrists tightly."Please don't hurt me!" she warbled."I-I was only doing what a girl *must* to survive! I was kidnapped young by evil men and horribly treated until I escaped, and—"

As her fear rippled through Audie, his anger drained. He felt shame for being the cause of it as the filth of the alley and the dark stairwell fought with her perfume and the smell of her skin. She blinked, awaiting his next move, and he fought the ridiculous urge to kiss her. He let out the breath he'd been holding."I cannot hurt you. But if I let go, you must promise not to run, or get someone to hurt me either. Perhaps what you did changed my life for the better Leah, or whatever your name is." Before she agreed he let go, and they stood staring at each other.

She inhaled."I can make it up to you in a bed, Audie."

He waved the suggestion away."I'd rather take you to a

better environment where we can converse. Perhaps over dinner without fear of a slung shot across the back of the head or a Mickey Finn for my beverage service. Any suggestions?"

She gave him a lovely smile, and ran a hand through his palm."I should love to go someplace respectable. I particularly favor the Palace Hotel."

"The Palace it is then."

"Oh, goody!" She jumped up and clapped her hands."Let's take a cab!" Leah grabbed his hand like she had when he was fresh off the boat, and pulled him up the alley toward Dupont."The cabs won't come down this alley; they get robbed too much, and it's almost dark. Can we stop at Dr. Shiffman's first?"

"Where?"

"I'll show you."

She hailed a horse-drawn Hansom cab on Dupont, and they settled on the red leather seat under a black canvas roof."The drugstore!" The driver nodded, turned the carriage around, and headed south."It's not far Audie, then to the Palace."

They proceeded through Chinatown and crossed Commercial past a sign depicting a large insect reclining in a field of flowers proclaiming **THE LIVELY FLEA.** Down two doors was one of a tall chicken with a red comb atop a red body, **THE RED ROOSTER.** Leah giggled."There's another name for that." They passed the **PARISIAN MANSION** with a Mercedes limousine out front guarded by two hulking gentlemen in ill-fitting suits. Red lights were coming on up and down the street as dusk fell."This is the French section ... at least that's what the madams would like the johns to believe."

They stopped before a sign reading **APOTHE-CARY-DRUGS-PRESCRIPTIONS** where a half-dozen ragged youths sprawled on the curb. As they pulled up, Leah sneered at a boy who wasn't older than herself with a yellow eyedropper in his hand and a bandana around his bicep. A girl was gouging a hole amongst the purple bruises on his arm with the sharpened point of an awl. He squeezed the contents of the eyedropper into a vein as she held the rag tourniquet and blood dripped in the gutter.

"Damnable hoppies, they give the whole town a bad name. Ugh!" Her breath rolled across his cheek as they stepped from the cab, giving those on the curb a wide berth.

A sickly-looking youth approached before they reached the door. "Fifteen cents? Help a poor boy with fifteen cents?"

"Back to the pit, fellow!" Leah pulled Audie past him. "That's how much a dose of heroin or nose candy costs. Ever tried Chief Wahoo's?"

"What?"

"Chief Wahoo's Indian Electric Tonic. It's the nicest stuff around. I can go all night on a half a bottle. Want to split one?"

"I-I suppose."

"I'm so glad you found me!" Leah wrapped her arms around his middle, stood on her toes, and kissed his cheek, only pausing for an instant to reach around the bulge of his gun. "We're going to have a wonderful evening." Her lips moved to his mouth.

After they had purchased a large green bottle of Chief Wahoo, the cab turned on Sacramento for Montgomery and headed toward the Palace. Leah handed him the bottle. It was square, with grape clusters and leaves molded into each corner rising to a round neck. On one side, words molded into the glass said WORLD RENOWNED, on the next CHIEF WAHOO'S, on the next INDIAN ELECTRIC TONIC, and on the last DUN-SMUIR CALIFORNIA. Elaborate crimson script on the paper collar claimed that it could cure syphilis, rheumatism, headache, diarrhea, and general ill health.

She snorted. "That's crap 'cept for the headaches. Sure great for a little roll in the hay though. Makes you feel like you can take on the whole world." She broke the wax seal and twisted the cork stopper, ceremoniously offering him the first swig.

He turned the bottle in his hands and examined the label. Surely this was one drink no one could have fooled with to drug him anyway. Audie took a slug. It didn't taste bad, and reminded him of sasparilla if it did leave a rather bitter aftertaste. He handed it to Leah, who promptly took three long gulps.

"Wahoo!" she yelled, making the horse jerk and prance before the driver calmed him back down, "Sorry!"

"Leah ... why did you rob me?"

Her hands tightened around the neck of the bottle as she studied his face before turning her eyes to the passing buildings. She bit her lip. When her gaze returned, they were brimming with tears. "I was only ten when they took me," she began, her voice disintegrating into a tremulous warble, "a little virgin girl from a farm in dear ol' Oregon. My daddy lost his money in the claims of the Comstock and was cruelly murdered in Nevada City on the way back to the Willamette Valley for the pittance left in his poke, and my mother was forced to take any job she could here, Audie. Sometimes the only job for a woman in dire straits is getting married, or ... or doing what *I* do. She toiled in the bowels of this accursed city and prayed for the Lord to save us, but she kept me dressed and fed, and read me my lessons too. Then one day a man offered her quite a sum in gold for first crack at me, but a girl of eleven. She hit him good with a fry pan, but he tied her up like a branded calf and had his way with both of us."

Audie gasped. "That is *horrible!*"

She took a swig and went on, "He was one of them lousy Rangers that used to haunt Portsmouth Square. I got the tongs

to get him later, goddamn his black soul." She spat on the cobblestones and dabbed at her mouth. "They threw what was left of
his filthy hide in the Bay. Such was my first experience with a man.
Since then, I've spent many a night with many a man yet trust
nary a one. Loneliness and sorrow have dogged me all the days of
my life, and only when I am laughing and gay do I find a single
moment's peace. One day I hope to marry well though, and escape
this prison into which I have been cruelly thrown by accursed fate."

"You speak quite well for a girl raised in such a way, have—"

Leah burped and pointed to their left. "This block's called
the Devil's Half Acre. More people been shot down here than any
place in the world I bet. By the way, Audie, how the *hell* did you
find me?"

"I happened to see you walk into that place. How did you
get back out anyway?"

"The *Bucket of Blood?* Are you crazy? I wouldn't go in
that hellhole! Never have!"

"But I saw you—"

"Not on your life! I was on my way down to Waverly Place
to give Charley Hung his due. His tong boys watch out for me,
and he needs to pull in cash to give the Suey Sings their cut, so
their highbinders leave him alone. All of us independent girls
give our share to keep the streets safe for ourselves. Otherwise
we couldn't show our faces when we cross tong territory." She
shook her head. "Sure glad I'm not some Chink singsong girl in
one of those damn tong cribs."

"What's a highbinder?"

"The guys in black you saw, the *Boo How Doy.* Tong hatchetmen, fella. Watch out for them. They'll split your skull way
before you dig out that gun under your arm. When they're on
their way to a fight, you don't see their queues though. They tie
them under those black hats, and that's how you tell. That's why

they're called highbinders."

"Who's Suey Sing?"

"*What's* Suey Sing. It's one of the tongs in Chinatown. On the legit side you got Sam Yup, Yung Wo, Kong Chow, Wing Yung, Hop Wo and Yan Wo, the Six Companies, but the tongs run the street and folks on the street got to pay them. There's the Mock Chins, Bo Ongs, Boe Leongs, Suey Sings, Hip Sings, On Yicks, Suey Ons, Bo Sin Seers, Hip Yings, Hop Sings—" Leah paused to take a breath.

"I swear I saw you go in that place."

"Nope," she shook her head, "I'd just got out of a cab on Dupont. The Bucket of Blood isn't my cup a' tea, Mister." She made a face. "You see any nice-dressed girls in that goddamn dive?"

"How old are you anyway?"

"Fifteen, Audie, only fifteen." Her cheeks bulged as Leah pretended to sob. She gave him a sideways glance, and snorted into her hands to hide a grin. "Think I'm redeemable?" Her eyes had a glazed look.

Audie felt a warmth in his face. His head was buzzing like a hot stove. "What the hell's in that stuff?"

"Alcohol, sarsaparilla, licorice root, nutmeg and cocaine far as I been able to figure … nothing bad."

He rubbed his eyes. "Damn!"

She pressed her lips against his throat, which brought the intended response in his groin in spite of his protestations. Nonetheless he succeeded in pushing her upright on the seat. "It's not proper to take a girl of such an age."

"For Christ's sake, fella," she exploded, "I been every way a girl can: inside out, upside down, with two men, with other women, hell, with—" she took three more gulps from the bottle, "rest assured you aren't defiling the innocent good sir. Anyway we're going to the Palace to eat, right? You said so. I can behave in such a place I swear. I've been there before. I was at the Saint Francis with a fellow who needed the company of an English Lady and brought me because I can talk like one. That was fun. Hell, betcha anything I can name more cities in Europe than you can."

"If you can, I'd like to know how."

"So are we going?"

"Yes. I said so."

"Good. I love the Palace." Her hand was under his belt before he knew it. "Oh yes," she murmured, "told you those hands and feet gave you away. They always do."

"Jesus."

Streetlights came on as he tried to keep her face out of his lap. They reached Montgomery and turned toward Market Street. In the next two blocks, better theaters appeared advertising acts he had heard of in places like New York and Boston, along with decent restaurants and the marble columns of a commercial exchange. The buildings of downtown were alight as they turned right on Market where the gilded crown of the Call building glowed eighteen stories above the street. Ahead on the left was the scalloped facade of the Palace Hotel.

The cab stopped before an arched entry of golden marble columns framing a gilded atrium. A uniformed guard tipped his hat to Leah and started her giggling again. They paid the cabbie and entered a spectacular court. Audie craned his neck to gaze at the tall pillars of dark golden marble on every side. Each floor was similarly pillared above the first, and lit with gilded candelabras holding electric bulbs. The echo of hooves resounded through the open door across the magnificent vault rising to a series of leaded glass windows eight stories over their heads. Live palm trees grew underneath a domed skylight in the roof that was set with floral patterns of stained glass.

She squeezed his hand. "It's so lovely!"

He could only nod in agreement and take her arm. He'd tipped the cabbie generously with Lorelei's money, noticing how Leah watched the gold tender notes in his hands as he doubted that he would ever recover his own money or possessions. Audie sighed. Then keeping her from any further trickery must remain his first order of business.

Musical laughter tickled his spine. Audie stopped in midstride with a gasp.

"What is it?" Leah's eyes had lost their glaze. Something seemed to flicker through them that made her seem far older. He felt as if he were under the gaze of Lorelei herself, watching him through the eyes of Leah.

"I ... suppose you've been approved."

Her eyes narrowed as she tried to define his meaning. He could feel the thrill of fear running through her quite clearly, as she prepared to offer herself to a stranger she'd already robbed. He took her by the arm, and turned toward the restaurant where white marble columns rose over a walkway topped with live palm trees and a floor filled with potted palms. They stepped up like a gentleman and a lady through a marble balustrade, where a man in a gold-trimmed white uniform bowed, and escorted them to a table.

XI.

The First Hunger

She clung to the cliff as the sea's breath beat upon her. The bellow of sea lions echoed off rocks as the sun sank like a bloody jewel on the horizon, knitting shadows into night. She took a ragged breath, and resumed her climb.

There was a ripple in the earth, and the tops of trees began to sway. Great redwoods shuddered from their roots, flinging dreaming birds upon the sky in a nimbus of needles and broken branches. The vault of sky grew yellow like the eyes of cats in firelight.

A bone-splitting howl arose from the stones of the earth that made her stomach lurch. She closed her eyes, sang the prayer a white-haired medicine woman had taught her, and began to climb again. Green sedges and yellow flowers shivered above her, spreading their petals in a soft rain. Gravel stung her face, then jagged stones. One cut her scalp. She bent her face to the damp earth beseeching the Mother, and grasped a root to climb higher. A stone caught her across the forehead, and she gasped. Blood ran in her eyes. She clawed at the cold soil, clinging to the breast of a living, raging earth. A third stone took her, and the sea swallowed her with a roar.

Lorelei detached herself from the Pomo Indian girl on that long ago day, as the blood-beating drum of the tribe filled her in one last rush. The girl cried out to her with others from death until Lorelei loosened the thread, and the dream faded. It seemed forever before she remembered what time she was in and who her lover was. She seized the silken cord beside the bed, rang the bell, and Wu appeared with a pot of tea and a cup on an enameled platter. "Get me some cold water," she croaked, "please."

Wu nodded, striving to hide his thoughts as always.

A smile flicked across her lips. "The Celestials have good reason to keep their thoughts to themselves," she said in perfect Cantonese, "for the big-eyed devil is abroad in this land, and Wu is but a pilgrim on this foggy coast."

"You speak beautifully," Wu admitted, "as a lady of noble rank would herself."

"I loved a Lord of the coasts when the Yellow Sea brought round-eyed brigands like sharks from the waves."

Wu only nodded again and attempted to veil his thoughts, but she caught the mixture of fear, awe, and imagination that made her a courtesan of demons, and an incarnation of love and lust. He went to fetch the water while striving to replace those images with the money she was paying him, even a plan to purchase a black ball of opium on Waverly Place. He was sending a thousand dollars in gold by the machinations of Wells Fargo Bank to Shanghai on the morrow to salvage his son's misadventure with the daughter of a wealthy trader. It was a sum worth many lives in China that the Woman had given him without his asking, placed in a camphorwood box with his son's name in red calligraphy upon it. Wu prayed daily that the Mandarins in charge would do just as they were known to do, and put the incident behind the silk curtain separating the privileged from those without connections. His son's head might already have left his body, although the Woman assured him that it hadn't. But tonight, he was going to get out of this house of the Woman from Heaven or Hell where he served his time. Wu sighed. This sojourn at the Golden Mountain was certainly a test of his mettle as a man of face.

Lorelei laughed, and the walls shook in sympathetic thunder and Wu fled the room.

When night fell she went to the rocks at Land's End where the Pomo girl had clung centuries before. Filling the head of the cove south of the point were three ornate glassed-in pavilions built by Adolph Sutro's Comstock fortune, holding the baths within. The outdoor pool of seawater was mirror-still in spring night. Sea spray glittered on stone, reflecting the glow from the bathing halls and the multi-colored tiles of their interiors. Coal smoke drifted inland from the stack of the powerhouse running pumps that changed the contents of the baths daily. The smoke crawled amongst the cliffs, covering the Monterey cypress on the hill in a pale shroud.

The voices of sea lions were as in her dream. She wore a plaid shirt and denim pants, with her hair braided in a glistening rope that caught the light of the baths. The wind of the Pacific slashed across her face as Lorelei listened to the dwindling crowd within the baths and the sounds of carousal from the Cliff House to the south. Its crenellated dormers were alight like a castle of ancient times, sparkling with electric jewels upon its towers. The central tower's windows glowed eight stories above the sea as the flags on its peak snapped in the breeze.

In a private dining room, men drank brandy and smoked cigars over beef and mutton as young women served them. Jessie Hayman had a glass of champagne in a bejeweled hand. This was her party, and she was making sure her guests were well cared-for. Like the curling smoke, Lorelei drifted to her, dancing amongst her thoughts softly as a flower petal on the wind. Jessie would make an interesting companion. It would be entertaining to make Jessie a lover, though her personality would stimulate a great hunger that could only be sated by a man, and perhaps leave Lorelei primed to kill at her next union.

There were candidates aplenty for that. That piece of shit Jules at the Municipal Crib was one. He'd screamed at her to return to her place when she'd appeared in his moneyed sanctum in the bowels of the Municipal Crib and reached for a gun. Lorelei had so enjoyed the feel of his throat crushing between her fingers. She sighed. Revealing that facet of herself to Audie would be a chore. She could go for a long time feeding a man's ego, stoking the fires of a lover's lust, but sometimes things found their way to their ancient purpose, and she couldn't predict when. Yet she so needed the acceptance of the good ones, something none before her had struggled with in thirty thousand years. The ancient weight of killing was a heavy cloak. She was astounded it remained invisible to mortal eyes.

Lorelei shrugged off the thought, and entered a tunnel cut into the cliff to a pavilion that allowed the viewing of sea lions. It had been closed for hours. The two souls following her glowed like phosphorescent candles in the night. They'd seen her on the rocks as she watched the sea. Of course she had known. She'd come for them, and now they were coming for her. They entered the shadows like coyotes, slinking toward their prey.

She felt the younger one's excitement as his heart beat louder. He was jittery with cocaine, and anxious to knock her to the damp floor. She inhaled his feelings like a vapor upon the air, and her own arousal grew stronger. He was a Mexican boy who'd seen much brutality in his short life in the camps and ranchos of central California, and likewise had grown cruel in his thoughts. He fondled an ivory-handled knife as he stared at her graceful form, imagined the Virgin of Guadalupe, and put the thought out of his mind to steel himself for the task at hand. He caught the scent of her hovering in the damp air like a wraith, and his cock stretched his canvas pants. Lorelei smelt the thick whiskey breath of the older one as his tobacco-blighted lungs labored. He stroked a lead-filled slung-shot intended for her skull.

She closed the distance in a blur and her right hand shot out, seized the older one by the throat, and crushed his windpipe, breaking his neck with a snap of her arm. The man made a sigh and slid down the wall. She threw the boy upon the floor and tore the pants from him. He bounced with the impact and gasped, to lie staring at the tunnel's roof. Lorelei commanded his penis to stand erect, dropped the men's jeans she'd slipped her long legs into, and lowered herself upon him. Her eyes were afire with the red of blood. She had no need to hide her purpose.

He stared in those eyes as his soul flowed into hers, drain-ing from his body. He shuddered, and cried out in a braided scream of pain and ecstasy as the world unraveled and spread with the river of his life broadening beyond his ability to retain it. He screamed, fighting to collect the thing he was from the spirit engulfing him. The boy bucked and heaved as she submerged him in the roar of that river. He was a babe in his mother's arms. He was a terrified boy hiding in a shed, raging at the rape of his sister. He was an angry youth who beat a girl much younger than himself and savagely took her virginity and then her life. He gave one final shout from his deepest core as she swallowed him utterly.

She took a shuddering breath and released his corpse from the grasp of her body. A trickle of blood trailed down her thigh on the floor of the tunnel. She wiped herself with his shirt, stepped into her jeans, took a body in each hand, and sprang out of the tunnel into the fresh wind of the sea. Life raged in her veins as she ascended the cliff face in a bound that took her twenty feet.

Moonlight danced in breaking waves as she fixed on the distant rise of the Farallon Islands, put down the body of the boy, and heaved the man at that distant mark. The broken thing cartwheeled in the wind, seeming to float upon the breeze until it was swallowed by the sea. The boy was lighter and went half-again as far. *Miguel,* his name was Miguel."Hello, Miguel."

A strangled cry answered from within her; Miguel's soul held in her own like an insect in the fist of a child. Lorelei dashed through twisted trunks of Monterey cypress until she found a cove that purled and seethed under the moon like the ocean in her heart. She dropped her clothes and stepped into the night-dark sea to bathe.

XII.

On Top of the World

Golden light nestled in the grain of finely polished wood, giving brass a warm glow and pooling in the snifters of brandy upon the immaculate white tablecloth. The music of violins and a piano came from the adjoining room, weaving a bright tapestry in perfect concordance with the ambience of their surroundings. It was a rich fabric of sound that reminded Audie of a peaceful sea with great boats plying their way, their decks full of light and warmth over tranquil waters. He rotated the brandy snifter in his hand, and watched the reflections in its purling depths. The rack of lamb was settling in his stomach quite nicely, and dessert was on its way. He stretched and yawned.

"Isn't this the tops?" Leah whispered as she watched the cart full of chocolate tortes and cheesecake approaching. Another waiter removed the remnants of her terrapin entrée from the table.

He yawned again. "Yep."

"Just like Mark Hopkins and Lady Stanford at the Ritz, or the ol' Queen o' England herself. You've spent more money on me than most men would for a week of bed favors Audie, and I must say thank you, sir." She placed her hands demurely in her lap as the waiter presented the confections of the Palace's bakery. "I should like that chocolate one with raspberry sauce please, and the cheesecake and two forks."

The waiter put both before her as her eyes lit up like a little girl's. Audie couldn't see using her, in spite of her profession.

The idea was simply too base at the moment.

She took a fork full of the torte, followed by one of cheese-cake. "Ummmm," She dabbed at her mouth with a napkin. Leah was conducting herself quite well. He supposed some men of standing actually *had* taken her in. How could she handle that kind of clientele ... and at such a tender age?

"Some man must have taken you under his wing for you to be so well behaved."

"I had the best patron in town. He loved me Audie. That might sound foolish to you seeing as I was with him for money, but he did. He's a scion of a local family out to delve into the underside of the City that he shall own a goodly piece of one day. He's a member of the Bohemian Club, and the Pacific Union. I studied in his library up on Nob Hill when his father was away on business. Learned a lot from one of the maids too-Monique. She trained in Classical ballet in Paris, and had a voice that could make the angels cry. Came off the boat from France and did a stint at Tesse Wall's after getting fired from the Bella Union. He preferred to share us when he had the opportunity."

"What's his name?"

"Audie, what kind of girl would I be to divulge that? Really. I should like to own my own establishment someday, and discretion is a fundamental principle of our profession."

"I thought you wanted to marry a good man and leave this life of sin."

"Well eventually, after all I'm only sixteen."

"You said fifteen."

"Ahem, you're not supposed to contradict a lady."

He glanced about the room. "Where?"

Leah's cheeks bulged, before they burst into laughter.

He tried some of her cheesecake, and it melted on his tongue. "I still swear that I saw you going into that dive that I found you in front of."

"Audie," her face grew serious, "I would be dead or a slave of the cribs should I go in there. Those lugs are trash. I'd probably end up like one of those girls in the ones they call cowyards." She shuddered. "*That's* a living hell! I'd rather die than be one of them."

"Tell me about them."

"There's not much to tell. They just stick you in a little room, and men come in and do whatever they want with you. You might save some money, but I doubt it. They take most of it back in room, board and doctor fees, and the girls spend the rest on booze and dope. The poor ignorant girls fall into that, the ones from some little farm somewhere. But the tong cribs are worse yet. They're actual slaves that they bring here from China ... and they often kill them when they're done. I doubt many of them ever makes it to twenty-one unless she escapes to one of the missions."

"Sure is odd that I thought I saw you."

"You imagined it. Get me some of that brandy would you?"

"Need you have another? Fifteen or sixteen, you—"

"Pshaw. Tessie Wall drank two whole magnums of Cliquot here when she was entertaining a Vanderbilt. One must learn to impress, and her girls are all my age. Don't be such an old fuddy."

Audie waved to the waiter, who brought two more glasses, and Leah lifted hers to her lips, swirling the crystal snifter under her nose like an experienced taster.

Audie inhaled the aroma of French cognac. "Maybe my mistress was working her magic."

"I know who that is."

"You do?"

"Of course. You were seen at Daroux's above the Orpheum

with Lucky Izzy, and this fantastic woman came in and took you out under her arm like a clutch purse."

"What?" He ran a hand across a reddening face. Leah was far more perceptive than he'd given her credit for, and it made her more attractive as he found himself becoming aroused by her intellectual felicity. The transition to appreciating her charms wasn't hard either. She obviously had more facets than he'd let himself believe, though what was true in her stories and what wasn't could take some winnowing-out.

"I've got friends, Audie."

"Were you really the daughter of a farmer? You just spoke of ignorant farm girls."

"No, but let's go listen to the music. Can you waltz? Chief Wahoo is making me want to get on my feet." She pulled him from the table, and he motioned for the bill. It came to seventeen dollars.

"That's the most expensive meal I've ever eaten," he muttered, before handing the man a five-dollar tip of Lorelei's money.

"It's nice to be spending somebody else's loot."

"Actually it is rather strange."

She laughed.

They moved to a small ballroom where musicians were situated along with a white-haired dowager at an ebony grand piano. As soon as Leah made to dance, they broke into a waltz. She snuggled up to him, and began to lead him through the steps. They danced alone for a good ten minutes, the scent of her perfume and rustle of satin a lovely interlude after a fine meal. He gazed down into her red hair and at the pale freckled flesh of her shoulders, throat and breasts. Here he was with a girl who had drugged and robbed him, and now he was holding her tiny waist and waltzing across a gilded room in the largest hotel in the world. His face spread a grin reflected by the wry expression of a musician. The man probably thought him a bumpkin out with a young lady of status who was trying to position himself within the upper echelons of society. Audie's grin grew wider.

She squeezed his waist. "I hope you're going to do me the favor of letting me make that other night up to you."

"Well, I—"

"Don't worry, I couldn't do that again." She sighed theatrically. "My uncle used to say that I was much too impetuous for a young lady and it would get me in trouble, too much book smarts and not enough living." She chuckled. "If he could see me now."

"Book smarts … your uncle? So you are from a good family. Then why are you—"

"Audie, I am exploring life. I don't want to go home if that's what you're getting at. There's nothing for me there, and I'd sooner kill that … never mind."

"Where are you from?"

"You want to know all about me, so how about I cut you a deal sir? Spend the night with me, and I'll tell you."

He gazed at the Corinthian tops of gilded marble columns against a high ceiling that was painted with classical nudes. Lorelei was expecting him back, and surely would find him. The absurdity of it all made him want to laugh. Perhaps it was the damn tonic he had drunk in combination with the brandy. "Why do you so much want to resume where we left off?"

"Because if somebody like that gorgeous Mademoiselle Lorelei or whoever she is gives you all this money right out of the hat, you must be the greatest cocksman that ever got off the boat in these parts, Mister."

"Oh,"

"I feel guilty for that Mickey Finn I slipped you. On my soul I do. I got it from two Chileno girls who do that all the time to johns down on Pacific, and I wanted to see what would happen. Curiosity I guess. It works, doesn't it?"

"It certainly does."

"Perhaps we'll use the Spanish fly instead. I've got some of that at home."

"That place you took me?"

"No, that was a place of assignation, not where I live."

"How did you carry me out of there?"

"There's a couple of fellows close-by for such things, and of course, if one of the clientele gets out of hand."

"I imagine if you'd had any trouble with me, I might have been feeding the fishes myself."

She fell silent, took a breath, looked up into his eyes, and batted mahogany lashes. "I have never killed a fellow, Audie, though the opportunity has presented itself aplenty. If that were to happen, I would throw in the towel and leave San Francisco forever."

"A lot of good that would have done me. What if some footpad or scoundrel had found me laying there in the dark and shanghaied me, or killed me out of simple wretchedness? Or done some unnatural act to my unconscious person?"

Her cheeks bulged. "Oh sorry, I was just visualizing it. That wouldn't have happened though, because I paid Junior to stay around and watch until you awoke. Otherwise you likely would have been hauled off by some Shanghai boys anxious to make their quota and awoke bound for Manila or Mandalay."

"Two of them nearly *did* get me!" He stopped dancing and stared in her eyes. He had no idea what she was doing in this world, if she was telling the truth, or why she would possibly want to stay considering the dangers. Obviously Leah had motives of her own, as well as resources beyond any mere girl of the street. "How can I believe you?"

"I can introduce you to Junior if you'd like."

"I think I'll forgo the pleasure."

"Well then, you got up and crossed Filbert Street, then headed into North Beach where you sat down by the fountain in Washington Square in front of the Flor de Italia restaurant. There your Mademoiselle Lorelei encountered you and took you to her house on Russian Hill."

"Damn," he shook his head. Obviously someone *had* been watching him, "I didn't see anyone else there at all, and what about those two—"

"You hardly saw anything at all. That stuff knocks you for a loop dearest. Well," she paused, "do we have a deal?"

Audie ran a hand through his hair. "Very well I shall have sex with you, but I admonish you that you must be on your best behavior."

Before she could answer, the musicians burst into applause.

They took a room that cost twelve dollars and rode in the gilded cage of an elevator toward the top of the Palace where they tipped the operator and turned right in a hall. Although it was one of the cheapest in the hotel, the accommodations were grand in the extreme, with a white marble fireplace trimmed in gold that had a huge mirror above it. A polished walnut bar and three brass-trimmed stools were in one corner of the room with the gleaming glassware behind it embossed with the crest of the Palace. The bed was huge and covered with a thick Scandinavian quilt. Leah bounced on it, and sat with her skirts spread out around her like some satin flower grown out of the bed. As he gazed upon her, Audie found himself quite ready for the moment at hand.

He took off his coat and draped it over a French chair by a window that gave a view of the Bay and wharves, with the dark rise of Yerba Buena Island halfway to Oakland. He hung his gun in its holster on the other chair and put his hat on the table. The lights of the Southern Pacific depot glowed before flat-bottomed sailboats full of cargo being unloaded by seagoing ships before they headed across the Bay toward Sacramento or south by rail. He counted fifteen steamers within his view and a dozen sailing ships, some no doubt salmon packets bound for Alaska.

The plans he'd made came back in a flash. What had become of them? Had it all been to escape the lot of a Minister's son in West Virginia, where every move he'd made growing up was presented for his father's approval? Did Lorelei always have to be so *right?* Here he was on top of the world's grandest hotel about to make love to a girl who's true name he didn't even know with an expensive meal in his stomach and cognac and Chief Wahoo in his veins. He chuckled. "I suppose it could be worse."

"What?"

"Things could be worse. When I awoke upon that hill the other evening, I was certain all my plans had come to naught. I wanted to—"

"Kill me?"

"No … but I certainly was angry. I should dearly love to reclaim my journal and my grandfather's pistol though. But now here I am, the kept man of a woman who … who is very different from the rest anyway, about to make love to a lovely young girl who has previously robbed me."

"Thank you for your forgiveness. I gave Junior the gun and shall try to recover it. I do feel bad about your journal. I would have kept it, but I was in somewhat of a hurry. He probably threw it away as he's not the literary sort. And I'd like to hear about how this Lorelei is so different, but right now I hope this shall do." Leah had hung her dress in the closet while he was ruminating on the Bay and draped her underwear on a chair. She was on her knees with her hands behind her neck, breasts thrust out like one of those poses on French postcards. Her long red hair fell down her back and framed her in a fiery halo.

His eyes skipped across her nipples and down her stomach to the thin dusting of reddish hair between her legs. He'd been with but one woman in his entire life, one very *different* woman. This wasn't the same. How could he even hint of what went on with Lorelei, the glowing distances that swallowed him in her embrace … *the sharing of blood?* A shiver ran up his spine. Audie still felt much the virgin as he took off his shirt.

Leah eyed his broad chest with approval and grinned. "Why Mr. Bond, you look positively shy."

"What's … what's your real name?"

She lay on the bed chin on her palms, legs crossed behind her with the black lace stockings on. The contrast was lovely against her fair skin. Audie noticed a pimple on her back, and couldn't help comparing it to the utterly unblemished flesh of Lorelei. Leah cocked her head. "Why?"

"I-I can't imagine going to bed with a woman whose actual name I don't even know."

She let out a shriek of laughter. "Then many a night has been spent in vain in *this* town!" Her blue eyes danced. "My real name is Suzanne, Audie. It's Suzanne."

"Are you telling the truth?"

"They say a woman can't lie when a man's got her heart. Know how to get a woman's heart?"

He stepped out of his pants. "I can guess."

She stared at his cock nodding like a fifth limb, and whistled.

It wasn't his Goddess, but it was wonderful. The brief trepidation he was damaged by what had occurred with Lorelei passed as the present overtook him. The little redhead became a muscular thing whose skin grew hotter as she opened to accept him, shrieking and panting as he found the depth of her. He was astounded he fit, and stared at her stomach wondering where it all went as he watched a pool of sweat dancing in her navel. Leah taught him all women could not easily take what he had been born with in full measure, but he quickly adjusted his strokes, and she was pleased with his consideration as well as his performance.

After their fifth bout, they fell into an exhausted sleep. The dream returned of a girl crying in the dark, fighting for air. He felt a great weight on her chest that was threatening to crush her. Cruel laughter echoed around her with the pounding of feet from above. Audie wanted to reach out and touch her, take her away from that horrid place wherever it was. He tried and tried, but he couldn't see her face.

He awoke listening to the never-sleeping traffic of the City beyond the window. Leah curled like a flower petal against his side nestled in the crook of his arm with his other hand behind his neck. He watched the play of shadows on the ceiling, and felt that dark room again like a weight on his own breast. Soon he must arise and leave Leah here ... *Suzanne.*

Lorelei. He should have gotten the telephone number of her house. Why hadn't she *given* it to him or even mentioned it? *Will she be jealous?*

Leah mumbled and shifted in his embrace. She nuzzled him as he began to consider sneaking out. As he drew his arm from beneath her, there was a peal of perfect laughter far too beautiful to be from any other woman on Earth save one. *"Thanks for the consideration, but I'm not jealous, Audie. Don't you recall I approved?"*

Audie glanced about the room for the source of that voice, though he knew he wouldn't find one. "That's ... good."

"However I do have need of your company. Leave her some money and a nice note. Suzanne's had much rougher adieus I assure you."

Audie slid off the bed and began to fumble for the paper and pen in the table alongside it. He sighed, put them down, and went to the ornate bathroom with his mistress chuckling in his skull. "So this is what it's like to be possessed."

"You're listening to Izzy a bit much with his tales of Liliots and succubae, but I'm grateful for your cooperation nonetheless."

"My God, I'm going from one woman's bed to another's."

"Oh, poor baby."

The water pressure was good even this high up, sustained by seven huge tanks on the roof. The man at the front desk had boasted that the Palace was certified totally fireproof even if the pipes in the street were disabled due to them, and the pleasure of a hot shower was enough to make him forget the world for a while. Audie lingered.

He dressed as Suzanne slept. Chief Wahoo had finally done his duty and departed, or more likely, Lorelei wouldn't allow her to awake. He wrote a note, and left money for breakfast and cab fare before he slipped out the door.

He almost ran into her in the hall. Lorelei was dressed in a plaid wool shirt, men's blue denim Levi pants speckled with purple stains, and tall boots to her knees. Her long hair was braided down her back. Audie wondered how she managed that even as his breath came out in a startled gasp. She took his hand, and all else no longer mattered as she led him to the elevator and out of the Palace Hotel.

XIII.

The Realm

"How was your night?" she asked as they climbed Russian Hill in a chauffeured motorcar.

"I'm sure you know." He rubbed his temples, astounded anew at the sublime creature beside him. He studied her skin, comparing it to Leah-Suzanne's soft young flesh already showing the flushing and bruising all mortal flesh would show as he left her dreaming. Flesh which would surely age and die. In a way Leah was well along on the process of aging and dying even now, as was he. Lorelei's skin was firmer and smoother, like an ivory raiment aglow from within.

"Your opinion flatters me, but I was rather too busy to pay attention to all your doings tonight."

"Really?"

She laughed, and their driver shivered as it rippled through his nerves like fingers on the strings of a harp. He glanced back, and when his eyes returned to the journey, he was watching her in the small square mirror he'd mounted from the roof for a view to the rear.

"Please watch the road." She turned to Audie. "Yes, really. I find some things quite inescapable. Sometimes it's so wearying."

"Did you go out?"

She nodded. "I've shown you a piece of that."

He felt the girl in a dark room with her voice pleading in a foreign tongue in meaning beyond words. "You certainly have."

"I took two tonight, though to far different destinations

than the one who touches your dreams."

He was silent when they reached her steps. He wasn't sure exactly what she meant or how she meant it, but a chill tickled him as they walked hand in hand to the high-ceilinged room where he would be her lover.

"You saw the girl dying in a basement again, Audie."

"Yes!"

"She was Mai Ling, who was sold into slavery at the age of eleven by her own mother to be raped in the bowels of a ship, auctioned like an animal, and dwell in the cribs of Chinatown. The slavers have but one appreciation of women. She was nineteen, Audie, nineteen years old and dying."

"Leah told me about the tongs."

"Yes, Suzanne. Suzanne really is her name by the way."

"Then you were watching."

"Only in part. Like I said, I was rather busy."

"I can imagine."

She sighed. "Not yet." Lorelei seemed far away even as that familiar current flowed from her hand into his. As they entered her bedroom, a charcoal cat with a torn ear jumped off the bed. She held out her other hand, and it rippled under her palm with a loud purr. "Do you want knowledge to the degree you think? I can love you and take you to only the good places, but it's true I long to share more. I need a partner for my own comfort, but I don't want to do it out of selfishness. I don't want to damage you or drive you insane either. That, Audie, is a fate that happens to men who aren't as strong as they fancy themselves."

"I assume it's happened before."

She tugged at her braid, shook it out, and brushed a strand of hair from her eyes. "Oh yes, oh yes indeed. I've made terrible mistakes. Like I said, I cannot truly see the future."

"In some ways you seem wiser than the prophets of scrip-ture." He gazed at her standing beside the bed, an angel in a Renaissance painting. "What the hell. Let's go."

"That's not youthful pride talking abetted by drink and drugs, and of course your exemplary performance with Suzanne?"

"Was I that good?"

"She thought so. She'll awake infatuated, so be prepared."

He grinned. "See what I mean? You *know* these things."

She swiped at her face. "I am trapped in youth over and over again, yet life passes me by as others find their fates. It's lonely … and here I am complaining again."

He traced her cheek with a fingertip. "What an incredible, beautiful curse."

"A curse it is." Her breath lifted his hair. "All right, let's see."

He was there in death beside others who had passed that way, struggling within the grasp of what could not be broken even as she held him apart and assured him it was only another's life before him. It was long done and not to be feared. Yet still, it was as if that life were his own.

He hovered on the universe of another man's soul, walking as an insect upon water with the surface bending but not breaking. He watched her take killers as they stalked women, reeling them in with her perfect beauty, drawing the substance of their beings into hers, to remember and live on. Yet somehow each was forgiven. He seized on that for his sanity, that flash of light that said she was on the side of the angels.

He inhaled the cold of winter mountains as a tall warrior stalked another man's lodge. The breath of hobbled ponies made clouds and sparkled on thick winter coats. His enemy was out hunting, and had left White Buffalo Woman alone with not even a child to stop the plan of He Who Sings, warrior of the Absaroka, blood enemy of Lakota since the world began.

All these hills had been his peoples', but the Lakota had driven them out of this good place they called *Paha Sapa:* Black Hills. Now he would take their Sacred Being who could talk to animals, take for his own the most precious thing his enemy had known and ravish her moon-pale flesh until she bore his child who would grow up with her power. He Who Sings saw a mighty son of their union, one who would drive the Lakota back into the plains from which they had come all the way across the Missouri and bring honor to his line until the end of time.

He glided past hobbled ponies to stand before her lodge, pausing to call on his youthful visions that had awakened at manhood on a lonely butte with only the sacred Pipe for company. Not a dog barked, nor did a pony snort, or stamp its feet. Clear proof his medicine was strong. The thrill of knowing her ran through him as his fingers touched the weighted hide flap to her lodge. He prayed to the four directions, took a breath, and flung it open.

She stood naked and smiling, and He Who Sings howled his vision-born song to the sky unafraid others would hear. He was close enough to touch her, and his arousal told him her power would soon be his own. Now she should fall to her knees, and acknowledge him master.

Her many-colored eyes became the color of blood, and he raised a hand to his face. When he took it away, he saw the Spirit Trail stretching across the vault above him as if the lodge skins had blown off in a great wind that blew her hair about the lodge as it closed around him like the wings of Raven. She mounted him with a shout, and the last moment of his life was filled with her laughter.

She held a reflection of the warrior's soul up for Audie to see, a wet scalp upon her bridle, a glistening trophy that yet *lived*.

She showed him Miguel, twisting in the place where she held him before he passed into the oblivion he'd made for himself. The thing that thought it was Miguel raged and cried out, unbelieving of his fate. He tried to cling to Audie, to come back with him to the world of flesh. Audie slapped Miguel away in an instant with the edge of his will, and wondered if he were indeed going mad. A feeling of sickness erupted, and threatened to overwhelm him.

"Easy, love, it shall pass."

She led him to calmer waters, yet a portion of him stood apart wondering if he could listen to any other voice again, or if he were doomed to wander the world an empty shade seeking some semblance of what he had known.

"What about men like me?"

"My lovers."

"You're carrying on your part of the conversation to make mine easier."

"Exactly. About men like you then: my chosen are the ones I share myself with as I've explained. Obviously I must eventually leave you also, but I'll wait until the time is right and you're the better for it. Afterward you will most probably live a good long life, and strong women shall be drawn to you, for they'll sense that which has awoken in you at our union."

"That's nice to look forward to, and I suppose I should like to get married eventually, but what about fellows like Bobby Giles?"

"Don't believe all you read in a dusty old paper, or in tomorrow's either. History is a conversation of the winners amongst themselves, or at least amongst the survivors. Bobby Giles was a lovely man."

"He was an outlaw."

"Indeed, and some so-called outlaws rage with the fire and

force of their souls in a wondrously unbridled form that makes my task easier as well as more pleasurable. But it's the same with women. You'll find that the dangerous ones are always the best in a bed."

"Present company included."

"Uh-hum."

"What about me? I'm no criminal."

"Do you know your future?"

He looked at the ceiling and ran a hand across his face. "You're not going to turn me into some kind of scofflaw, are you?"

She gave him a dimpled grin. "No, though I doubt you'll have much patience with temporal law again now that you've seen how limited it is. In your case it shall probably engender compassion. You grew up with a rather moderate Christian upbringing in spite of your father. The women in your family were lovely and nurturing, and you and haven't been roughed-up enough to despise folk in general. That boy Miguel would have had to work hard to be anything but what he was. His family was brutalized for five generations on the ranchos of California, from the Dons to the Anglo owners, but his particular cruelty was his own. He could have known feelings for others had he let himself, and I *couldn't* forgive his raping and killing a young girl. If you could have felt her death as I did," she sighed. "which was his intent with me, for that matter."

"If he had learned to care, if he'd tried to redeem himself after his crimes, would you have killed him like that?"

"Not unless he'd intended harm to me or some innocent, no. Absolution exists, call it Christian or whatever. It's far older than any creed, and one of our blessings. Did you find one death in me that wasn't justified?"

"No."

"Good. Can you imagine living this long with the weight of unjust killing? That would be unbearable. There is enough to my burden just seeing those I love pass by, loving those who are beyond help, and trapped in the warp of time and history."

"You are incredible. Everything I've ever known or studied—"

"Thank you. And you're still a sweet boy from my perspective." She kissed his brow. "We had a short time tonight, but you'll need to eat well when you awake. You took care of me and Leah like a stallion, and of course I've fed upon you."

"Suzanne."

"This morning it's Leah. You should get used to women changing roles as they change their minds. She's rather conflicted as she planned for you to be shanghaied, and now must deal both with her growing affection for you and a rather bothersome twinge of Catholic guilt due to her own upbringing." She laughed. "Are you going to see her tonight?"

"You leave me the choice."

"Of course. By the way her father is a Priest. You two are much alike in upbringing."

"A Priest? Then why is she whoring herself?"

"She's trying to have her own life. Her uncle was an over-educated cad who used her, and she escaped into the world early. Give her some lease if you intend to know her. Besides, she's only really worked the Uptown Tenderloin and the scions of Nob Hill, not the streets of the Coast. She was at the docks to see a girlfriend off who'd married well, and knew you were fresh meat so to speak, just off the boat and rather irresistible as I found you myself. Even that Mickey Finn trick was as she explained it. She can be a dangerous child, but you should be safe. Play with her if you wish."

"Thank you I suppose. Did you make me see her in that alley?"

"Yes. You had come so close, but your timing was a bit off. I was editing your life somewhat, with that interlude in the Bucket of Blood."

"That place was a hellhole."

"You forgot Izzy. You were supposed to meet him at Daroux's loft. He called my number excessively and gave Wu a headache. These telephones make such a racket with their damn bells."

"You gave your number to Jessie Hayman. Why?"

"Some things I keep private. I've already shared more with you than any woman on earth, and this is a rather spectacular first relationship for you if I may be so bold as to say. Just have Izzy quit calling. I can make him go wherever you'd like to meet him … and of course, you'll need more money." She was off the bed and across the room, and returned with a handful of bills. "Get some clothes for the country. That suit is beginning to wear thin on me although you could use another of those too. I'm letting you risk hanging yourself with so much cash, but I'll come if you're in real trouble."

"During the day?"

"There are ways to deal with that," she yawned, "and day is dawning. Let's get some sleep. You're adjusting to being nocturnal and have expended a lot of energy. More than you know."

"Can I call you on the telephone?"

"You don't need the number. You can always get in touch by thinking of me. But if you must have it, ask Wu. I've never used one. It may take a few years before I decide to."

"Thank you."

"Now come here."

XIV.

Jessie's Girl

Suzanne awoke alone, used the lovely shower, and put on the satin dress from the night before wishing she was in her loft on Kearney to change. She found the money beside the bed, saw the note, and read it:

My dearest Suzanne, I regret to leave in such a manner, but have been called away. Your company was both a surprise and an unexpected joy. Please allow me to see you once again. How might we meet? I am at Lorelei's house on Chestnut Street upon Russian Hill, previously called the House of Blazes, but have no inkling about your residence. I feel a great concern for your welfare amongst the riff-raff and blackguards of Chinatown and the Coast, and look forward to your returning to the better company from which you obviously came, and most certainly deserve. Please accept this money which is not for services, but for your breakfast and transportation wherever you need go. Respectfully Yours;

Audie Mitchell Bond, ESQ.

She folded the note. "Sweet."

Suzanne took a gilded elevator with a very friendly operator down to the Palace Grill and ordered poached eggs, smoked salmon, and coffee. Men with waxed mustaches and arm garters polished the block-long mahogany bar bathed in morning light coming from windows on Market. On his approach the waiter stroked his mustache, raised an eyebrow, and enquired as to her profession. She said that she was a secretary for Father Caraher, the well-known terror of every parlor house, saloon and melodeon in town, and he let the question go.

She stepped out on Market, crossed to the island along the Slot between trolley tracks, turned left past the Midway Plaisance, and headed past the pillared entrance of the Chronicle building. She passed the marble steps of the Baldwin Hotel on Ellis and headed west across Powell. On her left two blocks up was the handsome dark Victorian at 225. Between gilded columns on the third floor, a red silk curtain glowed in sunlight coming between the buildings from across the Bay. She stepped up the green travertine steps, smoothed her dress, took a deep breath, lifted the brass knocker, and knocked.

The stained glass windows shook slightly but didn't rattle, being well set in heavy oaken doors. There was silence within. She glanced up at the mirror over the transom, and noticed there was one on each side.

A Negro maid in a smart beige uniform opened the door."-May I help you?"

"You may, ma'am. I'd like to speak to Miss Hayman."

"Do you have an appointment?""

"No, her inventory's a bit rich."

The corners of the woman's mouth fought a smile before she gave Suzanne an appraising look."You lookin' for employment?"

"Yep ... I mean; yes, ma'am."

"Please come in."

Suzanne was led into a parlor with gold carpet, plush furniture upholstered in red velvet, and mirrors on every wall. Over a marble hearth was a gold-framed tapestry with homilies embroidered upon it admonishing against the use of profanity. The maid invited her to sit down, and she planted herself in a love seat.

She sat for ten minutes rocking her feet over the gold carpet. The golden clock in its domed crystal case on the mantle chimed eleven, and Jessie Hayman appeared. Suzanne stood, curtsied, eyed a stain on her satin dress, and slid her hand over it as she held up her skirts.

Jessie was very tall and dressed in green. The bun of her red hair had one lock half out at the back. Their hair was exactly the same color. Jesse had a palpable air of power that surrounded her like the expensive perfume she wore: a commanding presence much like men Suzanne had grown-up around."Well, what has the wind blown upon my doorstep today?"

"Good day, ma'am. I was wondering about employment."

"I see. And are you truly aware what the requirements are in my establishment?"

"Oh yes. I have heard the better gentlemen bra ... speak of your girls about town. And I am experienced, Miss Hayman."

"It takes more than mere 'experience' to be in my employ. Do you have a mack?"

"No, I detest pimps."

Jessie put a finger to her lips."So young, and without protection. You're spirited anyway. Then have you an education? I don't work with poor things off the farm. My clientele—"

"I have read the Classics, and speak Latin, French, Spanish, and a bit of German, Madame."

"Indeed?"

Suzanne nodded."And I know the Magna Carta, the Constitution, the Bible, and can argue the Law if the need arises."

"Oh, then tell me: from what land did Job come?"

"The, uh, the land of Uz. I'm better with the New Testament, actually."

"The Fourth Amendment says—"

"That one should be protected from unreasonable searches and seizures in our papers and property; a most useful thing to know in this profession when some copper is sticking his snoot in the door."

"And how does one of your tender years come by such learning?"

"I was raised on my uncle's estate in Burlingame, and have only recently come to San Francisco to pursue my emancipation."

"And who is your uncle?"

"Um," Suzanne bit her lip, "I'm loath to say, ma'am."

"You've been doing well up until now. Ours is a world of secrets, but you'll have to trust me, as I must by default hold them all. What was your name?"

"Suzanne Mae Callahan, but I go by Leah."

"So many do. Fortunately, we don't have one at the moment. Suzanne, it's necessary you tell me your uncle's name as he well might be a client, or at the least know one. It's only to avoid embarrassment in regard to some gentleman who might visit our establishment. Being discreet is—"

"A fundamental principle of our profession."

Jessie clasped her hands and laughed.

Jessie took her shopping that afternoon with another of her employees, a tall fair-haired girl from Los Angeles who went by Violet Adair. Violet said she was fifteen and had come to work the year before. They rode in a Rolls Phaeton limousine to the City of Paris, where Jessie seemed to have limitless credit. A woman began fitting Suzanne, and she had a spirited conversation with her in French about the Louvre that was joined by Violet, who'd been educated at a convent it seemed, and claimed her father built railroads. They skipped from one department to the next, and were served champagne and ladyfinger sandwiches in a parlor with a view of Union Square when they tired. They shopped for hours.

Jessie bought Suzanne four tailored suits, four street dresses, eight hats, two dress coats, (one plain, one fur-trimmed) twelve pairs street shoes, five dozen pairs of hose, six pocket books, two evening bags, a half-dozen street gloves and a half-dozen eighteen button evening gloves, seven evening gowns of French silk, seven negligees, twelve teddy slips, twenty-four nightgowns, six pair mules, two fur-trimmed evening wraps, seven pair evening shoes, nine dozen handkerchiefs, six blouses, and four-hundred dollars worth of fox fur wraps. The bill was six thousand two hundred and twenty-two dollars.

When Suzanne returned to her new home, she was shown a splendid room overlooking grape trellises above a back garden. The chauffeur and Bell made haste to carry the boxes and paper covered hangars upstairs, which were promptly hung in a huge walk-in closet by Starr, a young Chinese girl whom Jessie informed Suzanne was as of now her personal servant.

Suzanne sat on the bed watching the flurry of activity around her as Starr placed her shoes on a polished mahogany rack. She got up and wandered down the hall, and found Jessie in an adjoining room talking with Violet. "Miss Hayman,"

"Yes, Suzanne. You're wondering how I could possibly have such faith in you, seeing as you haven't worked yet."

"Um, yes."

"I came up through the same route myself love, and besides, I've got work for you this very afternoon. I'm sending you and Violet to the Poodle Dog in two hours to accompany two very important gentlemen, so prepare."

Violet came to her room with a silver box, took out a small green lozenge, and told her to insert it before sex in the washroom of the Poodle Dog. "These work. The fellows don't think they taste bad either."

Starr gave her a bath in lavender salts, shampooed her hair, and dressed her in a beige tailored suit with green trim. A two-strand dog collar necklace of diamonds and emeralds was placed around her neck, with matching earrings on her ears. Jessie appeared as Suzanne stood before a full length mirror lit by tiny electric bulbs in sconces shaped like petals of flowers. She drifted up in a rustle of satin skirts and placed graceful hands on Suzanne's shoulders. The two stood staring at their reflections with their red hair a perfect match, their eyes blue and green. "You could be my daughter."

"I'm overwhelmed, Miss Hayman. Can you tell me anything about the gentleman I am to see?"

"He's a friend of the mayor. Violet will inform you. The man's a guest of her regular fellow who is paying for his recreation as a reward for something. Do you know who Mr. Ruef is?"

"Sure, the guy who runs things."

"Correct, and keeping him happy keeps our little world safe from the slings and arrows suffered by the less fortunate. I don't know the gentleman's tastes, and don't intend to force you into any unpleasantness, but you must make sure he leaves the Poodle Dog *pleased,* Leah." Jessie's eyes were green as emeralds in the glass, and Suzanne nodded.

"This house has been here over fifty years since Dolly Adams built it with her earnings from the gold rush, and although I damned well earned it myself, I still consider having it both a privilege and a gift. It takes constant labor to simply *exist.* You have my promise I'll care for you as you do for me here. Remember that, love."

Suzanne answered her stare in the mirror with a nod. "You can count on me, Miss Hayman."

"Just Jessie, I'm always Jessie with my girls."

A gleaming black Siemens limousine waited at the curb, and the girls stepped in as the chauffeur held the door. Violet took off her pigskin street gloves, reached over as Suzanne removed her own, and the girls held hands as they were driven the short distance to Mason Street.

"I hear this one's younger at least," Violet whispered, "that old lug Ruef smells, but at least he can't hold his fire for long when he's drinking champagne. Just—*pop!*"

Suzanne giggled. "How long have you been seeing him?"

Violet groaned. "*Too* fucking long, but Jessie's adamant about it. He runs the whole damn town. All the Supervisors belong to him, and of course the mayor. If we need something, the best champagne, getting a girl out of jail, having a visiting Pasha or Sir Somebodyorother come to the resort Jessie's got it, the whole kit and caboodle. She gets a percentage of the refreshments at the Poodle Dog when we work there too, so be sure and get him to drink the good stuff."

"Do you know the fellow I'm to be with?"

"Just that he's someone who plays with the mayor in his orchestra, getting the special treatment from our dear Mr. Ruef for some favor."

Violet reached into her lead-beaded bag, removed a teddy slip and makeup kit, and took out a silver vial. She scooped a pile of powder on the end of a tiny silver spoon and offered it to Suzanne, who snorted it up her nose and passed it back again. The car pulled up before the **Poulet d'Or,** where the giggling girls were escorted up the steps by a doorman who looked like he'd been hired more for his pugilistic talents than social skills. They were escorted past mahogany tables under chandeliers where grinning middle-aged men smoked cigars and sipped brandy from crystal snifters. A man with blond mutton chop sideburns stared at Suzanne. He stood, bowed, and placed a gold embossed card in her hand as she passed. She glanced at the name *Crocker* on it and gave him a broad smile.

They were led up the stairs to the second floor, where they were let into a private room with a pool table, marble hearth, large oaken table set squarely in the middle of a purple Turkish carpet, and a small bar attended by the most effeminate-looking fellow Suzanne had ever seen with his hair in a shiny pompadour.

"Violet." A balding gentleman in an expensive Italian suit and a graying mustache draping his chin stood and bowed. His younger companion did the same a moment later. The young one wasn't bad looking, having curly brown hair and being clean-shaven. He looked to be no more than thirty, and was quite trim. Suzanne gave him her best smile. "And this is your new friend, Miss ... "

"Leah."

"Leah, of course. And this is my associate Mr. Christian Wiggins, in whose honor this little assignation attends to. Please, sit down."

It didn't take long to get down to business as Ruef was expected by his wife on Nob Hill, but they still found time to drink two bottles of Moet. Suzanne was amazed at Violet's capacity to consume champagne, but remembered what she'd said about Jessie's percentage and Ruef's dispositions. The cocaine helped too. Her head spun as the men escorted the girls to a fourth floor that contained bedrooms. Ruef disappeared into one with Violet, and Suzanne was led into another by Mr. Wiggins where a bottle of champagne sat in a pewter ice bucket before a canopy bed with gold silk curtains.

Suzanne excused herself to use the bathroom. She took off her smart beige suit and hung it on the door. She peed, cleaned herself with one of the thick washrags and coconut soap at the basin, and inserted the lozenge. She let down her hair, fingered the dog collar of gems around her throat, eyed herself critically in the mirror, and returned to the room.

Wiggins was on the bed masturbating, which made things easier. This might not take any time at all. She sat on the bed, and her fingers closed around his crooked cock. With any luck, he'd be done in a flash, and she could return to Jessie's with—

Wiggins grabbed a fistful of her hair and yanked her backward. Suzanne let out a yelp as he lifted her up and slammed her down on the bed with her face in the quilted silk comforter. He pushed harder when she tried to speak, smothering her cry of protest. She gasped as her cheek slid in saliva against the silk.

"So, little whore!" Wiggins slapped her savagely across her buttocks, leaving a sharp sting that seemed to hover in a hot cloud above her bare bottom. He kept pressing her face in the soft surface. Suzanne reached around with one hand, clawing at the fingers in her hair threatening to pull it out by the roots as her other hand tried to make enough of a depression in the comforter to breathe.

He wrenched her right arm behind her back, and her scream made the silk against her face tremble. The sudden violation from behind was a surprise. For an instant she thought he had simply missed the mark, until he rammed deeper and she screamed again.

XV.

Breakfast at Three

"Mister Audie, telephone call!" The voice of Wu came muffled through the polished oaken boards of the floor.

He groaned, rubbed his face, and lifted a purring cat off his chest. Lorelei stretched across the sheets beside him like a pale still life, making the breath catch in his throat. He stared at her nipples as they rose and fell with the flow of her breathing.

"Mister Audie! This man call all day too much! Please ... come talk *now!*"

"All right." He rolled across a stain of blood and grimaced, and stared at it for a moment. The headache was there, though not as intense. Lorelei had placed a bottle of Bayer's Aspirin and three bottles of Chinese herbs on the table. He took a sip of each, tore off the paper cover of the Aspirin with a brief glance at the German printed on it, popped the cork, and swallowed four pills. He rubbed his temples and sighed. He was as dependent upon her as a child for shelter, money, and food, yet was repaying it in a way surely as important to her as all three for him ... *more*. He gazed at bars of sunlight streaking across the far wall from between the curtains, and shrugged. Somehow the whole bargain seemed in perfect balance. He—

"Please!"

"Coming!" He grabbed a bathrobe, stumbled downstairs, took the black trumpet of the receiver from Wu, and leaned into the mouthpiece of the oaken box. Fried potatoes, eggs, orange juice, and coffee were on the mahogany table in blue china dishes. He'd planned to eat at Tony's for the opportunity to visit with Diana, but as he smelled the food his stomach growled. "Hello?"

"Audie! Things all right?"

"Sure, Izzy. Sorry about last night. I found that girl that I was looking for and—"

"The little whore? Unbelievable! Get your money?"

"Not exactly ... but I got some satisfaction."

"You rake. Don't tell me you made the little thing perform for the debt. You're a virgin no more with a vengeance, but four hundred dollars is more than a night full of girls and a couple cases of Mumms at a parlor house. You need some schooling on where your money goes."

"I suppose you want to catch up with me."

"You bet. I've been at a learned old man's home, going through some rare books and talking at length about your lady friend."

"A Rabbi?"

"Not exactly, he's a gentleman like myself only older. He's studied such things all his days, being of independent means with the time to devote to scholarly pursuits, and thinks you're the only person in the world having this particular experience at this time. He's explored the *Yenne Velt* a bit himself, that's the other world from whence he's absolutely certain she comes, and is considered a Rebbe amongst the educated of my people around here. He agrees that you've assumed a position that is both spiritually significant and absolutely mythic. But, let's get together and talk."

"I *know* I'm the only one. Listen: my stomach is digesting itself as we speak. Can you meet me at Tony's?"

"You bet. When?"

"An hour. I shall expedite a shower."

"I'm on my way, pilgrim."

"Good, good bye." Audie hung up and turned toward the bathroom, but found himself shoveling fork-fulls of eggs and potatoes Wu had left on the table into his mouth, and washing them down with orange juice and coffee.

Izzy was at Tony's when he arrived in conversation with Diana. They smiled as he came in the door. Audie took a chair, caressing the hard roundness of Diana's bottom as he did so, picking up where she'd left off.

"Hi, Mister late riser," she purred, "ready to eat?"

"I certainly am, my lovely friend."

"Tony's got fresh sole off his brother's boat. Ever have it? He cooks it in garlic and olive oil, with this—"

"No, but I'm sure it's delicious."

"The full course lunch then. Wine?"

"Coffee please."

"I forgot, you just got up with all that nightlife you're into. See ya in a minute." Diana gave him a blue-eyed wink and sashayed off.

His gaze turned to Izzy, who was fooling with an unlit cigar.

"Hello, Audie."

"Good afternoon Izzy. How was your night?"

"Saw a poor fellow get gunned down in front of the Orpheum. Over a woman I believe."

"Ouch."

"What's on your agenda? I mean before your nightly carousal with the Goddess?"

"I appreciate you're not calling her a demon or witch however you may feel. She detests that." Audie gazed out the window at a working girl arguing with a sailor. "She wants me to get some clothes, says I need some for going to the country."

Izzy ran the cigar under his nose. "These Cubans are marvelous. That war did a lot of good when it comes to the price of the things. Don't know if I could ever live where I couldn't get them again. Try one?"

"No thank you. What did your friend say about my woman?"

"*Your* woman? Audie, you may be *her* man, but she's far more than your woman I'd wager."

Audie let out his breath and nodded. "I stand corrected. She's far more and far greater than my woman. She helped me find Leah in fact. She made me see her where she wasn't, at least long enough for her to show up. Lorelei said she was just changing the timing a bit ... of our lives I mean, and I ran smack into Leah as I exited a doorway. Rather amazing."

Izzy's eyebrows knotted, and he stroked his beard. "So what's this little tart Leah up to? And what kind of satisfaction were you referring to anyway?"

"More than mere rutting, although we certainly did have a go. Leah's a runaway from a good family it seems, the illegitimate product of a Priest."

"Ho," Izzy leaned back and lit his cigar, "her too. Audie, we all are from the Cloth by way of birth it appears."

"What do you mean?"

"My father is a Rabbi in New York, yours is a Methodist Minister, and now hers is a Priest. From where?"

"I didn't get to ask. Lorelei told me that after she salvaged me from the Palace Hotel."

"Salvaged, the Palace? How did you end up there?"

"Leah took me. Her real name is Suzanne by the way."

"Did I mention that Leah is the name many women of ill repute use in this town?"

"If you didn't, others did."

Audie glanced at Diana approaching the table with bread and butter, her skin aglow in sunlight slanting through the windows. An aura seemed to enfold her. Something crashed across his vision, and he felt he was going to faint. Sparks crackled under his eyelids as his appetites began to merge. The scent of food and flesh made him ready to devour both the warm bread and approaching girl. He grabbed the edges of the table, and coffee splashed. A red drum pounded like a hammer throughout his being, threatening to crush all inhibition as something rose within him and lightening crackled under his eyelids.

When he regained his concentration, the bread was before him, and Diana was close enough to touch. He wanted to lay her upon the tablecloth, to feast on her in the afternoon sun full of dancing rainbows. He was a devourer of souls, sent to taste of all fair flesh. He squeezed his eyes shut, and opened them.

Diana stood blinking. Her lips glistened as she swayed on her feet.

"Are you okay?" Izzy asked.

"Huh? Oh … sure." She turned, took a step, and collapsed.

Audie sprang out of his chair and caught her as she went limp in his arms. His face was against her throat, and he inhaled the scent of her skin. There was a bruise on her collarbone that looked like it had been made by a mouth. She moaned, and he placed her on her feet.

Diana put a hand to her forehead. "Whew! What happened?"

"You just fainted in your tracks girl," Izzy said, "are you quite sure you're all right?"

Tony came from the kitchen wiping his hands on an apron as Diana tottered between Tony and Audie, holding onto Audie for balance. "Yes, I … jeez, Audie," she lay her head against his chest, "thanks for catching me. That's never happened before I swear."

Tony shook his head."Is it your time of month, or something?"

"No, and if it was it wouldn't be any of your goddamn business!" Diana stalked back to the kitchen with a snarl.

They sat down as Tony went back to work mumbling about foolish girls, and how hard it was to keep good help.

"What was that?"

"What, Izzy?"

"You did that. You were ready to ravish that girl right there, and she felt it. Holy Moses, that woman's turning you into Dionysus himself. I see it plain as day. Your lusts are unquenchable I'd wager. Did you wear out that little whore?"

Audie nodded with a mouth full of bread. He swallowed, took a gulp of coffee, and tried to return the conversation to what Izzy had found out from his learned friend."So what does your scholar say is the nature of Lorelei?"

"It's as I told you. She's appeared the world over by many different names and forms ... or at least her kind has, and he's in full agreement she's a Liliot. They show up at critical times as an auger of great change in human history, tempting the men who have a role to play. He's willing to wager his estate on it. He pawed through some very old books and wanted to begin praying to command her to appear before him to try and send her back to *Gehenna* or wherever she's from, but I thought the better of it. We don't want to set her off or something."

"Well, she's already admitted she's a Liliot or whatever, and I've accepted it. What do we really know about them anyway? She says that much of the disparaging stories about her kind are simply sour grapes on the part of men who couldn't accept what they are, and I believe it. Besides, I don't have any position of power here so I don't know why she'd choose me for that, but this town *is* ready for a good shake-up I'd say. I've seen more degradation than I knew could happen somewhere I care to call the country of my birth. Did you know the tong singsong girls are simply *killed* when they're used-up, when they're still but young girls?"

"The Chinks have their ways; that's a fact. How did you pick up on that, Leah? I mean Suzanne?"

"Leah only confirmed it. But Lorelei actually let me see … she let see me a girl dying. There is no one other than you I can tell that to who might possibly believe it of course."

"Say what?"

"She went to a girl in the basement of some awful place in Chinatown. I think it was a basement … and I *think* it was Chinatown. It could have been a dungeon for that matter. It was horrible, but Lorelei came solely to comfort her and take her … take her to the other side."

"You mean death?"

Audie nodded. "Her purpose is far more than either of us can imagine. Would someone evil be able to do that? She was that girl's only friend in the world, a light of salvation for a poor slave who was dying in a dark basement. How much more selfless could one be? I *saw* it, Izzy. Whatever else she is, Lorelei is a wonder of creation, and I must love her and honor her for what she has revealed to me, even if her true nature is a mystery as of yet. Mystery is her favored name for God, for that matter. Isn't that perfect?" He stared out the glass at the passing parade of mortal souls and ran a hand over his eyes. "Izzy, I realize this very moment that I love her with all my being. I can't tell you how grateful I am to be the one she has chosen for her consort, I—"

Izzy averted his eyes and stared out the window. "She could have made you see something that *wasn't,* you know. A Liliot has powers we can't begin to understand." He sighed. "You sound like some character out of classical myth Audie, who usually ends up dead from going where only the gods can tread. *Hubris,* you know. Listen to yourself."

"So what!" Audie's fist slammed on the table, and coffee splashed as the other diners turned and stared. "She *is* whom you suspect ... but far *more,* Izzy! She is a wondrous gift of creation that I have the honor and undying pleasure to submit to for this brief and passing moment which is my own life and that's all there is to the whole affair, so *there!*" Audie sat down hard, and diners muttered as they returned to their meals.

Izzy took the cigar from his mouth, having crushed the butt flat between his teeth. He took out an ivory handled clasp knife, and began to cut it off and shape it to a clean end. "Wow."

"I suppose that I am quite a curiosity to you by now."

"More than that pilgrim. Believe me, though, I envy you in a way. She's the finest woman *I've* ever seen, immortal or not."

"She's not immortal, Izzy. Someday she too shall die."

"I'd wager she's got a good whack at it from where I sit. How old is she?"

"She was born in sixteen seventy-nine or eighty, I forget which."

"A child compared to some of the Patriarchs. None of this even surprises me, which in itself is so astounding I can only sit here like a fool and relight this fine cigar." He leaned back in his seat, struck a match, and puffed it into a burn. "What are your plans for today?"

"Like I said, she wants me to buy some clothes, but I want to go down to the bad parts of the Coast and Chinatown where the singsong girls and cribs are."

"What the hell for?"

"There's a place I saw in a dream, but I know it's real."

"What will you do when you find it?"

"Just have a look around, and I think it's time to test some things I've begun to suspect about my own nature in regard to the reason she chose me in the first place."

"You're not winding yourself up to do something foolish, are you pilgrim? I know you're loath to hear it, and it probably won't make a whit of difference, but there are plenty tales of Liliots luring men to their doom through dreams only to be dropped into Hell."

Audie leaned back and closed his eyes, and Izzy flicked an inch of ash into the tray on the table and watched Diana serve two sailors until Audie opened them. "I don't think so, but it is something that I must finish. Will you be my guide?"

"Of course, and your backup partner. I have a cousin down there who can provide you with decent clothes, and then we can take a look at a few dens of iniquity. But remember: some of those Chinee lugs can cut a fly in the air with a hatchet, and they sure can cut you or bash your brains out way before you get to your gun, so listen to me when I warn you."

"Fair enough Izzy. Thank you."

XVI.

Down to the Coast

Izzy's cousin Mordecai had an emporium near the docks. "He tries to sell folks decent clothes before they get caught by the crimps, or spend it all on the girls."

"What's a crimp?"

"Sonsabitches who greet sailors with tales of women and high living. Shanghai guys who sell them to a Captain needing a crew. There are rooming houses that give sailors all the rotgut booze and slatterns they can handle, increasing the opium or chloral hydrate in their cups until they're like sacks of potatoes that they can haul to the boats, and those are the *nice* shanghai guys. They just drop 'em right through the floor into big rowboats after bashing them on the noggin at that place down at the foot of Jackson. Some never wake up, and they dump 'em in the Bay." Izzy shook his head, scanning the cobbled street for a cab as they descended the hill. "Some fools will go back to the same place again even knowing they'll be shanghaied. Figure a couple days of living it up free of charge with some fallen flower is worth waking up on another filthy tub I suppose." He shrugged. "Some life, but Mordecai's got some of them jobs on the better ships before they fall prey to those scum."

"That's admirable."

"Of course he's not above getting their money before some other guy does. At least they'll have good clothes on their backs, and sturdy shoes. Hey Sam!" Izzy hailed a horse-drawn taxi on Lombard. The white-haired black man driving pulled on the reins, and his steed pulled up with a snort and clopping of hooves. Sam grinned, and tipped his hat. Lucky Izzy was renowned as a good tipper.

As they rode toward the Coast, Izzy pointed out places, explaining who ran them and what went on inside. Travelers, sailors, men in suits, women in corseted dresses, Italian and Portuguese men with open-collared shirts, old women in concealing dresses with purple shawls, street-walking whores and a few East Coast tourists filled the streets. The dance halls, melodeons, bagnios and dives increased as they moved east. Izzy pointed out two big multi-story 'cowyards' full of girls: rickety three and four-story buildings peeling paint with mean-looking men guarding their entries. Red lights proliferated over doors and windows, ready for nightfall. A row of thrown-together shacks crowded an alley with drunken men waiting in line. A woman cried somewhere, as if in pain.

"Mordecai's on Front; he got the place twenty years ago. A shanghai joint was downstairs, the owner shot his wife, and somebody returned the favor with a shotgun. While the erstwhile management was dead, every lug in the vicinity looted the place, and somebody started a fire. Mordecai got it while it was gutted and rebuilt. There are good brick walls, and a brick-walled basement that was used for holding fellows while they were drugged and trussed-up for the boats that's dry and perfect for storage. He's made some great buys off ships that got stripped of their crews and re-sold the cargos over the years. It's a great location if you can handle the rough-and-tumble down here."

"Sounds like a solid citizen for these parts."

"Like a rock, pilgrim. Hey look, there's Oofty Goofty." Izzy pointed out a thin man coming down Battery from the direction of Pacific wearing a tattered suit and derby hat, carrying a baseball bat while tipping his hat to people.

"What is he doing?"

"He charges fifty cents to hit him with that bat."

"What?"

"Crazy, isn't it? Been around for years. Charges ten cents to kick him, twenty-five to hit him with your cane, and fifty for the bat. I've seen drunken sailors knock him across the street plenty of times."

"My God ... that's *madness!*"

"The fellow gets plenty of business."

A wan blonde appeared from the door of a building peeling green paint and whistled at Oofty Goofty. She brushed hair from her eyes and adjusted her blouse, having obviously just tossed her clothes on in a hurry for the pleasure of inflicting pain on the man.

Three women and a big man with a cigar in his mouth and bottle in his fist threw aside the dirty curtains and appeared in the windows. The dark-haired woman beside the man wasn't wearing anything at all above the waist, and her mottled breasts swung as she clapped her hands. The man lifted her to the windowsill by her crotch, eliciting a hoarse laugh that exposed gaps in her teeth. Audie grimaced as he scanned her florid face. "Knock the shit out of him, Louise!" she shouted.

The skinny blonde smiled, spat on her hands, rubbed them together, and held out a bill to Oofty Goofty. He handed her the bat, and began to fish in his pocket. "Keep the change!" she shouted, and swung the bat overhead with a grunt of effort. Oofty Goofty turned to catch the blow across the middle of his back. There was a loud *whack*, and he went sprawling in the gutter with his brown derby rolling in the street.

"Hooray!" came from the windows.

Louise curtsied, scratched between her legs, and held out a hand to help Oofty to his feet, who scooped up his hat, bowed, and placed it on his head. She planted a kiss on his cheek, handed him the bat, and went back inside.

"That is the strangest thing I've ever seen, Izzy." Audie said as they rounded the corner onto Front.

"Oh, even stranger than your lady friend?"

"Well ... "

Izzy laughed. "A hard way to make a living, pilgrim. Here's Mordecai's."

It was an open emporium on the ground floor of a smudged two-story brick building with a lattice-work of iron shutters on three sides. Clothes with yellow tags hung on racks, and were piled on shelves where rough-looking men browsed. In the middle of the store with a good view was a raised counter behind which stood a stout man who looked like a bigger version of Izzy, though his nose was a good deal redder. A dark-haired woman who likely was his wife arranged things in the near corner. A pretty girl who could pass for their daughter was doing the same at the other side of the place.

Mordecai was watching two sailors from his perch like a hawk, and Izzy and Audie were into the store before he noticed them. "Israel!"

"Mordecai! I bring you a friend, and a customer who needs apparel."

"You know you'll get the family treatment, eh, Israel?"

"I know you're worth the trouble anyway cousin. Audie here is newly arrived. He could use another good suit, but his paramour requires he be equipped for recreation in the country-side as well."

"What? Are you keeping a demimonde?"

"No," Audie began.

"Then have you got a rich one, with an estate already?"

"I don't—"

"A rich one anyway, but that doesn't mean to take advantage of the boy. I've been telling him how you've saved many a poor pilgrim from the clutches of crimps and blackguards, and I don't want my credibility challenged."

"I'll have my own daughter help him then. Obviously he's trustworthy. Just this morning, I had to split the noggin of some lout who stepped out of Nikko's across the street after a night of drinking and came crashing in here like a bull. Oy! He pulled down a whole shelf of Strauss's denims and tried to grope Esther." Mordecai held a thick-fingered hand over his head. "Great big Norwegian boy, a bloody Goliath of a Goy. Lucky I keep this cudgel handy." Mordecai reached under the counter and produced a three-foot dented black club with a heavy knob on its end wrapped in iron wire. He slapped it in his palm.

Esther approached and offered to help. Audie found himself staring at the fine pale skin of her throat, and fought an urge to run fingers across it. He tipped his hat and introduced himself, letting her guide him to a rack of denims while praying nothing like what he had gone through with Diana might come upon him now.

After Audie finished shopping, they sent Sam back with the purchases. Night was falling, and it seemed he could feel Lorelei waking like a flower blooming at dusk, smell the perfume of her flesh as she yawned and stretched. A glow rose from her skin as he gazed upon her in his mind, and he sighed.

"Well," Izzy offered, "Pacific's over there. What do you say we catch a hoochy-kootchy show?"

"I suppose. Is there a place to get a drink without a Mickey Finn and a trip to some boat in the Bay?"

"Sure, but stay close. The first couple of blocks are pretty bad. There's a place specializes in crews for whalers at the corner.

It's changed hands many times in fifty years and been burnt in three fires, but it's just as bad as the day it opened." Izzy pointed to a red brick saloon with a rusting anchor propped against a post out front. A smear on one of the ends looked like dried blood.

The scruffy blond man with a scar running down the side of his face who'd solicited Audie when he was just off the boat eyed them from the doorway."Have a good drink and a pretty lass, mates?" he said to Audie, having sized-up Izzy as not the type who would fetch money from a whaling Captain. A lead filled leather slung shot, the butt of a pistol and the sheath of his knife protruded from under his tobacco stained canvas coat.

"Tell Jimmy Laflin to shove it up his keester, mate."

The man made a barking laugh, followed by a few anatomical insults thrown at Izzy's back as they ascended Pacific Street. The place was coming alight with signs advertising beer, whiskey, lewd exhibitions, girls, tobacco and rooms. A theater's wide doors had gilded nymphs and satyrs in various forms of frantic pursuit and copulation, complete with erect penises as **HIPPODROME** glowed in foot-high letters on the marquee.

Audie was nearly run down by a White Steamer as he began to step off the curb with his eyes on the obscene façade of the theater."Whoof!" He sprang back through a tendril of steam onto the sidewalk just as a small body flew out the door of a melodeon. A bouncer followed, kicking the man in the head as he tried to rise. The man fell across a pile of horse droppings between two carriages, provoking snorts from the horses who mercifully stepped around him. Three urchins darted in to check his pockets as a puddle of blood spread around his head.

Audie stepped to the man's assistance only to be blocked by the big man who'd put him there, who showed crooked yellow teeth through a thick black beard."You want some too, lug?"

Audie clenched his jaw. "You're a lowly son of a bitch to treat such a little fellow—"

Izzy grabbed Audie's arm. "Not a good idea! It's not our fight! Don't know what it's about anyway." Izzy tipped his bowler hat to the scowling bouncer as he hurried Audie past the place.

In a few paces, Audie shook off Izzy's grip and turned to stare back at the saloon. "Damn! How the hell does someone enjoy themselves here with the threat of violence so prevalent? This isn't civilized, Izzy!"

"By only caring about their own self-gratification, pilgrim. The economics of this place are built upon it. Many will willingly squander their future for a few minutes of pleasure in their cups and the embrace of anything they can call a woman, or even a boy. The wheels of commerce have been lubricated by that truth since we first peered out of a cave, son."

Audie pondered that, comparing it to the overwhelming sense of selflessness he felt with Lorelei, and a feeling her existence was an answer to the painful world all around him overtook him in a rush. Perhaps she was an angel, sent to save the world through a finer and greater love. What did he know about angels anyway? Certainly they could be far more complex than he'd ever imagined, and some were said to do terrible things besides when the situation warranted. He gazed at the garish signs around him and imagined her rising above them on snow-white wings. He very much liked the idea. The memory of the bruised breasts of the harlot in the window while her friend attempted to harm the unfortunate Oofty Goofty flashed across his mind, and he scowled.

Laughter like the sweetest music poured through him like a brook. His nerves rang like a bell, and he stopped dead in his tracks. "Lorelei!"

"What?"

"She's watching!"

"Could she show up in a ruckus?"

"I suppose, if it were necessary."

"That would be something. I'd like to see it. Here's a good place."

Izzy turned into a large music hall called **The Thalia** past a teenage barker with a voice hoarse from shouting. Inside was a big room with a stage on which six girls were dancing to a ragtime tune played up-tempo on battered pianos faster than anything Audie had ever heard. They kicked high in the air as if doing the can-can as couples danced in no particular style he could discern. Girls in too-short satin dresses pressed against men in brown canvas coveralls, plaid shirts and denim, herringbone suits and bowler hats. An isle ran on each side below private booths where young women accompanied men at tables before red velvet curtains. The drapes behind one parted to reveal a man pulling his boots on upon a bed separated only by the curtain. Girls moved up the isles clad in bright red satin smocks that went barely below their buttocks with legs sheathed in black fishnet stockings as the cacophony of two pianos and shouts for liquor and beer from customers were underlain by the rhythmic pounding of the dancers' shoes on the scuffed stage.

Izzy stepped into a booth. "Come on. Let's see how long it takes for a couple of waiter girls to join us."

Audie wasn't sure what he'd said, but sat down in the din.

A girl appeared soon enough. "Champagne?"

"No, give us a couple steam schooners," Izzy said, ordering the local beer. He grinned as the girl moved away. "They try and sell that champagne to all the pilgrims. It's apple juice with some fizz added, and a dollop of grain alcohol. Easy stuff to dope too."

"Oh. Where's this place between the bottom and the top?"

"What?"

"The BOTTOM and the TOP!" Audie shouted over the music. "If the tong slaves and hop-heads cutting their veins are the very *bottom*, and the parlor houses and people drinking French champagne and dining at the Palace are the *top*, where would this be, on a scale of one to ten?"

"Oh," Izzy produced a cigar, "five, I guess. A plain old five."

"Just a place, then."

"Yep, just a place."

Two girls showed up at that juncture with the beer. One was tall and gangly with blond hair, the other chestnut-skinned and willowy with the cheekbones of an Indian. Audie gazed into her almond-shaped eyes and felt an intense bout of curiosity. Perhaps she was from one of the vanishing peoples of California, or even descended from some great fighting Chief he'd read about in dime novels. She certainly was attractive, though she looked rather tired. Before he could say anything at all, she was sitting in his lap. "Hey big blond boy, you a Norski sailor?"

"No, er, Miss, I'm from—"

The music rose to a crescendo as the pounding increased. He could hardly hear her words, and just watched the motion of her mouth. Her lips were full and dark like the color his arms got in a hot West Virginia summer, only becoming pink as they met the moist interior of her mouth around white teeth. Her tongue flicked, and nostrils flared as she spoke. His hand wandered to her breast, to be greeted by a bare firm thing under the thin silk blouse with a nipple that was stiff and erect. She folded into his arms, and he was kissing her.

After an eon, he pulled away from a mouth that grinned. She ran her tongue across the tip of his nose and squeezed the bulge in his pants. "This one's ready," she said to her friend, who was still trying to get on Izzy's lap. Izzy blew a cloud from his cigar around the blonde's face, and she looked like she was going to hit him.

"God!" Audie squeezed the brass rail separating the booth from the floor below.

"Want to go behind the curtains?"

Audie blinked. Her short blouse had ridden up. He saw a scar across her stomach, and his fingertips traced it. "What happened here?"

"Some lug I shouldn't a trusted tried to gut me with a Green River knife. Lucky I weren't kilt. You ain't a creep, are ya?"

"A what?"

"A *creep!*"

"No ma'am, I am the paramour of a goddess."

"Fuck!" The girl laughed, exposing two gaps where teeth were missing. "Well big fella, you can dip your wick for two bucks, one for the mouth. Make it three, and you can go 'round the world much as you like."

The seething unquenchable passion Audie had felt moments before was gone. Her proposal held no thrill, but rather made him want to leave on the instant. He glanced at Izzy.

"Thought we'd lost you there for a moment, pilgrim."

Audie threw down a five for each girl. "Here," he mumbled, "have a nice night."

The girls scooped up the money, and the one he'd thought himself in love with moments before smirked. "There's a place two blocks up you might like, boys in the booths and only a goddamn quarter." Shrill laughter bounced off their backs as they left.

They stepped into the crowds and continued up Pacific with Audie scanning the alleys on either side. An old Chinaman was packing up a fish stall in the dark and loading baskets into a cart. On the opposite corner, a red bearded policeman was screaming at a Chinese wearing a black bowler hat.

"Goddamn Chinee devil, take yer medicine!" The cop proceeded to cudgel the fellow about the head and ears with his billy club to the un-protesting silence of the tong man, who bent over and covered his head. The tong man's hat rolled in the street, and his queue hung to the cobblestones. As he stooped to get it, the cop kicked him squarely in the rear and the boo how doy went sprawling to the loud laughter of the Irishman. The Chinaman scooped up his hat and disappeared in an alley that was fragrant with trash.

"See that?" Izzy asked.

"Yes. Why did that Chinese behave so passively?"

"The tongs know you don't kill a cop unless absolutely necessary. It just brings trouble. That highbinder could have a dozen killings to his credit and probably could have taken that copper's head off pronto. Bet he takes it out on some unfortunate guy with a stall in one of these alleys or some poor singsong girl though."

They crossed Columbus again, and signs in Chinese appeared. A pagoda roof rose behind a red-painted fence as the sour, sweet and sickly smells of seafood, incense, and garbage mingled in their nostrils. A Chinese mother shepherded her boy across the street and glared at them.

The alleys grew narrower, and a girl waved from a doorway. "You likey good time, me give you so much, sailor," she hissed through dead white makeup, "your father he just leave."

Izzy chuckled. "That's an honor, pilgrim. It means you've got daddy's approval."

Audie stopped at a dark passageway between smudged brick walls where meat stalls were closed up, and figures moved in and out of the shadows.

"What is it, Audie?"

"Here," he said under his breath.

Two men in black silk shirts stood by a door at the end of the alley with arms crossed over their chests. He could see them though it was quite dark, and knew at the same time that they were certain he could not. He could *feel* within the walls behind them, feel the loathing and sorrow there like some tangled mass beneath dark waters. The sensation was familiar, familiar in a way he knew was the gift of Lorelei, for he had never conceived of such things days ago. Now he knew it like the feel of his own skin.

The boo how doy guarded a door where men of all races went after they had been inspected and allowed to enter. Beyond was where one paid to hold a girl in slavery, where all caring was lost. Here, customers could simply pay after they had killed a girl and return to their respectable lives. Here, at the end of Butcher Alley, Mai Ling had spent her short and awful life. Here she had died. "*Here!*"

"What?"

"*Mai Ling!* Her name was Mai Ling!" the name exploded from Audie like a festering wound had burst. It seemed to give the very air around him a sickly yellow light, echoing off the walls of the alley and sending two gamblers emerging from a basement scurrying. "She was but a *girl!*"

The two highbinders reached under their shirts in unison with eyes flashing in moonlight falling from a sky that was clean and full of stars. He could see their faces as he approached, with their broad cheekbones reflecting the streetlight behind him. He tossed off the hand grasping at his sleeve.

"Audie, for shit's sake!" Izzy fumbled with his Smith and Wesson while trying to cover Audie, but Audie blocked his view of the hatchetmen. "Audie, goddamn it, your precious Lorelei better

be watching you *now*, pilgrim! There's a lot more of those devils than these two, and this is tong territory! Audie, are you *listening*
to me? Goddamn it, you crazy fuckin' Goy, *stop!*"

He did stop, but ten feet from the hatchetmen. He could
see the glint of steel now, and the curve of a blade. This was
what had awaited Mai Ling when they had come and found her
still living but for the intercession of one who had stolen her away
in the forgiving night. A woman he loved with all his being, yet
whose very existence the entire world was blind to ... or con-
demned like a pack of superstitious peasants in the Dark Ages.
How many are inside?

"A hundred, but their numbers are countless." Her breath
caressed his cheek.*"If you go closer, I must give you the experience of
killing them. Do you want that?"*

Audie shuddered as if lightening had run through him, and
the hatchetmen backed into fighting stances. A blade hissed as
it cut an arc in the air. One of them spat out a curse in Cantonese, and showed him the very American gesture of a middle finger
raised in defiance. The sound of a hammer cocking came from the
boo how doy on the left, and the barrel of his pistol glinted blue
in moonlight.

*"I saved her from the knives Audie. You saw. Her soul has
a path to follow of its own making, a good one. Please return to
the street. I'll keep them here until you are safe."*

The world had stopped, and hung poised. Audie could hear
the labored breathing of the two tong killers and could smell
their fear-fear at his strangeness, fear at the light in his own eyes.

He turned his back on the hatchetmen and walked away.

Izzy backed up beside him, crab walking to keep up with
his gun on the boo how doy. When they reached the sidewalk,
he grabbed Audie's arm."Run!"

XVII.

La Questa Del Oro

The sojourn to the Coast and Chinatown had been quite enough for one evening. Audie had an overwhelming need to return to Lorelei, and very much hoped she'd be waiting as they caught a red lacquered horse cab to Russian Hill. When they came to Powell, a cable car was stopped in the middle of the street. Izzy tossed the carriage driver some money, got out, and swung aboard the trolley without a word. He'd been silent since their close escape and hadn't bombarded Audie with his usual battery of questions in regard to the matter. He merely tipped his bowler hat. "See you soon." His complexion was gray in the streetlamps.

Audie arrived at her door just as Wu emerged with two bags. Wu promptly put them down and signaled the cab to remain. A jolt went through Audie as the awful thought Lorelei might be leaving came to him.

She appeared a moment later in a wide black hat and black dress with the requisite corset not included, and her smile obliterated his fears. "Hello Audie!" She brushed lips across his cheek, and all was right in the world. "Well, you've seen a tiny part of what I have to live with every night of my existence. I've decided to take a trip this evening, and your bags are packed."

She stepped into the carriage, spoke to the driver in rapid French, and the man nodded as his eyes roved over her. Audie got in beside her, and the cab turned down the hill toward the wharves where boats rocked in dark clusters on the swells.

"Where are we going?"

"Out of town. It's a lovely night isn't it?"

"Yes." The sky was for once utterly clear of fog and the

smudge of the city's coal furnaces, and the stars were out. He wondered how they had seemed so brilliant from the dark canyon of an alley in Chinatown.

"Your soul was *focused,* Audie," she answered his thoughts, "all things become more intense at such times, as you were open to perception."

"Oh."

She squeezed his hand. "I didn't guide you to that place. You found it on your own initiative, by your own senses."

"How?"

"That which is in us all has awakened in you. The echoes of souls alive and dead are boiling up inside you like a kettle on a hot stove, and I very much don't want to see you blow your lid. I'm taking you out of town for a while to adjust, up to the redwoods, and I have some unfinished business to attend to."

"Adjust to what?"

"To your newfound sensibilities, and I don't want you killing anybody either."

"And to have me all to yourself, I suppose."

"Absolutely." Her cheeks dimpled. "You're starting fires everywhere you go. Remember what you did to that poor waitress? Our level of intimacy isn't common amongst 'mere mortals' or whatever, and it is spilling over to those around you. Women are quite sensitive to such things you know, and even Izzy was rather right about hubris in a way, at least as far as it being necessary to keep you from going overboard. Diana dreams of you, and Suzanne's searching the city for you at this moment. Even Jessie Hayman is putting out feelers, tipping people for the slightest word of your whereabouts like some infatuated child."

Audie gazed at the Bay. "I've had quite enough for a while."

"You are tired love, and for good reason, but you shall grow stronger."

"How could you have come to my aid against those hatchetmen?"

"Swiftly, dearest. I was on a very slippery tile rooftop overhead." She chuckled. "Lucky one didn't come loose and brain you. Look, there's our ride."

A small steamer was tied at the end of a wharf with her lights blazing and two short masts rocking on the swells with sails tightly furled. The low thud of an idling engine carried over the water as smoke drifted from its stack over the Bay. When the carriage stopped at the gangplank, Audie read the name off the stern: **La Questa Del Oro.**

The little Frenchman quickly unloaded their bags, and they were grabbed by a short muscular man with a black mustache and a wool watch cap on his head before they hit the ground. Lorelei thanked the cabbie in French, paid him, and greeted the seaman in Italian, calling him Carlo. Carlo made an expansive gesture with his right hand. He bowed, and grinned at Audie as he hustled their things onto the boat.

Audie stepped onto the deck inhaling the smell of fresh-cut redwood. Sawdust was in every crack and niche as the ship had just unloaded lumber from a mill along the coast. What did it cost to charter such a vessel? He was beginning to take such things for granted as the far more miraculous things he'd experienced were taking up his capacity for wonder.

The beat of the engine increased, they cast off, and the boat slipped out between two moored vessels. San Francisco glowed like a chaotic nest of dreams as he leaned on the gunwale.

"You've done well." She was beside him at the rail. "Your education is proceeding nicely."

"Not exactly the one I sought, dear lady."

"Are you sure?"

He inhaled the salt breeze as the boat rode the swells. The water pulsed with luminescence from beneath its surface like a thing alive. What *had* he sought? Surely he'd been given more than anything he'd asked for, yet he knew that somehow he'd asked for this. Something in him had called out, and Lorelei had answered as if it all had been arranged ... as if it was *ordained.* He laughed."Ordained, what a word for it!"

"That comes from your upbringing, but it could be graven on stone in our case. You're right, you were asking for my company. I heard your voice amongst that great riot in the night. I felt you coming when you were on a train crossing the plains, and I was on a steamer from Skagway. Even when I was taking my previous lover into my realm, I felt you growing nearer."

"I thought you said you couldn't see the future."

"Not all of it, not by a long shot."

Lorelei spread her arms to the sky, face aglow with the light of stars as she balanced on the rolling deck and Audie held onto the railing."This land is so full of beauty. If I could but spend one single, wondrous day just walking in it, listening to the birds and smelling the flowers."

"What will you do when daylight comes?"

"Sleep, Audie, though I can get around if absolutely necessary. Do you know what metabolism is?"

"The way a body regulates itself I believe."

"My body regulates itself differently from yours, to belabor the obvious. As you know, my system is sensitive to sunlight and finds it generally painful. It's the blood."

"What about it?"

"The fact that I live on it."

He felt that queasiness as before when Lorelei had explained who she was, albeit in the most gentle of ways. The rocking boat didn't aid in his dealing with it either.

"It's all right." She took his hand, and his head cleared

instantly. "Of course you don't like to think about it in that way. At least you have never thought of me as a witch, or an evil vampire." She shook her head. "That is just so appalling. If I can't wean a man out of that, we're done."

"A night with you that a man throws away is an entire world lost forever. The tragedy of a fool."

She grinned at the dark sea beyond the Golden Gate. "How poetic. You're learning fast. You're going to have a life that is admirable I'm quite sure of it."

"You speak of me as if of a child."

She gave him an impish grin. "Well … I'm ten times your age, after all."

His arms went about her wonderfully slim waist, their lips met, and the heaving surface firmed beneath his feet. He seemed to have the balance of a cat. Lorelei's breath was the breeze of the sea, her skin was a silken membrane across the water allowing him to walk on it at will. Being the consort of such a creature had its advantages. Audie put out of his mind more fearful thoughts along with the fading echo of his father's voice from a pulpit in West Virginia.

After a while, he noticed one of the Italian crewmen watching them from the forecastle, amazed they hadn't fallen overboard as they stood without support and quite aroused at the same time. Audie grinned over her shoulder, feeling the bone-deep envy of the man as he stood rocking in the arms of his angel … his *Goddess*. "I'm glad we're getting out of town."

"Of course you are. You have a lot to digest, and you need to put some distance between you and the Barbary Coast at the moment. Didn't I say I was taking care of you?"

"Yes." He paused. She was staring to the east as they chugged toward the Golden Gate, at the low rise of Alcatraz Island half a mile distant. "What is it?"

"It's someone whose spirit is strong after many years of cruelty, Audie. The soul of his people burns bright within him from the crypts of that damnable rock. To my eyes, it's a bonfire."

"Alcatraz?"

"The military prison. He's a Modoc Indian whose daughter was raped by a rancher, so he killed him. His mistake was seeing no crime in his deed and speaking truthfully afterward. They would have hung him in Alturas but for the intercession of a wealthy white woman who nurtured a secret love for him for decades." White teeth were in her lip as she ran a hand through her hair. "It might have been kinder. Such a place is worse than death for that man. If I were truly an immortal being whose will was law, he would be in the arms of that woman right now. I do long for happy endings."

"It sometimes must be horrible, knowing so much about so many. How do you keep from going mad?"

"Learning to be selective. I never would have made it to adulthood if I'd been like I am now from the beginning. It takes growing into."

"But you said your kind has always—"

"Yes, but I only knew what my mother had done up until the time she bore me, and that was filtered by her own life and not the really raw stuff, so to speak. Mothers seek to shelter their children from the brutalities of existence, even one such as mine. It only began for me as an individual at my first feeding upon a man. That's when the changes take effect for us."

"When was that?"

"At fourteen, the son of a bitch ... listen, can't you *hear* him? He's chanting to his ancestors."

Audie strained, but the sound of the sea and the perfume of her skin were all that came to his senses.

"Oh, of course not. I could make you, but I was hoping

you might be doing it on your own by now. In spite of centuries of disappointment, I always hope someone shall and usually they do. If we're together long enough, I'm sure you will too. His will is so strong ... " she sighed. "Oh well, the doors of perception are opening for you slowly."

"What did you live on until you were fourteen?"

"Food, silly."

"Just like me?"

"Yes and no. We didn't have the niceties of today living in a cabin west of the Massachusetts Colony obviously. The forest was thick and dark in those days, with many ancient trees and much game. The squabbling of the British and French was a bother, but most of the time no one knew our whereabouts but the Indians and the occasional Colonial who wandered into my mother's realm. The tribes brought us gifts and worshiped my mother to no end." She brushed a strand of hair from her face and leaned on the railing. "She had a strange idea of what was needed for a child. It had been so long since she had tasted mortal food herself that plain superstition had entered her from people in Europe she'd lived upon, and she'd begun to believe it. The Indians knew better, and I still wonder why it didn't make an impression on her since she took so many of them. I suppose that Irish stubbornness had made its way into her system once and for all by then. You spend centuries anywhere, and it's bound to have an effect. The Indians made an impression on me while still in the womb, and I was getting it second-hand. But then she was six hundred years old before she produced an egg that might be awakened by a worthy man in Ireland, and her sensibilities pretty much stopped developing back in the dark old days of the burnings and such." Lorelei gave the night sky a wry smile. "She did an awful lot of killing before I was born. Her rage would have made the First One proud. I've struggled with that facet of myself since the day

I saw her hung and burned to ashes. Sometimes it gets the better of me."

He studied her profile as she stared at the four tall smoke-stacks of a battleship moored near the receding shoreline, and fished for words. "That's … awful, Lorelei."

She chuckled. "Hell of a way to greet puberty. I truly doubt raw meat was necessary to give me a taste for the blood that would come later. I won't put my own daughter through that I assure you. It wasn't through the same processes at all, and my tastes were as any child's. I loved sugar plums and roasted chestnuts, and—"

"Raw meat? Ugh!"

"Like I said, it was different. Of course, I can survive on the food you eat if I have to."

"Really? Since I've never seen you actually *eat,* that's—"

"If you had my choice you'd give it up too. It's the results that are so appalling."

"What do you mean?"

"I can go without those particular bodily functions if you please, and besides, I'd grow old like that. I can eat like anyone on the face of the globe, but the source of my youth is yours, Audie."

"Then … there is no choice at all."

She took his hand. "Your education is progressing nicely."

Audie opened his eyes to a loud knock, followed closely by "Your breakafast!" in a thick Italian accent.

He got up, wrapped himself in a robe hanging from a hook beside the bunk, and wandered toward the barred entry. The swaying of the floor was as familiar as the previous night. He no-ticed a sliver of sunlight at the base of the door, and turned to check on Lorelei. She was beneath the covers, but for one slim foot and well-turned ankle that hung over the edge of the narrow bed they'd shared in perfect comfort. He rubbed his eyes and unbolted the entry.

The man who had taken their bags from the cab was standing with a tray in his hands covered with a cotton towel. Even in the salt breeze, the aroma made Audie's stomach growl. "The Lady, she says twelve o'clock sharp you take a' your food."

"Why, yes, thank you."

"You gotta live your life by day on the ocean, but she say a noon so a noon it is."

"That's fine, I—"

The man peered into the cabin for a glimpse of Lorelei, and the sight of one foot caused big white teeth to flash under his moustache. "That's a'some a Lady! Hope you gotta good night's rest, Mister ... "

"Bond, Audie Bond."

"Mister Bond." He grinned. "She speak Italiano like a real Lady. We gotta two omelets with a fresh mushrooms and tomato sauce my own a Mama make. And this a cheese—"

"That will do quite nicely I'm sure."

"And a fresh bread, and a coffee! You like cafe Italiano? I make you some more, you want it."

"Thank you." Audie took the tray with two servings. God knew he could demolish both. "This certainly looks nice."

"You bet!" The man held out his hand. "Carlo DeLeon, Captain a *La Questa del Oro* and a master a his own a fate. I cook it myself. When you gotta good boat an' a calm a sea, you can take a time to take a care a people. And a she's a very generous. That's a one fine a rich lady you gotta there."

"Thanks again." Audie glanced around for his wallet.

"No, no tip! This is the service the Lady has a paid a for, but you can do me a favor when you come on a deck."

"What?"

"Smoke a good cigar with me."

"Certainly, I'd be honored."

"Good." Carlo shook his hand. "Have a nice a breakfast then." He bowed, turned away from the door, and Audie saluted Carlo's back as he sprang up a ladder nimbly as a cat toward the bridge.

He made it onto the deck at half-past one, having finished both omelets and accepted another pot of the wonderful coffee from a big-eyed adolescent boy who appeared within fifteen minutes of Carlo's initial visit and spent time peering at Lorelei's foot also.

Audie leaned on the railing studying the coastline where green and auburn redwood forests, brush-choked hillsides, and clear-cuts full of stumps rose over rocky headlands. The white steeple of a church rose over false-front stores and saloons from which a road led to a river mouth with wharves. Wide-beamed boats were taking on logs by way of big cranes built upon redwood trunks driven into the sand. Beyond that a valley opened inland, and he saw a rail bed slashing through red dirt where it stabbed into green hills before disappearing in mist. They passed a river's mouth and cliffs crowned with wheeling pelicans and gulls. An osprey darted between the masts of the ship with a fish in its talons.

"It's a one beautiful country."

Carlo was leaning against the railing with hands clasped as if in prayer. Two big cigars were between his fingers. He offered Audie one with the end neatly trimmed and struck a blue-headed match on his rough canvas pants in an instant, cupping the flame against the breath of the sea.

Audie accepted the smoke and drew several times to get the cigar burning. He coughed just a bit, rolling the smoke in his

mouth to taste the fragrant leaf as Carlo deftly lit his own with the same match. "It certainly is. Where are we going?"

"You don' know?"

Audie shook his head.

"Then that's a two of us. She say just head north until we hear something from her."

"Oh." How would Lorelei manage to give directions while sleeping? *Perhaps through me.* She could do it if she had the mind. He leaned on the railing enjoying the smoke more than he expected, bemused at the idea of acting as her oracle, the mouthpiece of a woman.

"How did you meet a the lady?"

"She came to my aid like an angel in a time of need, and we've been together since."

Carlo squinted through smoke. "You must be givin' her the good time in the ways a amore for that kinda treatment." He grinned. "She's some kinda lady, that one. Where is she from?"

"Ireland I suppose."

"Ireland? A *Catholic* country! What a beauty! Those eyes are a something. I never seen such a lady anywhere with such a beauty. Excusa me, but a how old are you?"

"Twenty-two."

"She's not much a more, maybe less. Where does she get a her money? Is her papa a typhoon?"

"You mean tycoon. No, her father wasn't and he's dead."

"'Excuse a my manners, but … where does it come a from?"

"It comes to her." A pod of killer whales appeared like glistening black islands from the depths with their tall dorsal fins flashing under the wheeling wings of seabirds. Lorelei said she could hear their voices, and that their minds were of an order of intelligence that was very different but vast in its own way. She told him last night how she heard their voices through the hull and that some whales saw God as a whale in the sky, meaning the sun. Audie had never considered such a thing until she'd mentioned it, as if it were just another facet of a much greater, far more *real* world. He had so much to learn, *so much.*

Carlo stood gripping the rail, moving the cigar between his teeth with his tongue. It reminded Audie of Izzy: the same gestures, the same look of bone-deep envy blended with intelligent curiosity. "It *comes* to her? Is she ... she's a one a the ... the ladies of the—"

"The demimonde?"

Carlo nodded.

"No, Carlo, no. She has no need to ask for anything or to charge a fee for her company. Whatever she needs simply comes to her, and her father was a Lord in Ireland."

Carlo's thick eyebrows rose. "*Nobility!*"

Audie nodded. That explanation was as good as any.

XVIII.

The Keeper

Lorelei appeared at sunset in the red woolen shirt and jeans she'd worn taking Audie from the Palace Hotel with a broad-brimmed Stetson hat shading her face from the last glow in the west. She pointed east, and guided the ship toward a place where only cliffs and a dark shield-wall of mountains were visible, to the muttered protestations of the captain and owner.

Carlo was not happy leaving the sea lanes he knew, muttering about rocks and his inability to know what lay close-in. He chewed his moustache and grumbled as he took the ship closer, but fell silent when he saw the small harbor hidden from the sea. A few buildings stood before a wall of towering trees, with the yellow light of kerosene lamps glowing from their windows. They steamed for a lone dock where a dozen people came out to watch them, all of whom appeared to be Indians.

The ship reversed her engines and came to a stop in the water with her bow brushing the pilings. Carlo waved at the little settlement. "Not on any of *my* charts."

"Thank you." The gold coins in her hand glimmerd red in the last light of day. "Here's something extra for your services."

Carlo's mouth fell open, and he cleared his throat. "Grazi, Signori a!"

"If you proceed north to Eureka, you will find the railroad is washed out along the Eel, and the mills are desperate for boats to hall lumber to San Francisco Bay."

Without asking how she could possibly know, he bowed

and kissed her hand again. "We're off for Eureka!"

They stood on the wharf as the little steamer pulled away and chugged out to sea, and horses' hooves echoed from the forest. Her lips brushed his cheek. "We're going riding. Stay close."

"How far?"

"An hour's ride. There's a half-moon rising, but it's pretty dark in places for someone with your sight." A loon cried in the night as she sprang upon the black mount offered her by a tall Indian in a plug hat. Audie couldn't see his expression, but could feel the man's awe as Lorelei sat astride the animal with her white skin glowing in the wan light. He mounted a grey roan beside her, and the man handed him the reins.

They climbed grassy hillsides silver under a half-moon. The pale ghost of an owl cruised across their path. Lorelei made a musical laugh, and the bird hooted in reply. At the top, a yellow light was visible in a valley beyond where a homestead lay. A cricket sang a few furtive notes on its hind legs and fell silent.

"Only these few call to me.'"

"What?"

"The City is such a storm of souls, and one must walk with care in its confusion and shouting. Here I touch peace."

"It is peaceful."

"Here the dead outnumber the living. Below us was a village called Pekwei with enduring homes that had their names passed down for generations, and a sacred path to the sea walked for a thousand years. It's my nature to see them moving about from the strength of their spirits, and to touch them should I linger. But you'll meet those living who carry that world within them."

"Who?"

"Two tribes: Yurok and Pomo, and someone you'll know when you see her though you've never met in the flesh."

"Who?"

Lorelei let loose a howl that was answered by wolves from the next ridge. He shivered. "They're greeting us, love. Don't be afraid. They're the last of their kind here, and their hearts are so much easier to know than our own at times. They know such belonging they never even question." She sighed. "I envy them."

"That's easy to know for you perhaps."

"For you also, should you truly wish."

They descended to a pasture aglow in moonlight between the dark towers of ancient trees. A house of hand-split redwood planks and an ancient barn stood at the far end, and a dog barked. Lorelei thanked her mount for the ride as she dismounted. A huge pale mongrel appeared out of the shadows and leaned into her, standing like a statue as she scratched him above his swishing tail while the horse nuzzled her ear.

Two figures came from the house with a storm lantern illuminating their feet in a wobbly pool of light that reflected off the wide cheekbones of what appeared to be two Indians. The man wore a beaded headband, flannel shirt, jeans, and boots. The woman wore a hide dress and moccasins.

"Welcome back, you who never sleeps," came the deep voice of the man.

"My sleep is your day and my dreams are your waking, Toan."

"Our dreams are your seas to harvest, Song who Flowers in the Night. The tree of our lives drops its seeds for the coral basket of your heart to gather."

Audie glanced from Lorelei to the man. It had to be some kind of ritual.

"I *saw* you! I saw you come to her!" The woman cried out, and the crickets fell silent."Then she is truly dead, for you came as you had promised."

"She is, Ah Tsin. Do you wish to touch her?"

"Please!" The girl fell to her knees, and the yellow lamplight illuminated her lovely Chinese features framed by long black braids falling upon an elk skin dress.

Lorelei held out a hand, and Ah Tsin clasped it to her breast with an anguished cry. Her back arched like a lightening bolt had run through her, and Audie felt a blast of air upon his face as he stood rooted to the ground. The girl shook as she reached out to one that Lorelei held within herself, and had brought from the place where she had died to keep like a flickering flame in her own heart.

A lump filled Audie's throat. It was apparent why she'd come, as was his utter ignorance of what truly moved and mattered in the universe. His blindness had been as complete as his own self-absorption. He dug teeth in his lip, and tasted blood.

Lorelei carried Ah Tsin to the house as Audie and the man she had called Toan took the horses to the barn in silence.

XIX.

The Valley of Peace

She had shown him her reason for being, and the world was filled with light. The last bastion of Audie's critical mind collapsed in a million shards, as he knew a new God, a *Goddess,* whose love was manifest through this woman he adored with all his soul. He would worship her and die gratefully … *willingly* on the altar of her loins.

"Whoa, slow *down!*" Lorelei pushed him up, off, and out of her with one hand and a wet pop.

He swiped damp hair from his eyes, and gasped. "What?"

"Don't *do* that, Audie."

"What?"

"Become absolutely suicidal over me. You might trick me into … into actually finishing you, my beautiful, naive and innocent friend."

"Would that be so bad?"

"Gods, yes, I am not going to consume you. I have my own morals, my own ethics, and you are not for killing." She sat up on the bed, stretched, and cracked her neck. "That which I did for Ah Tsin takes a lot out of me. It would be far too easy to take all you offer tonight for the nourishment of my own soul, and you are just … just *too* willing. I couldn't live with it if I killed you Audie, I truly could not."

He ran a hand down her back, exulting in the silken touch of her skin as he listened to the thunder of his heart. He knew what she was talking about. He could feel it in his bones. It had been right before him all the time. "Human sacrifice."

"Yes, such is how it was when we ruled the hearts of men."

"Of course, it's so clear now. How someone could lay himself down in joy and consummation. How one could die—"

"Yes love, that's the way it began, and there will again come a time when I need that glorious subjugation of a spirit. A loving spirit will indeed die for me in the future, but not you, Audie."

A howling wraith of jealousy seized him in its crooked jaws, and green eyes bored bloody tunnels through his very soul. *Another* would be her beloved for all time. Another, whose face he wouldn't ever know would dwell forever in the house of her soul. *Another—*

"*Stop it!*"

He winced. "All right."

She giggled. "Oh Audie, you're getting the best sex in this world, and it's not enough."

"Yet ... you hold that one thing back."

"Yes, I *do*. You are supposed to live many years and do things. Don't allow yourself to become mad over me, please. I really don't need that on my hands right now."

He listened to the hooting of an owl in the night, inhaled the delicious scent of her, and his cock began to thump with a mind of its own upon his stomach.

"Don't. Not until you can keep some semblance of your own self, anyway."

"But, I've lost myself before in you."

"Yes, but you still kept your soul, your sense of self, somewhere safe beyond our union. An important part of you, your deepest identity, Audie, stood back and watched, but tonight you are absolutely out of control."

"I want to fuck you."

"And I want to fuck you with all my heart and soul. More than you can possibly know. You are the well from which I drink and the precious water of my life, but I need you to behave. You know how to do it if you don't think about it."

"Izzy was right."

"About the First Born becoming mad."

"It's so *nice* you know my thoughts ... it's so completely *right*. How can I ever be satisfied with any other woman again?"

"By keeping part of me within you as I keep you. My gift is freely given in that regard. Just don't make me kill you, Audie, with that goddamn worshipful stuff." She shook her head. "I don't deserve that kind of adulation anyway."

"I can, can't I?"

"*Yes!*" Lorelei sprang off the bed and hit her head on a beam with a resounding thunk. "Ow! Damn it!"

He exploded in laughter.

She sat down rubbing her forehead and laughed with him. They laughed until his stomach ached, and entwined giggling in the dark.

"You did that to bring me back."

"You're getting awfully good at knowing me."

"Thank you."

"You're welcome. Now, do we have our little self back to where he belongs?"

"That's rather patronizing you know."

Lorelei's eyes were huge. She tossed hair from her face and kissed him. "You're sure?"

"Yes."

"Then let's get back to where we left off, shall we?" She threw a leg across him and pressed her lips to his. "But," her breath echoed within him, "stay a *little* bit afraid of me, all right?"

They laughed again.

He awoke to Ah Tsin's voice in the kitchen and the smell of coffee. Sunlight peeked through a blanket over the attic window, and the deep voice of the man Lorelei called Toan said something in an Indian tongue. Ah Tsin laughed, and Audie rubbed his eyes. He had to ask her how she'd been spirited out of slavery in San Francisco to end up here, wherever it was.

He sat up and yawned. This morning he had no headache. *Afternoon,* it had to be afternoon. He checked on his love that no shaft of sun was upon her, and bent to kiss her.

"Call him Frank," she mumbled, "Toan is his sacred name and you're not even supposed to know it. He's Frank Flounder." Lorelei rolled over and drifted away to wherever she went during the day, though of course she was keeping track of his thoughts this very moment. The idea was comforting, yet somehow intimidating. "Good!" She growled into the pillow.

"Frank," he repeated. She was right. Dying could spoil a very good thing. *Do people ever have a belly laugh in the afterlife?* He couldn't picture it, but he couldn't have pictured his Goddess banging her head on that beam either. Perhaps such girlish tricks were called the trickery of a Liliot in generations past, but to him it was simply charming. *I'm charmed!* He caught a dimpled smile on her face as he pulled on his pants and shirt, and climbed down the ladder with a grin on his own.

Ah Tsin was stir-frying vegetables and elk meat in a pan over the wood stove with eggs frying in a pan beside them, moving things constantly with a wooden spatula as she carried on a spirited conversation in an Indian tongue with Toan.

"Call him Frank, Audie."

"Okay, Frank."

Frank turned. "What?"

"Nothing. Hello."

"Mornin'. You didn't get much sleep."

"Is it really morning?"

"Yep. How is . . ?" Frank glanced toward the ceiling.

"She's wonderful."

Ah Tsin handed him a mug of coffee. "Cream and sugar?"

"Cream, please."

He walked outside barefoot to piss, and found a spot a ways from the house under a twisted red-barked madrone. Chanterelle mushrooms grew around the roots, and he picked one. A green banana slug left a glistening trail in the damp grass as it made its glacial journey across the yard, and songbirds trilled and fluttered in the trees. A hummingbird darted amongst cherry blossoms.

Audie made his way back to the porch and plopped down on a swing hung by chains from the roof. He put his feet on the peeling railing, and wiggled his toes. Lorelei was absolutely right about getting away from the City, though her mission here was far beyond any mere favor to him. What of the gift she had given Ah Tsin? He'd felt the spirit of Mai Ling as if she'd been there amongst them, as if even the darkest death truly had no victory. The hair on the nape of his neck quivered.

"More coffee?" Ah Tsin was beside him with another mug.

She took his empty one, handed him the fresh, and he thanked her. Ah Tsin sat on the swing beside him, a beautiful young woman with golden skin that appeared totally hairless but for her shiny raven tresses. Something stirred in him, and he fought a sudden tear. "It's lovely here," he got out.

"Yes, so peaceful, but some ranchers are very cruel to the

Indians. The men of a Pomo family were wiped out south of
Fort Bragg just two weeks ago because they killed a cow for meat
and all the girls were raped. They fled with young men into the
forest, but their mother is staying with us."

"Where?"

"She's helping strip bark from tan oaks with Bessie Flounder for the tannery in Briceland. They're coming back for a
special ceremony and a sweat."

"Oh. Where's Briceland?"

"Inland a bit." Ah Tsin smiled. "Bessie is a great healer.
She made Elsie's bullet wound close up, and cured me of the clap
also." She gazed at the sky. "I thank Lorelei with all my heart for
bringing me here."

"You were a slave."

"Yes, a slave. Ten thousand men used me, and I was to be
disposed of like an old dog at the end of my service. Mai Ling,
my sister in spirit, and I escaped the cribs once, but the boo
how doy caught us. Something rose up in my heart like a dragon
then, and I fought. They took me bleeding and senseless to the
cliffs where the Golden Gate is to throw me into the waves. When
I opened my eyes, it was the first time I had seen the sea since the
boat from China and could breathe the good clean air. I was
only exulting that I finally was free to not die in some dark room
at the hands of a drunken fool, and wishing beyond hope that I
could take them down into the sea with me when she came."

"Lorelei."

"*Yes!*" Ah Tsin glanced up at the attic. "Yes, bless her forever! She cast them into the sea like chaff upon the wind and took
me in her arms as she did last night. She brought me here, and
the singing of ancestors and goddesses beyond counting surrounded me to bring healing to my soul. Did you know she
can fly?"

"What?"

"She can! We flew upon the wind, and I awoke in a sweat lodge. My wounded heart opened like a flower, and nothing but love and goodness has been in the world for me from that day hence. I only wish my sister Mai Ling could have lived to see it, but Lorelei could only save me because I fought."

"She saw goodness, Ah Tsin, I know it."

"Only in death," she stared at the tops of trees older than Christ, and wiped her eyes, "but I was given the chance to see Mai Ling cross over. What a *gift* to be given by that great lady! But you should know about her gifts. You are her lover."

"I have the privilege."

"Then you know who she is, but listen to me; the woman you see before you that I am now is another life that only she could have given me. I didn't know there was such a place, such a *world* from where I was kept. I could not speak this language that now pours from my heart in a torrent through my mouth from a seed she sowed there. My youth was used like a filthy rag by the dregs of the earth, and my only solace was in the arms of Mai Ling, my sister and my lover. Now I am one man's woman, and his wife amongst a free people where I am treated with dignity." Her eyes fell. "If only I could bear his child."

"Why can't you?"

She put a hand to her stomach. "They did great damage. I was only eleven and not yet bleeding, and many infections followed. It is a miracle Bessie could heal me."

"Don't you give Lorelei credit for that also?"

"Yes, but she gave me to a healer that the spirit of this good people would dwell within me forever, so I give thanks to the medicine woman of the Pomo Nation who cared for me."

"Perhaps Lorelei can help with your quest for a child."

"I would be so vain to ask such a thing! After she saved me

from death and gave me this life, how could—"

"You already have, Ah Tsin. She watches us from her sleep." He sipped his coffee. "I know she has never become fertile herself, but if anybody knows women's plumbing it's got to be Lorelei."

Ah Tsin laughed like a girl of nineteen.

He gazed at her with hands in her lap and a face turned toward nature. He couldn't imagine thousands of brutal men using her. He just couldn't. Audie shook his head. He was certainly getting a crash course on the tribulations of females. Where could Leah be right now? *Suzanne,* whose journey into prostitution was done as a lark and not in servitude. Most likely she was with some rich fellow right this minute, sipping champagne and laughing in a pampered parlor.

"Say, you didn't pee on the chanterelles did you?"

"No, I recognized them."

"Good, I pick them for my cooking. The food is ready so please join us. She says for you to eat a lot."

Frank told him the story of the valley over a breakfast that Audie had three helpings of with generous portions of fry bread and fresh butter on the side. As Lorelei said, a village called Pekwei had been on the site of the ranch for long centuries with a sacred trail to the sea down the valley of the Matole River. The men had been hunters, sailors, fishermen and whalers, and the oaks about yielded acorns the women leached and ground for meal. The forest was abundant in deer, elk, bear, and small game. The creeks teemed with salmon in their season, and steelhead and trout year-round. The coast gave them abalone, clams, shellfish, cod, halibut, sole, albacore, and all manner of things. Blue camas lilies grew in the valley bottoms whose bulbs supplied food, and there were other good roots, berries, and many other things besides.

"And wild honey," Frank went on, ladling some onto fry bread on Audie's plate, who promptly ate it and found it ambrosia. "We grow a garden, fruit trees, and raise chickens and some stock too. Only problem is we get shit on by white men, a few ranchers and present company excepted. But if you're with that Woman we got to treat you as a Sacred Being, so better get used to actin' like one."

"Well, ah … . thanks."

Frank's broad cheeks rose, and he cracked his knuckles in front of him. "Guess she'll be takin' you back to the City soon."

"Why?"

"She gets bored here."

"What?"

"She's wonderful and all that, but she's a trickster. She came here many years ago in stories handed down by our elders and caused big trouble. Young men went into the forest never to return. Older men left their wives, and fathers forgot their children." Frank shrugged. "She's not easy on the family way. You must have noticed that by now."

"Frank," Ah Tsin chided, "you were speaking to her in a sacred way last night, and I liked it much better."

"There is no conflict in my heart about my words."

She turned to Audie. "He has his own thoughts about her because of his ideas of women. Maybe if he'd—"

"She never *asked.*"

"She's a *Sacred Being,* Frank."

"I know that. Shit. But nobody said a sacred being couldn't do some dirt. They just can do it better."

Ah Tsin giggled. "She has to be special never to catch the clap."

"Yeah. I wonder how that works?" Frank glanced at Audie. "Ever ask her?"

"I never even thought about it."

"Must be love." Frank leaned back in his chair and guffawed. Ah Tsin put her hand over her mouth.

Audie chuckled nervously. He'd have to ask about that.

When Bessie and Elsie returned, Ah Tsin had Elsie show him where she'd been shot. The wound was two pink circles on her right side, one in front near her navel and one in her back. The sensation of a large caliber bullet passing through the elderly woman came to Audie with all the clarity of Lorelei, and he fought a sudden rush of nausea.

Bessie was a sturdy woman of some sixty-six years who wore her long grey hair tied in a thick braid wound with red ribbon. "So," she put a calloused hand to his face and turned his head both ways, "she picked you. Hum." She glanced at the frame of the sweat lodge. "Let's get ready for a sweat. We have a guest."

"The women are going in together," Frank explained. "They want to cure my wife's not having babies."

"How?"

"Women's things. Don't even want to know long as they do it. They're waitin' for the One Who Never Sleeps."

"Well, she's sleeping now."

"Don't bet on it. She'll appear when the lodge is ready. It's plenty dark in there. I'm gonna get a good fire goin', and they'll sprinkle water and a little dry sage on the hot rocks we pass in. That's Ind'n incense. My wife says the Chinee got nicer stuff, but it ain't sacred in our book. Ever been in a Joss house?"

"No,"

"I'd like to see Chinatown, but I'd likely kill one of them bow-wow hatchet sonsabitches soon as look at his goddamn slavin' ass."

"I'd probably help you."

"Be nice to try their food though. Ah Tsin can sure cook some fine Chinee stuff, and she's got a gift for anything that grows. Don't know when she found the time to learn."

"Perhaps in China, when she was a little girl."

"Yep."

When the sweat was ready, Lorelei appeared from the house in her Stetson hat and a Pendleton blanket. Her white skin flashed between the folds as she made the shade of the bay tree above the sweat lodge in two bounds. "Audie," She clasped his hand as the women stooped to enter the lodge, "I want you to go with Frank and take the logging railroad to the depot in Sherwood. There's a California Northwestern train heading to Sausalito every afternoon. You're to take it and return to San Francisco by ferry. Don't worry, I'll meet you. In fact I'll already be there."

"How?"

"In time."

"Wait," He grasped her hand as she tossed the blanket into the branches and stooped to enter the lodge. Dappled sunlight illuminated Lorelei's ivory skin, and she winced. Audie could feel her tolerating the pain as she lingered, and the words left him. She kissed him, disappeared within, and the perfume of her flesh lingered on the air mixed with the spice of the bay tree. He pulled the canvas cover over the door and turned to Frank, who was squatting beside the fire.

Frank stared at the door of the sweat lodge as the fire in the pit crackled and hissed. A cicada buzzed in the treetops, and he fumbled with a stick he'd been adjusting the fire with. "How are they supposed to bring in the rocks?"

"Don't worry Frank, we'll take care of it," Lorelei's voice came from the canvas-covered lodge.

Frank saddled the horses, and they left the little valley and headed inland through canyons of trees. Audie blinked in the daylight, unused to being up early as of late. The crimson bark of the behemoth was as red as Suzanne's hair. Curls of mist rose from damp duff and great green sword ferns at the redwoods' bases, wreathing the giant trunks in spirals as it burned off.

They came to where the hills were stripped, and shining piles of red bark lay amongst split trunks of trees in the slash and litter of logging. Audie could hear the whistle of a donkey engine in the forest as they approached a fence line where the grass was chewed down by cattle. They followed it toward the noise of the engine, and came upon where wilderness had given way to the determined efforts of man. Two men stood ten feet up on a springboard nailed into a cut in the base of a huge redwood, sawing methodically with a long springy blade, a *misery whip.* It seemed impossible that they could fall the giant tree, but as Audie watched, a sound like the bones of the earth being twisted by giant hands came to him, then a sigh as the air caressed a monster trunk hurtling through branches, followed by a crash that rippled through the ground beneath the horses' feet. Their mounts shivered, and danced sideways.

Audie glanced at Frank, whose face was a mask. "What are you thinking?"

"This grove has been sacred to my people since the world was made, in our thinking. Lotsa eagles up top, and I used to gather feathers they dropped when I was a kid. Young men and women went up for a vision on that rock where you can see the ocean. I did at fourteen, and there's one great big tree at the top of the canyon ... " his voice trailed off, and he ran a hand over his face. "There was, anyway. Come on, we gotta wait until the train's got a full load and ask the driver for a ride to the Eel."

The train sat on a spur ready to roll. Most of its flat cars had one great section of log upon them, though one had three that were only six or so feet in diameter. The leviathan directly behind the coal car was at least fourteen feet thick.

Frank waved to the engineer who waved back, and they exchanged words over the noise of the fireman stoking coal in the boiler as the engine got up steam for the climb out of the canyon. Frank was back in a minute. "Says you can ride on the coal car or on a log, but it costs five bucks."

Audie began to protest, but stopped. The exorbitant fee would get him where he had to go, and it was Lorelei's money. Certainly it was better spent than the ten dollars he'd tossed the two waiter girls in that melodeon on Pacific, to be rewarded by insults and laughter. He stepped onto the engine and handed the engineer his money.

"Hang on," the man yelled, "ain't no stoppin' her!"

Audie turned to see Frank leading the horses away. Frank stopped, waved, and disappeared in the ravaged forest as the engine began to roll. Audie climbed onto the coal car as a hot blast of smoke and cinders from the stack of the squat engine rolled across his shoulders. He would be a sooty mess when he reached the stage line. As the train lurched forward, he stepped off the coal car onto the great redwood log, and almost fell off when the bark moved under his feet. Audie dropped into a crevice of the huge trunk, clinging for dear life as the engineer grinned.

XX.

The Marathon

Lorelei staggered onto the beach with her hands on her knees. The swim had been too much after a run that had carried her one hundred twenty miles through dark forests, across cultivated land, and through towns where dogs barked while people commented on the sudden gust rattling windows. She hacked up seawater, and watched a rope of spittle unravel toward her feet. She took a ragged breath and pulled hair from her face, staring at the serpentine trail it left in wet sand as she gathered her last reserves for the dash to the house.

Swimming had been foolish. She should have taken a ferry, but she'd tossed her clothes somewhere along the way to feel the wind on her flesh while racing the wolves. She gulped air, sprang up the stone seawall to Jefferson, and dashed up Jones to Chestnut faster than a mortal eye could focus. She leapt to the second story of her house, found the window locked, and tore it open to fall like a dead thing upon the bed.

To herself, she stank, though any man would want her, probably worse for the strength of her scent. She let out an exhausted giggle at the thought, and groaned. She must feed soon and well. She clambered to her feet, and sand rattled on the hardwood floor as she tottered to the shower.

Wu came to the top of the stairs with a big Colt pistol in his wrinkled hand to ascertain it was only the return of the Accursed Woman and not an intruder.

"Wu!"

"Yes, Missy!"

"Fix me coffee, and beat six raw eggs with milk and honey in a mug. Throw in some cinnamon or something."

"You want *food?*

She let out an exhausted giggle, and gripped the tile wainscoting of the shower with trembling fingers. It crumbled like paper Mache in her hands. "Yes Wu, hurry up."

"Coming right now, Missy!"

After she forced down the unfamiliar mixture, she donned the clothes of the lesser classes, a simple dress of calico cotton and scuffed shoes. She threw a woolen shawl over her head, grabbed some money, and gave instructions to clean the bedroom and to call someone in the morning to fix the window and tiles post haste.

She'd take a cab. Her run had been quite enough for one night. It was three a.m., and the cribs were busy. Lorelei inhaled the moist breeze, and the scent of men welled up like desert blossoms after a rain. She was *starving.* She stepped out on the street and hailed a taxi, a black Ford Model N whose driver she guided to her door by whispering with her true voice. She jumped on the worn leather seat, and slumped against the door as the driver stared. "Six-twenty Jackson please."

The man blinked, and red mutton chop sideburns quivered before he spoke. He rested a thick arm on the front seat, staring at her from under heavy crimson eyebrows furrowed in distress. "What's a wonderful wee girl like ye goin' to the Municipal Crib, lass? Good Lord, ye won't last a week!"

"Don't worry for me, Alva MacNaughton. Take me to Jackson and Dupont, now."

The blood drained from Alva's face at the sound of his own name. "Dear God," he muttered, "forgive me transgressions." He put the car in gear.

She lay on the seat seeing the route through Alva's eyes and listening to the gears grinding beneath her. The roar of souls around her was deafening, and her ability to filter it was fading fast. Her head spun. She was sick to her stomach from the food, and she prayed they'd arrive swiftly.

The awful thought of taking Alva seized her as they sat at Union and Columbus waiting to make the turn. When the wheels began rolling, she let out a shuddering breath. Alva was a good man with a family. *How it would ravage them!* A wave of self-loathing rippled through her like an icy blade. She gripped the leather seat, and it shredded between her fingers.

But a block from her destination, she let out a groan. As they passed a filthy tenement at 730 Jackson, her weakened condition allowed the doings on the second floor to flood her being. Ah King's Parlor was filled with opium smokers, and she felt their inward-turning minds like creatures scuttling in a dark cave, pulling her down into thick black water where there was no clean air, no youthful blood to save her. Their souls spoke of an early, ugly death, and she had few defenses left in her own.

The sinkhole down the street was worse. Blind Annie's Cellar brought the noise of pipes bubbling in her brain, with painful hiccups as flames were sucked from brass lamps into bowls. She felt smoke curl up a stem into the riddled lungs of a woman who had once been beautiful, and for a moment Lorelei was trapped in that decaying body. She fought nausea, and fought to hold down the lump in her stomach. When they reached 620 she sobbed, and handed Alva the gold coin in her hand. "Keep it."

Alva weighed it in his palm and shook his head. "That's way too much, Lassie."

"For the seat."

Alva glanced at his ravaged back seat, and his eyebrows rose. "It's madness or drugs then. I don't know how ye know me name, but I cannot *stand* to see ya go in there lass! I honestly *cannot!"*

"Peace to you Alva." Lorelei was out before he could spirit her away to perceived salvation. She staggered on the steep sidewalk, staring at the tobacco-stained steps as the regular complement of policemen sat up from their lethargy on the stoop and stared back. There were only two, although she'd killed two of the mayor's cohorts at the Municipal Crib already.

The cops guarding the door from ruffians and over-zealous salvation types, as well as perhaps another murderer, glanced at each other and grinned. The older one twisted the end of his waxed mustache. "Didn't know anything *that* nice was workin' tonight, Danny."

"Any night, Pops. Billy Finnegan been improvin' the inventory since I had a night off, that's for sure."

Lorelei ignored them and stepped into Cooper Alley alongside the building. Before one of the cops could come around to see what she was doing, she sprang up the wall and landed on the roof to avoid the men waiting admittance to the girls below. She tore the lock off the door to the stairwell, and was in a hall with the smell of sweating bodies and over-used women all around her. She shook to her bones as she slipped into a room, and not being in any way selective guided the next man who reached the floor with the music of her voice. "Come in!"

It was the big doorman from downstairs, twirling the black truncheon with which this night he'd brained a West African sailor for the crime of his color. He'd gone on a bender to celebrate his deed, and had returned to his place of employment for some sport. He was still feeling mean, and he could be sure any mistakes with the inventory here would be smoothed-over. Any girl at the Municipal Crib was part of his benefit plan as he'd done his part for the boys at the Poodle Dog a dozen times with lugs who'd never left this building alive, and the occasional uppity girl who'd 'retired.' The memory of the man's skull spread across the floor of a dive on Battery Street filled his mind. He kept repeating the bloody vision over and over, as he swallowed from a bottle of Chilean Pisco brandy. Now it was time for some fun.

Lorelei felt that river beneath her feet welling up as the one before her stood unbeknowing under a red sun that had shown upon her kind since the world began. *Belay the guilt, Lassie,* her tired mind added in the voice of Alva. She let out an exhausted giggle, and was out of her clothes in an instant. "Hello."

His mouth fell open at the sight of her under the dim yellow bulb. When the shock had subsided, his eyes lit up in his ruddy features. "Damn, never seen a whore like you. When did you get here?" His tobacco-stained teeth flashed. "Gonna see some-thin' now," he guffawed, "come 'ere, ya pretty fuckin' white-arse bitch." He dropped his pants and pointed a dirty hand to his nodding penis with a grin.

Lorelei's fingers wrapped in his beard, and she threw him down and mounted him in a red rush. The big man gasped as the very stuff of life flowed out of him in a gush that caused his heart to tremble and miss its beat. He made one futile attempt to push away, growing transparent as every organ, layer of muscle, and living tissue surrendered the spark of life itself. He grew smaller as she took every drop of blood in his body, until his soul collapsed with a scream only Lorelei could hear.

She rolled the husk off her and stared at the yellow bulb on the ceiling as her head swam. The cheap brandy, opium and cocaine in his blood weren't welcome. She rose to her feet with a hand on the wall, regained her equilibrium, scooped up her clothes, and pulled the door shut behind her. Upon discovery the body would be disposed of by a management concerned with staying in business and protected by a municipal government of the same inclination. The gang at the Poodle Dog might miss some sleep though.

Lorelei stepped into the hall in front of a young man about to go into a room with a girl. She spun him on his heels, and he floated to her like a kite on the breeze. She tossed the girl his wallet."Here." The girl snatched it, and ran down the hall. He hadn't noticed, having eyes for Lorelei only as she pushed him into a room. This one was no arrogant killer, only a youngster looking for excitement. She'd let him live, maybe even leave a memory. She'd fed enough to try.

She left the Municipal Crib over the red roofs of Chinatown. She stopped at Stockton Street to drop in on the Fabulous Hotel Nymphia, a rickety three-story building built in the shape of a 'U' with a hundred fifty girls on each floor. She took four men there after eight at the Municipal Crib and headed home before dawn. Hot rushes shot through her body, and her head ached as she absorbed the blood of a dozen men, but she was as strong as ever.

She dashed through the streets though the fog was in and she could have walked and whistled a tune for all it mattered. The thought made her laugh as she stood on the cobblestones in front of her house with the cool mist delicious on her hot skin.

A milkman looked up from his rounds and saw a beautiful nude woman with hair to her knees and pale flesh glowing like a Chinese lantern. He muttered a prayer to the Virgin as the bottles slipped from his hands with a crash, and cream splashed over his shoes in a windfall for stray cats. The man ran to his wagon, shouted at his tired horse, and galloped down the hill toward Hyde Street with bottles rattling in the back of the whitewashed dray.

She watched him go as an angry soul roiled and churned within her. It was the thug of a doorman, kicking and cursing as he faded down a hole he couldn't vanquish with all eternity on his side. She would hurry him on his journey so she could get some much needed sleep. Otherwise, she'd be dealing with some wicked indigestion in the form of nightmares.

The healing of Ah Tsin had demanded far more than she'd imagined, but she was replenished after a terribly long day without sleep while the sun burned like a torch outside the sweat lodge and a night where she'd run a hundred twenty miles, swam San Francisco Bay, fed on twelve and taken one life, but her true achievement was the opening of two tiny paths from Ah Tsin's ovaries to her uterus.

One day, she too would know what it was like to carry a child. Meanwhile, the blood of a peasant girl from Kwangtung and a son of the Yurok Nation would be one. Such was Lorelei's gift to the future, and she could feel the line that this night would be conceived. Her heart tried to touch what was there and stumbled as she strained to hear that fragile song flowing in the river of thought and flesh that was the passing parade around her ... those yet unborn.

She stared into the sky, and gave up trying. She had to sleep and could only let the future happen. Still ... that was really something.

XXI.

The Demimonde

Audie shifted on the hard bench in the bow of the ferry and scanned the slips ahead as the boat reversed her engines and stopped to wait for an opening at the Lombard Pier. It was six twenty-two p.m., only two minutes behind the printed schedule.

Is she waiting?

The City came alight as a setting sun in the west gave her hills a ruddy glow. He searched for the familiar tower of the Ferry Building, but it was hidden by the rise of Telegraph Hill. The ride on the train had given him much time to think as he passed from redwood-shrouded hills through lush valleys, chaparral slopes, fields and vineyards. He'd opened his journal to make an attempt at describing her, but had descended into poetry that when re-read seemed mere babbling. He'd keep it. Perhaps it would make sense someday.

The journey seemed endless. How would she get back? When the log train had arrived in Sherwood, he was filthy, and paid a quarter to use a tub at a hotel. He bought a beer at a small bar downstairs and listened to the locals and other travelers waiting for the California Northwestern train. A rancher was boasting about killing Indians who'd killed his stock. Audie fought the urge to confront him, but he knew it would turn into a real fight. He finished his beer and took a walk with Bessie's wounds foremost in his mind. When the train stopped in Santa Rosa, he'd seen an Indian girl and thought for a moment it was Ah Tsin. She caught his eye and shot him a dark-eyed glare that softened as he continued to stare. When she turned away, her hair flashed rainbows in the sun, and he lost all bearing.

Where is she? He had so much to learn. It was far too soon for her to abandon him.

He got off at East Street, brushing off the drunks and panhandlers like bothersome insects. Was this his fate? Was he to become like them, the dregs and riff-raff of this wretched waterfront where a life was only worth the next bottle, a loveless tryst with a whore, or the rattle of an opium pipe? He groaned as a black funk threatened to engulf him. Audie was seriously thinking of doing some drinking as he hailed a cab on a strangely quiet afternoon for a ride to Chestnut Street. He spotted a congregation entering a church, and realized it was Easter. *Easter!*

The cab passed him by as if he didn't exist.

"Damn you!" He self-consciously tried to smile at two little girls in Easter dresses swinging straw baskets, and began the walk to Russian Hill.

"That's not our ride."

His heart stopped in mid-beat. The noise of the city abated as a silence deep as the redwood forest engulfed him. Then she was holding him with her cheek against his own. He wanted to fall into her grasp like Ah Tsin, to be carried away into her bed like a helpless slave. He was being an utter child about it, yet he couldn't help himself.

"You are indeed. Well, we both are fine as to our physical conditions. Now as to our emotional ones, I suppose you wish to bed me immediately."

"Need you ask?"

"No, but I enjoy it. By the way, Ah Tsin will have Toan's children. Their line shall be strong."

"That's ... good." He only wanted to be in her bed. The world no longer had any center at all, except for glorious Lorelei.

"Let's take a ride." She led him to a Siemen's motorcar with a red body and gold fenders, and the driver saluted as he pulled goggles down from his khaki cap and tugged at leather gauntlets, staring through the thick glass lenses at the curve of Lorelei's bottom as she entered the vehicle.

A grin stretched Audie's cheeks until they hurt. "Dear God," he dropped into the leather seat, "you have utterly spoiled me. Nothing and no one else will ever be enough again, Lorelei."

"Nonsense, your life's just beginning, and I still find plenty in the world that's fascinating and fun from the perspective of several centuries."

"One could if they were you." His hand slid under her skirt, to be grasped in a most welcome way by all that made life worth living. "That's the thing, just being near you. How did you get here so quickly?"

"I didn't fly."

"Ah Tsin said—"

"She's a lovely girl, but she's wrong about that."

"Honestly?"

"Honestly, I ran."

He laughed as he fondled her. "Like Mercury on an errand of the gods! Where are we going?"

She squeezed his fingers and spoke to the driver. "Take East to Market along the Bay."

The driver let out the clutch, and they headed toward the foot of Market Street. Gulls, eagles and ospreys perched on a thousand masts as they made the great curve of East along the stone sea wall and eventually turned right on Market at the Ferry Building. Up ahead the golden dome of the Spreckles tower was alight, and huge ads for beer shouted from either side of the grand avenue with its double trolley tracks in the center. Horse carriages and motorcars jostled for space on a day when all would be observant and quiet in West Virginia.

They passed Lotta's Fountain at Kearney, and passed the Examiner, Chronicle, and Mills buildings shoulder-to-shoulder on the right. The Palace Hotel stood on the left with its tiers of bay windows looking like a richly decorated cake. Audie craned his neck to examine the golden scalloped dome of the Call Building, glowing in competition with the Spreckles across the street.

A procession of Episcopal Priests and pedestrians in Easter finery gazed at the ornate vehicle as they passed, and Audie watched men marvel at the well-dressed beauty beside him. He slouched in his seat, wishing he wore a good suit of clothes today rather than the rough shirt, pants and suspenders.

"Don't be so self-conscious."

"Where are we going?"

"Jessie Hayman's."

"Why?"

"I'm going to arrange some company for you."

"Such as who?"

"Such as Leah, who is residing there."

"Jesus Lorelei, I—"

She yawned. "And I have business with the owner. You should be looking forward to this. Just watch how they treat you."

"Like a damn gigolo."

"Your appetites could get you in trouble without an outlet. I shan't have you thinking me some troublemaking Liliot who's out for her own nefarious purposes or any of that drivel and I'm making sure *you* behave as well. You were on the verge of killing people before we left if you'll remember, not that they didn't deserve it, and just look how one little night without me wore upon you. I have got to manage your growth, Audie."

"Without *you,* Lorelei. Not some selection of the demimondaine no matter how lovely they might be. I didn't *ever* desire such company and I still don't."

"I'm weaning you a bit from your habituation."

"If my habituation is you, I don't want to be weaned."

"Of course not." She kissed his cheek. "Suzanne shall be overjoyed to see you. She needs to rediscover trust in a man before she gets much older, and couldn't be with a better one in my opinion. And they do your laundry, serve an excellent breakfast, and give you the best shoeshine in San Francisco. Excellent champagne too. I might try some myself."

"You talk about us both as if we were mere experiments of yours, to simply be maintained when you're not around."

"Almost, Audie, but I prefer to think of you as experiments of life itself."

He inhaled the fumes of a wheezing delivery truck, frowned at a plaster gargoyle leering from a bank streaked with pigeon droppings, and sighed. "I'm rather acting the child, aren't I?"

"You've been struggling with your writing, and you're getting a tad bitchy. You haven't discovered how to deal with me as an author yet."

"I wrote something today."

"Yes. I believe it was about sex."

"It was about you. It was about this great mystery that I once called God that seems to grow more mysterious each moment. It was—"

"As I said."

They came to the marble façade of the Baldwin Hotel, turned up Ellis past Powell, and the dark Victorian with gilded columns and bay windows came into view. The red curtain on the third floor glowed, proclaiming that this was a worthy destination for gentlemen with both the inclination and the money. Audie had butterflies in his stomach.

She squeezed his hand. "Calm down young prince. I promise I'll take you home after this, by midnight at the latest."

When the motorcar stopped, he stepped onto the sidewalk and gazed up the green travertine steps at the oaken doors. The left one opened, and the Negro maid Lorelei greeted as Belle stood in the same uniform he'd seen her in when he and Izzy had passed on their way to Moshe the Tailor's a thousand years ago.

He took Lorelei's hand with a grin. It was all a great and mysterious game in which he was a winner. Thoughts of the miserable cribs of Chinatown and the cruelties of the Coast flashed through his mind, but were banished by the bright parlor in an instant.

They were in a room with plush gilt-framed red velvet chairs and couches with arms covered by silk dusters without a speck of lint. The seats were placed about a low glass-topped table below paintings of landscapes, and one of a beautiful red-haired woman reclining nude on a couch with a large black cat. Mirrors were on each wall, making the room seem larger and brighter.

Above the fireplace hung a framed tapestry in old English calligraphy, saying, **NO PROFANITY OR CRUDE LANGUAGE IN THIS ESTABLISHMENT** and under that **GOD BLESS THIS HOUSE.** The parlor was lit by a crystal chandelier that sent tiny rainbows across the room to be broken up by the mirrors, filling the place with pleasant light. A woman's skin would look good in that light, almost as good as Lorelei's.

"Please be seated," Belle said, and disappeared down a

gold-carpeted hall.

Lorelei was gone, and Audie sat on a love seat before the bay windows. A golden clock on the mantle chimed eight as tiny figures moved within its crystal case on horses chasing one another around a central cylinder of gold. He got up to examine it.

A hand touched his shoulder accompanied by a rustle of satin skirts and the scent of perfume, and he turned to gaze into the green eyes of the woman he'd seen at Daroux's. He was startled by her height and proximity, and the fact she'd approached without his knowing. Lorelei he could accept as her ways were beyond mere mortals, but this woman had somehow done the same while wearing those noisy skirts.

"Again we meet," Jessie said.

He reached for her hand in its white evening glove and kissed it. She wore an emerald choker that set off her no less green eyes and fine skin, skin nearly as flawless as Lorelei's though certainly prone to the buffeting of mortal wear. Even her breasts were similarly perfect. She sized him up much the same way he imagined her customers did for her inventory, and put fingers to her chin. "Well, she must know something." Jessie muttered.

"Um, I suppose, I—"

"Perhaps it's the lack of pretension I suppose, that, and of course something in the performance."

"I'm impressed by your obvious charms, ma'am. I haven't met anybody who could hold a candle to Lorelei until you, and to be honest, the second time is better than the first."

"That is a complement I cherish. For unlike your lover I have to work at it, dutifully and constantly." She smiled at his confusion. "Lorelei trusts me as she does you. Hasn't she told you?"

"She's ... she's hinted, I suppose."

"Well, we are allies in truth if not knowledge yet. Welcome to my establishment. The place will be busy in an hour, so you should be introduced to the girls. I understand you know Leah already, who'll be your guide."

"Suzanne."

"Yes. She gives you a great review by the way."

"Um, thank you."

"Nothing to be shy about in my company I assure you. Leah was one of those girls on her own without a mack. I thought she'd do well here, and she's rewarded my trust with exemplary behavior. Did you know that she speaks four languages?"

"I certainly didn't. Um … what's a mack?"

"A Maquereaux. In our business, we use the French version of the word instead of pimp, which is so vulgar. I only hire girls who can't abide such characters no matter what one calls them, girls with spirit and individuality. I let them keep all their tips too and I will never make them submit to things they'd not do, but find who has what particular talent and apply it where she is most useful. I haven't forgotten my own coming-up in the world they're in, and I endeavor to treat them as my own family. I do quite nicely off my share of the proceeds."

"Oh."

She took his hand and led him down the hall past a high-ceilinged kitchen with an old Chinese man slicing vegetables. They climbed stairs covered in more gold carpet and mirrors in gilded frames, passing paintings of girls upon divans and beds hung above the oaken wainscoting. "These are some of my best girls, many of whom have gone on to good marriages. If they've remained in the vicinity, I don't hang their picture out of respect for their present lives. All these either went to distant locations or have passed the pale."

"Dead?"

"Not all thrive, but I do still care for them. Some who

didn't perhaps the most."

"You and Lorelei are a lot alike."

"Thank you."

They started back toward the front of the house, and he peered in a bedroom where a long-limbed young lady was brushing waist-length light brown hair before a mirror lit all around with tiny bulbs while humming to herself. She gave him a radiant smile as they passed. The room was something a rich girl would decorate for her own comfort, done in pink with photographs and portraits in golden frames, though these pictures all seemed to feature a girl in the nude. He wondered if they were of her, and he wondered where Lorelei had gone to.

"She's left you in our company for a while."

He blinked.

Jessie placed him on a loveseat before another bay window with the gentle pressure of a bejeweled hand. "No introductions are required, so I shall leave you with Leah. My establishment is at your service. Anything or anyone you want, feel free to let someone know. There are pull cords in every room that summon servants. Lorelei shall return at midnight as promised."

Audie gazed at Jessie's breasts as she bent down and her lips touched his own. She put a hand on his cheek, and hesitated. Her teeth shown against her lower lip for an instant before she rose in a swirl of scents and was gone. He sat gazing at the door where she disappeared for a moment, yawned, and stretched his legs. A bath wouldn't be a bad idea.

Suzanne peeked from a doorway. She waved, gave him a dimpled smile, and bounced into the room in a lavender satin negligee. "Hi Audie!" She plopped into the loveseat and hugged him. "How have you been?"

"Occupied, but it seems you've done well for yourself

while I was away."

"Jessie is *so* nice. I have the nicest room and all these clothes, and she spent *six thousand dollars* for my wardrobe! And I can refuse to be with a fellow if I want to, and it's safe, too. I only hope I don't get fat eating in all those French restaurants. Did you know she gets twenty percent when men take me there too? And I get five, just for having dinner. Jeez! Of course they've got beds upstairs."

"I'm not surprised."

She stared out the window. "But what a smart lady. She started for Nina Hayman who used to run this place, who got it from Dolly Adams after she died way too young back before the pilgrims landed or something. People think Jessie's real name's Jessie Mellon, but it's really Annie Mae Wyant. I read it off some things in her desk, so don't say anything, all right? She's built this place to the tops, really the *tops*, Audie. We get Senators, Princes, Sultans ... everything. Did you know she turned down the Grand Duke of Russia in marriage? Can you *believe* that, she turned down a *Grand Duke?* Said she'd be bored. He sends her jewels on her birthday and tells the crowned heads of Europe how she's the best thing America has to offer, and the most beautiful woman in the world and such. You should see the tiara the Grand Duke gave her, all diamonds and emeralds. She loves emeralds although everyone calls her Diamond Jessie. And she's fun, and the other girls here are from all over too, and we get to go on trips sometimes to these mansions in the country all dressed up like we're on a Sunday outing." She giggled. "Happy Easter, by the way."

"The same to you, Suzanne."

"I was with Violet at the Stanford estate yesterday, but it's a secret of course. Violet's the daughter of a railroad tycoon in Philadelphia. She escaped from a convent in Los Angeles and made her way here from Sacramento when she was fourteen. The girl has spunk let me tell you, and she's *so* smart! You should meet her. She's my very best friend. Abe Ruef's in love with her, and Jessie never has a lick o' trouble with the coppers. She's the tall girl you passed in the hall. You can have her if you want. The three of us would be fun, huh? I've bragged you up enough already. Jessie says the whole place is at your disposal, which is pretty rare for a fellow no matter how much he's got. She's really taken with Lorelei I guess. She's—"

"And you're the daughter of a Minister."

She stopped in mid sentence. "Actually a Priest, Audie, a randy Catholic Father who wasn't supposed to be diddlin' a little red-haired Mick girl at all. He denies his paternity to the world rather than leave the Cloth, but he's established a trust for me that's handled by my uncle in Burlingame."

"Then what in Heaven's name are you doing here?"

She returned his stare. "And what are *you*, Mr. Minister's son?"

He shrugged. "Swept up by a goddess I suppose."

She shrugged right back, and gave him a theatrical sigh. "I earnestly seek to learn about the world, and the lusts that engendered me." Suzanne gazed at a limousine in the street unloading two gentlemen in top hats and tuxedos. "It hasn't all been a bowl of cherries. When I got to Jessie's, I figured I didn't have to worry anymore about being murdered by some black-hearted thug, but there's one sonofabitch in the mayor's gang I'd like to see taken care of someday. He was my first for Jessie, and I almost hit the road, but she bought all this stuff for me and we talked about trust and honor and such, and I couldn't bear to look at myself if I did. Besides, she's at the top of the game around here, nobody higher. But enough of my problems, Audie, I'm here to make you happy. And in spite of everything, I do still like to fuck."

"That I believe. What about your mother?"

She scrunched up her face and swatted the question like a bothersome fly. "She's married and I'm not supposed to rock the boat. She promises me something from the estate in her will, but I shan't hold my breath. The little hypocrite probably will give it all to the legitimate kids that don't even know I exist. Anyway my father comes from a good family and doesn't have any other heirs," she smirked, "I think."

"Right now I believe every word you're saying."

"Good. Listen, you should enjoy yourself while you're here. We are going to have a go aren't we? Jessie will just toss somebody else at you if we don't 'cause you're supposed to be here until midnight, and there's no entertainment scheduled. Sometimes we have actors do plays in the parlor, but not to-night. She says she and Lorelei have some business or something, but," Suzanne glanced at the door, and her voice dropped, "I bet they're in bed right this minute. Did you know all the madams have women lovers too?"

A Chinese girl appeared like a leaf drifting on the wind, and placed a bottle of champagne on the table with two crystal flutes. Ah Tsin and Mai Ling flashed before Audie's eyes. He felt warmth on his face as he lifted a glass to his lips.

His brief moment of melancholy was broken by Suzanne. "I missed you Audie, really! We never know what life's going to throw at us, but you're the most fun, and we're close in age too. Closer than most, anyway. You're educated and handsome, and to tell the truth, you're the greatest fellow I've ever had in a bed."

"It's getting rather thick, Suzanne."

"No, *really!* I don't know what it is. Jessie says it's something Lorelei saw in you too. Lorelei's incredibly stunning by the way. What's her story? She's the most beautiful woman I've ever seen, even more than Jessie. She doesn't seem to be afraid of anything, and I've never seen her put on airs. She's mysterious to say the least. I think she's royalty or something, but Jessie says it's beyond my understanding. That burns me up. People think you can't figure something out just because you're seventeen."

"You told me sixteen, and you told me fifteen the first time I asked."

"Sixteen, then. Anyway I missed you." She threw a leg over his lap, unbuttoned his shirt, and ran a palm across his pectoral muscles. "I love your chest," she giggled, "I love your whole body. You must have done a lot of hard work in West Virginia." Audie considered pushing her away, but changed his mind as she worked her magic. Finally she pulled away herself, and stood up to take his hand. "Ding-ding, all aboard for the bedroom."

"And a bath? I could use one first."

"Sure. We have a private bath and shower for each room. Nothing but the best at Diamond Jessie Hayman's Parlor House and Resort. I always have a bath in lavender salts before I go to bed and maybe a little drink of champagne, a puff on the pipe, and a massage from Starr."

"Starr?"

"That Chinese girl, she's my private maid."

"My, you do have it good."

"Yep."

He swept her up to a burst of giggling, "Let's go," and tossed her toward the ceiling.

Suzanne shrieked and laughed as he caught her, leaning back in his arms until her long hair brushed the carpet. "Oh, Violet …"

Violet appeared in a lavender silk smock and curtsied. Whatever Lorelei was up to, she knew how to watch out for him in the meantime.

XXII.

The Mayor

"This is becoming dangerous Abe." Eugene Schmitz stroked his neatly cropped beard, and stared out his office window in the new marble edifice of City Hall at brown, gray and speckled pigeons jostling for room on the sill outside. The one in the middle took flight, heading for the baroque dome of the Hall of Records looming out of fog across the street.

"Take hold, fellow." Abraham Ruef ran a hand over a balding pate. "I found Jules myself. How do you think *I* feel? You've got to keep your head on your shoulders for the hearing Wednesday. Stay focused. We'll have time to winnow out this madman and his killings afterward. Right now we must assure ourselves we have the blessing of time itself."

Eugene opened the teak humidor on the mahogany desktop, took out a dark maduro cigar, and rolled it on the beige blotter under his palm. "I was talking about Older and his damnable obsession with us. Have you seen today's editorial? Have you seen the cartoons by that hack in the *Globe*? He thinks he's another Nast, and is trying to make us look like clowns. I'm not going to jail."

"Fine, then we are both on the same track at least, and what brilliant ploy do you propose to solve this conundrum? I have one, and I can assure you that it is imperative, Gene, that we present a united front or fall in ruin like the hollow facades of great empires who came before. Let Older spout his bile in the *Bulletin* and the *Globe*. We have allies at the *Call*, the

Chronicle, and all the Supervisors in our pocket. And Phelan is the *ex*-Mayor, an impotent has-been who envies your position in this office to which he still aspires. He never got to serve in this grand new building, and wishes he still had the job. Twenty-seven years is a record for erecting such a monument to temporal vanity, almost as long as Tammany itself. There are builders, teamsters, bankers, saloon keepers, and parlor house owners whose continued existence is owed to City Hall largesse. They owe whoever is sitting in that fine leather chair against your backside a perpetual favor, friend. *You're* the Mayor now. Call them in!"

Gene found himself reaching under his desk to stroke a battered violin case. He fought an overwhelming urge to take the instrument out, and release the pathos of his situation in a torrent of music amongst the marble busts and columns of the rotunda below. The acoustics of the new building were quite good, and the vault of the rotunda was an unexpected joy when he played late in the evening after all else had gone home. He'd much rather be playing, or conducting his orchestra. He should stop at the Poodle Dog, sit Wendell down at the piano on the second floor, and play for an hour or so with a couple of stiff brandies and some female company. He stroked his beard and scowled. "You forgot Spreckles. He seems prepared to bankroll this thing forever." Gene stared through fog at the limp flag atop the Hall of Records. "Sometimes I hate this job."

"You love the easy parts, the parties, the status it brings, the celebrity you yourself have brought to it. In the end it's all one and the same. Lesser men have climbed higher and greater men fallen farther, Gene. Fate is both a cruel mistress and a jolly good slut. You never know which. We have judges, cops, and a man in Records across the street who can alter or destroy any document the Court cares to examine. I've had them sanitizing our tracks for weeks. And remember the cash and gold in that boodle box you've got under your bed, and the Southern Pacific stock I'm tendering to you in a fortnight. Nice to own shares in a monopoly, eh? Not to mention that lovely blond thing from Tessie Wall's resort you're going to the opera with and wherever else you please thereafter. Name's Cassandra by the way. Best of the bunch, and that's saying a lot. Thank your lucky stars, Gene."

The Mayor stared into the fog as he tapped the unlit cigar on a bronze replica of a gold nugget on his desk. "Who do you think killed Wiggins and Jules?"

"You forgot the doorman. What was the lug's name? They said he looked like a damn prune, as stiff as a board." Abe shivered. "Had four men with rubber gloves put him in a box and cart him off to some potter's field in Marin." He shook his head. "Don't think I'm not rather up about it. I still can't puzzle why the killer left every damn dime. He decorated his corpse with a veritable fortune strewn about the place like so much trash. Truly a madman!"

"Yes, a madman, a *madman,* Abe. We must be on guard! Lunatics aren't prone to civilized behavior, and at any moment may strike for reasons known only to their own black hearts."

"If he's mad his heart isn't black, only his sorely troubled mind. They're trying to heal such people nowadays in Europe and back East."

"What a time for philosophy!"

"And when is there? I often miss the cloister of the university more than all else. To have the privilege to reside in objective inquiry and speculation is a precious gift given only to the few. How I'd love to return to that state of affairs sometimes as the lumpen masses swarm and cry out for tawdry entertainments. But you're thirty-seven now and I'm an old man of forty-one, and we must gird up our loins for battle like the men we have become. Eh, fellow?"

"I suppose."

"You'd damn well better know." Abe stroked his drooping mustache as he walked to the window. He took off his bowler hat and ran a hand across a shiny forehead. "We're together in this all the way, whether we like it or not. I put you behind that desk, and I'm not going down without you, so you'd better pull your weight and bail like hell when this splendid craft we've built is leaking. I made you a rich man Gene, whose hardest work is riding in parades, going to banquets, and attending operas with the rich and powerful when some lovely isn't attending to your private needs."

Eugene stared at the floor avoiding Abraham's eyes. "And what is wealth without honor?"

Abe spun on his heels and caught one in the Persian carpet. He stumbled, and grabbed the hat rack beside a travertine shelf with a vase of chrysanthemums. The vase began to tip, and he righted it and scooped his hat up off the floor. "I can pull down this Tower of Babel much faster than it took to build it I assure you! And as far as philosophy goes, we can certainly continue the discussion at a future time and place while enjoying the fruits of our labors. *Now* is the time to come at those who would take us down with a broadside of our own! Far too many in this town have far too much to lose besides us. I have made preparations in that regard, but must count on your utter veracity. That sonofabitch prosecutor Henry's in for a surprise I assure you. My men are preparing it at this moment, but we must be tenacious. The battle is hardly joined, and please don't disappoint me as to your backbone."

"My apologies. These killings have me on edge. Wiggins played in my orchestra, and I recruited him into my staff after

I got this job and feel responsible. The condition they found him in has given me nightmares, Abe. And on the fourth floor of the *Poodle Dog!* How did the killer get *there?* We don't need some Jack the Ripper running amok in this town, especially one who preys on the customers of whores rather than the whores themselves." Gene wiped his forehead. "Thank God we had a closed coffin. His wife—"

"And Jules was my law clerk for seven years, and your besotted brother Herbert owns a quarter of that goddamn cowyard and won't keep his bloody mouth shut about the killings when in his cups, and people keep dying there in a *most* inconvenient way. Need I go on? Get that lout Dinan out of his office with some detectives. Get Biggy on it; he's jockeying for Chief and wants the feather in his cap. Work them *against* each other and you'll get better results. You're supposed to understand politics after all." Abe stared out the window before he squeezed his eyes shut, pinched his nose, and turned back to Eugene. "I've put two new doormen on at Jackson with a bit of education as well as muscle. They're ex-detectives themselves, artists with a pistol and a slung-shot, and smart enough to handle the results in an appropriate manor. Even without making the papers, rumors are running rampant about this mess. We've lost a bushel of business to the Mariscania and the Nymphia in the last two weekends you can be sure."

"I'll have Dinan raid the Nymphia. They own the Workingman's Party a fortune in fees."

"On what pretense?"

Gene shrugged. "Un-natural acts, the exploitation of white virgins, something or other."

"How's the lawsuit?"

"Tied-up, but we're bleeding them dry in the interim. I can switch judges again, and force them to present everything from the start if need be."

"They seem far too sanguine about spending money on it. These business disputes that become personal do no one any good but lawyers, and that's coming from one Gene."

"That I believe. How much energy is spent on this damn quibbling? My God."

"Well," Ruef donned his hat,"I have an appointment this afternoon that I wouldn't dream of breaking."

"Dinan?"

"That's your department. It's Violet actually."

"That's the first pleasant thing I've heard all day."

"Magnificent, isn't she?"

"Absolutely. Miss Hayman is an artist who paints her masterpieces in the flesh of nymphs. I've never known a girl of hers not to be of the highest caliber. She's our greatest asset in that regard, and she keeps Tessie on her toes trying to compete."

"Indeed."

"A drink before you leave?"

"I would be amiss not to."

Gene took a crystal decanter from the buffet against the wall while eying his beard in the mirror above it. He must get a haircut and trim before the opera. He poured two fingers of Hennessey into snifters, and snipped the ends off two cigars with a clipper from a pewter tray on the sideboard. He offered one to Abe, lit his with the same match, and toasted. They downed the cognac in one toss with heads wreathed in cigar smoke.

"Ah," Abe put his glass down,"now stiffen your spine and continue with the business of the City. I'll see you at the Poodle Dog this evening."

"Enjoy your company, Mr. Ruef."

"Without a doubt, Mr. Mayor."

Abraham walked through the rotunda past the statue of Justice, through bronze doors with scenes of gold miners and settlers, and down marble steps. At the Pioneer Monument in the square below he paused, glancing back at the imposing spire atop a dome costing more than any building in the West. The fog was breaking, and the gilded statue surmounting City Hall glowed against a blue sky with her torch held high to the heavens. A vision of Jules with his balls in his mouth flashed through Abe's mind as he stepped into his waiting limousine.

XXIII.

Shaking the Golden Mountain

The bell rang again. Wu rose with a scowl from his letter to distant Mandarins holding the fate of his only son to check on the visitor. Mr. Audie had left an hour before, and no deliveries were expected. He used the mirror over the transom to inspect whoever was seeking admittance from the street, and groaned.

Fong Ah Sing stood on the green travertine steps, staring into the mirror.

Wu gritted his teeth and rubbed his forehead. The Wah Ting San Fong Tong had finally found him, and had no doubt sent Fong to collect their regular dues plus the month Wu was in arrears. He'd heard that Charlie Sep Ye Hung was going to court, and no doubt needed to raise money for numerous bribes. And of course, there was the price of putting money on the heads of anyone who would dare speak against Charlie Hung, King of the Pimps.

Wu imagined Fong in chains on a steamer back to the Flowery Kingdom, where his own arrogant head would swiftly be parted from his body. Here, some thirty tongs and two thousand of their boo how doy had an iron grip on the sinews of the Chinese community. They'd grown fat and arrogant milking those who dwelt in the shadow of the Golden Mountain seeking their fortunes with which to return to China and respectable lives. The tongs made a joke of the Six Companies chartered by the Emperor to maintain some civilized control of Chinese life, and the wretched *Fan Kwei* authorities were no recourse whatsoever. They only made things worse.

He hesitated before opening the door. What would the White Devil Woman do if he let Fong in the house? The possibility of Fong challenging the Woman pricked at Wu's imagination.

What would happen? Fong specialized in keeping the girls of the cribs and the slaves of other boo how doy in line. He bragged of it constantly. Would she kill him? Wu unbolted the door, and bowed to Fong.

"Wu, I have been sent by the glorious Hall of the Flowery Mountain Arbor to assess your contribution to our continued prosperity, and by definition your own. Do you greet me in accordance with our needs?

"Of course, Fong. Only keep quiet and I will produce your dues."

"Ten dollars for the month past, and ten more for this one … as well as something for the trouble of my errand. You are fortunate I was sent, and not some hot-head anxious to make a name amongst the Hatchet Sons of the Flowery Mountain Arbor by blooding his blade." Fong glanced around the parlor. "Do you have a drink?"

"I have no sam shu, only French brandy."

Yellow teeth flashed. "Brandy will do nicely. You may serve me promptly Wu."

Wu led him to the high-ceilinged kitchen and offered him a chair. Fong adjusted his blue

silk shirt over his bulletproof vest of chainmail and the bulges of his hatchet and pistol, and sat

down. Wu poured cognac into a crystal snifter and bowed.

Voices of whales called across vaults of dark water as an angry hissing began at the seams of the world. A belt of blood-red sparks blossomed in the eternal night that is the bottom of the sea, throwing up plumes of heat that scalded her face.

She clung to a quaking cliff as the earth heaved and tried to throw her into the waves. Birds wheeled and cried as they were cast from sea-washed rocks into the sky. Redwood trees shook their crowns at clouds like angry fists, coming apart at the roots. Fissures split their trunks with loud popping sounds, echoing across the water like a thousand guns.

She lost her grip and fell into the sea. The blackness crushed her, making the bones of her chest splinter as she folded in upon herself. Yet she was still awake, still *living* as she became small beyond knowing.

Lorelei sat up with the echo of her cry hanging in the air. Something *wrong* was moving, something *close*. She blinked at sunlight streaming through the cracks in curtains Audie hadn't pulled tight enough, leaving trails under her eyelids.

Audie had arisen hours ago, and was in the company of Izzy Rothman debating the meaning of life and love from a Judeo-Christian perspective. He felt like a young lion that hadn't yet put the gift of his soul to the test of war. She wanted to reach out and stroke his mane, and tickled his self-awareness for a moment before returning to herself. She rubbed her temples, and yawned. A terrible thirst raged in her throat, just like the last time she had dreamt of the girl on trembling cliffs. She arose and donned her red silk robe.

What was her name?

Wu was downstairs with a Celestial whose presence had brought her sudden waking, who made her dreams dark, and full of rage. She touched Wu's mind and grimaced, before a smile spread her lips. Wu was determined to get Fong Ah Sing out of the house as quickly as possible, and was wishing the Woman from Hell would aid him just this once.

She exhaled."Fong Ah Sing," she called from the hall,"what pray tell is a filthy hatchet son of dogs doing in my home?"

The Accursed Woman's voice was louder than Wu had ever heard it as she stepped into the kitchen. She blinked as the afternoon sun falling from the windows stung her skin. Her eyes flashed pure red. *Let the dog see.*

Fong leaned back in his chair and began to fall against the counter. He righted himself, and cursed as brandy splashed on his fine silk shirt. He stood, back to the wall, his mind swarming with visions of girls he'd cut down for less. Fong sneered at the tall white bitch between him and the door. Her eyes ... they were *wrong.* He rubbed his own, but could not focus upon those eyes before they changed again.

Lorelei saw his memories as he'd lived them. She saw the dark basement of the"hospital"where Mai Ling had died, and smelt the stench that made Fong hold a handkerchief to his face as he entered on his familiar mission to cut the skulls of other girls as they lay laboring for breath crying out to their ancestors, as he would have cut Mai Ling's or Ah Tsin's.

She felt the sneer on the face of a girl beyond fear as she stared into Fong's eyes, and went down spitting blood as his blade cut her down the breastbone in one stroke. Her heart lay exposed between white ribs, beating in wet red glory in the lamplight as she lay upon a cold concrete floor. A mighty prayer went out from the girl, a last plea that demanded to be heard. The girl reached out as that sea rose to swallow her, her fingers sticky with blood in the flickering light of an oil lamp's single flame. Lorelei reached out to those hands and held bloody fingers in her own, hands that were dust and gone, yet alive within her grasp. Her face was radiant.

Fong stood paralyzed: a rabbit smelling the breath of the wolf.
"Wu, I shall take care of this. Leave us now."

Wu sidled around the kitchen toward the door, bowed, and
backed into the hall.

Fong hissed a warning and shouted, "Wu, you have the
temerity to leave my presence! Like—"

Lorelei's eyes were golden, a cat's in the branches of a
burning tree. "You have the temerity to breathe in mine?"

"What?"

As evening fell, a new *chung hung* reward poster graced a wall
in *Dupont Gai,* the oldest Chinatown in America, known to its
denizens as the Colony of the Golden Mountain. It hung at the
corner of Clay and Dupont where proclamations had appeared
on a wall in the battles of Face and Blood for five decades. In
red letters and perfect calligraphy, the chung hung heaped insults
upon the Wah-Ting San Fongs, calling them sons of dogs and men
without penises.

Upon closer inspection, the letters appeared to be written
in blood. At the end of the diatribe were the words *Loy gee,
hai dai; Come on, you cowards!* It was signed by the Hatchet Sons
of the On Yicks and the boo how doy of the Suey Sings. The
chung hung declared that the Wah Ting San Fongs would be
driven from the milk of the singsong girls within a fortnight,
and went on to proclaim that anyone who killed a highbinder
from the Hall of the Flowery Mountain Arbor would receive five
hundred dollars in gold from the grateful On Yicks and come
under their benevolent protection. Anyone who kidnapped
one of their crib women would likewise be given five hundred
dollars upon delivery to an On Yick soldier.

Most impressively, even to those who had grown callous of
the rhetoric of the tongs, the head of Fong Ah Sing was hung from

his queue by an iron stake driven into the bricks of the wall. His face was a mask of agony with sightless milky eyes frozen wide, staring at whatever he had last seen over lips pulled back from yellow teeth in a twisted grimace. The poster dared anyone to touch the head, and brought foul curses upon them should they do so, and upon their sons and unborn sons also.

Within an hour, shots rang out in a dozen places in Chinatown.

Izzy waved at the commerce of Market Street through the windows of Zinkand's Restaurant with his cigar. "There's a purpose to what she's doing. That's for certain."

"Of course, but so what? Perhaps her only purpose is to reside in the company of a lover and to enjoy the passing parade of our better nature somewhat like a collector from a higher realm enjoys her specimens. Who knows? It no longer plagues me Izzy, even if I must count myself as one of them."

"How can you be so accepting?"

"Because I can imagine an existence no finer, no richer, or more full of human experience. Because she keeps me aware of the transitory nature of our relationship even as I am blessed with the ability to see other times and places. To see *lives*, Izzy, that I had never dreamed of. I shall now endeavor to respect the indigenous peoples of this continent forever for instance. Previously I never gave the Indians much shrift beyond what I read in dime novels except to wonder why they seemed so without direction from my perspective. Their spirits called out to me from the very stones of the mountains in which I was born, yet I was deaf to them. No more. I know now the direction which I perceived to be a clear, linear progression toward some singular goal of our civilization, some 'Manifest Destiny,' was only an illusion in the eternal multiplicity of existence. Who was the Roman god of portals, Janus? I cannot even see God simply as my Father anymore. The other face of God is a *she,* Izzy, and Lorelei is her daughter. And the Chinese ... the slave girls of the cribs must be rescued! I plan to write and speak about what I have learned, I assure you."

"The Methodist and Presbyterian missions do a good job of rescuing Chink girls. And not all of them are slaves, by the way. Some are high class like some of the white ones. Ever hear of Selina, or Ah Toy? I don't know where they'd get all the cooks and domestic help without ex-singsong girls in this town. Damn grateful when they end up in a nice home on Nob Hill cooking grub for the nabobs you can bet, or tending to Jessie's girls at her resort for that matter. They are a treasure in a way."

Audie gazed upon Market Street. "There are many layers to the culture of exploitation."

Izzy chuckled with his head wreathed in cigar smoke. "May I attend your next lecture at the institution, Doctor Bond?"

"What kind of institution are you referring to?"

"Perhaps the halls of science. Perhaps the madhouse. Who knows? I don't know how anyone else would believe you when it comes to Lorelei. I hardly do, and I'm the one who told you what she was in the first place."

"Ah, but you really don't know. She's beyond imagining Izzy, though I know you'd like to try."

"Damn straight. I admit I wouldn't mind trying a Liliot out before I pass the pale if one like that's around. From what you tell me about this Ah Tsin, Lorelei has done some things that seem more like a *Shekhinah.* That's a bride of God in the Kabbalah, a divine female presence. It's hard to keep track anymore, what with these purported good deeds of hers like rescuing poor Chink girls. Damn confusing."

"I'm relieved that you've softened your stance on her. And

your company is enjoyed and appreciated, that we can sit and dis-
cuss such things. Would you order me more of that brandy?"

"You bet, pilgrim. You're paying for it anyway."

"She is. Money is nothing to her. I suspect she has hold-
ings in the temporal world everywhere. It must be easy—knowing
so much, being so beautiful, and lasting so incredibly long."

Izzy stroked his beard. "Child's play obviously." He frowned
at the butt of his cigar and crushed it out in the ashtray. "One left,
got to get more pronto. These Cubans are so damn cheap since
we taught the Spaniards who was boss. Arrogant sonsabitches
should never have sunk the *Maine*." He scanned the traffic on
Market.

"What are you looking for?"

"For one of the kids I know to run up to the Tobacconist on
Larkin. Don't feel like leaving our table just yet."

"Indeed, dessert is coming."

Just then three adolescent boys in white shirts, corduroy pants held up by leather suspenders, and flat woolen caps
passed the window. Izzy banged on the glass, and the smallest and
swiftest rushed to the door with dark eyes alight.

"Bepino," Izzy chuckled, "good work. Run over to Pete's
tobacco shop and get me a box of those Havanas. The ones
with the woman standing on the water with—"

"Sure, Mister Rothman, but please call me Bep."

"Sure, Bep. Tell you what, there's four bits in it if you hurry."
Izzy fished out a five from his pocket and put it in the hand of the
boy.

Bep grinned and was gone.

"A good kid there, Audie."

"He must be, to be trusted like that."

"One wonders what it's like, growing up in a town like this."

"I should think I would be hardened far more than West

Virginia, what with fleshpots, crimps and footpads around every corner. Jaded, to use the word. Thank God for the resilience of children." He smiled. "Lorelei looks upon us as children."

"For good reason I suppose."

Bep soon reappeared out of breath with a box of cigars under his arm. "Got to go," he gasped, "the highbinders are offering a dollar a pound for wildcat meat, and Paulo's father knows where there's a whole nest of them in Marin. We're taking my father's boat across to hunt in the morning."

"Whoa, don't you want your four bits?"

"Of course, I can buy enough bullets for all of us. Paulo has three twenty-twos at his father's house. Did you know they have fifty pound wildcats over there? That's *fifty dollars!* Bep snatched the money and ran from the restaurant, but not before tipping his battered cap with a flourish.

"Wildcat meat?"

"The boo how doy eat it before going into battle, Audie. They believe it gives them the strength of the animal through some mystical something or other. Guess there's another tong war brewing."

"Tong war?"

"Yep. Somebody really stepped on somebody's Celestial toes I suppose, and they're beating the gongs. Used to be they just used hatchets and knives. Nowadays it's pistols and shotguns, even bombs. Hope Lieutenant Price has the Flying Squad geared up. He can put a damper on the worst of it by putting a heel down now. I should call them from this establishment's telephone. It could be their first tip in regard to it, and they remember favors." Izzy stood up from the table. "Order me some of that German chocolate torte would you?"

Izzy returned with a look of satisfaction on his bearded face. He began to trim the end off a cigar and ran it under his nose before lighting it. He ran a finger across the torte on the plate before him, and tasted the frosting."That's the first he's heard. Next time there's a show raid on some place nice like Jessie's, it means I'll get the special treatment should I happen to be there. You have to keep your contacts in the world you know."

"Do they really raid places like Jessie's?"

"Very infrequently, but Father Caraher is on a tear, and there *is* an election coming up, so sooner or later we'll see one to impress those not in the know. Most likely they'll pick someone who's welched on their payoffs to the honorable police authorities or the Union Labor Party Ruef and Schmitz run. Kill two birds with one stone. The Twinkling Star Corporation's been in for a hell of a ride from them, that's their number one competition, and Ruef and Schmitz have been looking for an excuse to close their cowyard for a while. They run the Hotel Nymphia over on Stockton, a great big place I wouldn't visit with your dick, if you'll excuse the expression."

"No offence. Then the police raid the cowyards?"

"Sure, although the Marsicania on DuPont got a court injunction for the coppers to leave them alone for the last couple of years, which certainly puts a burr under some of the boys at the Poodle Dog's saddles. Interesting to see how that turns out." Izzy puffed on his cigar and twirled it in his fingers."Did you know they only use young girls to roll these? I hear virgins are the best."

"I don't know how that would affect the tobacco."

"Girls' skin is finer. They are by far the most flexible state of human existence. Haven't you ever seen one put her ankles to her ears?"

"Leah ... Suzanne can do that."

"See? And wouldn't a virgin be the best of all?" Izzy gestured with the dark shaft of the maduro."I'll show you some dancers in town that can contort themselves into pretzels, Audie, some but thirteen or so. They even—"

"None of whom are virgins I'd wager."

"No, but the skin of a virgin is more pure so to speak. It's greeted by the leaf of the tobacco as it is rolled, and the cigar takes up some of the essence of the young things they say."

"I'd never have thought that a Jewish student of history would believe in such folklore."

"It's dinner talk, something to go with this excellent brandy. You're my best company at such times, what with your tales of an actual Liliot that no one else believes but yours truly. By the way, Caruso is in town this week with the Conried Metropolitan Opera Company. Ever been to an Opera?"

"My father took me to one in New York years ago when he dragged me to a Methodist Synod. The Italian doesn't do much for me however."

"This one's in French I believe."

Audie leaned back and rubbed his chin. "I could bring Lorelei. She'd be a sight, more beautiful than all other women put together."

"The Belle of the Ball no doubt." Izzy drained his snifter. "You never foresaw any of this two weeks ago."

"Is that how long I've been in San Francisco?"

"Losing track of time, Audie?"

"Beyond measure. I really haven't been able to tell the days at all anymore. It could be—"

"It's Monday, April the sixteenth, nineteen oh six to be exact." Izzy fingered the fob of his pocket watch in a haze of smoke. "And nine forty-seven p.m."

"Then I have been disembarked on this peninsula for ten days, nine hours and forty seven minutes exactly." Audie shook a head pleasantly abuzz with the brandy as Izzy handed him a cigar. "It seems a lifetime," he stared at the traffic on Market, "several actually."

XXIV.

The Secret Garden

"I don't want to sleep." Her breath was across his cheek. "It's overcast and not at all bright today. I want to go to the Park."

"What?"

"I'll wear a big hat and do fine. I want to walk in the gardens and listen to the birds. I do so miss them sometimes."

Audie yawned, fighting the urge to drift off after an immeasurable time as her lover that left him disoriented and drained. "You want to go in daylight and tolerate the pain." He rose on an elbow. "Then once you lived the day. You can't miss something you've never had, Lorelei."

"As did those whose memories I hold, and I as a child as I've told you, and other things I'll explain later. Let's go to the Japanese Gardens. I only know them under the moon and stars. I do so want to smell the blossoms opening to the sun and listen to the morning songs of birds. I want to gaze up into the branches while those glorious colors are there and see clouds in a blue sky."

He began to speak, but sighed. She glowed with anticipation. "All right."

They took a carriage west from the old section of the City and turned on California toward the ocean. As they drifted south on Fillmore to Haight, the buildings became smaller, with open lots and broad margins along the streets. The amusement park at the end, The Chutes, sat empty in the grey dawn.

Its water slides and pools were given over to pigeons, seagulls and crows foraging for bits of food between hand-painted sideshow signs on bed sheets. They arrived in Golden Gate Park before the concessions were open, and passed the Conservatory with its gleaming white-on-white glass.

"I'd love to go in there, but the reflections would drive me blind. You should go later and see the water lilies. They're the largest on Earth."

"Sounds like you've seen them."

"At night. I love to watch the clouds pass in moonlight and listen to the things who call this place home. You can hear roots growing in the ground if you know how to do it, and the animals talking amongst themselves. I know their thoughts to some degree."

"And whales who speak of God. Nothing surprises me anymore."

"Let's get off here."

She asked the driver to stop, and Audie watched the man's entire body smile at the sound of her voice. He thought of all the death she had known, let alone caused, yet no longer felt any shock at it. That was another man who didn't know her yet. She was simply Lorelei: a magnificent creation of life who was destined to walk alone in the world in spite of her lovers. Neither did he consider her a Goddess at this moment, but somehow both more and less. She was a wonderful and unique person, one defined by her extraordinary, hungry soul far more than her temporal deeds and passing loves including himself. Audie reveled at the privilege of being beside her in the morning light. He felt her pain like a constant sunburn, and with his all wished her strength. Naturally she had a reason that he would learn in time, and naturally he was there should she have need to draw on what he could give to her moments in the eternal now they shared for a most indefinite time together ... which made it all the more precious.

Her gratitude was obvious: a primal state, like the sun and moon and stars. They walked hand-in-hand through mist on a flagstone path far beyond speaking. The Japanese Gardens appeared out of the fog with pagoda roofs glistening, surrounded by stone sculptures and looking like tiny temples inhabited by Oriental leprechauns. She chuckled at the image he conjured in his mind, and he didn't have to ask to confirm it. He didn't have to ask anything anymore.

They sat on a granite bench, and she leaned back and turned her face to the sky. Lorelei removed the broad black hat. Her hair fell to the leaves behind her, and dewdrops flew in a glittering spray. White hands gripped the bench as she endured light from an overcast sky. Audie could feel it beating on her eyelids, brighter and hotter than the strongest tropical sun for him he knew.

"I welcome the pain this morning." She inhaled the cool air, and let it out slowly. "Thank you, Audie, for you have come to love me for who I am."

"I have—"

She put fingers to his lips. "Shhhh," her luminous skin was reddening where it was exposed to the day, "you *love*, Audie. Not for the sexual fantasy that I am, or the power which you haven't begun to lust for. Not for the money I shall always have either. You love me because I *do* love, for you have come to see how it rules my being."

"More than I knew was possible for one heart. I was taught only Christ could have such love, yet have come to see it manifest before me in a living soul." He wiped his eyes. "You have redeemed me."

"Then I am your slave mortal man. My heart is upon your altar, just as you would offer of your own." Mourning doves began cooing from the eucalyptus and Monterey cypress overhead as the first shaft of sun touched them."Oh, so lovely," she sighed,"and the smell of flowers as they open themselves to the day. I do so miss the day. The sun on the trees ... "

"You said you would tell me why you have left it."

She was silent for an endless moment. Audie felt the beating of his heart."I can have the day, but I am not willing to pay the price of it. For each day I wake and walk in the sun, I must take the life of a good man the night before. Not a scoundrel the world can do without, and not a fool, but only a loving man with a heart that is open, who gives himself up to me willingly, with knowledge of what is to be. I must *kill* him, steal his entire future for the strength to face the sun." She opened her eyes to the glowing sky in the east, and squeezed them shut against her will."Such is my curse."

"A sacrifice."

A tear streaked her pale cheek."Yes." Mist beaded on her dark lashes. Her skin glistened as he stared at her profile against the glowing greens of trees and the reds and yellows of flowers. An iridescent green humming bird circled her as if she were a source of nectar revealed by dawn's light. Here he was with her in the *day,* perhaps the first mortal man to see her so in how long?

"When I was so ready to end myself ... I could have bought you but one day in the sun."

"Yes, for an entire precious life, but a *day!* Long ago when we ruled nations, we didn't live in the dark. We knew a selfless communion of souls with the best men of their generations, and lived—."

"You still don't."

"Oh Audie, do you believe that?"

A great weight rolled over him as Audie reeled from a hurt that was not his own but within her. Lorelei was opening her last hidden place to him, and was vulnerable as a child whose glorious heart was in his clumsy hands. Then this was her sacrifice; she would not live with his death no matter what it bought. Lorelei could not exist as a destroyer of all she cherished. She had chosen her nocturnal life not out of fear, but for the survival of her own soul."No!"

As the day grew brighter, she trembled with the effort to tolerate another minute. The sun broke through clouds, her face reddened, and her beautiful eyes squeezed shut. Tears ran down her cheeks in the glare. She folded in his arms and began to shake. He stroked her forehead, touching perfect the skin over that glorious and precious mind holding countless lives and untold secrets. She began a little laugh at his thoughts, but it shrunk to a tiny thing and diminished in a choked cry. Her breath rattled in her chest. A trickle of blood ran from her lips. He touched it with a fingertip, kissed it from her mouth, and it ran down his throat to blaze high in his heart.

Audie wept as he lifted her in his arms. She was lighter than a child as he carried her to the road and hailed a cab. The driver took one look at her, and suggested a trip to the hospital."She's all right, just weak."

"Just like a woman, always faintin' at the least little thing." The man cracked his whip across the rump of the big Clydesdale."I'd say she's in need of a good drink and a man's love. Too much sheltered livin' if you ask me."

He sat beside her, knowing that his blood was balm for her pain. She tossed in her sleep, and he gazed on her burned face as if seeing her for the first time. He wanted to protect her, stand before the world with the knowledge of what she truly *was,* and what he had become in her presence. *If they only knew!* Dreams of telling her story to the ends of the earth seized him, made his heart race, until his mind spun into a pit of exhaustion. *Can it be done without blood?* Audie put hands to her damp forehead and closed his eyes, striving to make her whole like Christ in a selfless act of healing.

Her voice came in a hoarse whisper. "I've killed six men since we met Audie, six souls who hadn't finished their journeys to wherever their lives were taking them." She moaned. "What if one had lived to find redemption?"

"It was just! I believe in you Lorelei, more than any other who has ever walked this earth! Nothing about you is evil, you—"

"I'm all right, really." She sat up and tossed hair from her eyes, and brushed his cheek with her fingertips. "But take off your clothes, if you truly want to be of some use."

XXV.
The Wealth of Ages

Audie awoke from the dream of a blazing marshland to Wu calling from downstairs. A huge blue dragonfly had droned over his head, and he'd been about to step on an altar under a blinding sun while staring into eyes beckoning with familiar beauty. The hand-me-down Winchester he'd hunted in the hills of West Virginia with had somehow become a bow and quiver. He'd dropped them in the reeds knowing he'd never see them again, and was about to take her outstretched hand when Wu's voice had interrupted him.

He rolled to gaze upon Lorelei. She slept on purple satin sheets beyond all pain. A perfect goddess again. Wu seldom seemed to come to their floor, which was fine, but Audie wished he had some method of alerting him besides shouting. He dragged his eyes off her and got out of bed.

He showered wondering where and how long ago that altar was and exactly what relation that woman was to his present love. She had to be an ancestor. An entire lifetime of study was in order. He decided to eat at Tony's, but checked on Lorelei one last time, trying not to be giddy or worshipful as his eyes dwelt on her stretched across the bed. Without conscious thought, he stuffed more of her money in his pockets and donned the shoulder holster before putting on his coat. Wu had acquired a friendly smile recently, and Audie paused to respond to it with a grin.

He was almost to the door when the telephone rang. Wu

ran to get it and announced it was for him. Audie returned to the dining room where the oaken box hung on the wall and put the black trumpet of the receiver to his ear. "Izzy?"

"Audie," It was the breathless voice of Suzanne, "I got your number from Jessie. You didn't tell me you had a telephone."

"Ah, hello Suzanne, how have you been?"

"Fine, but you'd make things better. Can we see each other tonight?"

"You mean at Jessie's?"

"No. I'm not here as a member of the white slave trade. I was thinking about going somewhere that we can be as regular people together, perhaps the Opera."

"Well ... I'd like to go somewhere besides, um, the same thing I suppose."

"We can keep our clothes on and have a wonderful time. I really do like you. I'm dying for some culture, and you're an educated student of life like me. Caruso is singing in *Carmen* at the Grand Opera House, and I have tickets to a private box. This gentleman simply forced them upon me after he was compromised by his wife's servant when he took me to the Poodle Dog for somewhat more than dinner. We could sit up there like Sir Bond and Lady Callahan with our retinue. I've got the dress for it."

"Is Callahan your last name?"

"Yes, guess I never told you. It's Suzanne Mae Callahan to be exact."

"No you didn't. Just one thing, do you promise to tell me the whole truth about yourself? No stories?"

"Sure, Audie, anything for a date."

"Well," he pressed the receiver to his breast. What would Lorelei do? The shock of seeing her helpless and hurting instead of the invulnerable being he'd come to know was evoking a need to protect her that was overwhelming. His teeth dug in his lip as he leaned into the telephone, and took a breath, "Suzanne, I am somewhat concerned about ... about Lorelei's welfare, she's—"

"That's quite admirable, but she's coming with us."

"She is?"

"Sure, Jessie's coming too."

He put the phone to his breast. He with all three women at the Opera, dressed to the nines, was just too much. "Yes," he chuckled, "yes, that would be marvelous, Suzanne!"

"Good," she giggled, "Boy, Audie, you sure are going to look like some kind of gigolo tonight."

He chuckled. "Why do people keep calling me that?"

"Meet us at the resort, seven sharp."

"Certainly. Suzanne?"

"Yes?"

"Did Lorelei put you up to this?"

"It was all of our ideas."

"Oh well, then fine, I'll see you."

"Good then, seven o'clock."

He left the house whistling. On the sidewalk, the present occupier of a line of Emperors of the United States and Protectors of Mexico was stopping a pedestrian, and Audie waved. The Emperor waved back, and returned to talking to a well-dressed man with mutton chop sideburns who was reaching into his pocket.

His eyes connected with Diana's as he entered Tony's and found a seat near the window. She sashayed over immediately. "Hi, Audie."

"Hi, Diana."

"How are you? No time to come by, 'cause you're eatin' at all the high-tone places?"

"Yes and no. I was out of town for a couple of days, up in the redwoods."

"Hear you been over to Hayman's Resort as a guest."

"You did?"

"Uh-huh. Think I'd do well there?"

"Somehow, I should hate to see it."

"Why?" Diana stood hands on hips and head cocked as he fished for a reply.

"I suppose just some residual sense of the romantic, some hangover from another life and another time."

"With the company you keep I guess so. Why do all these women treat you so good? It's not money, 'cause you're always spendin' theirs. I knew when I saw you that you were different, but jeez ... what have you got that keeps 'em comin' back, Audie?"

"It started eons ago when a goddess ruled the hearts of men, when they would give of themselves wholly and selflessly even unto death."

"That is so romantic. You must be a lover and a poet or something."

"Something, anyway. How about steak and eggs, and those potatoes Tony makes with green peppers and onions. Have him throw some of that red sauce on the eggs with Romano cheese. I'll have some of those hot peppers on the side too, and coffee, and orange juice, and of course sourdough bread."

"Gosh, you must be starvin'."

"Famished, with a hunger beyond the mortal coil."

"Comin' up, Mr. Lady's Man."

After the meal, he went to the wharves. Fishing boats were coming in as the sun touched the ocean beyond the Golden Gate with their triangular red sails like the wings of butterflies gliding over copper-colored water before the green reflections of Marin and Tiburon's peninsula. The rise of Mt. Tamalpais was ruddy red in the sinking sun with the trench of Mill Valley in shadow. Steam launches and ferries nosed amongst sailboats clustered between the Lombard and Fisherman's piers, leaving them in their wakes. Ospreys, gulls, and kittiwakes wheeled and cried over shouts in Italian, Greek and Portuguese as the writhing catch was unloaded in a chaos of silver flashing fish and pink crustaceans.

He leaned on the railing where he and Izzy had discussed the meaning of Lorelei and life, inhaling the salt air and absorbing the peace of the sea. Lorelei and life. *Life ... and Lorelei.* Down below a Catholic priest was blessing a boat while her proud owner stood with a hand on his son's shoulder as an image of the Virgin was held up by four young men upon a litter strewn with rose petals. The priest swung a silver censer and recited an incantation in Latin as the petals danced in the breeze around their feet and drifted into the water. Audie watched the red of some darken as they soaked in the sea, even as others seemed to float like jeweled drops of blood upon the water as they began their journey toward the open ocean. He took a deep breath, and closed his eyes. It was a good time to be alive.

He turned his gaze to the squat profile of Alcatraz and tried to *listen.* What about the Modoc man whom she had spoken of, waiting for the end of the world? Audie sent a wordless blessing to the nameless prisoner, whose good life was gone like the summers of years past.

He thought of that first vision in Lorelei's bed, of children playing, of the feeling of impending death already long past, and how it had torn at him that night. She'd wanted him to see it; of that he was certain. He'd heard Mai Ling's plea, and found where she had died on his own ... but where had those children lived? Perhaps the very beach on which they had played had been right here; things had changed so much.

How much luckier was he. How much more fortunate

that he had been robbed by Suzanne and lifted up out of his own dark night by the hand of Lorelei his lover. Glorious Lorelei, the last of her line. He blew a kiss to the Virgin, and headed back to prepare for the Opera.

She was fabulously attired in a large green hat with quetzal feathers, a shimmering green dress with a whalebone corset, tall black high heel boots, and black eighteen-button evening gloves when he arrived. She wore a series of diamond dog collar belle epoque necklaces that Suzanne had informed him were exact copies of Queen Alexandra's, who wore them to hide the scars of surgery on her throat. They glowed brightly on Lorelei's perfect one, interspersed with glimmering strands of seed pearls. A blood-red ruby at the bottom of a double rope of diamonds hung between her breasts with their exposed cleavage in the low-cut bodice cradling the deep red stone against glowing milk-white flesh. Audie rubbed his chin. He was dying to ask how she had got into the corset alone, as it required being cinched from the back.

She knew his thoughts, of course, but refused to tell him. "Some things should remain mysterious. I've taken you across worlds, but a lady's boudoir is her own business, and you must cultivate the habit of never asking other women things that I might readily explain."

"Well, I certainly don't wish to trample where a man isn't welcome."

"Then let's just be on our way."

After he'd changed into a tuxedo, starched white shirt, and purple cummerbund she had ready, they took a horse cab downtown. Lorelei told the driver to pass through Chinatown. Audie glanced at the driver's expression, and asked why she wanted to go the long route. It would have been easy to take Leavenworth to Ellis, being more direct, and they could avoid the more dangerous parts of the City by doing so.

"I want to see a few places."

A half-hour later she waved at two cops on the stoop of 620 Jackson as they descended the hill, who arose from their lethargy at the sight of her, grinned, and tipped their blue caps.

"Isn't that the place where the fellows were murdered?"

"Yes Audie, that's half the six, but that building across Dupont is what I really wanted to see." She pointed to a smudged brick structure down the hill with a red tile roof added to its gold rush era walls as the horses' hoofs clopped on the cobblestones and the driver stood on the brake.

"Why?"

"The basement, it's where the *Barracoon* is, a big room from the old days where the tongs hold their slave auctions. There was one for tonight, and I was wondering if the On Yicks would go through with it, what with the war and all."

"You know about that."

Her eyes flashed crimson. "I started it. It was impulsive. My mother taught me to stay out of view and never stir up crowds, and that most certainly applied to her. She couldn't seem to keep her eyes from going red when she wasn't thinking about it. It scares the hell out of people."

"Yours just did."

She ignored the comment. "But seeing as I'm the only one of my kind left, I'm doing what the majority dictates … or at least setting a precedent." She laughed. "They call that fetid hellhole the Queen's Room. It's where Ah Tsin and Mai Ling were sold eight years ago into the slavery of the cribs."

"Are they having it?"

"No. Everyone's afraid of getting killed or having their inventory purloined in a raid from rivals. I love that. I do so wish I could bring back all those girls who have died, to let them feel the fear tonight in the guts of the boo how doy."

"How did you start it?"

"With an atrocity. That's all that gets anybody's attention you know. Oh well, their days are numbered as are anyone's. God, I'm light-headed. It must be the sun this morning." She told the driver, who had a bemused expression on his face, to turn right at Portsmouth Square. "I've seen enough."

"All I've seen are buildings."

Four shots rang out from an alley to their right, followed by the thunder of a shotgun. The whine of lead pellets ricocheting off bricks made Audie reach for her hand and duck in the seat. His closed on her arm, but Lorelei was like a marble statue, ridged and erect.

The driver cracked his whip as they sped past a half-dozen Chinese running down a dark defile. Lorelei laughed, and waved. "You are crazy, acting like that in front of Stout's Alley!" the driver barked over his shoulder as he shook the reins, "You're wearing enough jewelry to cause a *dozen* women to be murdered! Get *down,* Madame, *please!"*

Lorelei fondled the blood red ruby between her breasts, held it to her lips, and blew the hatchetmen a kiss. "Loy gee, hai dai!" Her voice bounced off the iron-shuttered shops of merchants and echoed in the clatter of horse's hooves. The town's lone Stanley police car appeared as they reached the corner with its brass siren cranked furiously by an officer who held a shotgun in one hand as the car's boiler hissed like a cornered cat. She laughed again.

They made their way to Jessie's resort with the horses edgy and shivering. The team pranced sideways when they stopped at Powell for the cable car, and the driver cursed. "Damn nags, they've heard gunshots before, but something's got their goat tonight. I've got people to haul to Delmonicos' after I drop you folks off, and then the Opera." He shook his head. "Hope the rest of the night ain't like that trip through Chinatown. My hair is gray enough!"

A dog howled as if in great pain from somewhere close-by. Lorelei closed her eyes for a moment.

Audie turned to her as the carriage began the final blocks to Ellis. "What is it?"

"You feel it, don't you?"

He strained until his head ached, seeking something beyond the reach of his mortal senses that he knew was there. "What is it?"

"I don't know. There's something moving down deep in the world, but I don't know if it's physical, or in the human heart, or both. I don't even know if it's from our own species. The Bay is seething with the cries of distressed whales, and the souls of this city are so distracting when one tries to focus. It must have something to do with the sun today. I've been having this dream about this Indian girl." Her eyes flashed crimson. "I was *wrong!* There *is* going to be a slave auction, but very late tonight. I caught something strong from an On Yick who is quite willful, and he is going to make it happen. I do feel like doing something about that. And there's a fight going on two blocks over that's so annoying. Oh … someone was just stabbed. And Izzy's learned friend is praying for me to appear before him at a Rabbinical Court and give him a chance to banish me to Gehenna for that matter."

"Hell?"

"Correct." She squeezed his hand. "You've seen the door to Hell, Audie. It's at the end of Butcher Alley. Why in hell do they need another?"

"And you went there to rescue a soul."

"Thank you, although I only showed her what was in store

that she might pass joyfully. To pass in triumph is the last gift I can ever assist with." She scowled."I'm tempted to show up just to spite him, but he's got a bad heart, and he'd probably drop dead from fright and it would be my fault. And that poor man on Alcatraz is chanting for the end of the world. His song is so seductive for someone of my nature that it just makes me want to come to him with love and release him to his ancestors tonight."

"As for Mai Ling."

She ran a black-gloved hand over her face."I can't focus."

"I don't know how you keep from going mad, Lorelei."

"By keeping my attention on what pleases me, at least most of the time. I've driven good men mad before I learned to measure myself in their hearts. You were told."

"Izzy insists that's your true purpose on Earth, although he's also come around to admitting a desire for you, even a grudging respect. You both have the same tastes in religious literature for that matter."

"I only care what you think."

When they reached Ellis, a long black limousine was there with its driver leaning on the hood smoking a cigar. Audie held his arm out for her as she stepped down from the carriage, watching the man's wide-eyed stare as she placed a heel demurely upon the curb—a woman who could spring to the top of the building in an instant, or squeeze the man's throat until his eyes popped from his skull, should she have the inclination. He grinned at the game in which he had become a player: one of the lucky ones indeed. Izzy had explained how Audie's path was changed forever by meeting Lorelei as they sat at their first meal together. He'd been quite prescient about that at least. Of course, events seemed to shape themselves around her like the sea's currents around a coast or the wind over a mountain. Like the more real and permanent things in the world, Lorelei seemed to make her own weather, but this weather was comprised of the passions of living souls and the storms of the human heart. He took her hand, and they ascended the polished steps to a door opened by a smiling Belle.

XXVI.

A Night at the Opera

Suzanne was also in green when she greeted them in the parlor. Her auburn hair was perfectly coiffured, and she had a four-
strand dog collar of diamonds and emeralds around her throat. She
stared at Lorelei in obvious awe before she swallowed, grabbed
Audie's hand, and dragged him to the living room where a fire
crackled in the marble hearth. A bottle of Moet sat in a bucket
on a pewter stand next to a table with tall fluted glasses.

Starr appeared in a blue silk shirt and pants, poured a
glass of champagne, and handed it to Audie. She did the same
for Lorelei, then Suzanne.

Suzanne held up her glass. "To all things good."

Audie's eyes were for Lorelei only as she put the liquid to
her mouth and drank.

She emptied the glass and placed it on the table. "Am I
that strange?"

"I just … you know—"

"Yes I can drink, Audie. Eat, drink, piss, belch … even shit if
forced by circumstance. I told you that. Why so surprised?"

"Do you ever get drunk?"

Her cheeks dimpled. "Let's have another glass and see."

Jessie appeared in a green dress wearing a seven-strand
collar of diamonds and emeralds on her throat interspersed with
ropes of seed pearls. A large emerald hung between her breasts
exactly where the ruby hung from Lorelei's and in a matching setting. Hers were a mirror-image of the ones Lorelei wore, but with

emeralds amongst the diamonds instead of rubies. Her glowing red hair formed a shining bun without a single strand out of place. Jessie took Lorelei's hand and gave her a lingering kiss as Audie stood twisting his glass of champagne. She approached him and did the same. "Greetings, young prince."

"Hello."

"We have reservations at the Palace for dinner. I hear you favor the establishment."

Suzanne giggled. "And after the Opera too."

Lorelei gazed out a bay window at the narrow garden and drank champagne. The thin flute just touched her lips as she rocked from one foot to the other. A fire in the hearth threw warm umber hues that shimmered in the green of her dress and rippled across her legs, and she stretched under the caress of Audie's gaze like a cat in the firelight.

"Has Lorelei taken you to the Opera?" Jessie asked.

"No."

"It's different. Hold her hand, and you'll be able to understand the words in French, as well as what the singer is actually thinking. Just don't laugh too much, or people will think you daft. It is such fun."

"Really?"

"You should know better by now than to ask that."

"For the sake of conversation. One feigns shock and amazement to give the teller of the story some sense of purpose when it comes to these things, especially concerning Lorelei."

Jessie gave him a wry smile. "How sophisticated you've become in your brief stay." She pressed lips to his cheek, "Let's not waste this while it's cold," and refilled his glass.

He fought an immediate arousal, and nodded as he watched Lorelei accept her third glass. She shot him a glance, cocked an eyebrow, and put a hand to her mouth as a belch rippled her throat.

He laughed.

Suzanne bounced on her heels. "Time to go!"

Starr pinned a corsage of one red rose on each of the women's breasts, a carnation on Audie's, and Belle opened the front door. The driver stood beside the open door of the limousine with a gloved hand out for Jessie. Lorelei grabbed Audie by the belt and lifted him into the car next to Jessie as he was about to hold his own hand out, and jumped in with a giggle. Suzanne got in the seat across from them with her back to the driver. The rustle of satin and the smell of perfume filled the car.

Audie grinned. Here he was sitting between the two most beautiful women in San Francisco: a Goddess and a Madam, or perhaps a Demigoddess and a Demimonde. Either way it was wondrous. In fact, as Izzy had pointed out, it was *mythic.* He yawned and stretched. It would be nice to have one of Izzy's Cuban cigars right now.

"Not on your life." Lorelei kissed his cheek with her own marvelous scent hovering beneath the perfume. She was right of course. To obscure such loveliness would be crass.

They headed down Ellis past the marble eminence of Lucky Baldwin's hotel where men in tuxedos and women in evening finery were waiting for taxis doormen hailed as women chatted and men smoked cigars. They crossed the Slot and drove down Market. Audie craned his neck to catch the golden dome of the Call, blazing against the sky like some ancient pagan temple. There was a crowd of vehicles on Mission as they passed Third, already lining up by the Grand Opera House. The limousine approached the Palace's arched entry where a crowd was waiting to do the same. The driver took the car out of gear, and they sat idling in line.

"Can't you get us in now somehow?"

Lorelei laughed. "Well, Audie, I suppose I could cause

some pandemonium or perhaps toss these poor souls every which way like a bitch out of Hell throwing a perfect fit, but I suggest we wait." She waved to an aquiline-featured young man wearing a silk top hat, tuxedo, white scarf, a gold cummerbund below his starched white shirt, and a black bow tie who leaned on an ivory cane inlaid with gold. The man gave her a little open-palmed wave as he studied her with obvious fascination, wearing his lust like the women wore their gems. Audie didn't like him.

"That's John Barrymore," Suzanne said, "he drops by the resort every time he's in town."

"Barrymore the actor?"

Mr. Barrymore blew a kiss to Jessie, then to Lorelei and Suzanne. Audie scowled.

Lorelei slapped his arm. "Stop it! You're lucky you never met Alex Pantages the Vaudeville entrepreneur. He was one of my lovers in Dawson City. You'd get into a fight with him at the drop of a hat. And believe me Audie, Alex may be older and shorter, but he has a mean streak that doesn't give quarter even when most would walk away from a man down. He didn't thrive in the north by living an illusion. He robbed his poor violet-eyed lover Klondike Kate to start that chain of theaters he's building." Her mouth turned down. "I'm afraid I may have had something to do with that, but never mind. But wouldn't it be stupid if you were actually killed fighting for something you can never win or conquer anyway, that only can choose to come to you? I've seen that for two-hundred and twenty-six years, and I'm so weary of it that I could scream."

"He's young," Jessie said, "which is why you treasure him."

"The young ones are so full of life. So substantial in a physical way when one is crying out for fulfillment. Not to mention Audie's particular endowment here, and without all that dreadful baggage and cynicism as of yet. I found him a sweet church-going boy, which made him so accessible."

"As long as they can hold their fire when the goods are on the table."

"I never have that problem."

"Of course, you get to play both roles and they don't even know it." Jessie made a theatrical sigh. "Even I can't make a cock obey one hundred percent of the time, either to perform or to get lost. That would be marvelous."

Suzanne giggled as the driver strove to ignore everything. Audie felt his face grow warm. Lorelei and Jessie squeezed his hands as the car was waved in to unload, and he let out his breath. They disembarked as his companions held gloved hands to their mouths. A young man in a taupe herringbone suit lit up upon sight of Leah, while his wife was looking the other way, and she gave him a small wave.

Men and women dressed in finery of the highest station watched them pass as they followed a stiff-walking fellow in a white coat to a booth. Several of the women huffed audibly as their eyes landed on Jessie, and many a man's eyes brightened. An elderly gentleman with a white beard put fingers in his palm, clapped softly, and Jessie gave him a lovely smile. For Lorelei, the eyes roved in curiosity and fascination tinged with awe. Audie grinned back at the faces around them as they were seated in the high-backed velvet canyon of a booth.

Jessie put gloved hands on the tablecloth. "I have a light repast ordered for us girls as these corsets are no great joy. You, Audie, will of course want more, being a source of sustenance yourself for our dear companion. I would suggest the terrapin for Audie, fruit salads for us girls, and a glass of champagne for Lorelei."

"I'd prefer rack of lamb." Audie examined the waxed moustache of the waiter that curled up to his ears. It bobbed as he offered a bottle of Moet champagne for inspection: a green magnum the size of a tree trunk. Jessie nodded, and the waiter opened it with a flourish underneath a white linen napkin with the crest of the Palace emblazoned on it in golden thread. Suzanne laughed as it popped. He was impressed with how much champagne Jessie and Suzanne could put away, though he suspected Suzanne might have had the advantage of Chief Wahoo or something to that effect. Her eyes were dilated. Women used belladonna drops for that also, and he couldn't really tell.

"Yes, Audie," Lorelei responded, "and your first guess was correct too."

"He noticed the cocaine." Jessie whispered as she lowered a fork to her salad.

"Are you sure you can't read my mind?"

"I am beside Lorelei, who complements my own abilities most wonderfully." She reached across Audie's lap to rub Lorelei's leg, and her hand stroked his crotch on the way back.

He gazed in Jessie's green eyes. They seemed to change color like Lorelei's. As he attempted to blink the vision away, he saw a flash of blood instead. Audie swallowed, "I ... I'm seeing things it appears."

Just the trace of a smile crossed Jessie's lips. "Not at all, Audie."

Suzanne put a hand on Lorelei's, and two apparently young women two-hundred and ten years apart in age stared into each other's eyes. Audie was dying to ask what was going on. Was Suzanne now part of their secret also? Lorelei ought to tell him. She'd said that she was a mere youth in terms of her own span, and he wondered what the two might have in common. Might she be inclined to tell such wild stories as Suzanne, but with infinitely more effect? How dangerous could that be? He tried to hide the thought, though she'd certainly caught it the instant of its birthing. He thought of Frank Flounder, *Toan,* and his cautionary tale of what he claimed had been a visit by Lorelei or one of her ilk to his people a century before—a *Liliot* amongst the tribes of the redwoods.

Lorelei kissed his cheek and drank champagne.

They left for the Opera shortly before nine with the car having returned to the door. The driver smelled of whiskey, but managed to deliver them safely to the ornate entrance of the Grand Opera House two blocks away.

People ascended the marble steps as uniformed doormen did whatever they did for the sake of making people feel they were above the common folk with the hope of compensation in their eyes. Jessie pressed money into the hand of a young man she seemed to know, and covertly squeezed his bottom as he turned to help someone else before they passed through the gilded doors. The place buzzed under the Corinthian columns of the foyer. The Opera House was like a huge barn encrusted with gilt, and strewn with bouquets of flowers until it smelled like a wedding or a funeral. An usher showed them their box to the left of the stage.

Some three thousand people were arriving, filling the seats below and rows of boxes on either side. The floor was a sea of nodding heads and sparkling throats, with the flash of carnations in men's lapels. There were orchids, roses, and narcissus in bunches and bouquets, their scent mixing with the perfume of ladies wearing tiaras, diamond dog collars, and rose corsages as the orchestra tuned in its pit.

"Look, there's Rudolph Spreckels, son of Claus, the Sugar King." Suzanne whispered, pointing to a gentleman with a much younger woman beside him in a box across from their own. "That's his wife, isn't she beautiful? And look how *pregnant* she is! And there's Mayor Schmitz."

Lorelei was staring at the young woman beside Rudolph Spreckels with what looked like envy. Audie studied the Mayor, a sharp-featured man with a high curly pompadour and a beard trimmed like a dark dagger. He somewhat looked like the Devil in his black suit with a diamond stick pin in the lapel. The blonde beside him wearing a cream-colored bare-shouldered gown had a diamond choker around her imperially slim neck and looked to be not more than eighteen. Audie mused diamonds must be rather hard to come by on a mayor's salary, until he remembered the Poodle Dog and the Municipal Crib. There must be many such irons the Mayor had in the fire in a town like this.

"Everything you can imagine," Lorelei whispered, "but he's rather out of sorts tonight, what with friends dying mysteriously and worrying about court in the morning."

The Mayor was trying not to stare at Lorelei, as were most men in the audience and a good deal of the women. She was a diamond amongst the dross of humanity, shining before royal purple curtains at the back of the box. The young blonde beside the Mayor stared fixedly at her, but kept turning away when Audie sought to catch her eyes.

"That's one of Tessie Wall's girls with the Mayor," Suzanne said. "Every one's a blonde, and there's dear Violet with ol' Abe Ruef. She gave me such a *look*. Bet she can't *wait* to get out of here. He bought that girl Cassandra who's with Schmitz tonight too. She's great. We did a date together, and I'd like to get her to come over to Jessie's. And there's Chief of Police Jeremiah Dinan with his wife. He waved at Jessie when his wife wasn't looking, but you were staring at Cassandra of course. Oh, and there's Donaldina Cameron. God, look how she's looking

daggers at us! She's a Christian crusader out to close all
the cribs and resorts, and to rescue the Chinese slave girls
from the tongs." Suzanne took a handkerchief and waved
at Mrs. Cameron until Jessie put a hand on her arm to
make her stop.

Audie studied the white-haired woman in a box
across from them with the hard light of contempt in her eyes.
Lorelei was in turn watching her with a tranquil expression on
her own face. "She'll never know we are not enemies," she whispered, "how sad."

The woman found Lorelei's eyes, and Audie saw the hatred
in her own began to fade. Mrs. Cameron glanced down at her
hands, the orchestra began its opening theme to *Carmen,* and the
gigantic crystal chandelier hanging from the ornate painted roof
dimmed.

"What did you do?"

"Just loved her Audie, that's all." Lorelei removed her
gloves, took his hand, and did the same with Jessie. Suzanne
put her hand on Lorelei's arm.

Suddenly Audie could hear an argument going on behind
the curtain to the right of the stage. Madame Fremstad, all two
hundred pounds of her, was complaining in a thick Germanic
accent to someone named Antonio Scotti about the outrageous
fee Caruso was being paid. It was obvious that Caruso and the
Madame had no love for each other. Caruso had been quite
rude, as he was still livid about the drubbing the critics had given
his last singing partner for her performance in *The Queen of Sheba*
the night before at the Alhambra. Scotti desperately tried to calm
the Madame as the curtain rose, explaining that Caruso was a sensitive artist, and didn't mean to offend the Madame herself.

She huffed as she walked onto the stage to begin an aria.
Gott verdamnt! The little man is an artistic dwarf! A vain-glori-

ous idiot! A goddamn mental midget!"

The four in the box burst into laughter, and fell into muffled chuckling as heads turned toward them. Audie sat bolt upright, fascinated as the French the Madame sang ran through his mind. He could follow it as clearly as if it were from his own voice even as he realized she didn't know half of it herself beyond the pronunciation. Lorelei probably knew it by heart, as she'd most likely been to the Opera many times in many places. She knew the mind of the one singing anyway. *So this is how you perceive mere mortals.*

From behind him, a white-coated arm offered champagne. He took it with his free hand, a thank you, and a tip from money that appeared in his pocket.

By the time the short figure of Enrico Caruso appeared, the little party in their box was well along. Lorelei informed everyone Caruso wore a gun under his cummerbund against the small of his back, which was the cause of an occasional grimace under his makeup as it dug into him, provoking more stifled laughter from their box.

Jessie produced an ivory whale's tooth from her purse that was scrimshawed with nymphs and satyrs in a chain of lust running in a spiral around it rising to a silver cap. It looked like the relief upon the doors of the Hippodrome on Pacific. She opened the cap and extracted a tiny silver spoon from a trough in the side of the tooth. She took a spoonful of the powder within, put it to her nose, inhaled daintily into one nostril, repeated the act for the other, and handed the tooth to Suzanne.

Suzanne did the same, and spilled a bit of the powder between her breasts as she did so. She grinned and put a finger to her lips, touched the tip to the powder, and licked it.

Audie let go of Lorelei's hand. "What is that?" Caruso's voice was echoing in his mind in French, and he couldn't concentrate on anything else when he could understand every word.

"It's magic dust—" Suzanne began.

Lorelei took the horn and spoon from Suzanne's hands, snorted some of the stuff into her own lovely nose, and Audie's mouth fell open. "I can act like a foolish person occasionally, she whispered as she handed him the tooth, "plenty of time to be serious later. Way too much from my perspective."

Audie took the offered receptacle of cocaine and let out his breath. "Oh, what the hell." He took some of the stuff with the spoon and inhaled. It burned like snuff, and his first instinct was to sneeze. He did the other nostril, and felt a rush of blood in his brain. A fizzing sensation like carbonated soda roiled through his skull, and he gasped. Suzanne giggled.

"Wipe your nose," Jessie whispered.

Lorelei gasped. "I have got to pee!" They burst into laughter as she brushed a strand of hair from her face. "What's so funny?" She giggled, and disappeared out of the box.

"That's new," Audie said after catching his breath.

"Still think she's a Goddess?"

"You tell me, Jessie."

Jessie was silent for a moment as the opera sang on. "She's what all women would love to be, I suppose."

"Her burden is terrible and huge."

"She has let us both know that, still—" Jessie's green eyes reflected the footlights as she leaned her elbows on the brass railing, "I'd take the pain with the pleasure. There's enough in life anyway."

"The power would be tempting I suppose."

Jessie stared at him, and shook her head. "The *love!* You don't have to be a man to go where she goes when you're in her bed."

"How does she—"

"She doesn't have to feed, she can take anyone. Lorelei isn't just here for men, and her beloved are yet to be discovered. She's different than those who came before her, just as is this time in which we live. Have you ever visited the ruins of the Mediterranean?"

"Only read of them, and seen the pictures."

"I saw them in the company of a magnate of the White Star Line. Ismay was a cad, but the ruins made it worthwhile as we cruised the Aegean in his yacht. Off the coast of Turkey, I climbed to where a temple stood where the empire of Lydia reigned, and made love to a glorious shepherd boy on an altar under that huge Mediterranean moon. Quite a surprise for him I assure you. Remember Croesus?"

"The king who was so rich?"

"Yes. There was a rather strange goddess, a wild thing in the mountains of Anatolia beyond his kingdom who fed on the blood of men for her sustenance. From their *loins,* Audie. Her lover Attis cut his balls from his body when he made the discovery she was also his father, having been castrated by the Greek gods who had no affection for such a being who was until then of both sexes, which quite bothered the gods of the West I'd wager. The spilled blood gave rise to pomegranate trees on her mountain, Mount Agdos, and the fruit impregnated a young princess who ate of it." Jessie laughed. "I love those stories. Her father the King was ashamed, and sent her out into the country to have her bastard child in a shepherd's hut. She brought Attis into the world, and rather than kill him as ordered she gave him to the shepherd's family. He grew up in the wilderness to eventually become the lover of a wild girl who actually was a goddess who was his father through her blood. This being roamed the wilderness, and none could tame—"

Audie tingled from the drug as he strove to follow her sto-

ry. "I see you too are trying to puzzle the mystery of our mutual
friend," he finally got out.

"*Lover*, Audie, or should I say *beloved*. The priests of that goddess Cybele had to publicly castrate themselves when sanctified in
her service. Something to see as they performed the act in their
processions I suppose." Jessie chuckled. "I know girls who'd pay
to see that. The ceremony was called the *Hilaria*. The word hilari-
ous comes from it, but we've lost the sarcasm Romans attached to
it. They invited her to the Palentine Hill when their oracles said it
was the only way they could win the Punic War with Carthage,
but were horrified when they saw the spectacle of what they'd
welcomed. And those Romans had pretty strong stomachs
what with their own blood entertainments."

Audie rubbed his temples. "That's dreadful."

Suzanne made a face. "Ich."

"Boo!" They jumped in their seats as Lorelei burst through
the curtains. "That goddamn corset is the pits!" She'd lost the
offending piece of clothing, and a flash of white skin shone between buttons as she sat down. "Entertaining people with stories of my relatives again, Jessie?" She chuckled. "I do so want
to let my hair down too. Perhaps I'll go north next winter to enjoy
the long nights and indigenous residents. I never have to put it
up at all amongst the Indians."

They left during the sixth of nine curtain calls for Caruso
and rode to the Palace in an open carriage. A yellow moon appeared in the eastern sky as they turned on Market above the Ferry
Building, with its golden clock like a celestial body on the face
of the tower.

Audie smiled, sanguine in the knowledge he was on his
way to some wondrous saturnalia. His head was light, and he
felt an anticipatory thump in his groin. Lorelei had taken off her

hat and was pulling at her hair, removing barrettes and pins. A shimmering cascade fell over the back seat in the streetlights. She stood up in the carriage and held her hands out as her hair trailed in a light breeze. "Yes!" she shouted in a too-strong voice for a woman of this Edwardian age.

The horses bolted, and she was nearly thrown from the carriage. From another carriage behind came the shouting of the driver as his steeds pranced sideways. Dogs erupted in a chorus of howls to the south, where the working class neighborhoods began on the other side of Mission.

Lorelei sat down hard. "Whoa," she grabbed Audie's arm, "*there's* something!"

"You certainly spooked those animals."

"That wasn't me. There's a lot moving in the world besides yours truly. That was an earthquake, Audie."

"What?"

"Feel it? I've been feeling it all night, but I've been too caught up in my own doings to pay much attention."

"Just a little shaker," Jessie said as they pulled up to the Palace.

XXVII.

The Barracoon

Cruel laughter awoke her. Lorelei rubbed her temples, arose from amongst her friends, and stepped to the window. The moon hung high in the east over mountains behind Oakland and bathed the distant dome of Mt. Diablo in its light. She raised the casement to let the night air waft over her, and heard the honking of a horn and the shouting of a drunk below. Moonlight shone across the room's wainscoting of polished laurel, reflected in the crystal of the chandelier, and made the maroon satin wallpaper blue around the marble fireplace. A bedspread lay on the Persian carpet in a deep purple pile.

The breathing of Audie, Jessie and Suzanne was untroubled, for she had sunk them deep in dreams. They'd succumbed to her spell of sleep even as they were engaged in coupling and the bedsprings groaned beneath their sweating bodies. With the cocaine in their blood, they would have gone on past dawn, and she had business to attend to. She hadn't fed as it would have monopolized Audie, but had devoted herself to bringing all of them into a place where their loving was just beyond the attainment of mortals, and held them there as the orgasm that was her birthright devoured all separateness.

She closed her eyes and listened to songs of whales in the Bay. As was her habit, she began to come loose in time, and saw children playing on a beach, the lingering spirit of the Miwok people whose land this was. For a moment she felt as they did, that the world balanced on the back of a turtle. Did they worry about falling off? It felt like that as she held up a whole world for her friends to explore. But now she was unsettled, both from the silly drug she'd allowed into her system and the stimulation without release of sex, sans the ingestion of blood.

She glided to the bathroom to void the remnants of champagne, walked to the fifth floor window, and stepped onto a ledge five stories above Market. She didn't need to dress for the task at hand as the only witnesses would never speak a word of what they had seen. Most assuredly they would not tell.

She sprang to the roof, where a huge American flag snapped in the breeze aglow with light coming through the glass dome over the central vault of the Palace. She glanced past tattered clouds at pale horsetails of ice drifting high above the world in moonlight and leapt over Market in one bound. Like the breeze, she moved through the night over rooftops toward Chinatown to a basement under Jackson Street where a slave auction was getting underway.

There would be no raid. Lem Hip had paid the police, and the threat from the Hatchet Sons of the Wah Ting San Fongs and their allies the Mock Chins was greatly reduced by the presence of thirty of his own On Yick and Suey Sing highbinders. There were worthy guards in the alley, at the doors and on the three floors above watching every approach with guns and blades at the ready.

The boatload of girls had barely made it into port after a long layover in Vancouver, in which some meddlesome Crown authority had given his Captain ulcers with demands for further bribes, making this auction the most expensive in memory. A minimum of three thousand for the poorest girl in the bunch was not unreasonable with the market so constrained. It was necessity.

Charley Sep Ye Hung had sent his number one man, Lee Chuck. Lee Chuck had his own crib above the fish stalls of Cum Cook Alley, and Lem Hip's sources had informed him that he had just sent four girls to a 'hospital' in Cooper Alley to die now that a fresh shipment had arrived. Lee Chuck was here out of necessity also. Lem Hip grinned, and twisted his queue between long-nailed fingers.

His guards watched each bidder as he entered and moved to sit in the chair placed for him. Most came dressed in traditional garb, though a few wore dark business suits and bowler hats. Glasses of sam shu were offered by a perfumed courtesan in a traditional golden silk dress slit to the thigh. She hurried past the shivering girls with a scowl, and a silk handkerchief to her face, though they were all quite clean by the time they arrived at the Queen's Room.

Two bidders hesitated before tasting the liquor, and Lem Hip frowned. Those men were fools. No one would drug or poison such an assemblage and survive the repercussions, let alone keep Face. He stroked his queue, and sighed. It would be a great relief when the killers of Fong Ah Sing were found and summarily punished. Of course they could have taken a boat back to the Flowery Kingdom, or gone into hiding in one of the Chinatowns along the coast all the way to Vancouver.

Who knew? Lem Hip himself didn't believe for a moment the writer of the chung hung was an On Yick, and certainly his assessment was gaining ground amongst anyone with a thimble-full of sense between his ears. Charlie and Lee Chuck supported his view, which had made this twice put-off auction possible. It had been a good ploy though, hanging a man's head like that and writing the chung hung in his own blood.

How had they driven that spike into solid brick without attracting attention? His men had combed the neighborhood, threatening and bribing likely witnesses without any results whatsoever. *Very strange.* Lem Hip shrugged off the bad feelings brought by his contemplation of the killing and took a long sip of sam shu. The inventory was coming in.

Twenty-nine naked and frightened girls were being herded onto a platform in the middle of the room, the youngest being eleven and the oldest seventeen. That one would go cheap, having only three or four good years left. Then again, she was ready to go to work and looked healthy after the voyage. Lem Hip would take no less than three thousand for her also. Otherwise his profit would be not worth the trouble after paying the authorities in Victoria to release the *City of Peking* to finish her voyage, and buying an extra set of forged papers from his contacts at the Hall of Records saying all the girls were married to legal residents to avoid the Exclusion Act.

One of the youngest shrieked as an elderly man slapped her buttocks and made her bend over for inspection, to the laughter of the bidders and highbinders in the room. When satisfied she was not damaged beyond use, or perhaps even a virgin, he made a mark on a sheet of paper and moved to the next girl who was about fourteen. She dutifully bent over and spread the lips between her legs.

Lem Hip nodded. That one was obedient, pretty, and would fetch top money. Lee Chuck moved around to take a closer look at the girl while she was showing her teeth, and Lem Hip grinned. Dah Pah Tsin had coached her well in being compliant and dutiful, and he should complement the old woman for her effort. A woman to handle girls was a blessing in this business. No wonder Charley Hung was so filthy rich with a partner like that. Girls were always compliant at the hands of an older woman it seemed. He should find one.

The girls had been made to smoke *ah pin yin* before going on the dais, and a tall thin one tottered from the effects of the opium. She hissed at the man who made them bend over and show what they had between their legs, going so far as to raise her hand as if to strike him. The man cuffed her across the face with the back of a silk-covered arm, and she landed on the rough boards to loud laughter. Two Hatchet Sons jumped on the platform, grabbed her arms, and bent her over for inspection. One put his fingers in her, and spread her open as she moaned. Someone shined an expensive electric flashlight up her that he had saved for just such a moment to muttered comments of the other bidders and Hatchet Sons. The boo how doy turned her around, placed her feet on a certain spot, and commanded her to remain unmoving as they escorted the 'doctor' in charge of inspections down the line.

The girl put fingers to a swollen cheek. She brushed hair from her eyes, and sneered at their backs with a face full of hate, eliciting more laughter from the men. Whoever bought that one, her first lesson would be a good whipping and the servicing of a dozen lusty soldiers. After that she would be glad to settle down in the relative peace of the cribs. She had no chance whatsoever that a rich man might take a liking to her and take her somewhere she might service him alone, or perhaps even marry her. Men of Face do not tolerate surly girls. She was too tall as well and held her shoulders much too straight, instead of the inward-turning posture of submission.

He wondered if Number Two, the compliant one, might be so lucky. He could see keeping her himself if the bidding went his way, but she'd probably be the first to go. Lee Chuck looked ready to begin bidding on her before it was even proper. He'd get forty-two for that one, perhaps even forty-five.

A shout from the floor above and the pounding of running feet made him jump from his chair. For a moment, he wondered if Police Commissioner Drinkhouse had taken his money and betrayed him. It sounded as if the Fan Kwei had sent the Flying Squad even at this dark hour into the building as there was no gunfire, which would instantly greet any raid by the Wah Ting San Fong or the Mock Chins.

Dust drifted down from the ceiling between boards, and the yellow bulbs swayed as those in the basement waited for the splintering of furniture and cursing in thick Celtic brogues that would say it was the police.

There was a hoarse scream.

The black-hatted tong soldiers at the doors slid pistols and hatchets out of their shirts as four boo how doy shoved a red lacquered cabinet away from the far wall. The barred door to the tunnel that led under Jackson to the basement of a joss house was being opened in case they needed to flee. An On Yick slid a short Winchester shotgun out from over the door frame, and jacked a shell into the chamber. There was another scream from the room above, and three quick gunshots, followed by a gurgling howl. Lem Hip shuddered, as he envisioned someone being disemboweled.

Like a heard of cattle the bidders in the room began to move toward the tunnel, to the curses of Lem Hip, who was wishing bloody death on whoever was ruining his auction. Boo how doy were whipping the girls into a knot in the far corner at the command of Lee Chuck, shoving cotton blouses and trousers into their hands and commanding them to dress. The girls needed no encouragement, and began donning the clothes as the single row of bulbs over their heads went out.

Lem Hip blinked as darkness engulfed him. He pushed his way toward the tunnel where a light was moving down the passage, only to hear a shrill shout of one of the highbinders who was leading the rest under the street with a storm lantern in one hand and a pistol in the other. "Get away, Devil!"

It was the voice of the Hatchet Son who called himself Fat Choy, Good Fortune, who'd killed more enemies than any other man in the living ranks of the On Yicks. Fat Choy had laughed when six assassins caught him in Waverly Place two years ago. He'd sent four of them back to China in boxes, and left the other two horribly maimed. He wore a necklace when he went to war fashioned of his enemies' ears.

Lem Hip waited for the sound of Fat Choy's Colt pistol, but there was another scream, and the crowd in the tunnel turned as one and rushed back into the Queen's Room, stumbling over one another in the dark as they fled whatever fate had met Fat Choy. Something bounced against the tunnel wall and rolled to a stop against Lem Hip's feet. The bidder with the electric flashlight flicked it on, and Lem Hip gazed at the object that had touched him. It was Fat Choy's head. He gasped, slid down against the damp brick wall, and began to crawl toward the stairs.

The beam darted wildly about the room as dust motes drifted across terrified faces. Four boo how doy had their pistols trained on the door that led from the floor above, waiting for the attack they knew was coming. One of the Suey Sing soldiers seized the light from the bidder and held it as five men closed the mouth of the tunnel. The highbinder with the shotgun had it trained on the passage beyond the heavy iron slab as it ground shut on the concrete floor, and three boo how doy shoved the cabinet back in front of it, re-sealing the passage.

The lacquered wood exploded with a roar as the door was shoved through the wooden cabinet. The three men went flying with great splinters in them, to writhe on the damp floor. A gout of blood pumped from the throat of one, making a brilliant red arc in the flashlight's beam as the man's heels scraped on the planks. The soldier with the shotgun cursed, and aimed into the dark portal, his ragged breathing loud in the sudden silence of the Queen's Room.

Soft laughter came from the darkness beyond.

To Lem Hip it was most chilling, for it did not fit within his sense of the world, nor the bounds of conception for any sane man. It froze him where he stood. It was the pleasant voice of a woman, like music upon tranquil waters. He had a vision of willows over a misty stream, and pavilions filled with girls of the highest breeding. An Imperial Palace was the place for such a sound, not this hole hidden under Dupont Gai in a place some called Barracoon, like the Fan Kwei's slave houses of old.

The tall girl made a guttural laugh. "She's *here,* you shits!"

"Loy gee, hai dai!" A too-lovely voice came from the stygian blackness of the tunnel, and the sweetest scent wafted for an instant in Lem Hip's nostrils.

A brilliant flash accompanied the shotgun's report as lead pellets whined off the brick passage beyond. There was a chorus of clicks, as the man's hatchet brothers raised their pistols.

The flashlight flew from the hands of the Suey Sing soldier to go spinning across the platform where generations of girls had been sold, coming to rest as a pale form wreathed in dark locks darted through the light of the beam with the heads of six tong soldiers swinging by their queues. Lem Hip quaked on the floor, as he beheld a demon with eyes the color of blood whose laughter was impossibly beautiful. A warm hand closed around his throat, and the basement heaved with a jolt that sent bricks popping from the walls accompanied by screams as the beams overhead split asunder.

XXVIII.

April 18, 1906, 5:13 a.m.
The Broken Coast

Slolux leaned against the wall of his cell as he had every day
for the last sixteen years, praying to his ancestors to smash
this hell rock in the midst of the water. A yellow waning moon
hung in the west, greeting the gray dawn beyond the bars of his
window. Something flew out of a fog bank across the moon—a
great bird crossing the Bay. He closed his eyes.

A ripple began beneath his ribs as if his heart was near to
bursting, and a sound from the stone of the island became an
all-encompassing roar. He was thrown from his bunk as the
fortress of Alcatraz shuddered around him. The wall before him
collapsed outward as if swept by giant hands molding the mud
of men's lives to their will, and fell into a crack that opened
across the center of the island. The fat half-moon hung where
his window had been moments before.

Slolux rose to his feet and blew dust from his mouth.
He wiped his eyes, staggered around a gaping defile that had
appeared in the middle of the island, and out into the yard as
another ripple went through the rocks, like someone shaking a
blanket.

"There!" He lost his footing and sat down hard. Slolux
crossed his legs on the bucking stones, and screamed at the broken parapets in his mother Modoc tongue, *"There, y*ou bastards!
Sons of bitch dogs! Fuck you, and your mothers too!"

Slolux picked himself up again, slapped dust from his

gray prison dungarees, and lifted a door that had burst from the collapsing soldier's quarters like a bit of cottonwood down in the wind. He clambered down the rocky flank of the accursed island and tossed the door into the water, lay upon it, and began paddling toward the green hills across the Bay.

The voices of the deep were loud as he hovered where Lorelei had left him. Tendrils of his self reached out to touch her perfect flesh, her knowing presence that had become his sense of sanity as they walked beside that river. Without a mouth, he called across the depths of a pleasant sea where he had been lulled into near-forgetting. The songs of whales rippled through his flesh, the pleas of girls and the laughter of children. He was a young man standing before an ancient altar, fearless, and full of gratitude. He tossed in the current, winnowing those voices that stitched the seams of the world for the one voice that would grow ever clearer as he focused upon it, to become the song of his Love. He reached out with his entire being, but amongst the din of souls there was only an awful pit, a *void*. Utter silence, where once had been Lorelei.

She is dead!

Lorelei was dead and her line was ended. The golden thread of her heart was broken, and he would float forever in chaos as would a whole unknowing world. The rainbow-eyed girl who could ford that stream to the other side of longing was gone.

They were thrown into the air in a tangle of limbs, and six eyes opened to see the chandelier spinning about the room like a storm of diamonds in a fog-gray sky. A roar rose out of the bowels of the earth through the building into the bones of their bodies. Suzanne gripped him like a vice, buried her face in his chest, and moaned. Her mouth was hot and wet against his skin.

"Goddamn it!" Jessie shouted.

The mirror over the fireplace split. A brick dropped into the neat pile of logs placed in the English hearth with a dull thud, and a clatter as more followed. Then, silence.

Audie burst off a bed that had crossed the room, and tottered naked before the shattered window. Jessie and Suzanne stood before him covered with plaster dust from the ceiling that made them look rolled in flour, with their waist-length red hair at all angles. Their eyes were wide with terror as Audie swiped dust from his face.

"What!?"

"Earthquake, Audie, it's an earthquake!"

They stared at each other while the world trembled as if fighting for breath. Suzanne rubbed her eyes.

There was that sound again, growing from the ground like a million trains in the night carrying a thousand mountains, rushing like earthen waves on the backs of dragons. The hotel rocked like a bone in the mouth of a dog, and they were thrown to the floor. Audie bounced on the mattress and grunted as Jessie's elbow caught him in the stomach. The rattle of bricks popping out of the two-foot thick walls of the Palace and cascading down was a storm of horse's hooves galloping into the street.

Suzanne's eyes were as big as dinner plates. "Let's get the hell out of here!"

As they got to their feet, Audie glanced out the window. The Grand Hotel across the street had no outer walls, and he gazed into rooms where beds and tables hung over empty voids at a man who was about to urinate into a toilet that was now four stories below him. Audie wondered for a moment if he could hit the bowl.

"I'll be damned if I run out naked! If I live through this, people aren't saying Jessie Hayman ran naked and screaming from anywhere in this goddamn town. Fuck that!"

An adrenalin-fueled chuckle rippled Audie's lips. "I think it's over. Let's get our clothes on, ladies."

"I'm with you." Jessie began to rummage about for her dress as Suzanne did the same. "These are the wrong damn duds for a day like this!"

"You can say that again." Suzanne fought with her petticoat, made an angry little grunt, wadded it up, and threw it on the floor.

"Where's Lorelei?"

"Audie, don't worry. If anyone in this town can keep her ass in one piece, that girl can."

They went out into the hall where people stood dazed in various stages of undress. From suite 580 two doors down, Enrico Caruso appeared with a dusty beard. He glanced at the crowd and blinked before stepping back into his room and slamming the door that bounced back as the frame was no longer square. Curses in Italian echoed within, followed by shouting at someone in the room as if the man's incompetence surely had caused this.

They skirted the twisted gilt cages of the elevators, took the stairs, and joined a crowd fleeing onto Market and Montgomery Streets. As they made the sidewalk, a voice rang out from the fifth floor in the familiar tenor of Caruso. "*La fanta mi salva, L'immondo ritrova!*" came the words from an Opera, and several people applauded.

"Bravo!" shouted a white-haired gentleman clad only in a topcoat, crimson boxers, and shiny black shoes.

Jessie slapped dust from her dress. "I've got to check on my girls!"

Audie nodded. He took their hands, and they pushed through the milling half-dressed mass, he in his herringbone coat with his dusty shirt open, Jessie and Suzanne in green satin dresses sans makeup with their long red hair tied back and white with dust.

In the middle of Market, a streetcar lay on its side with a woman's legs protruding from beneath it. Electric cables sparked on the pavement. A man approached the legs, but danced away from a black cable as it began to rear up and strike out in his direction like a snake. They gave it a wide berth.

The north side of the street was higher as the curb had separated from the pavement, and they had to step up. The Midway Plaisance had clouds of dust floating from big green doors that had sprung open. A boy carried away a framed poster of The Girl in Blue. A man pushed a baby carriage full of whiskey bottles toward Union Square, where the Saint Francis Hotel stood shrouded in dust. The Dewey monument before it stood surrounded by shattered pieces of its base amongst ten thousand cherry blossoms shaken from trees in the square. The obelisk rose from their midst like the pistil of a flower throwing its seed to the wind.

The Chronicle Building swarmed with people as if the next edition of the paper were underway. Audie turned to look at the Palace. It seemed nearly untouched by the cataclysm, though the Grand Hotel next to it had lost its walls. The golden crowns of the Call and Spreckles towers stood in the first light of dawn as if no great shake had happened above Market, though the Call seemed somewhat off-plumb to Audie's eye. There was a flicker as flames appeared in a window on the sixth floor. Dark mushrooms of smoke rose to the south of Market.

They passed a pile of bricks three men were trying to remove from the sidewalk. One looked up at Audie and waved. "We got a fellow under here! Give us a hand!"

He'd turned to render aid, when he felt Suzanne's tug on his arm. "What's the use? He's dead!" The men looked at each other, shrugged, and walked away in different directions.

At Dupont the view to the north was utter desolation. The Chronicle building at the corner was relatively unscathed but for glass and plaster around its base and a few loose bricks people kicked out of their way, but other buildings were mere shells whose sides had sloughed away into the street atop pedestrians, carriages and motorcars. Smoke was rising from the direction of Delmonico's on O'Farrell. The exclusive Bohemian Club at the corner of Post had collapsed across the street within the ruins of the Shreve Building. Two men picked valuables out of the wreckage of a jewelry store on the ground floor as people and horses screamed. Broken water mains made fountains that washed blood into gutters, and a body rotated in a crimson whirlpool where the water ran down a drain. The hiss of broken gas mains came from all directions. A few blocks up Dupont was the chaos of Chinatown with multicolored piles of walls and red tile roofs at all angles. The ruins seemed to boil under a smoky haze.

Jessie put a hand to her mouth. "Can anyone be alive in there?"

An ashen-faced adolescent wearing a spring bonnet and nightgown tottered down Dupont, holding her bloody right arm and staring at the sidewalk. Audie ran to catch her as she collapsed on the pavement. Jessie swore, and began tearing the bottom of her dress into strips. She bandaged the poor girl's arm as best she could before a woman appeared, cried out the girl's name, and embraced her. They got up to go, leaving the two sobbing on the curb crying out to Jesus.

They stepped over big cracks in the sidewalk at Powell. The cable car turnaround had a car on it, but the tracks beyond had risen out of the ground and were twisted into spirals above the cobblestones. To their left, Market Street bulged as if a blister had risen from the flesh of the City.

"Gas main," a man said as he hurried past, "hear it hissin'?

She'll burn soon enough!"

The Baldwin Hotel at the corner was seething confusion with men piling belongings onto cars and wagons as women and children cried. People declared that they had to make for Telegraph Hill or Twin Peaks, as their elevations were safer, and a great tidal wave was imminent from the Bay. Others hurried in the direction from which Audie, Jessie and Suzanne had come, toward the Ferry Building and wharves for escape to Oakland or anywhere at all.

A man stopped piling trunks on a wagon when he saw Jessie. "Miss Hayman," he pointed up Ellis, "don't go that way! The whole city will burn! The water mains are broken, and gas is leaking everywhere! You must find a boat! Look, over there!" He pointed across Market to where the windows of a seven-story building glowed red. Flames licked at the lower ones as smoke billowed from its roof. The Call building was alight, with its gilded top sparking against the sky like a roman candle against the bloody clouds of dawn.

"I'll be fucked if I leave my girls to this!" Jessie snapped, and hurried up Ellis.

The house had shed some roofing, and the chimneys were collapsed. The gilt pillars around its bay windows were twisted at crazy angles, and the red silk curtain flapped in the breeze from the third floor. The heavy oaken doors stood open on the gilded parlor with their panels of stained glass strewn across the green travertine steps. A portion had been swept clean on which sat eight comely young women in bloomers, evening wear, and nightgowns, Starr with a blanket around her, Belle in a yellow calico dress with a loaf of sourdough bread, and Wa Chin the cook. At the sight of Jessie, they stood and cheered.

"How is the house?"

"It stands, ma'am," Violet replied, "but I don't think for long."

Jessie huffed, "We'll see!" and hurried up the steps.

Audie watched her disappear into the house as a feeling he had somewhere else to be engulfed him. The last twelve days had brought a sense of belonging he had never before dreamed of, let alone known. Now he felt utterly forsaken. Where *was* she?

Suzanne took his hand. "I don't want to stay here."

"Neither do I."

"Where shall we go?"

"I must go to Russian Hill, to check on Lorelei."

"May I go with you?"

He turned to the girl who had begun his adventure in San Francisco, swept her up in his arms, and embraced her. "What kind of creature would I be to refuse you? Of *course* you may! But you must dress in clothes that can hold up for a long time and take only money, as we must carry everything. I don't think you'll see this house again. The fires will get here sooner or later."

"What of the firemen?"

"They won't have enough water to put out one hundredth of the fires. All the pipes are broken. Didn't you see that water on Dupont?"

She nodded. "I won't be a minute. Want some breakfast?"

"With champagne?"

"Why not? While it's still cold at least."

He wiped dust from his face. "It would be wonderful to take a shower," and followed her into the house.

* **

Wa Chin produced a repast from the pantry that didn't need cooking, for the sound of gas hissed in the bowels of the house. They broke out Russian caviar, tinned Danish herring, oysters and French cheeses. The little party spread cambert on sourdough bread, spooned caviar, speared stuffed peppers from Mexico, and washed it down with Mumms champagne. It was one of the best meals Audie had ever had, there by broken bay windows and flapping lace curtains above an empty garden with grapes on a whitewashed trellis coming into leaf. After they'd eaten, Belle produced jeans and boots for him. Jessie had quite a wardrobe of men's clothes on hand.

Most of the fires seemed to be to the south of Market for the time being, and toward the Bay where the sky had a red glow lit below by flames, and from behind by a rising sun.

Jessie kicked aside broken dishes in the kitchen. "Here," she set a worn leather bag on the table with a thud.

"What is it?"

"Take a look,"

Audie opened it, and a small hoard of gold coins spilled out from a nest of ancient bills in morning light. He picked one up, and Suzanne took another. It was a near-new condition twenty-dollar double eagle, minted in eighteen-fifty at the San Francisco Mint.

"She wanted you to have this if you ever got separated. I'd say now's the occasion."

"Bobby Giles."

"What?"

"Bobby Giles, this is some of the gold he robbed from John Geary's offices in Portsmouth Square fifty-six years ago."

"Whatever. He's dead now and has a street named after him to boot, so I doubt he'll be looking for it. I'd put it in a good money belt like this," Jessie threw the aforementioned item on the table, "and then make like I didn't know it existed. Put the paper money in your inner pockets and the lining of your coat. Where's your gun?"

"Upstairs."

"Get it, dear heart."

"You're a wonderful woman to know at a time like this."

Jessie's emerald eyes brimmed with mirth. She poured a glass of champagne and held it in a toast. "I've got to check on my other girls and my house on Post. My neighbors there don't even know my profession. It's all stone and brick, and I can put up the girls there for the time being if it's not too damaged, and there's a limousine with a tank full of petrol in the garage across the street. Want to go with me?"

"I can't."

Jessie sighed. "I know. I suppose I was seeing if I could for just one moment snatch you away from her while she's somewhere else." She shook her head. "God, she's good."

"She is isn't she?"

"The best, Audie. Let's hope we both see her again."

"Why do you say that?"

"I can't feel her."

He felt as if he were struggling to awaken from his dream of the morning, and ran a hand across his face. "She can't be dead."

"No, she's very preoccupied I'm sure."

"We will stay in touch somehow."

"If she wills it and she's alive, it's a certainty."

They embraced as smoke rose from roofs a block away, rocking in each other's arms for a too-brief moment. Suzanne sniffed, hugged them both, and ran upstairs to change.

Suzanne returned in a smart pair of khaki jodhpurs, tall brown boots, a tan blouse with floral embroidery across the shoulders, and tan leather gloves. The pockets of the jodhpurs and a small lead-beaded clutch purse were stuffed with money and jewelry. Violet had braided Suzanne's hair into a red rope down her back. She looked ready for a ride in the country or a game of polo, and Audie complemented her.

"Rather more fitting today than satin, eh?"

"Indeed."

Violet gave Suzanne a kiss, squeezed her hard, and they embraced for a few breaths before Violet disappeared upstairs. Jessie reappeared in the parlor, where small bags of belongings were piled on the loveseats and couches. She was allowing only the very essentials as she had girls from houses on Mason and Divisadero to carry, and admonished them not to be greedy. She leaned a pump shotgun against the wall and tossed a bandolier of buckshot shells on the couch. "Lucky I'm prepared."

"Admirably as always, Madame Hayman."

They said their last goodbyes and stepped down to Ellis.

He wanted to get a look at their situation from on high, so they headed toward Mason and the slope of Nob Hill. A cable car sat buried amongst bricks and smashed wagons at its base. Horse hooves protruded from the wreckage. When they passed the Poodle Dog, the bartender from the third floor was stacking champagne bottles in a wheelbarrow. Suzanne snatched up a cobblestone, and with an excellent overhand pitch threw it at the tilted sign proclaiming **Poulet d'Or.** It bounced off with a resounding crack. "Good riddance!"

The man looked up in surprise, and her face split in an evil grin as she picked up another stone and threw it at him. "Eek!" he shrieked, dropping a bottle that exploded in green glass and foam before he sprinted up the crooked steps.

"I thought you enjoyed the high life."

She wiped a strand of hair from her face. "It's not so lovely with that bunch. Hope the fucking lot of them burn!"

They glanced up the steep rise of Mason where the mansions of Nob Hill glowed pink and white in morning sun around the cream-colored bulk of the brand new Fairmont hotel and the spires of Grace Cathedral. The castle-like parapets of several homes were collapsed, yet two tall chimneys that seemingly should have fallen first stood above a sagging roofline near the summit. Horse hooves clattered on the pavement as they reached Post, where an apartment building had collapsed, and groaning people filled the sidewalk attended by a group of nuns. A dozen mounted soldiers cantered up, gestured toward Nob Hill, and began shouting at every able-bodied man in sight.

When the Naval Lieutenant in the lead saw Audie, he commanded him to stop. "You, there, come with us! We need men to save the contents of the Hopkins Estate!"

"We have our own business and things to save." Suzanne shot back, "Why don't you get busy saving people instead of some rich man's loot?"

"It's a museum, and there are priceless artworks that must be preserved, young lady. Besides he has no choice." The sailor patted the butt of his revolver. "I don't like it any more than you, but I am authorized to shoot those who disobey. This city is under the emergency command of General Fredrick Funston." He wheeled his mount toward the hill, and gave Audie a quick glance over his shoulder. "Well?"

Audie glanced at the khaki-clad cavalrymen behind the Lieutenant with their Krag carbines across their knees, and shrugged. They followed the troops up Mason as they requisitioned more men, and headed toward the mansions and lawns of the rich.

Several residents were sitting on the grass having breakfast. Servants placed dishes on blankets spread across immaculate lawns that were now strewn with a variety of clothing and items. Clouds of smoke to the east passed across the sun, exposing views of Oakland and Berkeley that came and went. A tremor shook the ground, eliciting shrieks from the ladies on the grass until the sounds of falling masonry subsided. Their cups were refilled by servants, and they returned to their meals.

Working class people were hauling paintings and statues out of a redwood edifice crowned with turrets, dormers and gables on California Street under the watchful eyes of soldiers, stacking them on the manicured lawns between marble fountains and statues. Audie joined them. Suzanne visited with two ladies drinking tea brewed on a blue enameled stove that had been moved out of a mansion across the street with its gas disconnected, and returned to burning wood in the form of broken furniture.

A tall blond woman watched the goings-on from a window in the cracked beige facade of the new Fairmont Hotel. She wore a torn red crinoline slip, and smoked a tiny ceramic pipe with one bare leg dangling over the sill. She winked. Audie waved.

Soon he had no time for flirting, and was sweating under the weight of a marble Venus he and a big man in corduroy pants and rough hemp suspenders were made to carry to the sidewalk. Audie noticed the bulge of a slung-shot in the man's back pocket with the worn leather handle flapping over his belt. He looked like a tough lug from the Coast. "Didn't I see you on Pacific?"

"More than likely. These fuckin' soldiers went and shot my chum deader than hell, just 'cause he came outta a store with a couple a goddamn bottles a' rye and a little ivory necklace. Lucky I was takin' a leak. Told 'em I didn't know the lug, and they marched me and some others up here to save their fuckin' paintings while all the good swag burns."

"I'd belay that blackjack in your trousers if I were you."

"Not 'till it tickles the ear o' the next Johnny Bootstrap what gives me the opportunity. I'm makin' it back to the dear old Coast 'fore it's all gone up in smoke first chance I get. There's a big ol' safe fulla loot I bet nobody's guardin' in this mess in the basement of a saloon." The man looked Audie up and down, and grinned. "I could use a fella with a strong back. Wanta join me?"

"No, thank you."

"You look like a smart lug. What if I promise you a thousand bucks in gold? It's there, I swear."

"Money doesn't have much meaning to me anymore."

The man stared at him as they sat Venus's marble torso on the sidewalk. He put a hand on one of her breasts and smirked. "Then you're a fool. Chance of a lifetime, buddy."

"Whatever."

When the soldiers were elsewhere, he went looking for Suzanne, and found her sitting on the grass with several bored society matrons. "Audie," she sprang up, "these ladies are going to get the Lieutenant to let us go with a pass!" Her voice dropped to a whisper. "I told them my stallion Al Akbar is kept in the Park, and that I fear there are looters there. They think I'm the daughter of Colonel Worthington from San Mateo, so act like it. The one with the big hat is Mrs. Parker. Her husband is a Colonel at the Presidio under General Funston. Good thing I wore these riding duds, huh?"

"I suppose they would care more about a horse than the poor souls down there." He nodded toward Chinatown, the Coast, and the docks beyond. "How did you manage that?"

"I just talked about the Arab stallion I had in Burlingame, and it was easy. I *do* so miss him. Come, let me introduce you."

Suzanne dragged him toward the women on the lawn, and he tipped an imaginary hat in greeting. Mrs. Parker wished them Godspeed on their effort to save the poor horse, and the pass was initialed by the suddenly obliging Lieutenant before he marched more conscripts across the hill to Grace Cathedral from where he intended to fight the flames.

A handsome young man in a tuxedo and white scarf came up California Street from the direction of Union Square. When he reached the lawn, he wiped his forehead with a handkerchief, finished a quick nip from a flask, slipped it into his coat, and bowed. "Good day, ladies."

"Mr. Barrymore," Suzanne laughed, "you look ready for another night on the town."

"One must not let little things like an earthquake spoil the show, eh, Leah?" He kissed her cheek, said something in her ear, and Suzanne giggled and shook her head. His attention returned to the ladies on the lawn. "Does anyone have a spare cup of coffee … or perhaps tea?"

"Buelah," Mrs. Parker shouted, "fetch Mr. Barrymore coffee … and eggs Benedict while you're at it!"

John Barrymore bowed again and plopped down on the grass. The women clustered around him as Audie and Suzanne took their leave.

As they crossed the lawn, Audie noticed a short fellow with a beard carrying a painting. The man put it down, wiped his forehead, and stood looking over the city with the sleeves rolled up on his white shirt and a bow tie in his back pocket. His pants were held up both by a belt and suspenders, and his face was hidden by a bowler hat as he leaned into his cupped hands to light a cigar. "Izzy?"

Izzy turned in a cloud of smoke. "Hello, pilgrim!" He carefully hefted his coat with a heavy object in the folds of it. "Up early for a change I see."

"It's good to see you!" Audie turned to Suzanne. "Can you get them to make a pass for Izzy too?"

"I … suppose I can say he's my horse doctor."

"Say what?" Izzy glanced from one to the other.

"Let me try!" She ran back to the women on the lawn.

Audie shook his head. "She's not bad in a pinch. Very resourceful I must say."

"Not bad in a bed either. Leah's my favorite of Jessie's girls." Izzy flicked a piece of ash from his beard. "So, what have you been about?"

"I went to dinner and the Opera with Lorelei, Jessie and Suzanne last night. Please use *Suzanne,* Izzy, while we are about our present company. We retired to the Palace, and the earthquake awoke us."

"Doesn't sound as if you've been suffering. What did Lorelei do?"

"She wasn't there. I don't know what's become of her."

"Can't you ... you know, can't you talk to her or something ... like in your head?"

"Not now. It's like she's off the face of the earth."

"Guess she *was* supposed to presage a big shake-up. Damn." Izzy took a small brass telescope from his coat and extended it. "Maybe she's done her job here, Audie." He scratched his beard. "A Liliot presaging the waste of Sodom like one of the Greek Furies, or even one of those horsemen in that damn fool John's Apocalypse." Izzy took the cigar from his mouth and spat on the grass. "Would that the Council of Nicea had tossed John of Patmos out of the Christian Bible when they had the chance; it would have saved people a hell of a lot of grief." He squinted through the eyepiece. "It's something you should consider anyway, I mean that she's simply up and left."

"I hope she hasn't. You know ... that's what Lorelei said."

"About what?"

"About the Book of Revelations, she said the same thing."

Izzy put down the telescope. "Girl's got a good head on her shoulders for a demon succubus, I must admit." He put the tube back to his eye.

"What are you looking at?"

"Temple Emanu-El on Sutter—the fire's got to it. Hell of a lot of books there I'd hate to see lost, not to mention the Torah. Plenty copies of that though. Here." Izzy handed him the telescope.

Audie found the twin towers of the Temple after Izzy pointed them out. Flames were beginning to sweep up the right one to spout from the onion-domed copper top. It began to glow green as he watched, lit by fires within.

"Here," Izzy held his hand out.

Audie handed him back the telescope and watched the city burn. The Call tower was burning from the top down, leaving a blackened wreck as it went. The huge flag atop the Palace burst into flames as he watched. To the far right, he could see the tall dome of City Hall surmounting a skeleton of steel ribs with its marble walls shaken off. The dome of the Hall of Records wasn't visible at all, and must have collapsed completely. The big Mechanic's Pavilion across the plaza was shrouded in smoke, but he could just make out wagons loading wounded people from its interior as it had been pressed into use as an emergency hospital from which they now must flee. "It's all going."

"Yes, Audie, it is. My God, it's beautiful in a way. Look how she burns." Izzy handed Audie the telescope again and pointed to the edifice of the Temple. Both copper turrets were now alight in green flame, like a beacon of Armageddon looming over the shattered city at its feet.

Suzanne appeared breathless and smiling. "I did it! Izzy's my horse doctor."

Izzy tipped his hat. "Not bad, young lady."

"We're out of here!" Audie grinned. "Find us mounts, too?"

"Just a motorcar. It's only a Ford, but I hope that shall do."

"You sound more like your mentor every waking hour."

She beamed. "But we must return it to the Presideo tomorrow, I promised. Would you believe Mr. Barrymore was trying to get me to come to his room at the Saint Francis? The city's going up in flames, and all he's thinking about is another girl. He offered me every cent from his last show and his undying gratitude."

"You must have made an impression on him at Jessie's."

"Hope to shout."

Real shouts arose from the house behind them followed by two quick shots. The cavalrymen wheeled their mounts, and rushed to the other side of the Hopkins mansion with carbines at the ready as people hurried to see what the commotion was about. Suzanne grabbed Audie's hand, and they followed the soldiers around the building.

The body of the big man he'd been hauling the statue with was lying across a stone walkway and flower bed amongst glass from the solarium on the south side of the mansion. A pool of blood spread rapidly from his head around the roots of pansies and tulips, sparkling in a shaft of morning sun as it disappeared into the soft ground. Loud cursing came from within the house.

One of the soldiers motioned people away. "There's nothing to see here folks!"

"That lug tried to knock me out and get my gun!"

"It's over now Sir. He'll do no more mischief."

"Throw him in the wagon with the other blackguards, and put them on a good hot fire somewhere!"

"Yes Sir!"

Audie stared at the body of the man he'd been speaking with ten minutes earlier as the soldiers began to haul him away. One motioned to him. "Give us a hand here, would you?"

He helped them carry the body to a wagon hitched to two skittish mules beside a black Mercedes limousine. Blood drizzled from the man's head on the flagstones and left a trail to the curb.

As they lifted the body, he saw three more in the dray, all shot. Audie excused himself to escape into the chaos of the City.

XXIX.

A Dark Morning

Her fingers made bloody streaks on the damp rocks as she pressed her cheek to cold stone, before the earth bucked her into the sea and darkness crushed her.

Screams pierced her dream.

Lorelei opened her eyes and blew dust from her mouth. She rose to her elbows on the concrete floor, and gave a heave. The beam across her back scraped her bare flesh as debris creaked and shuddered above her. She heaved again, planks groaned, and she was on her knees. Faint light shone overhead. She sneezed dust as roof tiles fell like porcelain drops of rain in the ruins of this house of slaves they'd sheltered for generations, and slapped more dust off her exposed flesh.

She yanked a lock of hair from the boards and held up hands covered in blood. She couldn't remember whose. The cry of a girl shook her from her reverie as she stood in the hole she'd made where the three-story building had collapsed into its basement.

She lifted more beams and boards, and tossed the head of a boo how doy out of the hole of the Queen's Room. A woman shrieked as the head bounced across a rubble-strewn alley, and Lorelei giggled for a dizzy moment as she staggered under the weight of a beam. She could use some clothes.

A moan came from the cluster of girls in a corner of the collapsed basement. The floor had fallen in the middle, and most were unharmed, though no doubt scared half to death. She moved the heavy planks one at a time, until she could see them huddled together with round faces white with dust. "Hello," she said in Cantonese, "care to get out of here ladies?"

A tall girl nodded vigorously, while the rest only stared.

She felt terror in their veins. The memory of highbinders' heads ripped from bodies and still-beating hearts torn from splintered chests was fresh in their minds. She felt the image of her own eyes, flashing in their skulls like fire. Even if it had been in the dark, they'd heard every bit of it, and the blood-red glow of her eyes as she let herself go had surely horrified them. She supposed she did look quite the mess, but there was nothing to be done for it at the moment.

"Yes!" shouted the girl who had resisted the boo how doy. "Praise you, bless you, Goddess of Mercy! Goddess of Vengeance!" She slapped dust from her smock, and turned to her companions, "Come on you children. Would you look a goddess in the face and tell her you have no gratitude?"

The others rose to their feet but one, who remained with her leg at an impossible angle and a face pale with shock. Lorelei pulled the heavy beam off her and tossed it atop a pile of lumber. The girls gasped. She put her hand over the wounded one's eyes and used the gift of sleep. She placed her hands on the leg, straightened it, and set the bone's ends together, breathing upon it until the bleeding stopped. Lorelei closed her eyes and concentrated on a torn artery until it began to knit, then emptied the blood from where it had pooled between the muscles with a quick slash of a fingernail and pinched the flesh together until it held. The effort made her dizzy. She paused to get air. She tossed a tangle of hair from her eyes, splinted the leg with sticks, tied it with her own hair from the wreckage, lifted the girl in her arms, and turned to the rest, who stood huddled together in the chaos of the Queen's Room. "You cannot stay here."

She stepped into the alley and bent over a body there. It was the tall courtesan who'd served sam shu to the bidders. Her skull was crushed. Lorelei admired her delicate features for a moment before she peeled the golden gown off her and put it on. Day was coming, and the dress and the dust would help protect her, as well as the smoke that would thicken as fires ate the City. It certainly wasn't a day for traipsing around naked. She groaned. Days weren't for traipsing around at all.

She waved, and the girls followed in their white cotton smocks like a procession of ghosts. The one in her arms awoke and touched her cheek, like an infant exploring the face of her mother.

Brass bells from a collapsed joss house across the alley tinkled as a wall shifted and settled. Flames from candles that had spread to a pool of oil before a gilded Buddha flickered on his serene face as he smiled upon them, flames that would join others to dance like bright flowers where thousands were trapped. The cacophony of tormented souls across the city nearly deafened her.

From the tong cribs up the alley came wails of pain and grief. She put down the wounded girl to lift a wall pinning two others. A Hatchet Son stared from beneath a carved pillar ornamented with dragons as she pulled the girls out and set them on their feet. He whimpered, and reached out in pleading. Lorelei ignored him.

Tzu Mai, the girl who'd resisted the slavers, hissed, seized a brick from a collapsed wall, and brought it down on his face. The man made gargling sounds as bloody foam erupted from his lips. Tzu Mai spat on him and turned to help the injured girl walk. More singsong girls joined them from ruins on either side of the alley, forming a strange procession through Chinatown as they followed a very white woman in a bloody golden gown until they stopped at the corner of Jackson and Dupont.

A crowd milled as men shouted contradictory orders in

rapid Cantonese. Three different tongs were trying to make people empty a building where something of great value resided. A
man from the Sam Yup Company climbed atop an overturned
wagon, raised his hands, and shouted for people to ignore them
all, and save those whose voices rose from the rubble all around
them.

A highbinder hissed, and rushed at the man waving a hatchet.
The Sam Yup man stood in shock, only leaping down from the
wagon to run when the boo how doy was nearly upon him, and
the Hatchet Son's blade flashed as it swung at the red silken
skullcap on the back of the fleeing man's head. Lorelei put
down the injured girl, sprang over the crowd, and seized the
hatchetman by his queue to snap it like a rope. The tong man's
neck gave a resounding crack, and he dropped dead in the street.

The crowd fell silent as more Hatchet Sons reached for
their pistols. The Sam Yup man Lorelei had saved stood mouth
agape, with the blood draining from his face. The crowd backed
away as one from the tall woman who stood amongst them,
dressed like an expensive courtesan but not at all the same.

Screams came from the women, then many of the men
before people turned in every direction and ran up Dupont,
Jackson, and Ross Alley where mangled bodies were strewn
amongst fish stalls and smoke rose from piles of rubble. In a moment, there was only Lorelei and her girls with the body of the
dead tong man between them.

Tzu Mai put fingers to her breast and bowed. "Pray tell: why,
oh Goddess, are your eyes so red?"

Lorelei put hands to her face. The orgy of killing had let the
natural red of her eyes show through, and the sudden violence
of the earthquake had taken away any thought of it. They'd
been the glowing color of blood since she'd awakened. She covered her face, and willed them back into a bright blue-green with

just a hint of what lay behind. When she looked up, the girls gasped. Several fell to the ground in supplication with hands clasped before them. "Oh ... *stop* it! Please, you must save yourselves! I have others to help this morning."

"Where will we go?"

"To wherever your soul takes you. Just don't let those bastards own you again. *Fight!* Or at least go to the missions or something. I have got to be going." The morning light stung her face and shoulders. Her head was spinning from exertion and the lack of blood as a rising sun burned through smoke over Berkeley. She moaned. She couldn't function in the awful day ahead. She was ill already.

The realization that she must take a good man this very morning, take an innocent and loving soul if she were to use the day to save others came in a rush, and the roar of that river where she was less than an insect on a bobbing leaf deafened her. Lorelei staggered as if struck in the middle of Dupont Gai, as her birthright fell upon her shoulders with the weight of an ocean and a cruel joke. "No," she stumbled on the level street, "Mother ... I don't want this!"

Tzu Mai caught her as she fell and lowered her to the cobblestones. "Do not leave us, my Goddess!"

"I am *not* a goddamn Goddess," she sat up, "they don't die." She seized the girl's hand. "You have everything you need right here." She put a palm against the girl's breastbone, to let all she carried of Mai Ling within her find a home in the girl's thundering and worthy heart.

Tzu Mai quaked as she knelt on the cobblestones. "Oh!"

"Never forget that."

She kissed her mouth and was gone.

Alva MacNaughton knew he was dying as he stared through

the hole in his roof at the vault of heaven beyond. Red light began to fill it, but he continued to stare waiting for angels. Knowing that his daughter was safe made it all right. He'd swept the
girl up from her bed as a cornice on the Loma Vista apartments
next door had come down where she had lain, and it caught him
across the back.

His blessed wife Mary and daughter Chastity were here,
and though he could not move, he could feel their hands and their
tears on his bare arms. Alva took a deep draught of the breeze
wafting in where his front window had looked upon Post. It was
like the moors and the rocky seashore where he'd been born.
But damn it, breathing hurt.

"I told ye that life insurance was a godsend." He was
greeted by loud wailing."Now now, ye will be alright. Get me
gold watch and the things to remember me by, and take the
money in the garage under the slab. And there's a twenty dollar
gold piece in the box under the seat of the Ford. This woman
gave it to me the other night for a wee bit of a fare. It's a double
eagle, from—"

"Stop, I cannot stand it!"

"Stand it ye must, woman! I know ye got the mettle in ye, so
don't tell me otherwise. Ye must take the car to the docks for a
boat to me brother's house in Oakland. But come back and buy
a good piece o' land soon as the fires stop. The banks may let
the prices fall for a while, and ye can get a decade's jump ahead
of 'em."

"Daddy! You're not going to die!"

Chastity's words cut him like a knife, for he felt an abyss
within of blood and knew she was wrong. Sparks flashed under his eyelids, and he winced. His daughter's words were more
terrible than the pain in that he could not give her the one gift
she deserved: his life. He took a measured breath to rein in the

agony before he spoke again. "I shall be with ye always my love. I swear, I swear before God this day, but ye must go on to have the life I dreamed for ye, my daughter and my angel. Yer but a wee slip of a girl, but ye must be strong for your mother—"

"*Daddy!*"

A tremor shook the building, followed by a rattle of bricks from the Loma Vista next door. A woman screamed.

"Get out!" Alva barked, "Get out before the rest of the damn thing comes down!"

Mary sobbed. "I will never leave ye!"

"Ye'll do it, and be damned if ye don't! Think of our daughter! In the name of God, woman, think of Chastity!"

Mary wailed, standing on the tilted floor holding the quaking hand of their daughter. Chastity knelt in her white nightgown to kiss him on the forehead, and hot tears bathed his brow as her blond locks brushed his face with the wonderful clean scent of her like the spring air itself. With that blessed kiss, Alva closed his eyes.

He was in a meadow covered in heather and gorse listening to birds. The sound of the sea drummed in his bones as he sat beside a crumbling tower. He was that boy again dreaming of the family here beside him, knowing he would one day hold his daughter in his arms. Alva opened his eyes to tell her how he so loved her, but she was gone. He wanted to cry out, but held his tongue. He looked around nonetheless, and gasped.

Chastity's eyes were shimmering pools of light. Her hair was black, black as the ravens who saw all things both in the glory of summer and the deepest winter when other birds fled south from the cold and dark. The woman above him was gloriously beautiful, but surely, she was not his daughter.

"*You're a good man Alva MacNaughton … and I shall take you to that meadow by the sea.*"

"Glory to God!"

The woman's hair became a shining tent as her eyes grew larger. Her hand touched his cheek, and he could hear the rushing of the sea and the skirling of pipes. No, it was *voices,* voices singing songs he once knew but had somehow forgotten.

Alva laughed as warmth flooded his body and the pain left. He felt like a young highland bull. He was a wild young man loving wild young women whose laughter rang like silver bells as they ran across the rocky highland crags of summer with bodies swift as deer and hair like spun glass in the light of a great golden sun. They smiled with the radiance of the sun itself as they beckoned him onward.

He looked back once before following, and hovered over his wife and daughter who stood in the street crying. An angel's voice said that things were going to work out fine for his family before he let go. It was a promise he knew would be kept. He knew it.

Suzanne asked to drive as soon as they got out of sight of the Colonel's wife who'd insisted she be chauffeured by the men. She laughed as her foot slipped off the clutch, and the car lurched after they switched drivers at Jones and Washington.

They reached the intersection of Pacific where a three-story building had collapsed. She made a wide arc, and almost hit a man galloping up the street on horseback from the direction of Chinatown and the Coast. A loud boom made the horse rear, and the man jerked the reins, bringing the head of his steed almost to the horse's chest before he regained control. He swore profusely, and galloped away.

Izzy spun in the direction of Van Ness and almost lost his glasses. "What the hell was that?"

Suzanne came to a stop, put on the brake, throttled down the engine with the lever on the column, and sat listening. Another explosion came from just blocks away, followed by a gray mushroom of smoke and dust boiling over rooftops.

"Dynamite! They're dynamiting the buildings over there."

"What the hell for, Audie?"

"I suppose a fire line, Suzanne. Leave it to the army; blow up the City to save the City."

"That's crazy." She put the car back in gear for the climb up Russian Hill.

Up ahead a group of kids was coming out of a store staggering under armloads of candy, canned fish and meat. One boy wore three derby hats one atop the other, none of which would fit for years. A kid farther up the street shouted that troops were coming, and they scattered, leaving dry goods and food strewn in their wake.

A dozen soldiers appeared at the corner of Pacific and Levenworth, and leveled their rifles at the front of the store as the last of the youths poured out of broken windows with purloined goods falling from their grasp. Audie held his breath, but the men held their fire.

Izzy let out his."Lucky they're kids."

"Let's be gone!"

She dropped to first gear, and they climbed Russian Hill, stopping at the top where it was open to grass and vegetation. A man stood at an easel smoking a meerschaum pipe as people trundled belongings over the rise toward the Lombard and Fisherman's wharves with whatever possessions they'd fled with. He swirled a brush on his pallet, and added another stroke to what he was painting."Opportunity of a lifetime," he took the pipe from his mouth and gestured toward the south with the stem,"been downtown?"

"Yes, it's all going up in flames."

"Look at her now." The man waved the yellow pipe stem east

toward a riot of smoke and flame. Another explosion echoed as he put it back in his mouth. "That goddamn Fred Funston. I bet whatever's left in the vaults of Wells Fargo it's him ordered that dynamiting."

Izzy nodded. "I'd say you're right."

"Won't help. I'd like to get closer to the action, but I'd wager it shall soon come to me."

"I'd have to agree again, pilgrim."

When they reached the house, Wu was sitting on the stoop with his heavy old revolver in his wrinkled hand. He stood as the car made its way around obstructions in the street, and bowed.

"Has Lorelei been here?" Audie yelled.

Wu shook his head. "No, but I guard house until she return. Missy Lady very good to me. Rescue me from damn highbinder, and get my son out of big trouble in China with much gold. You think she come back?"

"If I knew Wu, I should be a happy man." Audie stepped into the house in a fog of doubt. He slapped the doorframe. "Where *are* you?"

"Thanks for your concern." Her breath caressed his left ear as if her mouth were an inch away.

He inhaled her scent fiercely, "You're alive!" he croaked.

"You've done fine without me, I hope you've noticed."

"Because I had to."

"It's but twelve days since we met, and you were alone and on an adventure beforehand. That's what attracted me to you in the first place."

"You know all I was beforehand ... but where are you?"

"Others need me far worse than yourself, though I'll try and meet you. Please remember I'm only one person. That's person,

Audie, even if a very different one. Time has diminished our dominion, and I can't be everywhere at once. Perhaps now you'll at least stop calling me a goddess."

"I have decided demigoddess is more accurate."

Lovely laughter rippled through him and shrunk to an exhausted giggle. Suzanne stared at him, wide-eyed.

"I like that. But I have a terribly busy day ahead and must attend to things."

"How are you getting about?"

"The good die also. It wasn't hard to find one who would know me and allow me to accept myself for who I am."

The nape of his neck tingled. "You came to someone—"

"And took his gift before I took him home. I can accept that in times like these far more than the random cruelties of this world. I'm in the company of my ancestors as if there were no time between now and then at all, but time itself is a fabric that twists in the river that takes us all. Willing sacrifice is made under the sky, and I greet the sun with grateful thanks to the blood of the innocent. If, that is, this damn smoke ever lets up."

A laugh balled in his throat.

"You might as well stay where you are. I don't think the fires will reach this far, and there's plenty of food in the house. Oh, and I'm glad Jessie gave you that gold. Thank Bobby Giles. You're really not that different in as far as he too came to see what truly matters in this world. His father was an Anglican Priest by the way. Now, I've got to be—."

"Wait! Will I see you again?"

There was a long pause. *"I think so Audie; I can't tell. There's another shortcoming in your Goddess."*

"Lorelei, if this is the last time we speak, I must know; what ... who are you?" The sea breeze danced around him as he waited. Gunshots rang out by the wharves. Something exploded in the west.

"Oh my love … who are you?"

She was gone. He inhaled, straining for any last scent of her, but there was only the smell of the sea and the incense Wu burned before a small gilded Buddha in his bedroom.

Suzanne grabbed his hand, "I *heard* her!"

"What did she say?" Izzy asked.

"She has business to attend to, and we may as well stay here."

Izzy pulled at his beard. "Damn! She came for the earthquake. I should have *known!* That woman is the very seed of Lilith, pilgrim. Holy Moses, I wish I could just sit down and ask her some things. God knows what she's seen … let alone what secrets have come down with her." Izzy slapped his trousers, and a cloud of dust floated away in the wind. "I can't believe I actually lived to *see* it."

"I don't think she knew the earthquake was coming. We were out last night, and she was quite carefree. She got rather inebriated. In fact, I'd say she was as unaware of what lay in store this morning as we were ourselves."

"A goddess … drunk?"

"Yep," Suzanne giggled, "hoppin' on the ol' cocaine too, and randy as hell to boot."

"What?"

Audie shrugged. "She says she's not a goddess Izzy, and I don't know why she would lie at a time like this. She got every bit as silly as we last night, and was more a girl out on the town than some magical being. After all I've seen her do, that was a revelation as big as anything else she'd shown me. She certainly isn't enjoying our misery. I know that. I know you have your doubts, but it's really not like her at all," he stared out a still intact window at Alcatraz where smoke drifted from the ruined fort on its crest, "although it's true some Indians who know her insist on calling her a trickster."

Suzanne smiled. "The women, or the men?"

"Both, I suppose."

"That's—"

Izzy snorted. "Ah well, then there's no credibility to it at all, right, Leah … I mean Suzanne?"

"You wouldn't understand, Izzy."

"Well gosh, Leah, I suppose she's spent her centuries using women as lovers."

"She has."

"Don't call her Leah, Izzy."

"Still, if even the Indians call her a—"

"Enough!" Audie held a hand up and turned to Wu, who had accompanied them into the house while hopelessly trying to follow the conversation. "Is there any water in this place?"

Wu nodded. "Good well here, very deep. Hand pump in basement. Plenty coal for heating."

"Then I think that I should love a bath."

"Girls first!" Suzanne's voice rang out from the parlor.

Audie sighed. She certainly deserved it.

XXX.

The Burning Day

Lorelei slid on bloody cobblestones as cannon fire rumbled over the rooftops. A rippling thunder followed, as charges of powder were lit at the corners of a building, and it sloughed into the street with a galloping roar and a cloud of sparks. Soldiers were bombing and shelling homes along Van Ness to create a fire line. Lorelei turned her attention from the shelling and gazed across Portsmouth Square at the castle-like parapets of the Hall of Justice, where she heard an excited babble from the mayor and his cohorts as they prepared to abandon their refuge.

She gazed at green bronze lampposts lining the square and felt rough hempen ropes tightening around throats of those hung fifty years ago here by the Vigilantes. She saw her mother tied to a stake, burning to the shouts of a mob. As San Francisco had grown in all directions from the Bay, leaving Chinatown, North Beach, and the Coast behind, the least of its citizens had found refuge here in the shadows. The denizens of the old City would be left to themselves while the military planned a defense of what General Funston deemed defensible—or worthy of it.

She came upon a crumbling adobe on Kearny where she'd met a young man bound for the goldfields fifty-seven years earlier, and the roar of lives past and screams of the present merged for a moment. Time roiled in confusion as the street bounced with an aftershock.

Lorelei put palms to ochre stones quarried by brown Californios at the behest of a flame-haired Irish gambler and touched the warmth of hands that had hewn them before returning to the chaos around her. So many were crying out, in so many names for God.

She walked up Jackson, and stopped before a building that had imploded as the earth beneath it turned to jelly. It was the Municipal Crib. Flames were beginning to blossom from it and cries came from the ruins. She tossed wreckage away until the head of a fifteen-year-old girl emerged from the remnants of a room. A framed Currier and Ives print of a New England farm was on the wall, and a drawing in the girl's own hand of a girl dressed as a princess on a chair with six white roses.

Lorelei lifted boards pinning her in a bed where she'd entertained men four times her age, snatched her up, and set her on her feet. "Watch out while I move these." She began doing the same for the sobbing girl in the next crib, whose leg was cut badly. "You must help each other." She said to the first, who stood tottering and staring as if drunk. "I can dig you out, but then you're on your own. I've stopped the bleeding. Tie this around her leg. Loosen it periodically so the blood does not pool and head for the Ferry Building or the wharves, and remember that money in your drawer. You'll need it."

"Oh, God!"

"Please don't ask for any miracles."

She made her way toward the wharves pulling stunned souls from the ruins. After a while she no longer spoke at all, but simply stood them up and slapped them on the behind to snap them out of their shock like children who had forgotten to run the bothersome errand of saving their own lives. Many were drunk or hung-over, with minds thick with opium and other drugs.

All the while the screams of those she couldn't reach twisted in her soul as she felt flames searing trapped flesh in a hundred places, flames marching from the south to join the fires around her.

A young man lay sprawled across his drawings of brigands, crimps, and whores in the ruins of a house wedged between a collapsed nickelodeon and a gutted saloon. Lorelei lifted him up from a pile of boards and placed him on the remnants of a wall. She sat beside him with an exhausted sigh and studied his charcoal sketches, leafing through them as gas lines hissed in the street. Water mains gushed in fountains, filling the alleys nearby as tanks on Telegraph Hill drained into the Bay. Lorelei brushed hair darker than night away from a face that had stood the glare of day but once in seven years, and nodded her approval. "Rather good, actually."

The young man gazed at the woman beyond beautiful beside him in a tattered golden gown. Dried blood stained her porcelain-white skin. Red flame from a burning wharf flickered behind her. He wiped dust from his eyes, and cleared a dust-dry throat. "Thank you."

"Now go help somebody." She handed the stack of drawings back and pulled him to his feet. "My, you're cute. Really wish I had more time fella." Lorelei kissed his cheek, and sprang across the street to tear open the door of a basement where nineteen Chinese gamblers were trapped, and water had risen to their waists.

Once they'd bathed, the three sat down to a meal Wu fixed over a charcoal brazier in the back yard. He'd reverted to his native cuisine in the throes of crisis, stir-frying chicken in a wok with vegetables and a spicy brown sauce Audie couldn't begin to place. Nonetheless it was delicious.

After the meal Izzy lit his last cigar in the spring sun as finches flocked around a pomegranate tree on the slope. Some of the unripe fruit had split in the quake, and red nectar bled down its branches. The birds tasted the bitter juice, fluttered away, and circled, crying in their thin voices before returning in a downward spiral to taste of it again.

A loud banging came from the front door, and shouting, "All out, by orders of General Funston! Evacuate immediately!"

"Goddamn it," Izzy growled, "why in hell have we got to go anywhere? We're fine right where we are."

Suzanne nodded. "I don't think the fire will get over the top of the hill. It's all grassy up there."

"And who's to watch Lorelei's house?"

"I stay here. You go talk soldiers. I go in basement, hide long time."

"Not a bad idea for the rest of us Wu."

Boots crunched on gravel. Someone had jumped the fence, and was coming around the side of the house. Izzy slid his Smith and Wesson out of its holster. Wu opened the door beneath the porch and ducked into the basement just as uniformed men appeared in the yard. Izzy stuffed the gun under his arm with a sigh.

"All out!" A young man in a blue uniform shouted from ten feet away.

Izzy waved his cigar. "What the hell for, soldier? The fires won't breach the hill. There's a well in the basement, and we can protect the house if —"

"These are *orders!* I am Lieutenant Balder of the revenue brig Bear, under the emergency command of General Funston in the service of the President of the United States of America. It is my duty to—"

"Whoa, slow down," Audie said. "Where are we to go?"

"You may proceed to Golden Gate Park, or endeavor to take passage on one of the boats from the Lombard Pier. If necessary, you may proceed to Fort Mason adjacent to this portion of the City for escort as you are in the company of a lady. Any attempt to re-enter the part of the City within the fire lines shall be turned back. Should you attempt to loot from commercial establishments, the Army as well as the men under my command have orders to summarily shoot you. You are to gather what you can carry and leave immediately."

"How old are you?" Suzanne asked.

The Lieutenant's face reddened. "Ma'am, seeing as you're a lady, I'd suggest you act like one."

"Just asking."

There was the sound of the car's engine being cranked out front followed by a curse, as the starter rod kicked back in the hands of a Marine when it sputtered to life.

Suzanne put hands on her hips and shot the Lieutenant a look of scorn. "You *aren't* taking that car!"

"Miss, it is to be requisitioned for the use of my squad. The vehicle will be returned at a later time."

"That's *Colonel Parker's* sedan! Mrs. Parker loaned it to me herself. How am I to explain that the goddamn Army took it?"

"We are Fleet Marines, ma'am. I will give you a written note to the Colonel, who should certainly agree with the necessity in this extraordinary situation. We have to patrol an area from Fort Mason all the way up East Street and—"

"Fuck you, you little Napoleon! You just don't want to walk! *You're* the looters, if you ask me!"

The Lieutenant froze, aghast at the language spewing from a young lady's lips. Izzy made a snorting laugh as the Lieutenant drew himself erect. "That will be all here. You have five minutes to gather whatever you can carry. I suggest you head for Golden Gate Park as there are tents and provisions being prepared for the arrival of displaced persons there." He saluted stiffly and began to move toward the front of the house.

"You damnable thief," Suzanne spat, "I shall have you posted to Terminal Island checking Manila steamers for vermin for the rest of your commission!"

The Lieutenant stopped. "Miss, I—"

"My name is Suzanne Mae Callahan, daughter of General Callahan, whose victories in the Philippines are well known, and under whom your damn Fredrick Funston *served,* and who is presently posted in Washington with the ear of President Roosevelt himself. Your own Captain, the redoubtable hell-roaring Michael Henley, is known to me personally and has dined at my father's table!" She held up the gold charm on a chain around her neck. "This is the very locket he presented me on my fifteenth birthday. Your Captain considers me his goddaughter! You take that car and you're toast soldier, or sailor, or whatever the hell you call yourself!"

The Lieutenant visibly whitened above his high blue collar before he turned to his Corporal. "Leave the vehicle." He saluted. "But you must leave with haste, please. We'll check back in an hour." He pivoted on the heel of a high brown boot, and the Marines were on their way.

"Wow," Izzy said.

"Very impressive, Suzanne."

"We get officers at our resort all the time. I know how those boys respond when you jerk their chains. Seen 'em throw their pants on and jump out a second-story window when they thought the Shore Patrol was in the parlor more than once. We know a fellow who sounds just like one that Jessie calls when they're getting tiresome. He comes in yelling bloody murder when it's time to clear 'em out, they scoot like rabbits, and he leaves with a kiss and a bottle of champagne." She huffed ."That Balder fellow will never get any service in one of the better sporting houses in *this* town again if I have my say. What a little worm, to order us around like that!"

Audie laughed. "Jessie was right. You're the best actress she ever had."

"She does have a talent."

"Where shall we go?"

"Let's go to the Park."

"The Park it is, Madame."

They loaded themselves into the car and headed up Larkin planning to turn on one of the east-west streets to the south and find an open route to Golden Gate Park. A rain of ashes fell, turning the City into a monochromatic desert. Izzy brushed them off his coat as they stuck in his beard and piled on his bowler hat. Audie and Suzanne's hair was gray. The south and east were a solid wall of fire and smoke, including a plume curling skyward on the other side of Nob Hill. Grace Cathedral was shrouded in smoke. Smoke rose from the direction of the Lombard Pier. The thud of explosions came at intervals from the west.

They hadn't gone far when they came to a roadblock manned by four men in rough clothing wearing white armbands, brass badges and guns. "Halt!" a man in a dirty woolen watch cap and stained canvas jacket barked as he leveled a double-barreled shotgun.

Audie stepped from the car followed by Izzy as the men eyed Suzanne. Audie held up his hands. "We are going to the Park, under orders of the military authorities."

"We're special militia, checking all passers-by under the orders of Mayor Schmitz and the Committee of Fifty."

"For what?"

"For whatever the fuck we want!" One of them said with a leer, eyes still on Suzanne.

"Leave the lady alone," Izzy growled.

"Do you have any valuables?" The leader asked.

Suddenly the gold around Audie's waist was a weighted chain ready to drown him. He squeezed the wad of bills in his pocket and shook his head. "No, we've lost all we have, and are simply seeking a place to sleep for the night in safety."

"We'll take the motorcar."

Suzanne sprang up in the driver's seat. "Not again!"

Audie winced. An aggrieved young socialite wasn't going to work on these types.

"Then again," her tone became silky, "perhaps I can take care of you gentlemen myself." She winked and ran a ring-covered hand across the cleavage of her shirt as the boom of dynamite echoed in the west. Shots rang out in the south as Izzy caught Audie's eye, and his fingers barely motioned to the gun under his arm.

"That's your cue, love."

Audie's gun was in his hand pointing at the head of the leader. Izzy's was trained on the others, none of whom had their own leveled as they'd been staring at the young redhead eyeing them coquettishly while toying with the buttons of her tailored western shirt.

"Well," Audie shouted, "I suppose I could blow your head off you worthless lug! Or you could tell your men to put down their weapons and let us be on our way."

"Drop 'em, you sonsabitches!" Izzy barked.

The guns clattered on the cobblestones.

Suzanne sprang out of the car and tossed the leader's shotgun in the back seat. "Search them for pistols! Never knew a lug like these not to carry something under his duds." She walked up to the leader, lifted his canvas jacket, and reached for the pearl handle of a Colt .38 protruding from his belt.

The man's arm wrapped around her neck, and he yanked

her in front of him and drew his pistol. His tobacco-stained teeth flashed in a grin. "Get 'em, boys!"

Audie's Smith and Wesson bucked with a roar, and the man's head elongated inside his dirty woolen watch cap before it spilled out in a pink cloud that painted the cobblestones. Suzanne let out a yelp, dove for a shotgun, and had it leveled it at his partners from the ground before she got to her feet. The three remaining thugs raised their hands in the air.

"Holy Moses!" Izzy got out.

Audie stood staring at the body sprawled in the street.

Suzanne made a face and flicked a glistening pink piece of skull from her khaki shirt that left a strawberry stain. "Finish searching these fuckers!"

They found a pistol, knife, and slung shot on each of them, tossed them in the car, and hopped in with a small arsenal clattering on the red leather seats.

"You can't leave us unarmed!"

"Why," Izzy shouted, "so if you meet some piece of shit like yourself you're not in a fix? You're lucky we didn't kill you all! Why don't you go find Abe Ruef and see if he needs any errands run, or maybe head over to the Municipal Crib? I hear it's plenty hot down there tonight."

"Fuck you!"

As they sped up the hill with a pop from the exhaust, Suzanne's hand left the wheel and squeezed Audie's knee. "I heard her *again*! She was right there, whispering in my ear. She saved us!"

He let out his breath. "She had to get my attention once she put you up to that." A vision of the man's head expanding in a pink cloud erupted, and he shook it away and turned to Izzy, who was fooling with one of the guns. "Did she cue you too?"

"What?"

"Lorelei, she set that up with those men to help us get the drop on them."

"Didn't hear a thing pilgrim; I was just using common sense. Good timing though." He glanced behind them with a gray face."Don't know why I didn't shoot. Anyway my hat's off to her. I'll never say a bad word about Lilith again I swear. That was *way* too close."

They reached Pacific and turned right into smoldering ruins. Buildings had sloughed into the street, and were blocking their path. Suzanne stopped the car and looked for a place to turn around. A tremor rattled bricks, rocking the Ford on its narrow wheels. The corner building behind them groaned.

"Look out!" Audie stood up in his seat."That one's coming down!"

They bolted out of the car and stumbled on the heaving street as the four-story wooden building began to lose its balance like a drunk. It leaned slowly out, hesitated, and cascaded in a torrent of boards and beams. When the dust cleared, the street behind them was a ten-foot deep pile of debris with the lion's claws of a green bathtub crowning the heap, pawing at the smoky air like a beast.

Izzy got up from the cobblestones and cleared his throat."Well pilgrims, back to the ol' shoe leather. Sure was nice while it lasted." He wiped his hand."Wish to God I had a cigar! If we head straight into Western Addition and bear south somewhere, we should hit the Panhandle of the Park before dark at least."

"I'm taking this shotgun. Womanly wiles can get a body just so far today."

"That's a commendable thought young lady."

Suzanne wiped a bloody strand of hair from her face as she

unbuttoned her shirt and reached for another fragment of the thug's skull.

They dusted off their filthy attire and began making their way over piles of bricks and boards toward the west. The morning sky was clear and smokeless in that direction, over a receding belt of fog that glowed like soft pearl over the ocean.

"Lafayette Park's not far," Izzy began, "and Van Ness is just past Polk. Got to be where they're doing that blasting; it's the widest street on the west side. At least the real military will protect us from more of those blackguards." The sound of explosions came from up ahead. "See?" Izzy said over his shoulder as he climbed a wall that had fallen into Pacific and formed a berm of red bricks. He stopped in front of the ruins of a tobacco shop on the other side. "Whoa!" He bent over in the rubble, and when his head reappeared, he had a cigar between his lips and a brightly colored box in his hand. "A Cuban! An Uppman, a whole damn *box* of 'em!" Izzy produced a big blue tip match with a wide grin on his face. He struck it on a brick, sat on the berm, and drew the smoke into his mouth with a look of contentment.

"Stop! Looter!" A shot rang out.

Izzy did a back-flip. His scuffed shoes were visible above the rubble berm for an instant followed by a thud, as he landed out of sight.

"*No!*" Audie screamed. Suzanne dropped the shotgun, and put hands to her face.

A dozen heavy boots pounded on the other side of the rubble as a squad of soldiers moved double-time toward where Izzy had been. "Shoot any more of them you find looting these shops!" came a voice of command that was far too young for the words it carried.

Something cold crawled up Audie's spine, and he drew the pistol from under his coat.

Suzanne seized his hand."No! You'll just end up dead too! Let's get out of here!"

They cut through a yard between two houses, trampling flowers and ducking under a leaning clothesline festooned with bloomers and petticoats. He threw her over the whitewashed fence separating the backyard of the house from one on Jackson. As he grabbed the fence and swung over behind her, a bullet whined past his head and shattered a window. They dashed between two houses onto Jackson, where the man in a taupe herringbone suit who they'd seen the night before at the Palace hung from a streetlight with a placard around his neck proclaiming **LOOTER.** His pants were soaked with blood still running from a hole in his chest mixed with the piss of fear. Suzanne gasped, and bit her knuckles.

They ducked into another yard, crossed to Washington, and passed a smoldering apartment building. A child's cry came from the wreckage. Audie skidded to a stop, lifted boards, seized a small hand, and pulled a dust-covered boy out who blinked and tottered on his feet.

She yanked on his arm."Hurry!"

They crossed Van Ness on Clay at a walk, nodding to soldiers forcing people from their homes up and down the street. Piles of belongings sat on the curbs: baby carriages, chairs, paintings, children's wagons, even an upright piano as people lugged possessions out of handsome houses that would soon be blown to rubble. An explosion a block away sent plaster and chunks of brick flying. They ducked their heads and broke back into a run.

Suzanne stopped when they reached Franklin, put her hands on her knees, and wheezed."Poor dear Izzy ... those fucking soldiers!"

"Shhhh, they're all about!"

"Audie, take me out of this place!"

"I should love to. Where?"

"I don't care!"

They made Lafayette Park, where a crowd milled on the grass. Soldiers were handing out blankets and filling jugs of water from tanks on the backs of wagons. Suzanne walked to the spout of a tank, put her head under the faucet, rinsed the blood and dust off her face, and dabbed between her breasts, then drank greedily from the stream.

"Stop that," a soldier barked, "you're wasting water!"

"What are you gonna do, shoot me?" Her shirt was half open from washing the remnants of the man's blood away and plastered by water to her breasts, and the private stared. "You boys seem to get pleasure from killing poor fellows who are only trying to find a moment's peace, so why not shoot a girl, you goddamn brave fuckin' *sonofabitch!*"

Audie pulled her from the head of the line, where the people she had stepped in front of were either grumbling or trying to get a better look. "Sorry sir, she's upset."

"Looks like she's a bit tetched, that's a fact." The soldier wrenched his gaze away from her breasts and went back to filling jugs.

They sat on a curb, and Suzanne's face flushed to near-scarlet. "Where the hell was Lorelei when they shot Izzy?"

He shook his head. "I don't know—perhaps attending to someone else's troubles."

Her jaw trembled, and she took a rattling breath. "I guess she can do just so much … but she sure saved us from those gunmen on Larkin." She ran a hand down his back. "Actually she just gave us the chance. You saved us, Audie."

A vision of the man's head exploding returned. Audie

wiped his face. "She certainly gave us a way out, but poor Izzy."

"He couldn't hear her, could he?"

"No, he couldn't." He stroked her red hair coming out of the braid Violet had made that long-ago morning, and rubbed her freckled shoulders.

She pressed a damp cheek against his. "I wonder how it is that she chooses?"

"What?"

"Who she helps, and who not."

"Perhaps it's just catch as catch can, just as we find ourselves. I know she's not all-seeing or anything like that."

"She sure sees more than we do."

"Yes, but it's a terrible burden. She's showed me that. She must hide simply to survive, and helping people seems to cause her nothing but trouble."

"I wish I could have her power for just one minute. Did you know she killed the sonofabitch who beat and buggered me at the Poodle Dog? Bet you didn't even know it happened ... I mean any of it. Jessie said Lorelei killed him, but I never told you. I couldn't let Jessie down, but I cried my eyes out when she asked me what happened with that guy. It was my first assignation in her employ, and I almost threw in the towel, but when I got back to the house Jessie took one look at me and knew." The muscles in her neck stood out, and her jaw tightened. "I'd rip those fellows who shot Izzy a new keister I swear! He was always so decent to me."

"I forgot. He was a customer too, wasn't he?"

"So was that poor fellow hanging from a lamppost. He was just a clerk at City Hall who wanted to write symphonies and was saving for a home. He played the cello. He was engaged and had bought a plot on Bernal Hill to build a house. He told me he wanted to have four kids, two boys and two girls." She wiped her face. "Do you think of me as a whore, Audie?"

"Well, I—"

"That's all right, I mean I *am* ... or I *was*. I'm never going back to it though."

"What shall you do?"

"What shall you?"

"I don't know anymore, Suzanne. Right now surviving is all I've been thinking of."

"I want to go to a university. That was my father's intention, and now I think I'll take him up on it. I'm well ahead of most anyway. I'd like to write books and live in the country ... and get another horse." She scooped up a cobblestone that had popped out of place and tossed it at a ragged rhododendron. "I sure don't want to be one of those stuffed chickens in a dress like that Colonel Mrs. Parker though."

An exhausted smile spread his cheeks. "What about Jessie? There's a lady I respect. In fact she gives a whole new slant for me on the whole profession."

"I love Jessie, but she helps her girls better themselves and even get out of the life. That's what I do love about her."

"Perhaps that's what Lorelei loves also."

"I know it is ... Audie?"

"What?"

"She's kind of the patron saint of the whores, isn't she?"

Audie stared at the buckled surface of Gough Street and began to chuckle. Her giggle joined his own, and they exploded in laughter.

Four men with pistols guarding a wheelbarrow with a hand-drawn sign saying **Bank of Italy** stopped at the sound and put hands to their guns. The man in front pulled at his thick mustache, fanned himself with a ledger book, and broke into a smile before motioning for his employees to stand down. "Well good afternoon, Miss Leah."

"Good day, Peter. I see you're not letting an earthquake spoil business."

"Not at all, Madame."

She gave him a tear-streaked smile, and he tipped his derby hat before continuing on.

She kissed Audie's cheek."Think she really *is* watching out for people like us? I mean some of the time ... for some of us?"

"I know she is. She saved a girl from the tongs whom I met amongst the Indians, and she," he clenched his jaw,"she rescued one from Hell ... the *real* Hell, right here on earth. Her name was Mai Ling. That throws all these demon stories into a cocked hat, I'd say."

"It's so nice to know there's somebody out there, somebody who's so much wiser and older, who loves us for who we are with all our faults and even sees whom we might become. I guess you have to have sex with her to hear her though."

"But you heard her when we were at dinner at the Palace."

A smile swelled her cheeks."It was driving me crazy Audie, Jessie and Lorelei I mean, and I thought I was being smart and sneaky when I snuck by her bedroom ... " she laughed,"of course she knew my mind and took me into her bed. That's why all of us were linked like that at dinner and the opera."

"I see why your uncle said curiosity would get you into something." Audie grinned."He couldn't have guessed what though."

"Yes ... but fuck him."

"Still, I should hope communicating with her is more a union of spirit between two people. Otherwise she could never keep up."

She took his hand."Let's be going now."

They made Golden Gate Park by evening along with a hundred thousand others. The once gleaming white Conservatory was a mass of broken panes and trampled foliage. Someone had strung a curtain across a concave concert pavilion from which a stovepipe protruded. She got a tent from two soldiers, and they put it up at the crest of a manicured hill. They had a view of Mt. Tamalpais across the Bay before the smoke closed in, and it looked like Russian Hill was burning after all. They acquired two jugs of water, and Audie spent the waning day digging latrines with a dozen other men.

By evening they were settled. Food was prepared in outdoor kitchens by women in dirty hospital uniforms, calico dresses, and torn silk gowns working together with their talk and laughter as welcome as the repast. They ate bean soup and sourdough bread in a haze of drifting smoke and retired with a single blanket as crickets sang in the rhododendrons.

"I want to move to Santa Cruz." She said against his shoulder.

"Why there?"

"I just favor the place. It's a beautiful bay with big trees, and nobody there should know what I've done here I hope."

"You really intend to quit the life?"

"Yes, Audie, I've seen enough of human nature in that regard. Remember how I said Dolly Adams, who started Jessie's place, died way too young?"

"Yes."

"Syphilis, Audie. They say she looked like a woman of eighty at twenty-six. She started at eleven on the Barbary Coast, swimming naked in a fishbowl."

He squeezed her hand. "What will you do?"

"Whatever it takes I suppose. We could buy land with what I've saved and that loot Lorelei left you and go into business. I could keep the books. I was first in mathematics in Parochial School, and Jessie had me do accounting. She even trusted me with the combination to a safe."

He ran fingers through her hair, which had come out of the braid entirely. "If all things were equal, that would be a perfect resolution, but I must know what has become of Lorelei."

"What if you never do?"

The question was one he couldn't answer, but felt no need to. What was a mere earthquake in the eons her kind had dwelt amongst the race of man? "She's not gone. She's got a lot on her hands, is all."

"Sooner or later she'll be. You're but a mortal man ... and she's *not*. You should be grateful for the time you've had anyway."

"I am." He rolled over and stared at the canvas wall.

She tightened her arm around him, and shivered in the cool night. "I wonder why she showed up here at all, what brought her now."

He let out the breath he didn't know he'd been holding. "So do I, Suzanne ... so do I."

She cried quietly. Audie rolled over and kissed her. She sniffled, hugged him fiercely, and climbed on top. Suzanne yanked off her bloodstained blouse, threw it against the canvas, and ran a blood-reddened finger across his cheek. "I know no one can be what she is, but she told me that we all have the same thing inside us ... even the most forsaken girl who's dying in a crib somewhere." She hiccupped. "She showed us that, and she says she's as mortal as we are, Audie."

"But I must know who she really *is*, and what brought me—"

"It's all a mystery. It always will be. Don't spend your life waiting for an answer from her. We can find our own."

"But … I so need to tell her—"

"Then do! You know she's listening." She shook her head, and a tent of smoky hair enveloped him. "Christ almighty, have some faith, Audie."

His laugh bounced her on his chest. "I never expected to take lessons in faith from you Suzanne, but you're right."

"She wouldn't mind if we kind of prayed to her, do you think?"

"Why not? She's put up with more than that."

Suzanne stared into space for a long time with a look of determination. "Then let's go there. That's her gift. We don't need Lorelei anymore."

The dark returned deeper than it had been for half a century away from the fires. She found a good man in the ruins of his home whose neck was broken, and stitched a channel between his brain and body long enough for him to perform for the last time. At the end she took him to where he would go on alone, stepped away from the light again, and drank the grace of his gratitude.

Lorelei stood amongst red fires under a crimson moon holding her hands to the sky like all her line, and felt their strength and approval. For a precious time outside the tolling of clocks and calendars, she was that very first Goddess, peering into a future she could only guess at.

She came to the Park and hovered over her friends tangled in sleep. She kissed them, not allowing them to wake, yet to know her in the depth of their dreams and her gratitude for the gift of their lives that made her own bearable. Lorelei rested her spirit within their tired flesh as within all the bruised and battered flesh around her, and felt that girl clinging to a cliff long ago. She stepped out amongst the dying campfires.

An infant awoke at the breast of her mother and wailed at

the smoky sky. Lorelei knelt in the damp grass above her. The child opened her eyes, and saw the wings of an angel against a bloody moon.

She kissed the girl and was gone.

The End